Westering Home

a Scottish Island Novel

D0976398

Audrey McClellan

Beaver's Pond Press, Inc.

Edina, Minnesota

ISBN 1-59298-014-7

Library of Congress Catalog Number: 2003107006

Cover art by Carla McClellan.
Eilean Dubh map by Jane Gordon.
Book design by Mori Studio.

Scottish country dance "Fàilte gu Eilean Dubh (Welcome to the Dark Island)" devised by Lara Friedman-Shedlov. Copyright by Lara Friedman-Shedlov. Used by permission.

"Eilean Dubh" and "Audrey McClellan/Thistleonia" are original compositions by Sherry Wohlers Ladig. Lyrics of "Eilean Dubh" are by Ladig/McClellan; "Sarah and Thomas" lyrics are by Ladig. Both music and lyrics are copyright by Sherry Wohlers Ladig. Used by permission.

Printed in the United States of America

First Printing: August 2003

07 06 05 04 03   6 5 4 3 2 1

Beaver's Pond Press, Inc.   7104 Ohms Lane, Suite 216
Edina, MN 55439
(952) 829-8818
www.beaverspondpress.com

to order, visit www.BookHouseFulfillment.com or call 1-800-901-3480. Reseller discounts available.

Dedicated to Mike, of course.

I hope you enjoy
your visit to
Eilean Dubh!
leis gach deagh dhùrachd,
(with every good wish)
Audrey McClellan

Contents

And it's westering home, and a song in the air,
Light in the eye, and it's goodbye to care.
Laughter o' love, and a welcoming there,
Isle of my heart, my own one.

Traditional Scottish tune;
words by Sir Hugh Roberton.

PART I

The Island

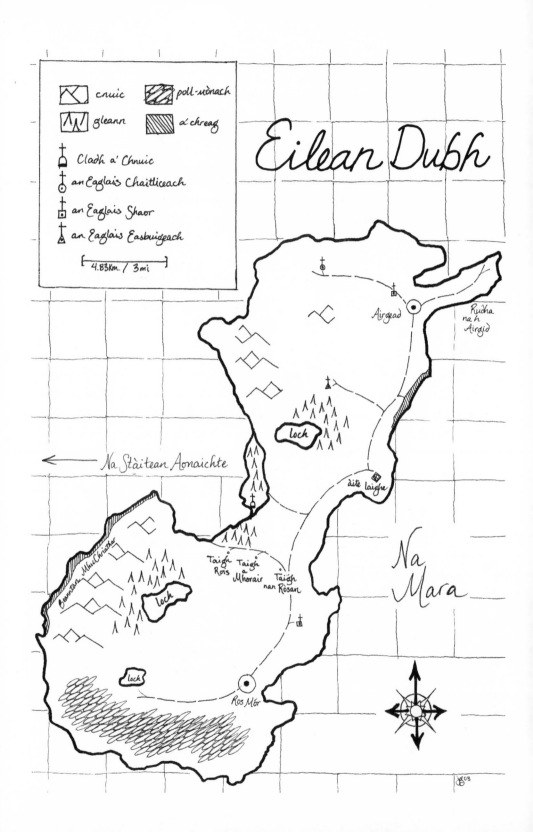

One

Eilean Dubh (pronounced ale-en dew), a small island located in the Hebridean Sea off the western coast of mainland Scotland; it is the largest island in the Middle Hebrides group. N. B.: geographers do not recognize a "Middle Hebrides," arguing that all of the islands so-called, with the exception of Eilean Dubh, are simply rocks in the sea.

Robertson's Relics and Anomalies of Scotland, 1923

*T*he Island was a dream floating on cerulean water, its outline etched by jagged crags covered with deep pine forests that were dark on the most sunlit days. It rose from the ocean as a silhouette hovering in the misty haar that made it impossible to tell where sea left off and land began.

Sailors had named it Eilean Dubh, the Dark Island, in the Gaelic.

Leaning on the rail of the Caledonian-MacBrayne ferry, Jean Abbott watched the Island come slowly into sight. The trip from Oban had taken three hours even though the distance across the Hebridean Sea was short. Thriftily, the ferry called at several other islands; Eilean Dubh did not have enough traffic for an exclusive route. Three times a week in summer, twice in winter, and that was pushing it by Cal-Mac standards.

The ferry lurched and stopped a considerable distance from the dock.

"Here's the pilot," said the man by Jean, gesturing at a small powerboat tying up to the ferry. "Only an Eilean Dubh native can guide the ferry past the rocks in this harbor. You can't see them but they're huge, just below the surface." He added cheerfully, "They'd rip the bottom out if we hit them."

Jean shuddered. "I hope the pilot knows what he's doing."

"Eilean Dubh sailors know every rock. It's taught them in the cradle. See those peaks in the west? They're extinct volcanoes. The theory is that massive landslides caused by a volcanic eruption poured across the Island, flattening this side. The rocks ended up in the water in front of us.

"The harbor wasn't navigable by a boat this big until World War II when the government dredged it to anchor warships here. Churchill was afraid of a German invasion through Scotland after a U-boat sank the *Royal Oak* in Scapa Flow."

He rambled on about Churchill barriers and submarines but Jean had stopped listening. She was picturing a torrent of rocks rolling down the mountains, obliterating everything in the way. Despite the violence of its geological history, she thought the Island resembled a delicate porcelain teacup dipped into the sea.

The ferry was moving again and the teacup's submerged rim was coming closer.

The man said, "Before World War II only boats with shallow drafts could make it into this harbor. The Island was cut off from civilization back then." He chuckled. "It's not a hotbed of activity even now. There's only ten people getting off here, most of us birdwatchers. Are you a twitcher?"

She looked so startled that he laughed. "No, I guess you aren't. American?" When she bobbed her head he went on, "A twitcher is a spotter of rare birds. Eilean Dubh is second only to St. Kilda in its population of nesting sea birds. Corncrakes, kittiwakes, Leach's fork-tailed petrels . . . and in the forests capercaillies, tree-pipits, willow-tits . . ." He smiled dreamily, then said, "Have you family here?"

"No, I'm just a tourist." Feeling she had to explain why she'd visit such an out-of-the-way place she added, "My ancestor came from here two hundred years ago."

"Oh, genealogist, eh?"

That was the easiest explanation. She nodded.

The ferry docked in a noisy medley of creaking wood and clashing metal. The ramp lowered, the lower doors opened and two cars and an old truck drove off. The watchers on the deck sprang into action, gathering up possessions, ready to disembark.

"Enjoy your holiday," the man said to Jean.

"Thanks. I hope you spot lots of birds."

Her suitcase had built-in wheels but it was awkward to manage with the smaller bags she'd tied to the handle. Still, she'd gotten it on the train from Gatwick to London, on the Tube to King's Cross and on the train to Edinburgh's Waverly Station, then to Oban and the ferry, and she was now expert in its handling.

She maneuvered it down the gangplank and looked around uncertainly. The ferry had arrived at Airgead, her hotel was in Ros Mór and she had no idea how to get there.

Passengers were heading towards a bus parked nearby. Jean followed, trailing the suitcase behind her over the rough paving, swearing under her breath every time it twisted and tried to topple over.

The bus driver sized her up quickly. "Are you wanting the bus to Ros Mór?"

"Yes," she said, relieved. "Are you it?"

"*Thà gu dearbh*, yes, indeed. Climb aboard, I'll stow your case."

With an exhausted sigh she got on the bus and settled into a window seat. The other passengers stopped talking and stared at her, then resumed their conversations. She couldn't understand anything they were saying. She realized they were speaking Gaelic, the language of the Highlands and Islands. Eilean Dubh suddenly felt very foreign to her.

But it was beautiful. The road south followed the sea, twisting and turning with the coastline. On the left waves crashed into foam against the rocks, on the right low whitewashed cottages sprawled in boulder-strewn fields. Streams trickled lazily through pastures sparkled by vividly yellow-flowered bushes and soft feathery lavender ones. Sheep were everywhere, faces deep in the grass, jaws working steadily.

The road rose high on top of a cliff that fell sharply away to the ocean and the bus rattled along on the left side uncomfortably close to the edge. There was no guardrail and Jean clutched the edge of her seat in terror. But an elderly woman in the seat beside her dozed, unconcerned, and the driver negotiated the curves without pausing in his conversation over his shoulder with the passengers.

The bus braked to a sudden stop.

Cows filled the road, some standing, staring at the bus, some meandering slowly along, one sprawled on the verge chewing in bovine bliss. They were the strangest cows Jean had ever seen, broad-shouldered, sway-backed and shaggy with matted brownish-red hair. All were adorned with horns extending a foot or more beyond their heads and each had ridiculously round ears and huge black eyes set in an elongated, wistful face. They look like giant teddy bears, she thought, and stifled a giggle.

The driver honked. Passengers laughed and offered suggestions. Finally the last cow, deep in thought, ambled off the road, the bus picked up speed and soon was racketing along at the same terrifying pace as before.

The road leveled, a village's outskirts appeared and the bus pulled into a shop-lined square. Jean pried her fingers from the seat. This must be Ros Mór.

She was the last one off. She stood with her suitcase, wondering where to go. The driver glanced at her, then pulled a handkerchief from his pocket, breathed on the bus's side mirror and polished it carefully.

"Can I get a taxi here?" she asked.

He considered, then shook his head. "Today's Tuesday, the taxi's down at the Seniors' Residence, taking a load of pensioners into Airgead for shopping. He'll drop them off and go straight home."

Her shoulders drooped. "Perhaps I can walk. Is it far to the Rose Hotel?"

"Just down the hill to the harbor."

"Thanks." It had been a long trip from Milwaukee the day before. She'd spent a less than restful night in an Oban bed and breakfast and had risen early to catch the ferry. Now she was so close to her destination. If she could make it down the hill she could finally rest. She reached for the suitcase.

"I can be taking you there, if you like," he offered.

"Oh, yes, if it's not too much trouble," she said eagerly.

"*Chan' eil.*" He grinned. "I always take hotel guests to the door of the Rose. You could have stayed aboard if I'd known."

The road to the harbor was short but very steep. Jean grabbed the seat as the bus dipped sharply, grateful she'd not had to walk. When they stopped by the hotel the driver swung her suitcase down. She reached for it but he shook his head. "I'll take it."

The Rose Hotel was a rambling whitewashed stone building set directly on the waterfront. In some places it was three stories tall, in others only two. Windows appeared unpredictably here and there and the front door was painted a cheery bright red.

Jean followed the driver into the empty lobby.

"Hang on, I'll give Gordon a shout." He disappeared through an archway and quickly returned with a middle-aged man with glasses halfway down his nose and a pencil tucked behind his ear. "Here's Gordon and I'm off." The driver was out the door before Jean could thank him.

The other man beamed at her. "I'm Gordon Morrison. You must be Mrs. Abbott from America. Have you had a good trip?"

She'd been asked this question by nearly every Brit she'd met and by now she was tempted to respond frankly. No, I haven't, the plane was packed, the flight was bumpy and the food only slightly less appalling than that on the BritRail train from London.

But she said none of that. "It was okay but I'm glad to be here."

"You must be tired. Come sign the register and we'll get you settled."

Her room was up a flight of stairs, down a corridor, up another flight and around a corner to the end of the hall.

"I'm sorry to put you so high," Gordon said, "but we've this large party of birdwatchers and they wanted to be on the same floor. This is the only room left with a sea view but we can move you down next week when the birdwatchers leave."

The room was decorated in floral chintzes and the front wall had a double window with a cushioned seat. Below, the ocean glowed slate blue, still except for gentle ripples pulsing beneath the surface. "It's beautiful," Jean said.

"On a clear day you can see twenty miles out to sea," said Gordon proudly. "Of course, there's nothing to look at but water. But early tomorrow morning fishing boats go out. You might like watching, if you're wakeful."

He handed Jean her key. "Will you be wanting dinner? We start serving at six."

"Yes, please." She was starving.

"I'll set up your table. I hope you can find your way downstairs. The Hotel's a mixty-maxty, knocked together from old fishermen's cottages. Easy to get lost." He left.

All she wanted to do was undress, clean up and sprawl on the four-poster bed. The shoes came off first, then jacket, blouse and skirt, then the bra that had been pinching her for the last three hours. Stripped to tights and panties she washed off the travel dirt.

She was tempted by the window seat but it would have meant dressing again or giving passing Islanders an eyeful. Instead, she lay down on the bed and dozed off.

The phone woke her. "Gordon, Mrs. Abbott. Do you not want dinner?"

"What time is it?"

"Almost seven-thirty. We quit serving at eight-thirty."

"Sorry, I fell asleep. Be down in ten minutes, okay?"

"Brilliant."

She dressed, then started down the hall. Left turn, stairs, left turn . . . no, that was the television room . . . right turn . . . down the stairs. Triumphantly she walked into the lobby, then realized she'd no idea where the dining room was.

She followed the corridor until she came to a large cheerful room full of tables and chattering diners. A serious-faced teenaged girl hurried up. "Mrs. Abbott? I have your table ready."

Jean had prepared herself for the inevitable woman-alone place back by the waiters' station so she was pleasantly surprised to be shown to a small table tucked in front of a window overlooking the sea. The meal was even more of a pleasant surprise. Fresh trout, rolled in ground almonds and fried. A potato dish rich with cream and butter. Tender baby carrots with broccoli tips. A sharply sweet glass of Chardonnay.

When the waitress brought her cheesecake, Gordon was behind her, carrying a tray holding a crystal glass with an amber-colored liquid. "It is the custom of the Rose to greet guests on their first night with a dram of malt whisky. This is Talisker, from the Isle of Skye."

She picked up the glass, trying to look pleased. Her experience with whisky was limited to her husband's choices, any of which would take the chrome from a boat hitch in Jean's opinion. She sipped cautiously. "It's nice, thank you," she said, smiling bravely while the whisky burned its way down her throat.

Gordon smiled. "*Fàilte do'n Eilean Dhuibh*. Welcome to our Island."

It did not seem polite to leave any whisky in the glass and besides she was beginning to enjoy it. What had been fire was now a warm glow from mouth to stomach.

She realized fatigue, wine and dinner were having a predictable effect that the whisky was definitely accentuating. She stood up. She walked with dignity as far as the lobby but needed the help of the stair rail to make it up the two flights.

She had just enough energy left to locate her toothbrush and undress. Then she fell into bed. She didn't get up the next morning to see the fishing boats, nor did she hear them. It was her best night's sleep in four months.

Two

They met, they lingered together for the least fraction of time, and that was enough.

Robert Louis Stevenson

a smiling blonde woman extended a friendly hand to Jean the next morning. Her accent identified her as English, not Scottish. "Hullo, love, I'm Sheilah. Welcome to the Rose. Gordon's my husband; he's the manager and I cook. Is your room to your taste?"

"Fine, and dinner was wonderful."

"Thanks." Sheilah looked at her visitor curiously. American visitors to the Island were rare. Most tourists were English or European, interested in bird watching, hiking and getting away from it all. She wondered which category her guest fell into but she never pried and said only, "The weather's lovely today, if you're going walking."

"Yes, I think I will," said Jean.

After breakfast she unpacked, then walked the waterfront from the Rose to the lighthouse at the harbor entrance. From there she watched the fishing fleet straggling back in. She bought a sandwich from a dockside vendor and sat on the pier to eat it.

She enjoyed another superb dinner at the Rose, then went to her room for what she knew would become a weekly duty: writing letters home.

To Russ, her estranged husband, she wrote a short formal letter advising him of her safe arrival. It was her duty to tell him that but she'd no intention of letting him think she'd forgiven the lapses that had driven her from her home to a tiny Scottish island.

Her son Rod, a computer science student at the University of California in Berkeley, got a chattier note. That came easily because she was used to communicating with him by frequent, brief e-mails.

Her letter to her nineteen-year-old daughter was harder. Sally knew nothing of why she'd left and must be wondering why her mother was three thousand miles away from home.

She started that one several times before achieving the right touristy note. "You'd love this place, Sal. The Island is beautiful, all different shades of the most unbelievable greens, but the mountains are dark and mysterious, almost black at the tops." Her enthusiasm for the Island's beauty carried her through several pages.

After the letters she was at a loss. It was too early for bed and she hadn't brought enough paperback books in her suitcase. Television, she thought, and went looking for the TV lounge.

She had the room to herself. Once she'd mastered the controls she discovered there were only four channels. The news program was terse; nothing much had happened in the outside world. The weather report covered so large an area that by the time she'd figured out where she was the report was over. She thought the forecaster had said, "Rainy with sunny intervals," and "sunny with rainy intervals," for all of Scotland.

On the next channel she found a program called *Classic Theatre* and the play was *Jane Eyre*. She settled down to watch and was content to go to bed afterwards.

Her next few days were the same: walks, good meals and television. She realized she was going to have to start her genealogy research soon but she felt too emotionally drained to think about it. She would take it easy for now.

After four nights of television her luck ran out. A by-election was being held somewhere in Scotland and one channel featured a political debate between two men in suits who looked uncannily alike. A science program was on another channel, an American re-run on the next and the last had switched to a Gaelic language format. She watched that, bemused, for a while, then turned it off and wandered down to the lobby in search of something to read.

Her waitress was there. "Enjoying your holiday, Mrs. Abbott?"

"Yes, it's very relaxing."

"If you'd like an after-dinner drink the residents' bar is down the second hall."

That was something to do although she didn't want more liquor. But the bar was smoky, noisy and crowded and it took all her courage to go in.

Sheilah was there, chatting with Gordon who was tending bar. "Mrs. Abbott, how are you keeping? Drink for you, love?"

"Gin and tonic, please."

Sheilah said, "Are you enjoying your walks? Tomorrow will be fine again. If you're wanting places to explore there are hiking maps at the front desk. Help yourself." She rose. "I'm off. Dishwashers to empty and tables to set for breakfast."

Sitting by herself at the bar Jean was no longer uncomfortable. She recognized some of those around her as guests she'd seen at breakfast and others as hotel staff.

At a table in the room's center a man sat alone, his broad-shouldered, long-legged frame dwarfing the chair that held him. He stared somberly into a glass of golden liquid.

Amazed, she realized she knew him. The sharp profile and jet black hair held some strong connection with home but she couldn't put her finger on it. How could someone she knew from Milwaukee be here?

But he didn't look American. His lean face had a curiously refined European look: pale skin, high cheekbones and a long elegant nose. Not a handsome face, but it drew the eye and held it.

Jean stared and wracked her brain.

Gordon pulled up a chair by him. Not once did the other smile though Gordon was obviously trying to cheer him up.

When Gordon went back to the bar she could stand it no longer. She got up and picked her way through the room to his table.

"Excuse me," she said.

He rose politely halfway from his chair and looked at her. His eyes were the most startlingly blue she'd ever seen. No, this is wrong, she thought, I'd remember those eyes. But she had to say something. She blurted, "Don't we know each other?"

He looked at her down the long elegant nose for a moment. The blue eyes became distant. He said coolly, "Sorry, I don't think so," and sat back down.

Dismissed, Jean felt herself turning red. To her eternal chagrin she was a blusher. She took a step back and bumped into a man standing by the next table. His beer sloshed.

She apologized, pulled herself together and exited the room with as much dignity as she could muster. Outside she felt the hot blush beginning to subside. He thought I was trying to pick him up, she decided, not realizing that a pick-up in the Rose's residents' bar was as likely as a spaceship landing in Ros Mór harbor.

Humiliation overwhelmed her and she scampered upstairs to her room. Suppose he's staying here, she thought, I'd have to see him at breakfast. Well, of course he's staying here, stupid, he was in the residents' bar. He was drinking, perhaps he won't remember me tomorrow. She resolved to be cool, collected and to look carefully through the glass door before entering the dining room. If he was there she'd skip breakfast and take a long walk.

Three

Most Islanders live by fishing and crofting,
the Highland practice of working a small plot of land,
which they tend with great care, nourishing the ground
with dressings of seaweed, animal droppings and fish carcasses.
Thus enhanced the crofts provide vegetable crops
for their human residents and feed for the beasts.

Robertson's Relics

*N*ext morning the thought of missing Sheila's scones seemed much worse than running into a man who'd snubbed her publicly. I did nothing wrong, Jean told herself. Who does he think he is?

She put on a becoming green turtleneck and slim skirt, determined to march into the dining room with all flags flying. She put on walking shoes, too, in case she lost her nerve and had to hotfoot it out.

As it turned out he wasn't there and she spent her entire meal jumping nervously whenever the door opened. Still, the scones were worth it.

Since she was dressed for a walk she walked. She climbed the steep hill from the harbor to the High Street square where shops were clustered. Each shop front was painted a different color. There was pink, peach, deep green, yellow and even one lilac, all trimmed with white. The painting had obviously been done years ago; the colors had mellowed into the soft tones of an Impressionist painting.

She peered into the windows of the butcher's and the baker's and admired the bright glassy eyes of fish arranged artistically on ice in the fishmonger's sparkling-clean window. The greengrocer's shop spilled out onto the sidewalk, vegetables and fruit in neat rows. Bunches of flowers sat in a bucket of water.

The sun hid behind a hazy overcast and the air glowed with a clear white sheen, reflecting the light bounced off the sea nearby. There was almost no one out. Twice people passed on the other side of the street, glancing curiously at her, but apart from that she had the square to herself.

She passed an estate agent's yellow-toned storefront, then turned back when she saw pictures of houses in the window. "Estate agent" must mean real estate agent, she decided, studying the pictures. Several were large houses with large prices. She hadn't realized Eilean Dubh possessed such mansions but a closer look revealed that the houses were located in Edinburgh, York and someplace called South Croyden. The cottages pictured were more reasonably priced but all were in Cornwall and Devon.

On impulse she opened the door and walked in.

A bespectacled man in shirtsleeves and tie sat at a desk and didn't stir until she said, "Hi." He looked up, startled, then rose.

He sized her up quickly as a visitor and spoke in the formal, beautifully enunciated English she now recognized as the hallmark of Eilean Dubh Gaelic speakers, for whom English was a second, infrequently-used language. "Good morning, madam. May I assist you?"

"I'm looking for a place to rent."

"Oh? In what part of the country are you interested? We've lovely self-catering cottages on the Cornish coast, perfect for holidays."

"Here on the Island is where I wish to rent," she said, her answer coming out phrased as an Islander would say it. "I mean, I'm staying at the Rose and I'd like to rent something for several months."

"Please sit down. My name is Tòmas Mac-a-Phi."

She moved to the chair he offered. "I'm Jean Abbott."

"From America. What part?"

"Milwaukee." She expected a blank look but he said eagerly, "But that is near Chicago, is it not? Perhaps you are knowing my cousin Angus Carrothers? He emigrated to Chicago ten years ago and has a bake shop there."

"Sorry, I don't know many people in Chicago. It's a huge city."

"*Thà gu dearbh*, yes, of course. Silly of me. Now you are wishing to rent . . . "

" . . . an apartment or a small house."

"I'm afraid rental properties are difficult to find here. Most people own their crofts and the rights that go with them." When she looked confused, he said, "A croft is a small farm with rights of grazing, peats harvesting, and so on. You don't wish to become a permanent resident? It's difficult for crofting rights to be transferred to a non-Islander and there are seldom crofts for sale. Our people are very stable."

"No, I just want a place to stay for a few weeks."

"Ah." He paused. "Nothing comes to mind right now." But with the Islander's typical inability to say no outright he added, "If I think of something I will contact you at the Rose."

She stood up, disappointed. "Thanks for your time."

"A pleasure. Enjoy your holiday on Eilean Dubh."

Out in the beautiful day once more she paused, wondering where to go. She had nearly completed the circuit of the square. Only one shop remained, its front a deep cool blue that seemed to merge into the sky above. Its sign said something incomprehensible in Gaelic but the word "Co-Op" was painted in elegant letters on the window.

Once inside she saw it was a kind of general store. One side held groceries, dairy and freezer cases. The other was like a small town department store with everything from stationery to hardware. She wandered into the lingerie aisle, worked her way through clothing, turned right into linens and ended in a corner packed with bolts of cloth.

She lingered, fingering a flowered calico. The dusty fabric odor reminded her of similar stores in the small towns of Door County. For a moment she was there, looking for curtain material for her family's cottage on Sister Bay. With her daughter Sally, and husband Russ and son Rod next door in the hardware store. Back when her life was safe and predictable. Homesickness loomed, tears prickled her eyes. You need lunch, she told herself and headed for the door. She stopped short.

Her mystery man was there, chatting with the two women at the cash register. They looked at him admiringly as he waved his long-fingered hands about, expounding on some point that amused all three. His face shone with life and intelligence and even at this distance she could see the sparkle in the blue eyes.

Jean froze. There was no way she could leave the store without passing him. She moved into the lingerie aisle, turned her back and pretended a deep interest in a counter full of cotton underpants. Automatically she began looking for her size and found a pair in a virulent shade of puce. She clutched them, realizing she was eavesdropping on the conversation behind her.

It was, of course, in Gaelic. So he was not a visitor like herself, he was an Islander and there would be many opportunities to bump into him. Might as well get it over with. She steeled herself to turn around and walk out.

"Do you require assistance, madam?" said a voice in careful English. The younger clerk was at her elbow. Realizing she was clutching the puce panties and feeling absurdly like a shoplifter Jean stammered, "Do you have this size in other colors?"

"Permit me." The clerk took the panties and looked at the size, then opened a drawer and rummaged through it. Pulling out a handful she announced triumphantly, "There's white as well, madam."

"Oh, good," said Jean, feeling even more foolish. "I'll take two." Hopelessly she realized that not only had she committed herself to a stay at the cash register, she'd also be embarrassed by the purchase of an item of an intimate nature, and an ugly one at that.

She realized she hadn't brought her purse. Relieved, she said, "Oh, sorry, I don't have any money, I was just out for a walk. I'll stop back another day."

"Yes, madam. We've an ample supply in that size. I'm sure there will be some left when you return."

"Thanks," said Jean. She turned and fled. To her immense relief he had left; the older woman was alone at the register. Shaken, feeling more foolish than she'd ever imagined feeling, she headed for the Hotel, glancing from side to side in fear of encountering the mystery man again.

By the time she got to the Rose she'd straightened her shoulders and was holding her head up. Really, there was no need to carry on like this. Was she going to keep on dodging around corners just to avoid a man who had probably forgotten both her and last night's encounter?

She marched to the dining room for another delicious meal and began to entertain serious worries about her weight. Food this good would fatten her like a Christmas goose.

Gordon came by. "The newspapers are here. Yesterday's, of course, but I've two London papers and one from Edinburgh if you'd like them."

"Thanks. May I take my coffee out on the patio?"

He looked puzzled, then brightened. "Oh, of course, into the garden. Why don't you select a chair and I'll bring you a fresh cup and biscuits for afters."

Ensconced in a sunny corner of what she now realized was called the garden, Jean sipped coffee and nibbled on Sheila's delicate cookies while she scanned the papers. But everything she read about seemed far away. She put the papers aside, closed her eyes and settled back to do some serious day-dreaming.

"*Gabh mo leisgeul*," said a deep voice. Jean woke with a start and looked up to find herself staring into a pair of astonishingly blue eyes.

Abair rium mun abair mi ruit. Speak to me ere I speak to thee.

Gaelic proverb

*H*er first thought was that he was even taller than she'd realized when she'd seen him in the Co-Op. Her eyes had to travel up a long way to meet his, past a lean figure in jeans, a sweater as blue as his eyes and a Harris Tweed jacket that had seen better days.

"Excuse me," he said in English this time. Jean's eyes focused uncomfortably on his. "Don't we know each other?"

"Well, really," she said, outraged. "Of all the nerve." Whatever she had expected from their next encounter it had not been that he would throw her own words back to her in mockery, with a perfectly serious expression on his face.

"Sorry?" he said, puzzled.

Jean said coldly, "We established last night that we don't know each other."

"Last night?" He ran a hand through the black hair until it stuck up wildly. "*A Dhia.*" He hesitated. "May I sit down?"

"If you insist."

He drew over a chair and sat for a moment, apparently at a loss.

Jean said, "Well?" The situation was beginning to get on her nerves.

"This is most awkward, but would you please tell me the circumstances under which we met last night?"

"We didn't meet, that's the point." Then, as he looked baffled she said, "It was in the residents' bar. I thought I knew you so I spoke to you. You made it clear that you didn't know me and you didn't want to."

He winced. "Was I dreadfully rude?"

"Well . . . " Saying it aloud made it seem rather petty. "I thought you thought I was trying to pick you up." Memory made her cheeks color.

"*A Dhia*," he said again. He bowed his head for a moment, then said, "Please forgive my rudeness. It's not much of an excuse but I received upsetting news yesterday and I was not feeling sociable. I was in a bit of a . . . funk, as you Americans say. I'm not usually rude to ladies."

Jean said, "Oh, it's okay. I suppose I took it too seriously but I was embarrassed. I was so sure I knew you."

"Last night's encounter explains why I felt that way about you but I don't think we've met. Perhaps I remind you of someone."

"Perhaps." He seemed so distressed she decided to be friendly. "My name's Jean Abbott." She held out her hand.

He shook it firmly. "I'm Darroch Mac an Rìgh, I live on the Island. Where in America is your home?"

"Milwaukee." She expected him to look vague but he said, "Where the beer comes from, *nicht wahr*?"

"*Jawohl,* but we are not all German there and we have lots to offer besides beer."

"And you don't like being called a suburb of Chicago." He looked triumphant at her start of surprise.

"Have you visited Milwaukee?"

"Once, years ago. Does the German restaurant in Old Town, the Strudelplatz or something like that, still flourish? The potato pancakes were wonderful."

"Altplatz, it's called. Yes, it's a landmark, it'll survive all the inhabitants." They smiled at each other, common ground established.

"Well, now. What brings a lady from Milwaukee to Eilean Dubh?"

"Do I have to have a reason?"

"Aye, of course, no one just comes here. It's part of the charm of the Island. If you don't have a reason, make one up. I love a good story." His smile sparkled first in the amazing blue eyes, then migrated down to the well-shaped mouth. Jean stared, fascinated.

He looked at her cup. "More coffee? Wait for me, I'll be back straight-away." He was gone before she could respond.

He returned carrying a tray with a coffeepot, another cup and two crystal glasses. He refilled her cup, then set one of the glasses down next to it. It held a dark golden liquid. "I've brought you a whisky. Whisky is the customary drink for all ceremonies here, including the ceremony of making amends."

She looked uncertain. "I don't have much experience with whisky. My husband drinks Johnny Beam or whatever but it's too strong for me."

He wrinkled his beautiful nose. "This is quite different, a single malt, our Scottish drink. This is the Glenmorangie, refined and elegant. I always think of it as most suitable for a lady." He lifted his glass and said, "*Slàinte mhath*."

"*Prosit*." She lifted her glass but he shook his head. "No, for your first sip of whisky on Eilean Dubh you must make the toast in the Gaelic. *Slàinte mhath*, good health."

"Okay, slan-jah vah." She sipped carefully. The whisky was very strong but it had a pleasant aftertaste, rounded, mellow, faintly sweet. "I could get to like it," she conceded, "although I'm more used to a gin and tonic."

"A *Sasannach* drink," he dismissed it. "For the English. Here on the Island you should drink whisky."

"And speak Gaelic."

He grinned and corrected her. "*The* Gaelic. *Thà gu dearbh*, of course."

"I can't help wondering . . . what was the news that drove you to drink?" She was instantly appalled at herself. She knew personal questions were off-limits to Brits.

To her surprise Darroch said, "Would you mind if I told you about it? If I'd had a sympathetic ear last night I might not have behaved so badly."

"What about Gordon?" she said, betraying that she had been watching them.

"Gordon . . . well, Gordon thought I shouldn't be concerned about my news. He wanted to cheer me up, I wanted sympathy."

"Go on. I feel sympathetic."

"I received a letter from my ex-wife, inviting me to her wedding."

"And you're still in love with her?"

"*A Dhia*, no." He was horrified. "I have not loved her since she told me she'd gone to bed with another man." Jean drew in her breath sharply. "No, the letter brought back the anguish of that discovery and of the divorce. Happy memories, too, of when we were married. I had such high hopes for us and I'd failed."

"Was it your fault, if she was sleeping around?"

"Why wasn't it my fault? What did she need that I couldn't give her?"

"Maybe it isn't our fault, maybe it's theirs," Jean said bitterly.

He caught on quickly. "What, you too?" he said.

"My husband confessed four months ago."

"*A charaid*, I am sorry." His beautiful voice was deeply sympathetic.

Jean felt both comforted and oddly like crying. She finished the whisky, not noticing the warmth in her throat this time. "You first, tell me about your wife. Ex-, I mean."

"She's an actress, she took a part in a film in France. I was working and couldn't go with her. She had an affair with her leading man, very handsome and notorious for getting his co-stars into bed. A fool I was, to think she could resist him." He sighed, thinking of his charming, empty-headed wife. "What hurt the most was that she assured me it was part of the job, that in a romantic film people always have affairs to help develop their roles. Absolute twaddle, of course. I might have understood if she'd said she'd fallen in love."

He smiled. "Your turn. What was your husband's excuse?"

"He says he likes the thrill of the chase and he doesn't get that in marriage. Then some psychological . . . twaddle, that's a good word . . . about being addicted to adultery. Which I took to mean he'd had other affairs. I was right. He admitted it."

Jean looked past the garden down to the pier's end where sunlight gleamed off high tide. The whisky had lowered her inhibitions; tears were running down her cheeks. Darroch's innate kindness made him pull out a handkerchief and gently dab them away.

Touched by the gesture, she said, "I've been married twenty years and have two children. How about you?"

"Three years, no children."

Jean sighed. "You're the first person I've told about Russ. No one knows."

"Lucky you. Adrienne's affair was all over our circle. That's why she told me, because she knew someone else would. She wanted to be first so she could coax me into forgiving her.

"One of my friends tried to tell me about it after I knew." His voice sharpened and became waspish. "'She's a tart, old chap, at it for years. Everyone knows, just waiting for you to find out. Can't help it, the silly cow.' I'm afraid I hit him. I have a distinct memory of him looking up at me from the floor and saying, 'Dear boy, I was only stating the obvious.'"

He shook his head. "Poor Max, everyone takes a swing at him eventually. Most irritating man I know and never afraid to say out loud what everyone else only whispers."

Jean said, "I left town before anyone found out. Our kids don't know, they think I'm nuts to run off to a place like this." She looked at him and something clicked in her brain. Mentally she added sideburns and beard to his face and said, "You're an actor. I saw you in *Jane Eyre* the other night, isn't that right, Mr. Rochester?"

He smiled. "Aye."

"That's why I thought I knew you." She peered at him more closely. "But there's something else . . . something I thought of but couldn't quite . . . My goodness! You're the Magician!" she gasped, eyes widening.

"I used to be." His manner changed subtly. He was still friendly, but reserved.

Jean picked up the change. Of course, he was used to being accosted by fans. Perhaps he was tired of being hassled and that was why he'd snubbed her in the bar.

She tried to speak coolly. "My daughter and I watched your show on public television starting when she was nine. We loved it. We taped all the episodes and watched them over and over." Their imaginations had been captured by the BBC fantasy show about the young Victorian music hall performer who suddenly developed the ability to perform real magic and used his skill to fight evil-doers. It had been funny, romantic, and quite addicting and its tall hero, in claret-colored frock coat, lace ruffles at throat and wrists, had enchanted both Jean and her daughter.

Now the real man flashed her the smile that had charmed them from the television screen. "I'm glad you liked it, I always enjoy hearing that. You'll have seen my ex-wife then. She was the Magician's assistant the last two years of the program."

"The little blonde? In the short skirt and tight blouse?"

"We had a new producer who thought we should add some sex appeal. To a children's program." He shrugged, the thought processes of television producers being incomprehensible to normal people.

In Jean's opinion and her daughter's the blonde hadn't improved the show but she said only, "I'll write my daughter Sally about meeting you. She'll be thrilled. Maybe it will make my coming here more acceptable. It was hard to explain."

"What did you say?"

She looked rueful. "Damned little. I made my plans secretly, told them Monday I was leaving Tuesday." She was silent, remembering Sally's astonishment. "Mom! All by yourself to a little teeny island? Why?"

"My story is I'm doing genealogical research on an ancestor from here. It's true, partly. But I would never have come here if I hadn't been running away from home. The truth is I thought this would be a quiet place without distractions, to think about what to do with my life."

"Your family is from Eilean Dubh?"

"One of them."

"What was his . . . or her . . . name?"

"All I know is that his first name was Ùisdean and he was known as Hugh."

"Ùisdean is the Gaelic for Hugh. You don't know his surname?"

"Not his real one. It's a long story. Perhaps you don't have time right now?" She eyed him doubtfully. The light on the sea had changed. The afternoon was turning into the long twilight of midsummer that would last until midnight.

"Are you having dinner in the Hotel?"

"Is it that late? Yes."

"May I join you? Then you could tell me your long story."

"Sure, if you'd really like to hear it," she said, flattered.

Darroch stood. "I'll be right back." He headed for the Rose's kitchen where he discovered Sheilah pulling something smelling delicious from an oven. Her pretty face red from the heat, she struggled to settle the heavy tray on top of the stove. Then she noticed him. "Darroch! *Ciamar a tha?*" How are you? It was one of the few bits of the Gaelic she'd mastered.

"*Glé mhath, tapadh leat. Agus thu?*" he responded politely.

"I'm fine. Just the usual pre-dinner jumble."

"Can you accommodate one more for dinner, love? And is it venison pie?"

"Yes and yes. Murdoch's delivery."

"Ah, his cousin the Duke's factor's been culling the herd."

Sheilah nodded. "Brought me the deer Wednesday."

"The Duke's loss is our gain. Sheilah, please set a place for me with your American guest. We've been chatting."

"Yes, all right." If Sheilah was curious about this she didn't ask. Her mind had already turned back to dinner preparation.

When he returned, Jean said, "I'm going to my room to tidy up. I must have mascara smeared all over."

"Not at all," he responded gallantly. In fact, whatever eye makeup she was wearing had smudged from her tears. It gave her a disarmingly rakish air, like an old-time movie star. "I'll wait for you in the lobby," he said.

Five

*The angel said, "There is a laird who has been
driving out his tenants . . . He is now forever doomed to be
alternately bitten by serpents and have his wounds
licked by fiery hell-hounds' tongues . . . "*

From the vision of Hell of the nineteenth-century crofter-seer, David Ross

*W*hen Jean came down fifteen minutes later she'd changed clothes and put on a terracotta colored turtleneck and a black skirt. She'd repaired her eye makeup and brushed her hair to a red-brown sheen.

In the dining room, Darroch persuaded her to try the venison pie. The only venison she'd ever eaten had been shot in northern Wisconsin and was laced with unexpected fragments of metal. She ventured tactfully to inquire how carefully she should chew tonight's meal.

He chuckled. "Not to worry. This deer lived fat and happy and was dispatched with one careful shot to the head. Murdoch's cousin does not believe in damaging the merchandise."

"Is that Murdoch the . . . what do you say . . . Helicopter?" She'd learned from Gordon the Island habit of identifying people by physical characteristics or jobs to distinguish those with similar names from each other.

"Murdoch the Chopper. He has lots of cousins and puts them all to good use. The one who supplied the deer is a Highland duke's factor. When it's time to thin the herd he tells Murdoch and he collects a deer for Eilean Dubh. No one here has ever asked if it's with the duke's permission."

"Free enterprise."

"Well, it's an old Highland custom, living off the crumbs from the lord's table, scrounging what can be scrounged."

She wondered at the bitterness in his voice. "I thought the clan system ensured that the chief looked after his people."

"That broke down in the nineteenth century when the chiefs realized they could make more money by booting their kin off the land and running sheep instead. 'Four-footed clansmen,' people called the sheep. The chiefs needed money so they could go to London and ponce around at Court, hoping to get in good with the power brokers so they could find ways to add to their estates and purses."

"I've read about that. The Clearances, wasn't it, when people were evicted?"

"Aye. Many who were cleared off their crofts were given worthless land that wouldn't grow food. To escape starvation thousands emigrated. Sometimes the chiefs gave money to help them leave, sometimes they just turned their backs.

"Scotland lost a lot of population that way; you can see burnt-out cottages all over the Highlands. Their homes were burned over the inhabitants' heads if the factors didn't think they were getting out fast enough." He said grimly, "Every ruined cottage is a nail in Scotland's heart."

Jean shivered. "Did that happen here?"

"We were lucky. Both our harbors were impassable except for fishing boats so we were isolated up to the twentieth century. Isolation meant no Eilean Dubh laird was invited to Court until after Victoria. They'd barely heard of us in London before then."

"But people did emigrate. My great-something grandfather did."

He leaned forward. "Tell me about him."

Their meals arrived before Jean could begin. "My goodness," she said after the first few bites. "This venison pie is superb."

He smiled. "Aye. Sheila's an example of what happens when the Island gets hold of someone. She's a professionally trained chef, came here one summer to help Beathag and Tearlach MacDougall start their restaurant. A couple of weeks after she arrived she met Gordon at a *cèilidh*. They fell in love, married and amazingly Sheilah prefers to stay on the Island and help run the Hotel.

"Someone with her talent could be very successful in London. She's from the East End; her family thinks she's daft, spending her life in this remote place. Sheilah says she likes it here." He smiled. "The only reason she'll give is that she likes the sunsets."

"Like that one." Jean pointed out the window where the sun was setting in a flaming puddle. It was almost excessively gaudy, like a musical show with too many dancers in rhinestones. Hot pink, blazing coral and cool lavender-gray clouds jostled in the slowly darkening sky.

Darroch leaned back in his chair, stretched out his long legs and gave her the full benefit of the blue eyes. "All right, let's hear about this ancestor of yours."

What a charmer, thought Jean, remembering the bemused women in the Co-Op. She took a deep breath and launched into her story. "I was executrix for my great-aunt's estate in North Carolina. I found letters in her desk and a note saying they were written by my great-great-something grandfather Ùisdean. Am I pronouncing that right?"

"Oosh-jan. Go on."

"The letters had been written to someone on Eilean Dubh named Mòrag."

"Gaelic for Marian."

"Is it?" she said in surprise. "Marian is a family name; it's my middle name. The letters were in Gaelic but I found a translator at the local university. He only did the first one, he said the language was archaic and he didn't understand the idioms. He did establish that they were sent to Eilean Dubh but returned to Ùisdean in America. The cover letter said Mòrag was dead and the writer requested no further contact with her family.

"That was the first I knew of the Eilean Dubh connection. We knew we came from Scotland but we didn't know from which part. Ùisdean was a mysterious character. He started as a fur trader and built up a business bringing supplies and settlers over the mountains to frontier settlements. Very risky because the mountains are dangerous. Our family story was that he seemed to have an inborn understanding of them, knew when it was safe to travel and when it wasn't. He could almost smell a snowstorm coming."

Darroch said, "Because he was an *Eilean Dubhannach*. He had to be able to read the weather to survive here." Jean's story fascinated him. He'd only met three North Americans who could trace ancestors to Eilean Dubh.

"When I couldn't find much information about the Island I realized I'd have to come here to learn more. So here I am, thanks to my husband's fooling around."

"You don't know Ùisdean's last name?"

"Not his real one. My maiden name is Greer, the name he adopted in America. The envelope with the letters was addressed to him but the last name was torn off. The family's always wondered if he changed it because he was an outlaw. Greer doesn't sound Scottish, does it?"

"It's not an Island name. How did you know before the letters that you'd come from Scotland?"

"Oh, that was no secret. Ùisdean was proud of being a Scot. We've always been proud of that. But because we didn't know his real name or where he came from we couldn't join a clan or wear a special plaid.

"In America in the eighteen hundreds, no one cared where you came from and secrecy about your background was common. Lots of people were running from something and what mattered in America was brains and hard work, not family."

"So you're ancestor-hunting. What do you hope to find?"

"It would be interesting to learn who Ùisdean was and about his family but that was a long time ago. It doesn't matter now." She stared out the window. The sun had disappeared but brilliant purple streaks in the sky mourned its passing.

"I want to know the place he came from. What it was like back then, what it's like now. Why did he leave? Who was Mòrag? If along the way I pick up a cousin or two that's a bonus. I'll stay a few weeks, poke around the cemeteries and museums.

"I can't afford to stay at the Rose forever and if I keep eating Sheila's meals I'll resemble a balloon. But the estate agent was dubious about finding anything to rent."

"We've always been short of decent housing. I suppose you'd want all mod cons."

"What? Oh, I get it, electricity and indoor plumbing. Yes, it can be simple but I don't want to rough it too much." She added, "I'd like to hear some real Scottish folk music, too."

"We have *cèilidhean* every other Friday night and all we play is traditional music. There's one this Friday. I'd be glad to take you."

She was delighted. "Wonderful. Since you're answering all my questions, could you find someone to translate Ùisdean's letters? I brought photocopies. I'd like to read them word for word."

Darroch said, "I'll look at them for you."

"Would you? That's very kind. But you must be busy, I don't want to impose . . . "

"Not at all, I'd enjoy it. I don't often get to see material in eighteenth-century Island Gaelic. If I get stuck there are others who'll help, like Isabel, our librarian and history expert. She'd love to see them."

He considered her other needs. "I could give you an Island tour. We've just one museum, in Airgead, but it's packed with things. And I'll show you the cemetery. I enjoy visiting it."

"I'd love that."

"Tomorrow? No, I've got Co-Op business all afternoon. But it's in Airgead. If you came with me you could start in the library. Collect you at one, shall I?"

At her nod and smile he said, "I'm away home, then, if we're set."

"I'll walk out with you. I like to look at the harbor at twilight."

"You and Sheilah. She'll be sitting on the steps now."

She was. Darroch said, "Here's someone else who likes our sunsets, Sheilah."

She said, "Take care, Mrs. Abbott. These sunsets get under your skin. You'll be another one who never wants to go home."

I don't have a home any more, thought Jean, suddenly depressed. She said goodbye to Darroch somberly. He looked at her searchingly but said only, "Tomorrow, Jean. Don't forget."

"I won't." The two women watched the tall figure stride up the hill. "Does he live near here? Or is his car parked somewhere around?"

"He's walking home. It's a couple of miles. All these Islanders love to walk," observed Sheilah. "Haven't gotten into the habit, myself."

"He'll walk off that wonderful dinner," said Jean. "I'm going to have to step up my activity level or I won't be able to get into my clothes. You really feed people well."

Sheilah shrugged off the compliment. "It's not cooking for every day. When people here eat out they want something special."

Jean said, "He's nice, Darroch." And a fast worker. Bemused, she realized that she'd disliked him intensely this morning and by sunset she'd agreed to not just one, but two dates. If they were still called dates in this day and at her age. Nonsense, she told herself, he's just being friendly. But his attention was a boost to her ego all the same.

"Yes, he's lovely." Sheilah paused. "Is he taking you somewhere tomorrow?"

"To Ar - gatch, is that right? To the library."

"A pretty drive and you'll enjoy meeting Isabel, our head librarian. Are you doing research?"

"Looking for an ancestor."

"Better you than me, I hate genealogy. I come from the East End of London. Everyone there's related and everyone knows who your great-greats were. I like the anonymity I have here. Of course they all know Gordon's family and where his skeletons are buried but I'm the mystery lady. They speculate endlessly about my antecedents."

Jean didn't want to admit that genealogical research was only her cover for visiting Eilean Dubh so she said, "Oh, I like poking around in old books and papers. You never know who you'll find among your relatives."

Sheilah chuckled. "One of my ancestors was hanged as a highwayman and I'm sure there were others just as shady who didn't get caught." She stood. "Breakfast at the same time tomorrow?"

"Yes, please. Good night." She stared at the sea a while longer until the last rays of sunset had faded. It was still light out but she decided to go to bed. Tomorrow sounded like a busy day.

Six

A surprise invasion of Eilean Dubh was always impossible
because of the razor-sharp rocks in the harbors. As a result
the Island enjoyed centuries of peaceful isolation unheard of in Scotland.

Robertson's Relics

*T*rue to his word Darroch arrived promptly the next day. He and Gordon were in the lobby, chatting in the Gaelic.

"You're one of us, I hear, Mrs. Abbott," said Gordon. When she looked puzzled, he added, "Your people came from our Island."

"Only one."

Gordon smiled. "That's enough."

Outside, Jean stared at the car parked in front. It was a Bentley, a sleek black sedan and it seemed enormous to Jean who'd gotten used to the miniature British cars. "Is this yours?"

"Aye." He patted a fender fondly and opened the door for her.

The inside was dark gray leather with a dashboard of polished walnut. "My goodness, this is beautiful. I've never ridden in anything so elegant."

"Pure self-indulgence on my part, bought in the first flush of success of *The Magician*," he said. "Gas mileage is appalling but on Eilean Dubh distances are short. And she's fifteen years old and not produced any more so I tell myself I'm preserving a classic. I didn't dare drive her in London so I brought her up here."

The engine purred so quietly and the ride was so smooth she could hardly believe the car was moving. She slanted a look at him. He was a curious mixture, she thought. The car was obviously valuable but his clothes, though well cut and hand-tailored, were worn. The cuff on the jacket sleeve closest to her was frayed and the leather elbow patch was shiny with wear.

When they passed a road two miles from town he slowed and gestured to the left. "That's my cottage, second one down."

It was an ordinary cottage of whitewashed stone with a shingle roof, like others she'd seen on the Island. Nothing put it in the class of the Bentley.

She remembered Airgead from her arrival. The town was set upon a flat plain uphill from the harbor, the mountains behind framing it like a theatrical backdrop. The same mix of softly painted stores as Ros Mór lined the square. At the far end stood a huge Victorian brick mansion and by it was a smaller building of stone.

"The stone building is the museum, the brick one the library. We'll start there."

They entered through tall wooden doors into a long hall. The room on the left had obviously once been an elegant drawing room with an enormous marble fireplace and an oak-beamed ceiling. But it would have been recognized as a library anywhere, with rows of bookshelves lining the walls and marching down the center of the room, and a large desk by the door.

The young woman behind the desk brightened, seeing Darroch. They exchanged greetings and she waved toward the office beside her. He rapped on the open glass door.

A gray-haired woman glanced up from her desk. Darroch said, "Isabel, *mo luaidh*, I've brought a lady from America to meet you. Jean Abbott, Isabel Ross, our librarian."

"How exciting!" Smiling, Isabel came forward to offer her hand. "Whyever have you come such a long way to our Island?"

"She's looking for an Ùisdean," said Darroch.

Isabel said, eyes twinkling, "An Ùisdean? Has she lost one?"

"An ancestor," he replied and the story was begun.

Isabel listened carefully. "So you want to identify Ùisdean?"

"Yes," said Jean. "Do you think it's possible?"

"Not easy, but possible. A problem is that source material will be in the Gaelic."

"Oh, my," Jean said, dismayed. "I never thought of that."

"I can help with translation," began Darroch but Isabel shook her head. "No, you would not have time for all she will need. Let me think." They sat in respectful silence while she tapped her pencil, then snapped her fingers.

"What if we find a student who's having trouble with English? You could tutor him or her in return for translating."

"I'd be glad to help a student with English. I've done ESL—English as a second language—tutoring. But I'd pay a translator. I wouldn't expect a person to work for free. Kids want paying jobs."

"We'll find someone and you can work out the details." Isabel said, looking at Darroch, "Liz."

"Aye." To Jean he said, "Liz Thomas is head of the English Department at the High School. She will know who'd be good at your project. Shall I ring her, Isabel?"

"No, I'll be talking to her tonight; we're planning a walking holiday on Jura next month. We'll find someone, Mrs. Abbott."

"It's Jean, please, and thanks very much."

"*Glé mhath*," said Darroch, glancing at his watch. "I must run, I've Co-Op business that will take hours to sort. *Mar sin leat*," he said and left.

Isabel said, "I'll get you started on your research. There's an unpublished history of the Island that's translated; it'll give you background." She took a thick manuscript from a filing case and handed it to Jean. "Come into the library, I'll show you around."

"It's a beautiful building," said Jean, following Isabel into the reading room.

"Built as the Laird's mansion in the 1860s. Laird Alasdair gave it to the Island in the early twentieth century. Unfortunately, beautiful old buildings don't make the best libraries. You'd be shocked at the trouble and expense it took to wire it for computers."

"You have computers?" said Jean.

"Aye. We're entering all our holdings into a computer catalog. Quite a job, but we've invaluable source materials for Highland history and development of the Gaelic that scholars need. We've also added computers for the public to use for word processing. We'd like to make the Internet available but the phone lines are shockingly old-fashioned. We can't connect modems without putting half the phones in Airgead out of order." She sighed. "The Trust's given us a grant for the work but we have to get British Telecom to do the modernizing . . . " Her voice trailed off wistfully. "Here's a table for your work. If you really get stuck into your research we'll find a shelf where you can keep materials."

Jean began with the manuscript history, which said that the origin of the earliest Islanders was unknown but the author speculated that they were the mysterious Picts, the first known inhabitants of Scotland. They were subsequently overwhelmed by Celtic invaders from Ireland in curraghs, small flat-bottomed skin-covered boats that could easily maneuver past the harbor rocks.

The Vikings, the Dark Ages scourge, managed a few inroads, enough to contribute genes for fair hair and blue eyes, but their longboats couldn't make it through the rocks. At other times, shipwrecked sailors clinging to bits of their boats had been washed up on the shores and assimilated into the population, first as slaves, then as free men.

Several boatloads of survivors of the Spanish Armada debacle were blown up to the North Sea and around the top of Scotland. Their contributions were Spanish names in certain families and physical characteristics, jet-black hair the most distinctive.

Desperate fugitives from the Jacobite Risings of 1715 and 1745 trickled in. They contributed an enduring aversion to the English and the London government. "Treacherous as a *Sasannach*" and "shifty as a member of Parliament" were Island sayings surviving to the present day.

Covenanters, mutineers and refugees from the Glorious Revolution, the Industrial Revolution and the Clearances all found their way to Eilean Dubh and all added their blood and beliefs to the Island mixture.

The responsibility for bringing Christianity to Eilean Dubh was that of a saint who floated to the Island on an oak leaf, leaves being a popular form of marine transportation for early Celtic saints. He was Saint Daragh, which, modernized to *darach*, meant "oak" in the Gaelic. Jean found this especially interesting, given that the saint was an ancestor of the Mac an Rìgh clan, since priests in ancient days married and had families.

On the way home in the Bentley, Jean studied Darroch. Becoming aware of her scrutiny, he glanced at her. "Is something wrong?"

"No . . . I was just looking for the halo."

"What?" He gave her a startled glance, then understood. "Oh, you've been reading our history. Isabel wrote that."

"What, she's I. Ross? I didn't guess. It's excellent work."

"Aye, it should be published. That's on our list of things to do."

"I've never met anyone who could trace his ancestors back to a saint."

He laughed. "Alas, sanctity is not inherited and I am quite without a halo."

"It's just that no one I know, even the genealogy buffs, can trace back to . . . well, that must be the Dark Ages. It's phenomenal."

"Not at all, most Islanders can. When we identify Ùisdean you will, too."

As her eyes widened he said, "Ours is a very small Island and careful family records have been kept. The Islanders had to know to whom they were related and how closely because they recognized years ago that birth defects could result from inbreeding. Before couples could marry they had to submit their names to the keepers of genealogies to see if they were within the proscribed limits of blood relationships.

"What began as a means of keeping families healthy ended up quite ritualized. All these records were part of the oral tradition, very important in Celtic societies. *Sgeulaichean*—storytellers—recited genealogies at ceremonial gatherings. That's how family records were passed on before the age of writing."

Jean relaxed against the leather seat, absorbing the information. "So if I find out who Ùisdean was I'll find an entire recorded family tree."

"Right."

When they reached the Hotel, Jean said, "Thanks so much for today, Darroch. It's been fascinating. I'm looking forward to more work in the library."

"*Miorbhuileach*," he said. "Remember the *cèilidh* is Friday night. I'll pick you up at seven-thirty."

When Sheilah told Gordon of Jean's research, he dug out newspaper clippings his father had collected about Eilean Dubh's history. Jean started making notes about what she was learning. Someday, perhaps, her family might be interested.

Seven

*The native language of Eilean Dubh is the Gaelic,
considered by linguists to be the purest example of that ancient and noble
tongue in all Scotland, since it has been neither changed nor influenced by
outside sources. The accent is lilting and musical, and lends itself well to
their exceptional body of native song. The Gaelic has a tenacious hold on
the inhabitants and English has made few inroads.*

Robertson's Relics

*F*riday arrived. "What do you wear to a *cèilidh*?" Jean asked Sheilah.

"Nothing warm. You'll get hot dancing."

Darroch was waiting that evening when Jean came downstairs. Gordon was there, too, and both men were wearing kilts. Jean thought Darroch looked particularly dashing. "What a beautiful plaid," she said to him. It was pale blue and dark green, with red and white lines criss-crossing.

"Tartan," he corrected. "It's the Mac an Rìgh tartan. Representing the four elements of Eilean Dubh: blue for the sky, green for the sea, white for the water in the burns and red for blood." She looked shocked. "Well, in the old days red might have signified clan warfare, the Mac an Rìghs were an argumentative lot. Nowadays I prefer to think of it as the lifeblood of our people."

He looked at her with pleasure. He was quite enjoying having a woman to squire around again. In London he had plenty of flirts in the theatrical set but all the Eilean Dubh women his age were married or otherwise unavailable and he would not play the fool by chatting up some awed, wide-eyed youngster half his age.

And Jean was pretty as well as interesting, delightful to look at as well as talk to, with clear green eyes and hair an unusual shade of brown. The color of whisky, he thought, bemused.

"Shall we go?" He'd brought the Bentley although the Citizens Hall was only a few blocks away. He was not sure how an American would feel about walking; he knew they loved their cars. But she wanted to walk along the pier.

The old-fashioned, high-ceilinged Hall was alive with the babble of over a hundred voices, but a quiet wave of respect preceded Darroch across the floor and a ripple of excited, though muted, interest followed him. The men stopped their conversations to greet him warmly and the women looked at him with the flirtatious deference reserved for an attractive, unattainable man.

Jean was getting plenty of envious attention, fueled by his hand on her shoulder steering her through the crowd. He introduced her to everyone as "our American visitor." The *Eilean Dubhannaich* smiled and greeted her in careful English, inspected her discreetly and asked if she was enjoying her holiday.

Sheilah and Gordon were sitting in the front row. "I've saved you places, Darroch," said Sheilah. "I wanted Jean to have a good view since it's her first *cèilidh*."

"You'll have someone to sit with while I'm on stage," Darroch said to Jean.

"Are you performing?"

"Aye, my friends Màiri and Jamie and I play a bit of music." He turned to the woman who'd sat down by him. "*Feasgar math, a Bharabal,*" he said. "*Ciamar a tha?*"

"*Glè mhath, agus thu?*" The niceties observed, Darroch made introductions.

Barabal Mac-a-Phi was in her mid-thirties, plump and unstylish, but her brown eyes were sharp and alert. She shook Jean's hand firmly.

Sheilah leaned over and said, "Gordon's not playing tonight, he had bad luck in the kitchen." He held up a hand with a bandage on the index finger.

"What do you play?" Jean asked.

"Accordion. It'll have to wait 'til the flesh I sliced knits up." He looked rueful. Sheilah said, "Hazard of the cooking trade."

The program began with bagpipe tunes by a large black-haired man whose face turned red with effort as he played. The music filled the hall and did queer things to Jean's senses; she could feel the hair tingling on the back of her neck. There must be something to the idea of Scottishness in the blood, she thought.

Children performed next. Little girls and one boy danced the Highland fling. A girl in her teens read a poem in the Gaelic.

Then three people filed on stage. One was Darroch. He was escorting a woman to the piano bench with as much ceremony as though she were the Queen. A gorgeous cascade of brilliant red-gold hair flowed halfway down her back. Darroch sat down by her, next to the piano.

An astonishingly handsome man, tall, trim and muscular, carrying a fiddle, took center stage. His hair, tucked carelessly behind his ears, was sunlight blond and his features were beautifully regular: large expressive eyes, perfect nose, authoritative mouth.

He surveyed his audience coolly, tucked the fiddle under his chin and began to play, weaving a shimmering cascade of notes into a melody of great beauty. Jean's jaw dropped.

He finished. The audience reacted with a respectful silence and then an enthusiastic murmur of approval. The fiddle player ducked his head slightly in acknowledgment.

Jean sat stunned.

Barabal leaned over and said, "Did you enjoy that?"

Jean clasped her hands together reverently. "He's incredible."

There was a flicker of disappointment in Barabal's eyes. Then she said, "Aye, he's reckoned the handsomest man on the Island, is Bonnie Prince Jamie."

"What? Oh, yes, he is good looking. But he's absolutely the best fiddle player I've ever heard. Technically and lyrically." Barabal looked at her with new respect. So it was music, not appearance, that impressed the American.

Darroch came forward. He seemed to be the group's spokesperson and what he said in the Gaelic drew chuckles from the audience. Then he began to sing.

His voice reminded Jean of the whisky he'd tried to teach her to drink: full, warm and mellow, smoky and sweet but with an edge to it. It was not a professionally trained voice but he had full control and great stage presence. Even though she couldn't understand a word, Jean was entranced. He sang:

Fhir a' bhàta no hòro éile,
Mo shoraidh slàn leat 's gach àit an teid thu.

The audience joined in the chorus with him. Jean picked up the melody on the second repetition and by the third she was singing, very quietly, most of the simple words of the chorus. She thought it was the most beautiful tune she'd ever heard. She turned to Barabal at the end and demanded, "What is that song called?" The need to learn it had become an urgent need.

"'*Fear a Bhàta*'," said Barabal, then, taking pity on Jean for not having the Gaelic, said, "The boatman, in English. It's about a sailor who makes promises to young lasses he doesn't keep. It's not one of ours, it's from the Highlands."

The group finished their set with a riotous duel between piano and fiddle while Darroch sat listening. The audience's murmur was sustained and appreciative.

When Darroch returned to his seat, he looked for Jean's reaction and was astonished by the rapt look on her face.

"What wonderful music," she said. "I would like very much to learn some of it. Especially the boatman song, what is it . . . air a vata? I definitely want that one. Can I get sheet music for it?"

"Do you sing?"

"Yes, folk music. American, English and Welsh, but I've never heard anything like what you sang."

Welsh, he thought, and wondered where she'd learned Welsh music, but the dance band was setting up on the stage and the audience was clearing the floor of chairs.

"Come meet Màiri and Jamie, my musical partners," Darroch invited as he carried their chairs to the side of the hall. "They're husband and wife."

"Oh, I'd love to meet them. They . . . and you . . . were terrific, just great!"

He said, amused, "Don't say that, they'll think you're a gusher. Just say it was nice, or fine, if you want to go overboard."

She raised her eyebrows but followed obediently in his wake across the floor. When they came upon Jamie and Màiri and she was introduced, she said quietly that she had enjoyed their music very much. She could not resist a sly glance at Darroch to see if that was an acceptable comment. He grinned at her.

Jamie, who was even more staggeringly good-looking up close, was cordial and in his reserved Scottish way, friendly, but his wife was different. Màiri fixed Jean with a challenging look in her cool blue eyes, her pretty face sharp with disdain. "You are a tourist? Staying a week or two, are you?"

Jean answered, "For a couple of months."

"What for?" demanded Màiri bluntly and Jean stared at her.

"Màiri means that not many people come to Eilean Dubh and no one stays above a fortnight so she wonders what your particular interest is," interposed Darroch, who seemed to be trying to avert an outbreak of hostilities.

"Really, Darroch, I can speak for myself," snapped Màiri and tossed her head, red hair flying. "And that was not what I meant to say at all. Good evening, Mrs. Abbott, enjoy your holiday." And she stalked away.

Jamie and Darroch looked at each other and Jamie shrugged. Darroch said something in the Gaelic that made the other man laugh and Jean wondered if it had been a typical male comment about women.

In fact, what he had said was, "Cordial as ever to strangers. We must get her a job in the Tourist Office." To Jean he said, "You mustn't mind Màiri, she'll be friendlier when she gets to know you. She's . . . ah . . . shy."

With difficulty Jean restrained herself from an unladylike snort. Màiri was shy in the way that Adolf Hitler had been shy. However, one woman's hostility wasn't going to slow her down. She turned to the hall where the band had announced the first dance.

"Come try this, if you like. It's quite easy." Darroch offered her his hand.

Jean loved dancing and this was a simple couple dance in waltz time. She fitted easily into his arms and grinned at him. "Do you have this much fun every Friday night?"

"Every other Friday and it takes us till Tuesday to recover. If we had *cèilidhean* every week we'd never get any work done." He swung her merrily around the floor. To her surprise after the first repetition she'd changed partners and was dancing with the man in front of her and so on around the room.

Darroch retrieved her at the end of the dance and took her to the sidelines where he vetted the invitations to dance she received. "'Highland Fair,' aye." 'St. Bernard's Waltz' got an approving nod. 'The Black Dance' he partnered her in himself. But he shook his head at 'Strip the Willow,' 'Màiri's Wedding' was vetoed, and an invitation to dance 'The Eightsome Reel' got a cold stare and a firm comment in the Gaelic to the inviter who slunk away.

"Imagine," said Darroch to Jamie. "He must know she's a beginner, what a daftie to ask her for that."

"Gormless," Jamie agreed.

Jean, watching the dancers hurling themselves about, turning each other in complicated patterns, thought she recognized some of the figures from square dancing. Darroch called it Scottish country dancing. She liked it. The dances she tried made her feel as if she were flying and the music was intoxicating. Something else to learn, she thought. Eilean Dubh was really going to stretch the boundaries of her mind.

Eight

*W*hen Darroch left her to offer his hand as partner to a dignified older woman Jean found herself standing with Jamie and Màiri. She searched her mind for a safe topic of conversation where Màiri was concerned, doubtful there were any. As a result she blundered onto the wrong subject.

"Darroch's been really nice to me. I appreciate it," she said and was alarmed by a flash of jealousy on Màiri's face. Uh-oh, mistake, she thought.

"Yes," said Màiri. "He seems to like you." Her tone was surprised. "What Darroch says is important here." Watching Jean, she added, "He is the laird of Eilean Dubh, you know."

Jean knew some reaction was expected. "I didn't know. Um . . . what exactly is a laird? I've never quite understood."

"The Mac an Rìghs have ruled Eilean Dubh since the seventeen hundreds and Darroch is the senior member of the clan. He's the hereditary ruler, the laird."

Jamie cleared his throat. "We don't have an hereditary ruler, *m'eudail*."

Màiri said haughtily, "It's the principle of the thing. The feeling is there."

"The principle of what thing?" Darroch walked up behind Màiri, who looked guilty.

"Màiri was explaining to me about lairds," said Jean into the sudden silence. Jamie was gazing off into the hall, smiling to himself.

Darroch swung around and stared at Màiri. "Just what was your explanation?"

"Your friend asked me what a laird is. Why don't you tell her, Darroch?" She stared defiantly at him.

Darroch said carefully and deliberately, "A laird is a useless remnant of the bad old days when rapacious chieftains extracted all they could from their people and then expected loyalty, soldierly duty and unquestioning obedience as well. Anyone called a laird today is that only because of the deeds, or misdeeds, of his ancestors and with no regard whatsoever to his qualifications for leadership, the brains in his head or the nobility of his soul.

"At least so my great-grandfather said." He nodded courteously at Jean, then glanced at Màiri. "Would you say that he was right, *a Mhàiri, mo chràdh?*"

She gave him an enigmatic look. Then her pretty mouth curved into a smile. "A strathspey, Darroch. Let's dance." She held out her hand. His eyebrows still raised disapprovingly, he let her lead him onto the floor.

Jean followed them with her eyes. She said to Jamie, "What was that all about?"

Jamie sighed. "Well, you never can be sure with our Màiri but I think she was testing you."

"Testing me? Why?"

He sighed again. "It's a wee bit complicated. She feels it her duty to vet any woman in whom Darroch shows an interest. She still feels responsible that she couldn't save him from that *arpag* he married." He watched the dancers. "Darroch and Màiri were lovers, you know."

"Um . . . well, no . . . I had no reason to know." Jean was embarrassed and intrigued. This had gotten very personal very fast and these *Eilean Dubhannaich* spoke their minds without hesitation.

"Oh, yes, lovers, promised to each other since they were sixteen years old and devoted friends for years before that. They would be married now had they not both been so stubborn."

"What happened?"

"Darroch took a notion to become an actor. He won a scholarship to an important acting school near London and he wanted Màiri to live there with him after they married. She refused to leave Eilean Dubh. She said it was her home and she intended to stay here and work for the Island's good. So they broke it off."

"Oh, dear," said Jean. "How sad."

"Yes, there was much gnashing of teeth and rending of bosoms, I understand, for they were desperately in love. But it happened for the best. Darroch became a successful actor. Màiri decided to work her father's croft. She went off to study agricultural economics and music at Sabhal Mór Ostaig, the Gaelic college on the Isle of Skye. That's where I met her."

He was suddenly silent, remembering, as he often did, his first sight of Màiri Ross. She'd been running to class in the rain, red hair flying out behind her like a cloak, the wind plastering her clothes to her body in a most enticing way. Entranced, he'd followed her inside, only stopping when she disappeared into a classroom.

Jamie loved art. He'd spent much of his time in the high school library leafing through art books instead of studying and the Pre-Raphaelite artists were his favorites. Rossetti, he thought, looking after her, the *Beata Beatrix* come to life before his eyes.

He was known as Handsome Jamie and the girls were mad for him. Not only was he beautiful and from childhood the best fiddler Skye had produced in years, he was also charming, good natured and an incorrigible tease who could reduce the most self-possessed young woman to helpless giggles with his attentions.

An older woman seduced him when he was sixteen and once he'd discovered the pleasures of sex the kirk's teachings on that subject flew out of his head. Any number of girls were willing and eager to engage in a cuddle after Friday night dances, and when he took a job at a Portree hotel he found that tourist girls on holiday were even more willing. He made love to English, French and Dutch girls, a new one every week as guests came and went.

Playing Jack-the-Lad in as close-knit a place as Skye had its disadvantages, not the least of which was the disapproval of his parents, his three brothers and his minister. But it was not until one of his flirts became hysterical with jealousy and made a scene at a dance that it dawned on him he had the power to hurt women badly.

He could not stand that. He retreated into himself to do some thinking and grew up in a week. He had brains, good grades in school and he was meant for something better than being a hotel clerk and the playmate of tourist girls.

His parents worked a small croft and his whole life had been bound up in crofting. He loved the predictable rhythms of each season's work from lambing to harvest. He relished the hard physical effort, the good exhaustion after a day's work, the constant pitting of his wits against nature. He enrolled at Sabhal Mór Ostaig, down the road at Teague, sure that he could make a living from crofting if only he could learn enough about it.

Then he saw Màiri running through the rain and knew he'd met his destiny.

He said, coming back to himself, "It was a year after her breakup with Darroch and she was still desperately unhappy. She went to classes, studied in the library and spoke to nobody. Then one day I was walking down the hall in the music building and heard piano playing coming from a practice room. It was a tune I'd never heard before . . . and I was very familiar with Gaelic folk song . . . and played so beautifully, so mournfully it would break your heart.

"I eased the door open and peeked in and saw a creature with hair like coiled copper rippling down her back, sitting at the piano. Of course I knew who she was. I'd had my eye on her and that hair for ages but had never been able to figure out how to meet her.

"Oh, she was lovely. I was bewitched, so I did the only thing I could think of to do."

"What was that, Jamie?"

"I had my fiddle with me so I took it out and began playing, improvising on the melody as I picked it up from the piano. She hadn't known I was in the room. Her whole body stiffened when she heard the fiddle but she kept playing to the end of the song before she turned around. I fell in love with her at that moment." He sighed, remembering. "And that, Jean, was the beginning of a beautiful relationship."

He'd been determined to have her and it took him a terrifyingly long week to win her. Màiri, her heart still aching for Darroch, had hesitated before letting Jamie make love to her in a private little glen he'd discovered at Tarskavaig, in the woods above the college. As he waited in agony for her to decide whether or not to yield herself, a procession of English, French and Dutch girls chanted in his mind, "Now you know what it's like, Jamie."

He'd pressed his ear against her belly and when she demanded to know what he was doing he'd said, "I'm listening to our children."

She snapped, "I suppose you know what color hair they'll have."

"One red and one blond," he said promptly.

"I suppose you have the Sight," she mocked.

"Aye," he said. He'd never before admitted it to anyone but she had the right to know if they were to be together. Her eyes grew big with a Highlander's superstitious awe. "It's not important. This is important," he said, and moved on top of her. Her surrender was complete; she took him inside her and neither looked back, after that.

They'd married, moved to Eilean Dubh and bought her parents' croft. The *Eilean Dubhannaich*, after sniffing at Jamie suspiciously like fastidious cats, decided he was one of them. His astonishing beauty awed them as much as his Skye version of the Gaelic, supposedly the purest in the Highlands, amused them. And when he played his fiddle at *cèilidhean* the Islanders were struck to respectful, amazed, silence. He won them as he'd won Màiri.

His smile of reminiscence lit up the room. Jean, fascinated by the smile and intrigued by his romantic story, said, "So you think Darroch and Màiri did the right thing, not getting married?"

"I think they would have driven each other mad even if Darroch had not wanted to become an actor and stayed here as a good little crofter laird. Their personalities would not make for a tranquil union."

"I take your point," she said and for the next few moments they watched Darroch and Màiri dancing together in the elegant rhythm of the strathspey, smiling challengingly at each other across the set.

After a while she said, "Why is there no hereditary laird any more? There are still dukes and things."

"It goes back to Darroch's great-grandfather, Alasdair Darroch Mac an Rìgh, at the turn of the century. He was the laird's heir and his father wanted him to be the first of the family to have a university education. He sent Alasdair to the University of Glasgow.

"One day Alasdair heard a rabble-rousing Socialist chappie . . . it may have been Lenin himself . . . give a speech on the aristocracy's oppression of the poor. He was instantly converted. He formed a Karl Marx club at university that nearly got him sent down. He denounced World War I as a capitalist plot to exploit the lower classes and not only refused to serve but went home and discouraged other young men from enlisting.

"When the old laird died and Alasdair inherited he called a meeting and announced that he was renouncing the title for himself and his descendants. He said the men should get together and form a governing council and that each man, including himself, would have one vote, all equal. Three years later he persuaded the men to extend voting rights to women by the oration he gave at his mother's funeral.

"He gave the family mansion for a library. He gave Mac an Rìgh heirlooms to create the museum. He divided up all the lands in his family's holdings into equal parcels and announced that every man could draw a lot for a croft. That meant they'd all own their crofts, they'd no longer have to pay rent to a landlord. Almost unheard of, in the Highlands, tenant ownership.

"He stunned the Islanders by drawing a lot himself and that was all he retained of the family lands. With his own hands he rebuilt the *taigh dubh* on his croft into a fine cottage. That's where Darroch lives today. The Islanders named him *An Tighearna Dearg* . . . the Red Laird. Darroch admires him immensely."

Jean said, "But Màiri called Darroch the laird. If the title was abolished why does she call him that?"

"Partly it's Màiri showing off to impress you with her Highland queen mixty-maxty, but remember that Scotland in general and the Highlands in particular and Eilean Dubh in double particular, if there is such a thing, are the home of the clan system. Loyalty to the chief is bred in our people. Alasdair renounced the title and styled himself just one of the mob, but the aura of the laird clung to him and clings to his descendants.

"Darroch can go to a Co-Op meeting and people will disagree with him, vote against him and even shout at him if the meeting gets heated, but if you watch them closely . . . the sense that he's someone special is always there. You can see it in their eyes. They want his opinion and his approval. It drives him mad to think anyone might defer to him or agree with him because of his ancestors.

"He calls it 'that laird business' or if he is really annoyed 'that bloody laird business.' I won't sully your ears with his Gaelic phrase which is even more forceful."

Jean was silent, then said, "Umm . . . you probably don't know . . . I'm married."

He looked at her, curious at the change of subject. "I didn't know."

"Darroch and I . . . we're just friends. Perhaps you could let Màiri know that. I mean, because I'm married she doesn't have to worry about me."

"I'll tell her." He looked doubtful. "But I don't think it'll do any good."

She changed the subject. "That governing council must be doing a good job. The Island seems prosperous."

"The Trust turned our economy around. Astonishing what an influx of private capital can do. Auld Alasdair would be scandalized, good Socialist that he was."

"A Trust? What does it do?"

"Its commitment is to preserve traditional life and culture on Eilean Dubh. In reality that aim is stretched a wee bit to include things like hospital equipment, a van for the Seniors' Residence, books for the library. Its first and probably most important act was to set up the Gaelic Playschool Màiri runs.

"Next it revived the Co-Op. Alasdair's son set it up in the nineteen thirties when the cooperative movement was very big in rural Scotland. But it was foundering, had lost direction. The Trust brought in experts from the University of Edinburgh and Sabhal Mór Ostaig to get it up and running again. It was completely reorganized and now it's the center of our economic life.

"The Co-Op stores replaced the village shops in Airgead and Ros Mór that were going out of business after the war and up through the Thatcher regime. The shopkeepers were older people retiring with no children to carry on. Too many Island young people stayed in the cities where they'd gone to work during the war.

"Co-Op stores are owned by the members and managed by the workers. Because they're big they get good wholesale prices and pass the savings on to customers. And they pay dividends to members so that's another source of income for us all. The Co-Op doesn't compete with the independent shops still in business but it supplies everything else needed."

"It sounds quite idyllic," Jean said.

Jamie considered. "Well, I wouldn't call it that, exactly. We have our problems."

"Such as?"

"Well . . . let me see. The kids are all right. They've too much work to do at home and school to get into mischief, apart from the occasional burst of graffiti and practical jokes. They have to leave the Island, though, to go to university, and then it's touch-and-go as to whether or not they'll come back after they've seen the bright lights.

"No drugs problem, but I suspect there's hidden alcoholism. Winter's hard on the men. They're used to being busy on their crofts and they sit around when the weather's bad and drink more than they should. Women always find something to do, don't they, knitting clubs, coffee mornings, tea parties. But men haven't the knack of keeping busy.

"Health care . . . the hospital was tarted up with Trust money but we're wearing out poor Ros MacPherson, our only doctor. Ros gets interns from Edinburgh, trying out the rural practice idea, but no one wants to stay. They want to go to London and make a fortune curing the common cold, not work twenty hours a day for a bunch of troublesome Scots. But we've a grand corps of nurses, local girls. They take some of the load off Ros.

"What else . . . well, money's always tight. Crofting's about the riskiest thing you can commit your life to, ask any farmer. Almost all of us raise sheep and whatever can go wrong with the daft buggers will go wrong, always. You'd lose your supper if I told you the disgusting diseases they're subject to. We're just waiting for the sheep equivalent of mad cow disease to surface; that would put paid to the market for lamb which isn't grand to begin with.

"Fishing's as risky economically and it's terrifyingly dangerous. The whole Island goes rigid with fear if a storm blows up while the fleet's out. We've had many tragedies through the years and nothing can be done about it; it's part of a fisherman's life.

"What have I forgotten? Oh, aye, the people. Mostly good-hearted, well-behaved and well educated. Scots insist on good schools. We're the best-educated people in the world; that goes back to auld John Knox. But everybody knows everybody else and feuds and grudges are centuries old. They're not keen on new ideas, they're suspicious of outsiders, and they can be irritatingly strict in their religious practices when it suits them.

"And they're passionately inquisitive about everyone else's business and they love to gossip. It's like a disease, no one is spared. They would have torn me to shreds when I came here if they weren't all terrified of Màiri."

"I can understand that," said Jean, then wished she hadn't. "Oops . . . I'm sorry . . . "

"Not at all, I'm quite terrified of her myself." He grinned. "Have I frightened you away? Look on the bright side: we've no traffic jams, few accidents and no car thefts. Everyone knows who belongs to which car, a thief could never get away with one.

"So that's our little Island. It's not all thistles and heather and bagpipes, here on Eilean Dubh, but we must like it because we stay put."

"It's an unusual place," Jean said.

"There's a vitality here that few rural areas in Britain can equal. I love Skye where I was born but Eilean Dubh is a far more interesting place to live. There's a real sense of community and purpose here. And Island music is very fine, quite unspoilt by contact with the real world."

"I'd like to learn some of the music," she said as Màiri and Darroch reappeared.

Màiri looked suspiciously at the two heads so close together, lost in conversation.

Jamie said, "I am just telling Jean about our Island, and she is saying how unusual it is."

Màiri was prepared to ignore Jean but Darroch, always ready to talk about his beloved Eilean Dubh, responded eagerly. "Aye, it is that. The world's biggest small town. Or is it the smallest big town? I forget."

Jean said, "There's an almost magical quality to the place."

Darroch shook his head. "This is not Brigadoon, bonnie Jean."

"Oh, no. I meant the scenery. The mountains, the sea, the fog. Sometimes the Island seems to be hovering in the air . . . "

"And other times it lets you down with a splash," said Jamie. The three *eileanachan* grinned at each other.

"More often than not," growled Màiri. She took Jamie's hand to lead him to the dance floor and condescended to nod stiffly at Jean.

Wow, progress, Jean thought.

Darroch attempted to explain Màiri's coolness as they walked back to the Hotel later. "You mustn't mind Màiri," he said. "She doesn't like the English or anyone who speaks English. She sees them as threats to her language. Which they are, of course."

"Yes, I understand. I'm sorry that's the case, I sort of like her. She's . . . a character." She realized that could be construed as insulting or patronizing and glanced at him, remembering that he and Màiri had been lovers and were clearly still close.

He said wryly, "*Thà gu gearbh*, yes indeed. A very strong character." He gave her a sidewise grin.

"I hope she gets to like me," said Jean, but she wasn't hopeful. "Anyway, Jamie is the most wonderful fiddle player I've ever heard . . . " Discussing Jamie's wonderfulness keep them occupied the rest of the way to the Rose.

At the Hotel, Darroch remembered her request. "About learning our music . . . "

"I'd like to, very much."

"I have a trunkful of sheet music at my cottage if you'd care to come over and go through it." He watched happily as her face lit up. She had meant it, then.

"Oh, yes, please."

"Tomorrow afternoon?"

She nodded.

"*Glé mhath*. I'll collect you around one, then." They smiled at each other and said good night. Jean fell asleep with bits and pieces of music running through her mind.

Nine

I see her in the dewy flowers —
I see her sweet and fair.
I hear her in the tunefu' birds —
I hear her charm the air.
There's not a bonie flower that springs
By fountain, shaw, or green,
There's not a bonie bird that sings
But minds me o' my Jean.

Robert Burns

*N*ext morning Jean sought out Sheilah who was in the kitchen making desserts. "Sheilah, Darroch has offered to teach me some Island songs," she said.

"That's brilliant," said Sheilah, rolling out pie crust. "The music's beautiful, you'll love it. Do you play an instrument?"

"I sing and play the guitar. I was wondering, though . . . " She did not quite know how to phrase her question. "Darroch's asked me to his cottage to look through sheet music and try a few songs. . . "

"And you're wondering if that's the musical equivalent of going to look at his etchings?"

Jean nodded, embarrassed.

Sheilah said, "Darroch's got more charm than any six men put together and he could probably seduce the Queen if he put his mind to it. But he's also one of the most honorable people I know. Completely trustworthy. If he's invited you over for music, that's what it will be." She looked at Jean. "All right?"

"Yep," said Jean, smiling. "I thought so."

Darroch picked her up in the Bentley after lunch. It was a short luxurious drive to the side road that led down to the sea. His was the second cottage from the road, past a tiny house with a thatched roof.

He opened the unlocked door and showed her in. "*Fàilte gu Taigh a'*
Mhorair. Welcome." He shivered. "It's a wee bit chilly. I'll build a fire. Have
a look around." He knelt by the fireplace and began criss-crossing peats into
a neat pile.

What had been several small rooms had been knocked into one large
one, framed by whitewashed walls three feet thick. A fireplace sat dead
center on the right wall, its mantel and chimney-breast taking up nearly a
third of the space. Bookcases filled up the rest and most of the front wall.

The back wall held two large windows, a desk with a computer under
one and a sink under the other. A stove and a tiny refrigerator, half the size
of an American fridge, flanked the sink. A table and chairs sat on an elderly
oriental rug on the left, where another window offered a view in a different
direction.

Jean was drawn immediately to the window over the sink. Through it
she could see all the way down to the sea, for the land sloped sharply into a
rocky hill leading to a pebble beach where waves lapped.

Darroch, coming to the sink to wash his peaty hands, said, "Grand view,
isn't it. I had those windows put in. I wanted to put them into my mother's
cottage—it's the first one up the hill—but she said no. She said she'd seen
enough of the sea during her years and big windows made her feel cold."

Jean turned to the window by the table where the view was down hill
over a stretch of grassy knolls and huge rocks. She could see a cottage like
Darroch's. "Màiri and Jamie live there. Their cottage is called *Taigh Rois*,
the house of the Ross family," he said, following the direction of her gaze.

He put a kettle on and assembled cups on a tray. When the kettle whistled he rinsed the pot with hot water, threw in tea, added water and put the
pot aside to brew. "Would you want to sit on the sofa and I'll bring in our
tea."

While they sipped he told her about his house. "I've modernized it a lot.
I put in a new fireplace and night storage heaters. And skylights upstairs and
as many windows on the first floor as I could without the house collapsing. I
wanted openness, views and light." He had added polished wood floors
throughout. "Warmer on bare feet than the old stone floor."

Jean thought it was charming and told him so. He smiled, then set his
cup down. "Well, now. What shall we look at first?"

"Air a vata."

"Do you read music?"

She nodded.

"Brilliant." He was kneeling in front of a trunk full of books and sheet music. "I'm musically illiterate, learn everything by ear. Màiri plays it for me on the piano until I've got it. But I collect sheet music." He handed her a yellowed paper booklet labeled *Old Scotch Songs*. "This is ancient but it has the nicest version of the words."

Jean examined the song. The music was not difficult but the words were daunting. "I'll need help with this. The language is like nothing I've ever seen, except for Ùisdean's letters. Could I buy some beginners' tapes to help with pronunciation?"

"I've some I can lend you, if you like. You'd do me a favor if you tried them. Several publishers send me tapes for Gaelic learners, wanting an evaluation, and it's hard to find time to listen to them. And since I know the language I'm not the best person to judge."

"Sure," said Jean. "I brought a cassette player with me. I'm as ignorant as they come about the Gaelic. I'll give them a good tryout."

He smiled at her again. What a particularly nice smile it was, Jean thought. His eyes, framed by thick black lashes, were strikingly navy-blue in this light. And his nose was quite the most elegant one she'd ever seen.

He said, "Let's start with the chorus. *Fhir a' bhàta, no hòro èile, mo shoraidh slàn leat 's gach àit an teid thu.*"

She repeated the lines until she thought she had them. Than he sang the chorus and she hummed along. Finally they sang it together and then he said, "Now try it alone."

She was hesitant but gained confidence as she sang.

Darroch looked at her thoughtfully and said nothing for a few moments. Jean said uneasily, "I can try it again if that wasn't right."

"No," he said slowly. "That was grand. I was just thinking what a lovely voice you have." In fact he was quite struck by its quality: perfectly pitched and always on key, a soprano with true high notes and a touch of huskiness on the lower ones. Its warm sweetness made something inside him reverberate. A true folksinger's voice, he thought, and like a typical Gaelic singer's in its purity. What a find, and she wanted to learn their music.

He said, "Do you think you have it enough that you could sing the melody while I harmonize?"

"Yes." That went so well he was soon teaching her the verses. The words came slowly because she was having a hard time fitting the sounds to the letters on the page. "Dh" was a particular challenge. It was "yuh" in some cases and "guh" in others and she couldn't anticipate which it would be. Finally she closed the book and her eyes and concentrated on mimicking him. "If you recorded the words on tape I think I could get them."

"I'll do that, but don't worry, you've nearly two weeks to learn them before the *cèilidh*."

"Umm . . . what?"

"You'll sing at the *cèilidh*. Màiri and Jamie and I will back you up."

Jean suddenly thought she was moving into some high-powered company. "Darroch . . . I don't mind singing, I love performing. But isn't it a little . . . cheeky . . . isn't that your British word? . . . to sing in the Gaelic when I've only been here two weeks?"

"Nonsense, people will be complimented. Besides, you and I will sing that one together as your encore after you've sung a song in English."

She was getting in deeper and deeper. "Encore? Suppose no one asks for an encore?" The thought was enough to make her palms grow cold and moist.

"Oh, they will, *mo charaid*. I'd not worry about that." He smiled, anticipating the audience reaction. The Islanders were passionate about music and they'd love her.

"All right. I'll do it but only if Màiri approves."

"Màiri?" He raised his eyebrows as high as they would go. "Why Màiri?"

Jean could not answer; she shook her head. Instinctively she knew that Màiri would speak out if she thought the American was encroaching.

"All right, Màiri will have to vet you. Now what song in English do you want to sing? It'll be quite a departure; we've never had an English-language song at a *cèilidh*."

Great, thought Jean. Not only am I intruding into their sacred language and music but I'm introducing an alien culture as well. I'll be lucky if they don't kick me off the Island. Still, he should know, she'd have to trust his judgment. And the thought of performing for an audience again, one that did not consist entirely of schoolchildren, was tempting. "What shall I sing?"

"Whatever you like."

Together they ran through American and English folk songs in Jean's repertoire. Darroch knew many of them and he sang harmony, his mellow voice blending with her sweet clear one. Jean was luminous with pleasure.

"Oh, it feels so good to sing again! I think we sound well together, don't you?" Without waiting for an answer she said, "I wish I had my guitar. I don't know what to do with my hands."

"You play the guitar?"

"Play it, hide behind it, cover up forgotten lyrics, you name it. It's my prop and support. I've never sung in public without one."

"Hang on." He unfolded his long legs and went up the iron spiral stair-case to the floor above. He returned carrying a guitar case and put it in her lap. "Try this."

Wondering, she opened it and was too stunned to gasp. Inside lay a gor-geous guitar, decorated with Celtic knotwork on the sides and crowned with a rosewood soundboard. She stared, not daring to touch it.

"Go on," urged Darroch. "Take it out."

Reverently she lifted the instrument from the case. She ran a hand over the top, touching the strings delicately, then plucking them. Predictably they were horribly out of tune. She bowed her head over the guitar, murmuring to it.

Darroch smiled, recognizing the bonding of musician and instrument. He'd seen it in Jamie, who always crooned to his fiddle and polished it lov-ingly before putting it away.

"Darroch," Jean said, "I can't. This must be very valuable, I wouldn't dare." But her fingers lingered on the strings.

"Come now, *mo charaid*, what is a guitar for but to play and the poor dear's lain in her case so long. I bought her when I was doing a nightclub turn after *The Magician* became popular. I've a rare weakness for beautiful instruments and I couldn't resist her." Once he'd bought an exquisite little spinet piano and presented it to Màiri. Transporting it to the Island had been a challenge but worth it: Màiri had been speechless with pleasure; she'd trembled when she'd first run her hands across the keys.

"I saw the guitar in a shop and had to have her. My excuse was she'd help me learn to play and my agent thought I should accompany myself on an instrument. But I'm useless, can't find the right places to put my fingers. In the end I gave up and hired an accompanist, much better than my plunking. I put her away after the nightclub engagement and I've felt guilty. She's like a princess locked in a tower, silent and lonely.

"Tune up, let's hear her," he urged. "There's a pitchpipe in the case."

"I don't need that." She bent her head over the guitar, tightening strings. She played a simple tune, marveling at the depth and beauty of the sound. Then she began the accompaniment to *Fear a' Bhàta*.

When she had mastered that they sang the whole song together, then smiled at each other, well pleased.

"That'll wow 'em," said Darroch in satisfaction. "You're a natural, Jean, aren't you. We'll practice the next two weeks until you're comfortable with the Gaelic. Take the guitar to the Hotel with you. Gordon will find you a quiet place to work."

"I couldn't, Darroch. The instrument's far too valuable. I'd be terrified something might happen to her."

"Nonsense, she'll be safe as houses with you. Now play something else."

Unconvinced but very tempted, Jean didn't argue. They spent the next couple of hours exchanging songs until the phone rang.

Màiri, at the other end of the line, said, "Hello, *mo bhràthair*, will you come for supper tonight? I've a fine huge mess of trout to fry."

Darroch said, "Well, I've a friend here, Màiri . . . " She interrupted, "Bring him along. There's plenty," and rang off.

He was left staring at the phone. Typical of Màiri, he thought, but then decided, why not? He wanted her and Jamie to hear Jean and now was a perfect time. The thought that Màiri might not be pleased to entertain the American he brushed off. Once she'd heard Jean sing all would be forgiven.

"Màiri's invited us down for a meal and I've taken the liberty of accepting. I hope that's all right?"

Jean's heart sank. Màiri's dislike had been so obvious that the thought of being her guest was daunting. "Are you sure she won't mind my coming?" She realized how ungracious that sounded. "I mean, I'd be delighted, but if she doesn't like . . . "

"Strangers," Darroch finished. "This will be a chance for her to get to know you."

"Okay," said Jean, resigned. "When does she want us?"

Darroch liked immediate action. "Let's go now. We can help set the table. We'll take the guitar and have more music after we eat."

"Shouldn't I call Sheilah and tell her I won't be there for dinner?"

"I'll call and arrange for Gordon to leave the front door unlocked for you. He likes to lock up at eleven and I'm sure we'll be later than that, once we get going."

They set off for *Taigh Rois*. It was a beautiful evening, the sky a clear deep blue. Rather the color of Darroch's eyes, Jean thought. She braced herself for confronting Màiri in her den, comforted by the knowledge that Jamie at least had been friendly.

Nothing ventured, nothing gained, she thought.

Ten

Praise the Lord, we are a musical nation!
Dylan Thomas

The door to *Taigh Rois* swung open at Darroch's knock. Màiri said, "Darroch, you're early . . . " and stopped short.

"*Feasgar math, m'eudail.* You remember Jean. We've been sharing music this afternoon."

"Aye," Màiri said flatly. "Still here, are you, Mrs. Abbott? Come in, then."

Darroch said, "I'll hang up our jackets. Carry on cooking, *a Mhàiri*; we'll be in to help in a minute."

Jean whispered, "You didn't tell her it was me you were bringing, did you."

"She didn't give me a chance," he whispered back. "Courage, she doesn't bite."

Jean was not at all sure of that, especially when they reached the kitchen and Màiri snapped in the Gaelic to Darroch, "Now we'll have to speak English all evening, I suppose."

"It would be the polite thing to do," he replied, refusing to be drawn.

Jean said, "May I help with something?" She knew she'd feel more comfortable if her hands were occupied.

Jamie came in the back door before Màiri could respond. Pulling off his muddy work boots, he said in surprise, "*Feasgar math*, Jean. Where did you come from?"

"We've had a musical afternoon," said Darroch, "and Màiri has kindly invited us to supper."

Jamie, glancing at his wife's rigid back and at Jean's tense posture, guessed there was more to it than that but wisely declined to probe further. "Lovely to see you again," he said. "Shall we have a glass of wine?"

He opened a bottle and poured four glasses. Màiri ignored hers and slapped a trout fillet into a pan of hot fat. The violent splattering seemed to relieve her feelings and she said, "Will you peel these potatoes for me, someone."

"I'll do them," said Jean. She settled the bowl in her lap and picked up the knife. At least I'm armed now, she thought, looking at the sharp blade.

Jamie said, "You've been singing together?"

"Aye, Jean wants to learn our songs."

"How can she sing our music when she doesn't have the Gaelic?" snapped Màiri, flipping the fillets with unnecessary vigor.

Jamie took the potatoes from Jean and put them on to boil. "These will never be done in time, *mo ghràdh*, you've started the fish too soon."

"I know that," Màiri answered crossly. "I'll use them for breakfast tomorrow. There's plenty of fish. We'll have that and bread and salad tonight."

"As for the Gaelic," said Darroch, "she can learn the lyrics by imitating me until she picks up the language."

Màiri snorted and Jean found herself agreeing. From what she'd heard of the Gaelic this afternoon she didn't think it was a language one just picked up.

They ate their dinner in a polite truce, Jamie and Darroch keeping the conversation going. By the end of the meal Jean felt as though she'd been playing Twenty Questions, so many answers had she provided about family, Milwaukee and the United States. She was interrogated with an exquisite Island courtesy that was gentle, unobtrusive, but nerve-wracking nonetheless.

Darroch, she thought, irritated, seemed to be enjoying the tension, smiling to himself as though he possessed some secret knowledge. Màiri was unrelentingly brusque.

They washed dishes. Then Darroch said, "Well, if you musicians don't have dishpan hands to nurse, what about a little music?"

"If Jean doesn't mind," said Jamie gallantly. "If she hasn't had enough today."

"Oh, no, I'd love it," she answered. It was after all one of the more unusual dinner parties she'd attended, with her hostess openly hostile. Perhaps music would soothe Màiri's savage breast.

Màiri frowned but went to the piano and lifted Jamie's fiddle off the top. "You first, *a Sheumais*."

"Give me a hand. I've a mind to play '*Mo Ghille Dhubh*' and it sounds better with the piano."

Listening to Jamie's fiddle as he improvised, wrapping sinuous notes around the melody, Jean felt a great stab of envy. Imagine being able to spend an evening with a spouse making music. At the song's end she said as much to Darroch, who replied, "They have two grown children, twins, both musical. The four of them together make the house rock. My ears ring all the next day but it's worth it."

Jean sighed and settled back, content to listen. After a particularly dazzling performance by Jamie on another tune she said to him, unable to resist, "You know, you're just wonderful."

He blushed. Màiri sniffed. "Americans and their hyperbole."

Stung, Jean forgot guest manners. "It's not hyperbole! He's a wonderful fiddler and anyone would say so who's got two ears to listen with!"

Jamie said hastily to avoid bloodshed, "Your turn, a Dharroch. Give us a song."

"I've a better idea. Let us show you what we've been working on. No, better yet, sing something by yourself first, *a Shìne*."

She was trapped. Jamie waited, politely expectant, Màiri glowered, a "show-me" expression on her face, and Darroch looked supremely confident. He nodded at her. "Anything you've a mind to sing." He lifted the guitar case from beside his chair, opened it and handed her the instrument.

Màiri said, aghast, "Darroch! Your rosewood guitar!"

"*Thà gu dearbh*. She didn't bring her own so she's using mine."

The temperature in the room dipped a couple of degrees but oddly enough Màiri's reaction stiffened Jean's spine. She settled herself on the chair, thought a moment and chose her favorite Stephen Foster song.

I dream of Jeannie with the light brown hair,
Borne like a vapour on the summer air.
I see her drifting where the bright breezes play,
Happy as the daisies that dance on her way.

Màiri and Jamie were thunderstruck. "*Miorbhuileach*," Darroch said softly. "Your song, isn't it, Jean with the light brown hair." Pleased with himself, he lifted an eyebrow at Màiri who ignored him. She demanded of Jean, "Sing something else."

"More Stephen Foster, please," murmured Jamie, his eyes closed in rapture.

So she chose another that she thought might be familiar to them.

Let us pause in life's pleasures and count its many tears
While we all sup sorrow with the poor.
There's a song that will linger forever in our ears,
Oh, hard times, come again no more.

Jamie picked up his fiddle and began to play. Their eyes met and they collaborated as though they'd rehearsed together forever. When they finished they looked at each other for a long moment.

"Wow," said Jean.

"And that's no hyperbole," said Jamie. "Wow indeed." He held out his hand and she put hers into it. "*Fàilte do'n Eilean Dubh, a Shìne, mo charaid.*" He kissed her hand.

"Ummm . . . thank you."

"*Tapadh leat,*" said Darroch. "The Gaelic for thank you. May as well get started."

She repeated the phrase until he nodded his approval.

Màiri said gruffly, "I . . . well . . . you've a fine voice, Jean." Jean realized it was the first time Màiri had called her by name.

Darroch said, "Here's a song Jean liked when we sang it Friday night. We're working on it for the *cèilidh* next week." They sang *Fear a' Bhàta*.

"*Mìorbhuileach,*" murmured Jamie. Terrific.

"I want to get in on this," said Màiri and jumped to her feet. "Come to the piano." She jerked a kitchen chair over and patted it impatiently. "Sit here, Jean. Has he taught you '*An Ribhinn Donn*' yet?"

Jean got up, flashing a look at Darroch. "I think you've passed the audition," he said, smiling, and stretched his long body out on the sofa. He put his head on a pillow, closed his eyes and prepared to be entertained.

They played and sang until voices were hoarse and fingers sore. Jamie's marked preference for American music amused Jean. He knew all the names: Leadbelly, Bix, Woody, the Carter Family, Pete Seeger. Jean admitted to a love of country music.

"Hank Williams?" asked Jamie and simultaneously they burst into song.

Your cheatin' heart will make you weep . . .

They sang it until they forgot the words and had to stop, laughing.

Màiri sniffed audibly.

"Do you like Richard Thompson? And Marty Robbins and Sandy Denny? Your voice reminds me of hers," Jamie said as he shook out a cramp in his bow hand. "How about bluegrass, do you play it?"

"A little. Damn, I wish I had a mandolin, my cousin in North Carolina taught me to play one two years ago and I'd have time to work on it here."

Jamie turned to the sofa. "*A Dharroch*, have you got a mandolin in your closet?"

"What? A mandolin? Do you need one?" he said, eyes still closed.

"He's quite capable of calling a music store in London and ordering one," said Jamie softly, grinning at Jean. "And I'm quite shameless when I want something for music making. Jean, why haven't you come down to the residents' bar on Thursday for the *seisean*?"

"I heard the music last week but I thought it was a private party."

"Ach, no, it's a right stramash, anyone with an interest in making music shows up. Why don't you come with me this week? It's too rowdy for Màiri . . . the music, I mean, not the people, they're safe as houses. Darroch doesn't come either. He prefers Gaelic music and we play everything on Thursday nights. I'll come by about 8:30, take you in, introduce you around." As Jean was digesting that he turned to the sofa and said, "*A Dharroch*, you lazy *diabhol*, come sing and give us a rest."

So he came and leaned on the piano and with a mischievous grin sang a song unaccompanied. It was a charming tune but judging by the heightened color in Màiri's cheeks and the grin on Jamie's face it was rather naughty.

"It's as well you don't have the Gaelic yet, Jean," said Jamie. He got up and brought from the sideboard a tray with a bottle of whisky and four glasses. He poured them each a generous amount. "*Slàinte mhath, a Shìne*," he said ceremoniously and they raised their glasses to her.

Jean took a deep breath and hazarded a guess. "Umm . . . tapa lot." She saluted them in return. "Slan-juh vah." In her nervousness she took too deep a gulp of whisky and choked. Darroch patted her on the back while she coughed.

"I'm teaching her to drink whisky but she hasn't quite got the hang of it," Darroch said. He glanced at the clock and was startled to see it was nearly midnight. "Good job none of us have to work tomorrow."

"Speak for yourself," said Màiri. "I've got to go into the school, I've tons to do."

"Are you a teacher?" asked Jean.

"Teacher, manager, shepherd of volunteers, cook. I've done it all."

"Is it a private school?"

"It's a Gaelic playschool, intended to help our under-fives keep our language," said Màiri. "We think that by reinforcing it at the earliest age the children won't abandon it. Children acquire more language by the age of five than at any other time."

"Our problem," said Darroch, "is that although the kids speak the Gaelic at home, they're exposed to English on all sides, radio, television, films, everything that's fun. So English seems more appealing. We end up with situations where the parents speak the Gaelic to their children and the children understand but respond in English. Our language has to bring them as much satisfaction as English. It can't just be the language of home, it has to be in our workplaces, music and media if it's not to fade into something the old people speak and the rest of the world ignores."

Jean said, "And you have to keep the language alive to keep the community alive, don't you. We have more immigrants in the United States now than at any time since the early nineteen hundreds. We have the same situation: parents want their children to keep their language but everything tells the kids that English is what they need and want.

"I think it has to do with building a sense of community, of making people want to preserve what makes them unique, language, music, literature . . . the heart of their culture. It gives kids self-respect if they respect where they came from."

She added, "But your world here is not the same as the one beyond the Island, is it. And when two civilizations clash the winner is going to be the one that offers people most: education, jobs, entertainment. If the ads for microwaves are written in English and you want a microwave, English is going to seem more useful."

Darroch said, "You understand about this."

"I was an English as a Second Language tutor working with Mexican immigrants, then Hmong. How many students do you have? Who teaches in your school?"

"About fifty students," Màiri said. "I design the curriculum based on material from our Playschool Association and our teachers are mothers of the children who are enrolled. Each one gives a few hours a week and we pay them a wee bit. It helps supplement their incomes. Crofters always need that."

Jean looked at Màiri, took a deep breath and plunged. "I think your school is a great idea. Do you need any help?"

Màiri said, "We always need help."

"I'd be glad to do something. I like working in schools and I've lots of time."

Màiri stared. "You? What could you do?"

"When I volunteered at my kids' schools I brought my guitar and taught them American folk music they wouldn't otherwise have studied. Of course you wouldn't want music in English and I can't work with the kids because I don't speak Gaelic . . . the Gaelic. But I could do other things."

With her earlier hauteur Màiri said, "Can you rebuild our roof? Or glaze window panes?"

Both Darroch and Jamie turned on her but Jean was unfazed. She'd had plenty of experience, dueling with two argumentative teenagers. But she was exasperated at such obvious provocation. Really, would the woman never come down off her high horse?

"You must have paper work. Do you need a filing system set up? I was office manager at my husband's firm for several years. Do you have a computer? I'm good at word processing, I could type letters or reports. And I can do spread sheets."

One word caught Màiri's attention. "You know something about computers?"

Jean was on solid ground. "Oh, yes," she said. "We've had computers at home since there were home computers. My husband's a software developer. He brings equipment home and turns the family loose on it . . . Apples, Macs, PCs . . . you name it, we've had it. As soon as we got used to one he'd get rid of it and bring in something new and improved."

"The school's got a new computer." Màiri avoided looking at Darroch whose gift it had been. "I can't make head or tail of it. I could just manage the old Apple but this one has me baffled."

Darroch said, "Did you call their tech support?"

"I couldn't get through, I can't wait on hold forever." To Jean she added, "It's a damned devil."

Jean said comfortingly, "They're all like that until you've wrestled them into submission. And of course, as a last resort, you can read the manual."

"I tried that," said Màiri. "It's gibberish."

"The manuals are always gibberish." Jean glanced at Màiri. "My daughter Sally and I have a saying: men and computers are the two orneriest objects in the universe, but at least you can turn off a computer."

Màiri gave a shout of laughter. Jean added, "And there hasn't been a decent operating manual written for either of them."

There was a muffled snort from one of the men listening and Jamie said in his laconic way, "I'll make the tea, shall I?"

"Aye, if we're to have any it looks as though you'll have to. I'll help." Darroch stood, smiling.

Màiri was now fully focused on Jean. "You really think you can get it to work?"

"Sure. When would you like me to start? And where is this school?"

"Tomorrow morning? It's by the Citizens Hall, across from the square."

"Okay, I'll walk over."

"You don't have to." Màiri was suddenly conciliatory. "I'll pick you up. Eight-thirty?"

"Oh, no, you don't, *a Mhàiri*, my little slave driver," Jamie said, bringing teacups. "I'll not have you rampaging around at sunrise, I promised myself a lie-in. Ten o'clock at the earliest, Jean."

"Okay, I'll be ready."

The two women looked at each other. Màiri smiled first, the corners of her mouth turning up as reluctantly as if she'd never smiled before. Darroch, watching them, knew he'd just witnessed a major skirmish.

Full marks to you, Jean, this time anyway, he thought.

Eleven

I would like my children to speak Gaelic. What can I do?
Speak Gaelic to them if you are a Gaelic speaker.
If not, perhaps a neighbour or a friend can help,
or send your child to a Gaelic playgroup.

From a *Communn na Gàidhlig* leaflet

*N*ext morning Jean got her first look at the Playschool, a stone building by the harbor. Inside were two classrooms full of toys, books and a playhouse, a tiny kitchen and an office separated from the rest by glass walls. Màiri led Jean into the office.

Jean's eyes went immediately to the computer and she eyed it appraisingly. Oh, yes, I remember you, she thought, you were the one before last. I hope I can remember all your little tricks. She sat down in front of it. "What do you want done?"

"Correspondence. Saving snack recipes that've been converted to large quantities. Minding our budget. Equipment inventory." Màiri ticked off items on her fingers.

"Okay, give me the inventory. I'll start with that." She focused her attention on the computer. Màiri watched, then turned to her work of organizing lesson plans.

After a couple of hours she made tea and brought Jean a cup. "Milk and sugar?"

"Both, thanks," said Jean without looking up. At the end of another hour she pushed her chair back. "Okay. I've proofed it twice and I think I've gotten everything from your notes but keep the paper copy for backup till I can save it to a disc."

Amazed, Màiri took the pile of lists and scribbled notes Jean handed back. "You're done with the inventory?"

"Yes, but there is one thing. Most of this was in the Gaelic. You'd better proof read it. I may have misread someone's writing."

Màiri said, "I'll have to translate the budget into English. I didn't think of that."

"What a nuisance, but you'll have to or I'll never get things into proper columns. It won't matter with reports as long as I can read the writing." She shrugged off thanks. "I enjoyed doing it. It's easy on a computer."

"If you know how," said Màiri dubiously.

"Want me to show you how it works? I can come back Monday. In fact, I'll come in mornings and work on stuff for you, if you want. Except for Fridays, that's my day to go to the library in Airgead."

"I don't want to take up so much of your time . . . "

Jean said, "Listen, Màiri. I like to keep busy and I think your school's a great idea. I'm glad to help. Tell me what you want me to do and I'll do it. But also tell me when you want me out of the way. If you do that we'll get along fine."

Màiri was unused to so much American frankness but she found it curiously reassuring. The boundaries would be clearly drawn and neither would encroach upon the other. She said, "Would you want to go up to the Hotel for lunch? My treat. It's almost two so Sheilah can probably join us. You'll enjoy talking to her."

"Yes, I know that. Great, let's go." They walked to the Hotel and when they parted after lunch they were close to becoming good friends.

Sunday was very quiet. Sheilah had explained to Jean that Gordon, a Free Presbyterian, observed his kirk's injunction not to work on that day.

"I'll leave cereal out for breakfast and you can help yourself to milk and juice and scones. And are sandwiches all right for lunch, and cold game pie for dinner? I'm afraid it will have to be self-service but you can eat where you like, kitchen or dining room or your room, wherever you are comfortable."

She looked at her guest anxiously. It seemed inhospitable to leave Jean so much on her own. The Hotel's other guests had cars and could drive to the Island restaurant that was open on Sunday.

Jean said, "It'll be like home, puttering around a kitchen. Make sure things are labeled, though, so I don't wolf down Monday's meals by mistake." In the end she took a tray up to her room and read a book while she ate. It was quite restful.

Monday morning she was up promptly and walked to the school. When she came in the room was awash with three- to five-year-olds, all jabbering at once in the Gaelic while they removed coats and caps. Jean grinned over their heads at Màiri, said "*Madainn mhath*," in her best accent and disappeared into the office, shutting the door behind her so she wouldn't blurt out something in forbidden English.

Màiri, who'd half suspected Jean might not turn up, was delighted to see her. She'd put out three months of reports by the computer. Jean busied herself with them.

At teatime Màiri brought in two women. "This is Mrs. Abbott from America. She's helping with our computer; she knows all about it. Barabal Mac-a-Phi and Catrìona, wife to Ian the Post."

"Call me Jean," she said and held out her hand. She did not intend to get locked into Old World courtesy titles; she was going to be unabashedly American. "Hi, Barabal, we met at the *cèilidh*."

"Aye, I remember." Barabal's brown eyes were appraising but her smile was friendly. The other woman was a pretty blonde with an intelligent face. They sat down with Jean for their tea break and once again she underwent a gentle polite interrogation. She was a curiosity, she realized. A tourist who didn't act like one, and moreover a tourist who'd been accepted by Màiri.

She answered their questions with good humor. Catrìona had never been off the Island and was very curious about America. Barabal was far more sophisticated. She'd been to Edinburgh.

When the phone rang Màiri answered, then said in surprise, "It's for you, Jean."

She stared, not understanding, then seized the phone, fearful that something had happened to her family in Milwaukee. But it was Darroch.

"I've finished my work and I wondered if you'd like to visit the cemetery up on *Cladh a' Chnuic* this afternoon. I'm free around two if that would suit you," he said.

"Oh, yes, that's fine."

"The Hotel, then, Jean," he said and rang off.

Màiri, who had recognized the voice, stared at her searchingly and Jean felt compelled to offer an explanation. "We're going for a cemetery crawl this afternoon. Looking for ancestors."

"With Darroch," said Màiri to the other two who looked suitably impressed and very curious. But Barabal said only, "Wear heavy stockings and good stout boots. Trousers, too, if you have them. The thistles in that cemetery are something shocking."

Twelve

She gave her life for her people and her people gave her all their love.
Inscription from Lady Eilidh's tombstone,
translated by Darroch Mac an Rìgh

*B*ack at the Hotel, Jean ate lunch, dressed for thistles and was ready when Darroch arrived.

A mile beyond his cottage they turned off the main road into a driveway leading up *Cladh a' Chnuic*. On top of the hill was an ancient cemetery ringed by gnarled trees, all leaning in the same direction, shaped by the ever-blowing wind. He parked and they walked to the graves.

Jean loved old cemeteries. She wandered among the stones, trying not to step on the graves, although it was hard to tell which was path and which was grave. Most were marked only by tiny stones without inscriptions and many stones were broken or crumbling. They need a cemetery beautification committee here, thought Jean, remembering the well-kept family graveyards of North Carolina where committees sponsored tidying-up visits every two months.

Jean wondered aloud whether any of the stones covered relatives of hers.

"Undoubtedly," Darroch replied. "This is the largest cemetery on the Island. Because of intermarriage among families everyone has someone buried here." It should be better looked after, then, Jean thought.

He paused by the largest monument. The statue was of an angel with a baby in its arms. "This is the grave of my great . . . " He counted on his fingers. " . . . great-great . . . " He lost count and gave it up. "Many times great-grandmother. She died in the seventeen hundreds. The monument was erected in the last century. The graves surrounding hers are mostly those of children."

"Why is that?" asked Jean, looking around. There were many small mounds, far too many for one woman's children.

Darroch knelt on one knee by the monument. He slipped easily into a storytelling mode; it seemed as natural to an *Eilean Dubhannach* as talking about baseball was to an American.

He began, "Late one winter a terrible epidemic broke out. We think it was diphtheria, brought to the Island by dying sailors washed ashore in a small lifeboat, put off their ship when they became ill.

"Diphtheria starts with a sore throat and a low fever. Then in the worst cases a thick membrane forms across the back of the throat. It may close the throat entirely, or the bronchial tubes may swell, or the membrane may become detached and lodge in the air passage. Victims suffocate or choke to death."

He sighed. "Of course no one had any immunity because it was a new disease to the Island. People began dying and the disease spread. Severe cases of diphtheria can last weeks and if victims don't get proper rest and food they may die of heart failure.

"Lady Eilidh . . . that's who's buried here . . . was a happy young mother of two boys and two girls. She was adored by her husband the Laird and by the Islanders. She looked after the welfare of the sick, elderly and poor, all the things that responsible aristocrats did in those days. She was especially devoted to the Island's children.

"She and the Laird were lucky when the epidemic broke out because their children had been ill with some winter ailment and confined to their nursery. They hadn't been mingling with the village kids as usual so they hadn't been exposed to the sickness. In fact, the Laird's family knew nothing about it. The Laird did, of course, but he had not told his wife because she was exhausted from looking after her four. He knew she'd be frantic about the epidemic.

"It was a nursery maid who told Lady Eilidh. She'd come to ask permission to go home to look after her family. By then the death toll was high, nearly one-third of the children were dead or dying.

"Lady Eilidh was horrified. She begged the Laird to let her go to the villages to help. He refused to allow her to risk infection.

"She was distraught at not being able to help her people. Late that night she slipped out, saddled a horse and set off to see for herself what could be done. She went first to Airgead where the epidemic had started. It had nearly run its course there and people were either recovering or beyond help. She got a villager to ride with her to the south, to Ros Mór.

"There the epidemic was in full swing. Nearly all the children were sick and the adults either ill or exhausted. She took over the largest house and brought in children who had no one to care for them. She nursed them around the clock. At one point she was caring for ten children by herself and she did that until others were recovered enough to help her."

He looked at the angel, standing on tiptoes on its plinth, the baby cradled in one arm while the other arm stretched to the heavens. "Only two of the children she nursed died. She cared for the rest until they were out of danger. Then she got sick.

"The villagers cared for her devotedly. On her orders they would not let the Laird in. She knew he must survive to look after their children and the Island. She died on the fourth day after she became ill. She choked to death.

"That was the end of the epidemic. She was the last to die."

Darroch took a handkerchief from his pocket and wiped his eyes. "That story always makes me *deurach* no matter how well I know it," he said.

"She was buried here, surrounded by other victims. One of the children she nursed died on the same day and is buried in her arms. The last child she cared for was a little girl, named Eilidh for her. She was orphaned by the epidemic. The Laird was afraid she'd be blamed for his wife's death so he adopted her."

He pointed to a grave lying crosswise below Lady Eilidh's. "That's her grave. She worshipped Lady Eilidh's memory and vowed to be buried at her feet. She grew up in the Laird's family and married his eldest son. She became as venerated for her charity and compassion as Lady Eilidh had been. She was my great-great-something grandmother."

Jean's glance at him was thoughtful. So that was what it was like to have a family history linked to one place.

Darroch smiled. "Well," he said. "Why don't you have a look around. The eighteenth-century part of the cemetery is over there. There's no readable stones left but it'll give you a feeling for the place. I'll wait for you on the bench up the hill."

"Sure you don't mind?"

"Not at all. I often come up here to look at the sea."

Jean went from stone to stone, increasingly dismayed by the cemetery's condition. Thistles were omnipresent and rubbed menacingly against her jeans. A long hideous vine had snaked its way from the edge of the cemetery into the outer row of graves. Her gardener's instincts flared.

When at last she made her way up the hill he turned away from his contemplation of the waves and smiled at her. "Find any relatives?"

"No." She blurted, "Darroch, would anyone mind if I did some weeding here?"

He looked at her, astonished. "You want to weed the cemetery?"

"Well, it needs it." Then, afraid she'd been rude, she added, "I've got time on my hands, I like to garden and I hate weeds. I'd enjoy some good outdoor work."

"If you want to do it, *a Shìne,* no one would mind. You'll need tough gloves, some of these weeds sting. Would you like a hoe? My mother had lots of gardening tools. When do you want to start?"

She had to stop to think. Her days were getting crowded. "It will have to be afternoons. I'm promised to Màiri and the Playschool in the mornings."

He hadn't realized she'd made such a commitment. "You'll need a ride. Màiri could drop you off after Playschool. Have her stop by my place and you can take your pick of tools in my shed."

Màiri was happy to take her to the cemetery the next day. "What are you going to do up there?" she asked.

"I'm going to remove the weeds from Lady Eilidh's grave."

Màiri would have liked to ask her why, but she had learned by now that the American was full of energy and enjoyed having work to do. If she wanted to weed the graveyard why not? If Darroch's surmise was correct, she had ancestors buried there, so she had every right to care for it.

Jean was grateful for Eilean Dubh's cool weather once she began in the cemetery for she worked up quite a sweat. She had not realized that thistles had such deep roots. She had gathered a large pile of dead vegetation when she realized that the sun was beginning to move downward in the sky.

She peeled off her gloves and picked up the hoe. She glanced around for a place to store it, then decided she'd better take it with her. She realized she'd made no arrangements to get back to the Hotel.

Oh, well, she thought, it was only two or three miles and she could drop the hoe off at Darroch's when she went by. She hoisted it over her shoulder and started down the road.

She had underestimated the time she'd spent in the cemetery and overestimated her energy. By the time she walked half a mile her feet were complaining, the hoe weighed a ton and there was no place to rest.

When a small red van with the Royal Mail insignia on the door came over the hill she moved to the side of the road. It stopped just beyond her and the driver leaned out the window. He sized her up and spoke in English. "Is it a ride you are wishing?"

Astonished, Jean hurried up. He said, "This is the post bus, if you are wishing a ride to Ros Mór."

"That would be wonderful," she said gratefully. She put a foot on the step, then asked, "What is the fare?" She stared up at him. He had a pleasant face framed by sandy hair falling over his forehead.

"Three shillings."

Damn, she didn't have her purse. She took her foot off the step. "I'm sorry. I forgot to bring any money."

He said, "You can be paying me the next time you are riding, if you want it."

"Oh, yes. Thanks." She climbed aboard. The hoe clanked against the top of the bus door. The driver looked at it curiously but said nothing.

Afraid he'd think she had been digging up wild flowers or something equally dreadful, Jean felt compelled to explain. "I've been weeding. In the cemetery."

He nodded, as if it were customary to pick up a tourist with a hoe who'd been weeding a cemetery. He said, "You are the lady from America, is that right? My wife is telling me of meeting you."

"Who is your wife?"

"She is Catrìona and she will be working in the Playschool. I am Ian Ross, the postman."

"I'm Jean Abbott. I remember your wife. She's the pretty blonde."

He smiled at last, a smile that warmed his face. "*Thà gu dearbh*, the very pretty blonde."

After that, conversation lagged. Jean was feeling her afternoon's exertions in her lower back. She always overdid when she started gardening for the season. She closed her eyes and leaned back.

The next she knew Ian was talking to her. "Mrs. Abbott, we are at the Rose."

She roused. "Thanks." When she stood up the hoe fell at her feet with a resounding clank. "Drat," she murmured and bent down to pick it up. Maybe Gordon could find a place to store it.

Ian could not resist commenting. "Do not be forgetting your hoe," he said.

"It's not my hoe, it belongs to Darroch Mac an Rìgh. I was going to put it in his shed when we went by but I must have fallen asleep."

Ian said thoughtfully, "I can be leaving it off for you. I am just going by his cottage on my way home."

"Would you? Thanks so much. And I'll be sure to pay you next time I ride. Do you come this way at the same time every day?"

He nodded. "*Thà gu dearbh*, yes indeed."

"I'll see you tomorrow. Bye." She went into the Hotel and staggered upstairs straight into a hot bath. She fell asleep in the tub and almost missed supper.

Thirteen

Yes, as the music changes
Like a prismatic glass,
It takes the lights and ranges
Through all the moods that pass;
Dissects the common carnival
Of passions and regrets,
And gives the world a glimpse of all
The colors it forgets.

Alfred Noyes

*J*ean was happy. She'd begun her ancestral research, she'd found work to do and she was making friends. And she'd gotten her music back, realizing how much she'd missed it. It was as though there'd been a hole in her soul without it.

Jamie came by Thursday night to escort her down to the *seisean*. The bar was smoky on the public side, worse in the residents' bar and Jean all but gagged. There was a particularly pungent reek to cheap British cigarettes.

At the entrance to the room Jean took a sudden step back, nearly flattening Jamie who put a hand on her arm to steady her. "What's amiss?" he said.

"I can't go in, it's all men. I don't belong in there."

Jamie held up the guitar case. "This is your passport, *mo charaid*."

She looked at him as if he were mad. The men assembled in the bar did not look like musicians or even music-lovers. Several were in their sixties, with white or grizzled hair; most were leathery-skinned and weather-beaten whether twenty-five or fifty. Work shirts, sweaters, old trousers were the costume. There wasn't another woman in the room and the only familiar face she saw was Gordon's, behind the bar.

Jean advanced into the room only because Jamie's index finger was planted firmly between her shoulder blades.

"*Feasgar math, feasgar math*," he said, nodding to all. They nodded and greeted him, staring at Jean. She felt herself growing red and hoped it wasn't noticeable through the smoke haze.

Jamie headed for a table near the room's center and to the one chair with someone sitting in it. He stood by that chair, looking politely down at its occupant who stared up at him, baffled. "*Cathair dhan a leadaidh*," said Jamie firmly. The other man stared at Jean as if she were an apparition. Then suddenly light dawned. "*Thà gu dearbh*," he said and scrambled to his feet.

"*Tapadh leat*," said Jamie. He drew out the chair. "*A Shìne*," he invited.

She seated herself, smiling uncomfortably, and hissed at Jamie, "What the hell are you doing? You're making a spectacle of me."

Jamie sat down by her and said, "Ach, lassie, have you not noticed? You're not exactly invisible to begin with." He grinned. Then he raised his voice and said in the Gaelic, "Gather round, lads. We've a friend with us tonight."

The men shuffled closer. Several, at Jamie's nod, sat at the table. Jamie stood and said, "This is Mrs. Jean Abbott from the United States. Introduce yourselves," and he pointed at a man on his left.

"Somhairle Mac-a-Phi *as sine*," said that individual and they continued around the table with names.

Calum, the man next to Jean, said, "Are you a Gaelic music scholar, Mrs. Abbott? We've had several come to record us."

"Oh, no," she said, embarrassed. "I just want to listen to your songs, maybe learn some of them."

"Do you sing? Or play?"

Niall, on the other side of Jean, leaned forward. "Ach, Calum, do you not see the lass has brought an instrument? Unless Jamie's given up the fiddle."

"I brought it," admitted Jean.

"Ah. You'll maybe give us a song or two tonight? What do you sing?" he said with as much of a drawl as he could manage, "We're mighty partial to American country western music here."

"Well . . . I sing mostly folk music, but I know some country."

A tall man placed a glass of dark beer in front of Jean and a pint in front of Jamie, who nodded his thanks regally. "Ah . . . tapa lot . . ." said Jean and there was a general chuckle. She was becoming used to the kindly laughter that followed her attempts to speak the Gaelic. Only Darroch took her seriously and would correct her or nod approvingly if she got something right.

Gordon came from behind the bar with his accordion. "That's it for now, lads. If someone's really desperate with the thirst just pour it and leave the money by the register." He sat down at Jean's table in a chair obviously saved for him. He said casually, "I happen to know that the lady'd like to hear some of our songs about the sea."

Somhairle Mac-a-Phi was shocked. "Sea songs? Do you think them suitable, *a Sheumais?*"

"She doesn't have the Gaelic, man, it won't hurt her to hear them."

Somhairle said stubbornly, "Rough songs are rough songs and I for one will not be singing them in front of a lady."

Several of the older men nodded solemnly in agreement.

Gordon winked at Jean. "Perhaps you're right. It'll have to be love songs, then."

The tall man who had brought the beer began suddenly to sing, unaccompanied. He stood in the middle of the room, his reddening face serious, his voice deep, rough and melodic. He sang with great emotion, gently rocking back and forth on his heels.

Ochòin a ri,'si mo ribhinn donn,
Dh'fhag mi fo nhighean 'us 'intinn trom!

Jean sat quite still, mesmerized. When he'd finished there was a nod of appreciation. Jamie poked Jean and whispered, "'My Brown-Haired Maiden.'" When she looked at him, startled, he added, "He sings it in memory of his wife."

Then Gordon began to play a reel on his accordion and Jamie joined in. Chairs were drawn up, instruments were pulled out. Jean tried to look inconspicuous, painfully conscious of the rosewood guitar at her feet. It shouldn't even be here with all the smoke, she thought, and wished she'd tried harder to persuade Jamie to leave it behind.

She was allowed to listen until they quit for a round of drinks.

Sipping her beer and wishing she'd brought a tape recorder Jean tried to sort out in her mind what she'd heard. Her head buzzed with melodies. She was concentrating so hard on her thoughts she missed what Jamie was saying until he spoke her name loudly.

"*A Shìne.* Your turn." He had the guitar out of the case and was handing it to her.

"Jamie . . . I . . . what on earth could follow all that?"

"Anything. Don't worry, *a charaid*, Gordon and I will go wherever you lead."

Every man in the room was staring at her. Jean went cold with stage fright, sure her voice would come out in a terrified croak. Finally she thought of something to sing, checked the tuning and began "The Wildwood Flower."

I will twine with my mingles of raven black hair
The lilies so pale and the roses so fair.
The myrtle so bright with emerald dew,
The pale and the leader and eyes of bright blue.

After her first tremors she discovered she was enjoying herself as the song absorbed her and the rosewood guitar rang like a hammered dulcimer. Around the room heads nodded in time.

When she finished Jamie began without a note's pause "Hard Times" and she sang that with his harmony on the chorus, forgetting her self-consciousness in the pleasure of making music. When Gordon began "The Banks of the Ohio" in his lugubrious voice she added her soprano.

Then only say that you'll be mine,
In no other arms entwine
Down beside where the waters flow,
Down by the banks of the Ohio.

Darroch entered and paused out of sight by the door while Jean, Jamie and Gordon sang. He saw, looking around at the rapt audience, that Jean was the success he'd expected. He smiled in satisfaction.

I took her by her lily-white hand,
Led her down by where the waters stand.
I picked her up and pitched her in,
Watched her as she floated down again . . .

There was an appreciative murmur when they finished and much interested peering at Jean.

"*A Dhia beannaich mi*, that is beautiful," said Somhairle, who like nearly all *Eilean Dubhannaich* had an excellent command of English and had understood the words easily. He wiped a tear from his eye, unashamed.

Calum said, "Is it singing for a living you do, Mrs. Abbott?"

Somhairle said, "I am wanting to teach you *'An Gille Dubh Ciar Dubh,'*
Mrs. Abbott. It will be just suiting your voice. No one's really sung it well
since Mairi *Bhàn* MacUaine died, rest her soul."

Niall said, "Will we be having that country-western song next, Mrs.
Abbott?"

Jean glanced at Jamie. "Well, 'Your Cheating Heart?'"

Before they could begin Darroch stepped forward and the room went
absolutely silent with shock. The Laird had never before attended one of
their *seiseanan*. He looked at Jean, the drink in front of her and the men surrounding her. The corners of his mouth quirked up. "I didn't know God
made honky-tonk angels," he said.

"What?" she said, astonished to see him. "Oh, the song . . . I don't
know all the words."

"We'll have to learn it one of these days," he said, grinning.

When he walked around the table, Jamie and Gordon hissed to the
others, "Shove over," and everyone moved hastily so that there was room
when Darroch took a chair, casually inserted it next to Jean, and sat down.

The silence grew into a little buzz of satisfaction. The married men now
had a rejoinder to the wives who complained that they spent Thursday
evenings drinking beer and making music. It was all right. The Laird was
there. And because Island men loved a tidbit of gossip as much or more than
Island women, here was a tasty morsel to spring on their ladies: Darroch had
come because of the American woman.

Some of them had second thoughts about relaying that information,
since it was widely known that a woman had never attended one of their
seiseanan . . . until now.

A glass of whisky appeared as if by magic in front of Jean. She stared at
it in surprise. Darroch nudged her. "Laphroaig, twenty years old. A rare
treat, and a compliment."

"Oh." Well, if it was a compliment she knew how to accept it gracefully.
She picked up the glass, waved it vaguely in the air, said *"Slàinte"* in her very
best pronunciation and sipped. The peaty odor singed her nostrils, the
smoky sweetness of the whisky enveloped her mouth. She swallowed slowly
and at that instant realized what all the whisky fuss was about.

There was a response of *"Slàinte"* as the others lifted their glasses. Niall
came bustling over carrying a pitcher of water. He aimed it at Jean's glass. Her
hand and Darroch's came over the glass at the same time. Both said, "No."

"Ach, Darroch, it's no proper for a lady to take her whisky neat," said Niall. "Dinna be such an old stick, man," said Calum. "Have you no heard about the lassies being liberated?" He put his arm around Niall and steered him away, grinning over his shoulder at Jean.

Jean took another sip. "This is amazing," she said, holding up her glass to look at the rich warm color of the liquid.

"Aye. And how is your evening going?"

"Wonderful. The guys have been very nice to me and it can't have been easy for them to accept a strange woman in their midst."

"You're not all that strange, and besides they're fair chuffed to have a pretty woman to show off to."

Well, that was a new idea. She'd never thought of herself as a pretty woman in the center of an admiring group of males but on the other hand he seemed perfectly sincere. She eyed him intently. "I thought you usually didn't come to these shindigs."

"I had a special reason for coming tonight. Umm . . . what is a 'shindig'?"

Before she could answer Jamie came up to the table with a large bear-like man, brown-bearded, with pale blue eyes and a serious expression.

"Here, Jean, you must meet Kenneth Morrison. It's him who's done the collecting and writing down of Island songs."

"I am pleased to meet you, Mrs. Abbott. *Feasgar math, a Dharroch.*" The two men exchanged polite nods. "Am I right in understanding you do not have the Gaelic?" he said with a courtly bow in her direction.

"*Chan'eil,*" said Jean, practicing a phrase from her tapes, "but I'm working on it."

"I have many songs in the collection that would suit your voice to perfection, but of course they must all be sung in the Gaelic."

"I have taught her songs and she's learned the words by imitating me," said Darroch.

Kenneth shook his large head sadly. "Not the same thing, dear boy. Our songs must be sung with complete understanding of the words or the unique flavor is lost. You must be a Gaelic speaker."

Jean was suddenly depressed. How long would it take her to learn the language well enough to sing in it?

"Although . . . " He stroked his beard thoughtfully. "Perhaps I could teach you the words, explain the nuances, parse the grammar so that you grasp the full beauty of each song. It would take work, long practice sessions . . ." He watched her with a hopeful gleam in his eyes.

Jean opened her mouth to say that she was very ready to devote the time needed if it would give her access to Island music, but Darroch forestalled her. He said something in the Gaelic to Kenneth that was both short and to the point and the other man flushed guiltily. He said quickly, "Of course you would be there as well, *a Dharroch*."

Darroch was mollified by his inclusion in the proposed *seiseanan* and listened as the two began to talk about music. Kenneth had an extensive knowledge of Scottish music. He seemed to have met most of the key performers of the last thirty years and Jean listened as stories of Jean Redpath, Silly Wizard, Dougie MacLean, Run Rig, Christine Primrose, rattled off his tongue. Darroch's attitude was polite with no signs of disbelief so she concluded the stories were true.

They finished by setting a mutually agreeable date, Monday next, to look over Kenneth's music collection. Darroch said casually that he would pick Jean up and take her to Kenneth's. When Kenneth moved on, Jean asked, "What was that you said to him in Gaelic . . . uh, the Gaelic . . . a while ago?"

He smiled, all innocence. "Only that you would need a ride to his cottage. He lives in the back of the beyond."

Hmmm, Jean thought. He was making a pass and he was warned off. She eyed Darroch thoughtfully.

The men began to drift back from the bar and there was more singing and a fiddle solo from Jamie that left Jean weak with admiration. She gazed at him in awe. Darroch whispered into her ear, "I wish a lass would look at me the way you look at Jamie."

Jean said, unembarrassed, "I can't help it, he's terrific. I honestly don't think he's human when he plays the fiddle. He sort of . . . glows."

"I've noticed that," said Darroch. "Especially when he plays in the dark."

The object of their admiration lowered his fiddle and looked at Jean. "Right," he said. "You promised me bluegrass."

"In aid of that . . . " said Darroch. He reached under his chair and pulled out a case no one had noticed him carry in. "I'll open it, Jean. The case is not very clean." He lifted out an instrument and placed it in her lap.

"Dear heaven," said Jean. "It's a mandolin." She stared at Darroch who was smiling, pleased with himself.

"I told you," said Jamie to Jean, and to Darroch, "but however did you manage it so fast?"

"Ah," Darroch said, looking even smugger. "Jamie, you ken Paddy O'Hara, the *Eireannach* who lived on the Island a while back?" Jamie nodded. "He's in Inverness now, running a music shop. I rang him and asked could he get a mandolin. He said he'd ring me back. I expected it to be several days but he called in twenty minutes. It seems the secondhand shop down on Castle Street has had a mandolin in its back room for well over a year and Paddy'd been keeping an eye on it, thinking someone would want one some day. All he had to do was walk down, buy it and give it to Murdoch to bring to the Island. It's not pretty but perhaps it'll do the job for now."

Jean cradled the mandolin and crooned, "It's lovely." She bent her head to the strings and Jamie slid out of his chair to crouch by her. They put their heads close to the instrument so they could hear over the room noise.

"I think it's a good one even if it's a wee bit battered," he said. "Can you tune it?"

"You tune it like a violin. Does this sound right?"

Jamie listened and nodded. "Try it, play something," he said.

She plucked the strings for a moment or two and then had an inspiration. "This is an American Civil War song, about a soldier who didn't come home."

We shall meet but we shall miss him,
There will be one vacant chair.
We shall linger to caress him,
While we breathe our evening pray'r;
When a year ago we gathered,
Joy was in his mild blue eye,
But a golden cord is severed
And our hopes in ruins lie.

The mandolin set off the song beautifully. The room quieted to listen. When she finished Somhairle sniffled unashamedly and said, "You do know some lovely sad songs, Mrs. Abbott."

Jamie tucked his fiddle under his chin and said, "Bluegrass now." To Jean's astonishment he began to play "Turkey in the Straw." Instruments reappeared around the room and joined in when he moved to "Foggy

Mountain Breakdown" and "Old Joe Clark." Jean tried to keep up on the mandolin, gaining confidence as she played.

At the end, Jean said, exhausted, to Jamie, "Well, thank God that's over. I was terrified you were going to light into 'Orange Blossom Special.'"

He grinned. "It crossed my mind."

"Had enough?" said Darroch.

"My fingers are bleeding; it must be time to go. I've had a smashing time," said Jean.

"Perfectly good Gaelic expression . . . *s' math sinn*. It means, that's fine." He picked up Jean's sweater from the chair and draped it over her shoulders, then retrieved the instruments. They left to the accompaniment of cheery goodnights and reminders to Jean to come next week. "The bar's closing but some of the lads will stay behind after the door's locked."

"I'm ready to go. I feel as if I've run the four minute mile."

"Wait till next week. Now that they know you the gloves will be off," said Jamie.

They said good night to Jamie outside the Hotel. Jean said, "I'm going to sit on the bench. I need a breath of fresh air. It was so smoky in there I was beginning to sound like Marianne Faithfull."

"I'll sit with you a wee bit if you don't mind," Darroch said.

They sat and stared out at the gooey range of mud banks. The tide was out. "Gorgeous, isn't it," said Darroch ruefully.

"I like it fine, it's real. It's not like some picture postcard."

"Picture postcards don't smell of fish," he said, wrinkling his elegant nose. He put his arm across the back of the bench. "You've been here nearly two weeks. What do you think of the Island?"

"It gets better every day. I've been treated so well by everyone. I can't thank you enough, I know it's because of your friendship they've accepted me. I don't feel like a tourist at all."

"It's when folk start being rude to you that you'll know you're not considered a tourist," he said, but Jean found it hard to imagine that the courteous and gracious *Eilean Dubhannaich* would ever stoop to rudeness. Except for Màiri, of course, who was a law unto herself.

The dark clouds parted and a full moon sailed majestically into sight, her light so bright that they blinked. The moon seemed to pause, posing against the cloud-streaked sky. They watched in admiration.

Darroch turned to Jean, illuminated by the moon's rays. Strong profile, firm chin and a mass of hair that was black in the moonlight, gold in back from the reflection of the hotel lights. Head high, feet planted confidently on the ground. A handsome woman, he thought, and so American.

"'How sweet the moonlight sleeps upon this bank! Here we will sit . . .'" she paused, stymied for the rest of the line.

" . . . 'And let the sounds of music creep in our ears . . .'" He nodded back at the Hotel where a faint sound of singing could be heard from the residents' bar.

Jean sighed, looking up again. "We don't have this kind of moon in Milwaukee. Sometimes up in the north woods, but never in town."

"It's because we have so few street lights. See how dark the Island is. You can really see the stars. We'll have to go up *Cladh a' Chnuic* one night when the moon's full. There's more stars up there then you've ever seen before, I guarantee."

Wouldn't that be as romantic as all get out, thought Jean, abruptly reminded that she was sitting by a very attractive man. She could feel his arm behind her, warm and strong.

His hand gripped her shoulder. "Look," he whispered and pointed to her left.

The sky was pierced by a shower of diamonds, each one flaming into a burst of illumination, then fading to black. Jean counted twelve flare-ups after it occurred to her to start counting.

Darroch turned from the spectacle to watch Jean's reaction and saw the lights reflected in her eyes like tiny stars. Deep inside him something stirred.

The meteor shower died away. He watched, staring at her mouth when she wet her lips with the tip of her tongue. An invisible thread tugged at him and without conscious thought he leaned toward her.

A cold wind blew up from the mud flats and twitched Jean's sweater like a bony hand. She shivered violently.

He straightened. "You're cold, *a charaid*," he said. "Go in to your warm bed."

They walked to the Hotel. A moment of hesitation, then he bent and kissed her on each cheek, exactly as she'd seen him kiss Màiri. She thought about kissing him back but decided it was safer just to say, "Good night, I mean *feasgar math, a Dharroch*."

"*Oidhche mhath*, good night, *feasgar math* is good evening," he corrected, smiling at her as she went in.

In her bedroom she was suddenly too tired to analyze the nuances of the last five minutes but they'd left her feeling warm all over. She'd not need the blanket on her bed tonight.

Fourteen

Dust as we are, the immortal spirit grows
Like harmony in music; there is a dark
Inscrutable workmanship that reconciles
Discordant elements, makes them cling together
In one society.

William Wordsworth

After Thursday night's pub visit, Jamie said casually one evening after dinner while Darroch and Màiri were doing dishes, "Jean, I know you want to learn our songs. But would you ever want to get together with me and play other music?"

Surprised, she said, "What other music?"

"Oh, fool around with country western, Appalachian, jazz. I don't get a chance to play anything but our music except on Thursdays and that's just a pick-up *seisean*. Màiri only likes Gaelic music and there's no one on the Island as good as her . . . except you."

She was touched and honored that a musician of Jamie's ability would make such a request in such terms. "Sure," she said, "I'd really like that. When?"

"Some afternoon? I take Wednesday afternoons for myself, don't do any croft work. I stay home and read or fiddle around."

"Okay. Gordon's given me a practice room. Wednesday afternoon come over and we'll fiddle around together," she said, then blushed as she realized how that sounded.

Jamie chuckled. "I'll stop by around one, then, shall I. And Jean . . . don't mention this to Màiri, not at first. She'll disapprove." He grimaced.

Jean was dubious about keeping secrets from Màiri but Jamie must know his wife. "Okay."

He arrived promptly after lunch on Wednesday, fiddle case in hand. In her practice room they eyed each other. Then Jean said, "Where do we start?"

"Wherever you'd like."

She shuffled through the music books she'd brought down from her room. "Here's a book of American Civil War songs. They're sentimental but the tunes are lovely, especially for a fiddle. How about this one?"

The years creep slowly by, Lorena,
The snow is on the grass again.

Jamie joined in and afterwards said, "That's lovely. We could play that at the *cèilidh* . . . or at least on Thursday nights. Maybe we'd better save the *cèilidh* for later, come to think of it. We don't want Màiri to get the idea you're leading me astray."

"Would she really think that?" asked Jean, eyes wide. Trouble with Màiri was the last thing she wanted.

He grinned. "Lass, when I can predict what notions Màiri will get in that red head . . . " He left the sentence unfinished. Jean shook her head. She could never tell when he was joking.

They'd put the Civil War songs aside when they heard a knock. "Come in," she said.

Gordon opened the door. Uh-oh, she thought, we're too loud and we're disturbing the Hotel. But he was smiling expectantly and carrying a tray with a teapot and three cups. "Is this a private *cèilidh* or can anyone join in?" he asked.

"The admission fee is a pot of tea and a drop of whisky wouldn't come amiss, if you want a hearty welcome," said Jamie. He cleared music off the table so Gordon could set the tea tray down.

"Be right back," Gordon said.

"Will you be mother, Jean?" asked Jamie. She looked puzzled. "That means, will you pour the tea?"

"Is there a special ritual to it or do I just pour?"

"You ask each person what they take in their tea. Milk goes in the cup first, then tea poured through the strainer, then sugar. Stir it and hand it round." Jamie eyed the tray. "What, no biscuits?" he grumbled.

Gordon reappeared, clutching his accordion and a tray with three glasses of whisky and a plate of cookies. Jamie rubbed his hands together happily.

"Good man, Gordon, *mo charaid*." To Jean he said, "Island survival tip, Jean. Never miss a chance to have Sheila's biscuits and Gordon's whisky."

Jean, munching a delicate lemon bar, mouth full, nodded her head.

After they'd finished their tea Jean said, "I like these Island customs like afternoon tea and whisky but they're hard on the waistline. You folks are always eating."

"Aye," said Jamie, "but you notice we work hard too. We work it off." Carefully he wiped his hands on his handkerchief and picked up his fiddle. He played a short exuberant jig and finished it off with a flourish. "See, I burned up three biscuits with just one tune." He grinned at Jean. It must work, she thought. There was not an ounce of fat on his gorgeous body.

Gordon picked up his accordion and began a spritely jig. Jamie joined in and Jean experimented with a mandolin accompaniment. Playing without sheet music was challenging but fun; it took all her concentration. At the end she decided Jamie was right. She'd had a workout.

They had subsided happily into a set of waltzes when Sheilah popped her head around the door. She clicked her tongue. "Musicians," she grumbled good-naturedly. "Have you lot no work to do? And you, Gordon . . . dinner prep in ten minutes."

"It's hen-pecked I am and no mistake," sighed Gordon lugubriously.

Jamie said, "Aye, the lasses rule the roost around here. I'd best be off or I'll be sleeping in the truck tonight. Herself will have plenty that wanted doing yesterday."

Jean was alarmed until it dawned on her they were joking. "I'll peel potatoes if that will get you back in Sheila's good books, Gordon."

"Worth a try," he said, and winked at her. "Give us a hand carting the dishes, *a Sheumais*."

In the kitchen, Jamie set the tray down and turned to the other two. "Next Wednesday, same time, *ceart math*?"

"Okay, I mean, *ceart math*," said Jean, pleased, and Gordon said, "I'll give you time to work together and then join you, if I may, assuming I can slip away from the trouble-and-strife."

"I heard that," said Sheilah. She took the tray from Gordon, set it down by the sink and handed him an apron. "Work," she commanded.

"Can I help?" asked Jean.

Sheilah said dubiously, "You're a guest, love, it doesn't seem right."

"Nonsense," said Jean. "I love cooking, I miss my kitchen and I'm bored out of my skull with inactivity. Give me something to do."

"The devil finds work for idle hands," said Sheilah. "Call me Auld Nick." She tied an apron around Jean and gave her lettuce to wash.

"I'm awa' before she finds an apron to fit me," said Jamie and slipped out the door.

The ice broken, Jean found herself venturing down to the kitchen often. Sheilah was chronically short of help since the young people she trained so expertly usually left for well-paying hotel jobs on the mainland. Gradually she got used to thinking of Jean as a helper and not as a guest and began to give her tasks like preparing vegetables. Jean sat happily with a pan on her lap and a knife in her hand and worked while they talked and she watched Sheilah.

She began to pick up little niceties of the chef's trade, like a foolproof way to make gravy without lumps and how to melt chocolate without scorching it. The day Sheilah entrusted her with stirring a delicate pudding was the day Jean felt she'd arrived.

"You're becoming such a help I should give you a discount on your room rate. I've never had a Hotel guest who'd work in the kitchen."

"Consider it an exchange for letting me have the practice room," suggested Jean. "Not to mention the tea and the whisky. Besides, I'm learning your cooking secrets. It's an education watching you." It was true; Sheilah was both an expert and an artist.

"I wish I had my own kitchen, I miss it. I love being here in the Hotel, but . . . "

"I know," said Sheilah sympathetically. "Are you homesick for your family too?"

"Ummm . . . " said Jean and stopped. No, she thought guiltily, not at all. Except for Sally, whom she really missed and to whom she wrote long letters every week (and received equally long replies), she found her Milwaukee life had faded to the back of her thoughts. She'd become so busy and so absorbed in the everyday activities of Eilean Dubh it was as though she'd always lived there.

Funny, she thought, how easily she'd become part of this community.

PART II

Jean

Fifteen

There's ane they ca' Jean, I'll warrant ye've seen
As bonie a lass or as braw, man;
But for sense and guid taste she'll vie wi' the best,
And a conduct that beautifies a', man.

Robert Burns

Four months ago it would not have crossed Jean's mind to come alone to a Scottish island so tiny it wasn't on the map. Four months ago she was a happily married mother of two, solid citizen of Milwaukee, Wisconsin, living the life that had been organized for her before she was twenty, organized before it had barely begun, all because of a few careless minutes of passion that had gotten her pregnant at nineteen.

She'd made the best of it, in her cheerful, compliant way. She put aside her college education and married her lover Russ. She learned to cook and keep house. They bought a home, sold it and bought another, finally acquiring a charming five-bedroom colonial overlooking Lake Michigan in an expensive neighborhood.

It took all her energy to keep everything running smoothly. All the housework devolved on her. Russ was good with the children and they adored him but he was useless around the house. When he'd offered to help with the vacuuming he'd knocked an irreplaceable crystal out of the chandelier. The only laundry he could be trusted with was his own underwear which he happily washed in scalding hot water. And he hadn't a clue about cooking.

Any suspicion that he might be inept on purpose to get out of helping disappeared when he proved equally inept in the workshop: pictures he hung fell down, pipes he cleaned backed up and toys he put together disintegrated.

It was a great relief to everyone when their son Rod picked up a hammer at six years old and drove his first nail straight and true.

But Russ was good-natured, gregarious and hard working. He was a skillful lover. He was a shrewd businessman. His deficiencies were forgivable.

When Rod and Sally were old enough to go to school Jean became a room mother, the volunteer whom teachers could call on for any task. Music was her particular joy and she loved bringing her guitar to school and teaching the children American folksongs. But in the eighties' recession, faced with falling sales and canceled contracts, Russ let staff go and asked Jean to be office manager. By the time that panic was over the kids were in junior high and definitely did not want their mother involved in their school.

So Jean, at last, went back to college. She finished her English degree and began thinking about graduate school and a profession. She considered becoming a librarian or a teacher but employment prospects in Milwaukee weren't good and she couldn't move away for a job. She examined college catalogs and dithered.

The children grew up. Rod went to Berkeley to attend graduate school in computer science. Sally started university in Madison and moved on campus.

Jean found things to do. She helped form a folksinging trio, playing coffeehouse gigs. She volunteered. She gardened. She took gourmet cooking classes. She joined a book club at the library. Russ taught her how to use a computer and when the Internet began she was one of the first to start surfing. Russ was making an excellent living by then, bringing home fistfuls of money.

Life was comfortable, safe and quiet and she thought her marriage was the same until one night when Russ felt the need to confess.

He was seated in front of the fireplace when Jean brought in the coffee tray. She was pleased with the coffee, a new flavor she'd discovered. Russ loved flavored coffees. She waited for him to take a sip.

"This is good. What is it?"

"It's tiramisu. From the Co-Op."

Eyebrows raised, he said, "How can you stand to go in there? The people are so grubby, like hippies."

Jean had never understood Russ' antipathy to the Co-Op. She liked it and its earnest, intense volunteers and she found the vast array of nuts, seeds, grains and unidentifiable substances endearing. And their coffee was the freshest in town and cheaper than in supermarkets.

"Oh, I suppose I have some folk-singing ex-hippie left in me," she said.

She lifted her legs and put her feet in his lap. Sometimes he welcomed this, sometimes it seemed to annoy him. His attitude towards intimacy had puzzled her in the last few years. Sometimes he made love enthusiastically and sometimes it seemed he was only going through the motions.

Tonight his mind seemed far away.

Jean didn't object to his silence. It had been a busy day and dinner had been a lot of work, her own recipe for lasagna that she thought had been a triumph. She wished he would rub her feet because they hurt from standing, but otherwise she was happy to relax.

Russ said abruptly, "Jean, I have something to tell you." He lifted her feet from his lap and deposited them on the floor. Surprised, she sat up.

"I have been having an affair."

The world stood still. "What?" she asked blankly.

"I have been having an affair. For two years."

Jean blurted, "Why?"

The question surprised him; he'd thought she'd ask with whom. "I don't know . . . I can't seem to stop myself," he said, rattled.

"Oh. It's happened before, then." Her spine was slowly turning to ice.

"Yes."

"How many times?" If the earth had opened up she would have hurled herself into the gap, so deep was her humiliation.

"Two or three." In reality it was five, counting a couple of brief trysts at conventions, but Russ, who kept a careful half-ashamed tally, could not bring himself to admit that.

"I see," Jean said. She rose, picked up the tray and walked to the kitchen. After a moment he followed her, carrying his cup.

She was loading the dishwasher, her face frozen and empty. She took his cup. "Thank you."

"Jean, let me talk to you about this . . . "

She looked at him and for a moment he caught a flash of anger in her eyes so intense that he found himself shriveling.

"No. Not tonight. I'm tired."

"But . . . " he could not stop himself from saying as she started the dishwasher and turned to leave. "Don't you want to know with whom?"

"No. What does it matter?" Her voice held deep despair. She walked out, leaving him staring after her. She turned. "Please sleep in a guest bedroom tonight."

She was silent and withdrawn for the next few days. She could not bring herself to talk to Russ even though he coaxed and pleaded and finally stormed at her in an effort to evoke a response. She only turned away and retreated to their bedroom, closing the door behind her.

Her life with him was a lie. Everything in her life began to seem like lies. Love vanished. She felt as though she loved no one, not Rod, not Sally and certainly not Russ. She was empty of feeling.

She unfroze, briefly, when Russ insisted on confessing further. By then she was wondering who his lover was. It did not help to learn it was Mary Lu, his office manager, a frequent guest in their home. Her bitterness deepened as the weeks crept by.

Self-doubt gnawed at her. She stood in front of the mirror. She was not beautiful but she thought she was attractive: bright green eyes, nice features, hair an unusual red-brown. She kept her figure trim by brisk walks and twice-a-week workouts at their health club. She was good-natured and affectionate and she enjoyed and sometimes initiated sex. According to the books, she was doing everything right.

What was wrong with her that caused her husband to seek other women?

She retreated into herself. Communication between them came to a halt and it drove Russ mad. He tried everything he could think of to get Jean's attention, pleading, raging, needling, but she remained frozen and distant. Curiously enough, he had no desire for sex with his mistress but he was desperate to make love to Jean. She had never failed to respond to that.

Russ was not a deep thinker when it came to his relationships with women. One night, frustrated beyond reason, he stood outside their door, the door she'd shut against him. He opened it, stepped inside and listened. Her soft breathing told him she was asleep. He threw his robe on a chair and made his way carefully to the bed.

She did not stir. He slipped in beside her.

She was wearing his favorite nightgown, the one that buttoned all the way down. He undid the buttons carefully and pulled it open. He put one hand on her breast and the other between her legs and caressed her until he found a responsive wetness.

Jean's dreams, since Russ' confession, had been awful: dreams of her happy family life when she'd been sure of her husband's love, dreams that changed suddenly, trailing off into a terrifying unknown. If the dreams had been bad awakening was worse, reality turning into a long bleak future stretching before her each morning.

Now she came slowly awake to the awareness of being made love to, enjoying it, responding. Russ used to wake her like that often, blending her dreams into the most exquisitely erotic experience. Now he sensed the perfect moment of her arousal, moved on top and thrust into her. She arched toward him, her climax flooding her body.

Awareness returned abruptly and she had a sudden vision of Russ on top of fubsy-faced Mary Lu. Her revulsion was immediate and complete. She began to struggle as he drove deep, groaned and collapsed on her. She wept, tears spilling down her cheeks.

When she moved frantically under his weight he rolled off to lie beside her and put his hand possessively on her belly. "Ah, Jean," he said. "You're still as hot and tight as you were that first time up by Lake Michigan, remember?"

Hot and tight. Was that twenty years of marriage, summed up? "Get your hand off of me," she snapped.

"Jean . . ."

"Get out of my bed."

He crawled out awkwardly and stood up.

"How could you? How could you do that while I was asleep?"

"You wouldn't talk to me . . . I thought it might help. And I wanted you."

"Get out of my room, you . . . you . . . " Her voice trembled. What epithet was harsh enough for a cheating husband? "You rat!"

"It's our room, Jean. Our bedroom."

Furious now, she searched frantically on the bedside table for something to throw at him and found her little Waterford crystal clock. She hurled it and had the satisfaction of hearing him yelp just before the glass shattered on the floor.

"Jean, you're being unreasonable . . . we've got to talk . . . we'll talk tomorrow." He stumbled awkwardly through the darkness to the door, bouncing off furniture, cursing at the pain in his shins.

"Get out of my room! Get out of my life!" she shouted, control gone.

He left, closing the door hard behind him.

Jean leaped out of bed and ran to the shower where she scrubbed at herself, sobbing. Of all he had done this was the worst, to make love to her while she was half asleep and could not control her response.

Back in the bedroom she sat on the bed and felt total despair. She was well aware of the urgency of her sexual needs; she'd always wanted more lovemaking than Russ would give her. He'll use sex to get me back and it will work, she thought. He'll keep on doing it until he wears me down. The gloves were off and he would use every weapon he had to win her back. And there was no lock on the bedroom door.

She looked at the remains of her beloved clock. It had been a birthday present from Russ two years ago. She picked up the pieces and put them in the wastebasket.

One of the shards of glass pricked a finger and a drop of blood welled. Her heart hurt as though it was full of glass. She sat on the floor and cried for her shattered clock and her shattered life.

She had cried this hard only a few times before. When Russ had left her years ago, before they were married, telling her casually one night that he was going off to college in New England. When her father had died suddenly of a heart attack. When her mother had died the following year, after a short, intense struggle with cancer.

She cried until she was sick to her stomach, cried till her bones ached and her eyes burned. When she was cried out, common sense took hold, as it always did with her. I've got to get out of here, she thought.

In her frozen fury she'd been planning to leave him for several weeks now, with no idea of how to do it. She had money of her own, inheritances from her mother and great-aunt in good investments, but the income was just enough to rent a small apartment, with nothing left over. By rights Russ should give her money to live on but she could not bear the thought of confronting him and enduring his trying to argue her out of leaving. She wanted to pack, disappear, be gone by the time he came home.

It was obvious she'd have to get a job and support herself but there was not much call for an English major with no experience beyond being a homemaker. Then it dawned on her there was one thing she was good at: computers. They'd had computers for years and she could do anything with them short of making them sit up and beg.

But in her first interview she learned personal experience meant nothing, it was education that counted. And her second interviewer's polite boredom turned to pointed interest when he realized she was married to one of the country's leading software designers. "What's he up to these days?" the interviewer said casually and Jean envisioned herself working there and being pumped daily by a competitor for details of Russ' work.

She reluctantly faced the fact she had no marketable skills and no chance of finding a good job.

An idea entered her mind. Several summers ago her great-aunt Marian had died and Jean, as executrix, had gone to North Carolina to settle the estate and sort out the enormous old house, filled from attic to basement with family papers, antique furniture and oriental rugs.

Whenever Jean thought of that summer she felt the sweat on her brow, smelled the dust of the attic, heard the insects humming in the heat. The house was not air-conditioned and the summer was relentlessly hot.

When she finally got to the contents of her aunt's desk she discovered a pack of old letters written in a language she'd never seen before. A translator determined that they were love letters sent from someone named Ùisdean to someone named Mòrag in a place called Eilean Dubh and that the letters had been returned because Mòrag was dead.

Jean knew that the founder of her family had emigrated from Scotland but knew nothing else. She went to the local library and learned that Eilean Dubh was a small island in the Hebridean Sea. The trail stopped there; she could learn no more.

The idea took hold. She would go to Eilean Dubh and find out about her ancestor. It was the perfect excuse to leave, get away from home and family while she thought it all through and decided what to do about her marriage.

Her travel agent had never heard of the Island but several sessions on the Internet yielded the information needed about transport and accommodation. In five days she booked her flight, made a reservation at one of Eilean Dubh's two hotels and packed.

She announced her plans at dinner to a startled daughter and an aghast husband and caught the plane to London next afternoon.

Once she had arrived on the Island she knew she'd made the right decision.

A month later she was even surer, though the glamor and novelty of Eilean Dubh was wearing off, replaced by something deeper and far more interesting. She began to look closely at this place in which she now found herself.

No one had much money. The cheerfully painted shop fronts and their sparkling windows trimmed buildings long past their prime. The *Eilean Dubhannaich* wore their clothes past their prime, too, and their cars were ancient. Darroch's middle-aged Bentley moved through them like a swan through a flock of geese.

There wasn't much to do on the Island besides work. The sole movie theater up in Airgead never had first-run films. The Island newspaper came out only twice a week and newspapers from outside arrived a day old. The four channels of British television presented, for the most part, an appalling mixture of American re-runs, dreary documentaries, silly game shows and incredibly boring political broadcasts, only occasionally enlivened by a program such as *Classic Theatre* or a Britcom.

The library was a bright spot, with an ample, well-chosen collection in English. "There aren't enough books published in the Gaelic each year," sighed Isabel. "So we make do with English." Jean got a library card . . . "ticket" it was called here . . . and helped herself, carrying home armfuls each week, her reward after her Friday research slogging.

Homesickness began to creep into her mind as she got used to her new surroundings. She missed many things about America. One day she suddenly stopped in the middle of the Co-Op and looked around at the plain over-head fluorescent lights, the dreary linoleum floor, the shelves of unfamiliar, drably-packaged foods.

She had a sudden vision of her favorite store in Milwaukee, elegantly lit and carpeted. The huge deli counter with bowl after bowl of salads, sliced meats, cheeses and comfort foods like meatloaf and potato pancakes, to re-heat if the shopper didn't feel like cooking. The coffee aisle with twenty-five flavors of coffee. Dairy cases with twenty flavors of yogurt. Produce aisles with jicama, radicchio, thirty salad dressings and nineteen kinds of olives. Frozen bagels, breads, fancy desserts. Much of it was stuff she never bought and would disdain eating but she liked knowing it was there.

She stood in the middle of the Co-Op's prepared food section and found herself looking at canned sausages. She burst into tears.

She put down her basket and fumbled in her pocket for a tissue. Another shopper entered the aisle. Horribly embarrassed, Jean bent so that her hair swung forward to shield her face. She seized a can at random from the shelves and pretended a deep interest. She found herself reading the label of something called Marmite and it sounded so nasty that she almost gagged. She put it down and tried to swallow a sob.

"*Feasgar math*," said a cheerful voice and she turned and looked into Barabal's face, which immediately expressed concern. "Whatever is wrong, Jean?" she whispered.

"Homesick." It was all she could make herself say.

"Ah. Come have a cuppa." Barabal picked up Jean's basket and her own and marched to the cashier's counter. "Keep a watch over these for us, will you. We're going for tea." She shepherded Jean out of the store and down the street to the teashop.

The shop was known for the strength of its "cuppas" and Barabal poured Jean's and added plenty of milk and sugar to take off the edge. Then she waited until Jean had taken a few reviving sips.

Jean said, shamefaced, "Imagine a grocery store making you homesick."

Barabal said, "I remember the summer I spent working as a child-minder in Edinburgh. Every time I walked down Prince's Street I passed a little antique shop. One day they had a creamer and sugar bowl on a silver tray in the window, like the set my mother had. Her prized possession, only came out for Sunday evening tea. I started to cry, right there in the midst of the shoppers. It's a wonder no one called the police, great Highland daftie, howling away."

She sighed. "Always walked on the other side of the street after that. Well, you couldn't give Prince's Street the skip, could you? That would have been even dafter. But I was certainly homesick. Came back to Eilean Dubh at summer's end and never have had the least desire to leave."

There it was again, that deep attachment the *Eilean Dubhannaich* had for their Island. Poor and old-fashioned though it was, they loved it. Jean pondered that and wondered if she had the same attachment for Milwaukee. She decided she didn't. Milwaukee's neighborhoods had character but as a whole, it was just another city.

But she had deep feelings for her own country, America. She'd always gotten teary-eyed when singing "The Star-Spangled Banner." Was she missing her country now or just its material comforts? Shallow, she decided, you are a shallow person, to miss fine grocery stores and fancy foods and a hundred channels on television, few of which had anything worth watching.

But she had no desire to leave the Island and go home. There were things here that mattered more than the ones she'd left behind. She ran through them in her mind: music, friends, her work with the Playschool. Darroch. Especially Darroch. If she went home she'd miss him desperately.

The implications of that thought made her deeply uncomfortable and she shoved it into the back of her mind. "Thanks, Barabal, I feel better," she said, even though she was only partially comforted. She'd work the rest of it through later.

Who was she, really? Housewife or free spirit? Mother of two or care-free folksinger? Vacationing American or forlorn stranger on a tiny Scottish island? Who did she want to be?

She wanted to be somebody with a purpose and mission in life. Her best friend was a nurse. Russ's sister taught learning-disabled children. Russ's brother was a social worker. She'd only gotten her B.A. two years ago and she wasn't qualified for any kind of a job beyond flipping hamburgers.

She and Russ had gone out to dinner one night with three other couples, all six of them professional people. "What do you do, Jean?" asked one of the wives, a lawyer. She had a no-nonsense very short haircut and wore a sleek black suit, its skirt reaching precisely to the knee.

Russ answered for her. "She's just a housewife," he said jovially. "Her job is to look after the kids and me. She's great at it, too."

"Oh," said the lawyer. "How lovely to have children and stay home with them." Her tone suggested that it was not quite as lovely as all that. "How old are your kids?"

Interest faded rapidly when Jean revealed they were teenagers. No one wanted to hear about teenagers unless they were brilliant and had entered medical school at 16, or incorrigible and bailed out of jail innumerable times. No one cared about nice, well-behaved, only slightly goofy teenagers.

There was a definite pecking order among the wives present. The pediatrician's opinions were received solemnly by the group, then the lawyer's, then the teacher's. At the bottom was Jean, the little homemaker. She thought her opinions were as well thought out and as cogently stated as the other women's but they were listened to and politely ignored. "Hmm, well . . . interesting," and the conversation flowed on around her.

Still, she didn't think it mattered, beyond her momentary pique, until Russ said in the car on the way home, "That Elise . . . she's something else, isn't she?"

Elise was the pediatrician, tall, blonde, weighing about ninety pounds and still boasting an impressive bosom that Jean, unkindly, thought was created from wads of tissues.

"Beautiful and brainy," Russ sighed.

Jean felt very unimportant, awkward and stupid. She used to be brainy, too, and if not beautiful, at least pretty. Where had the real Jean gone?

Falling asleep that night curled against Russ' unresponsive back . . . he had not been interested in sex and that hadn't done anything to bolster her self-esteem . . . she thought, I must do something with my life. She'd fallen asleep with a firm resolve to consult those college catalogs.

But next morning, caught up in four breakfasts and two lunches to prepare, appointments to be made, and half a dozen phone calls needed for her volunteer work, Jean postponed her goal of becoming somebody to whom people listened. It could wait until she had more time.

Later she thought it would have been some comfort if Russ's affair had been with someone like Elise . . . real competition. But Mary Lu, his office manager, dumpy, not too bright, but convenient . . . that wasn't love; it was just a tawdry office affair. A man happy with his home life wouldn't have gotten involved.

Something must be wrong with her.

Rain. It began one morning as a light shower and hung on as clouds moved over the mountains and stalled. The sky turned gray and stayed that way day after day.

The usually cheerful *Eilean Dubhannaich* grew dour as the clouds hovered. Gordon moaned about a leaky roof and growled at Sheilah, who snapped at the hotel maids. Barabal complained about her eldest son's behavior. Catrìona fretted because Ian the Post came home every night with soaking wet feet and the Co-Op was out of wellies in his size. Màiri was sharp with Mrs. MacQuirter *as sine* who'd brought her little Fergus to Playschool with a bad cold. The shopkeepers grew quiet and their lively banter with their customers dwindled to brief action-oriented exchanges regarding merchandise required.

Even Jamie, normally the soul of even-tempered serenity, became morose. "May as well move back to Skye. It couldn't possibly rain any harder," he mumbled.

The weather took its toll on Jean too. Now two months into her stay on Eilean Dubh, she entered the period of her greatest unhappiness. It was partly the rain; she'd never experienced anything like a Hebridean island in monsoon season. But other, odd, things could set off a wave of depression that would hang over her all day.

There was a man on Eilean Dubh who from the back resembled Russ: tall, square shoulders, blond hair. The day she caught sight of him walking through the square with his arm around a woman was the day that, blinded by tears, she'd walked into the edge of a shop door. That had called for a prolonged sit-down in the shop with a cold compress held to the rapidly purpling bruise on her forehead. Little Mrs. Cailean the Crab, the shopkeeper, had been most upset.

Jamie and Darroch knew what she was going through, Jamie because he always knew and Darroch because he'd been there himself three years ago. He could recite by heart the stages of grief through which she was traveling: shock, denial, anger, guilt, depression . . .

He could always tell when she'd had a bad night by the circles under her eyes and the slump of her shoulders. And she was growing thinner, losing weight, something of a miracle on Sheila's cooking.

Both tried to help her as best they could. Both knew an open expression of sympathy would bring tears and embarrassment all around. So they adopted more subtle methods.

Jamie used music. He could always produce a new tune or a new approach to an old one that would lift her out of her misery and leave her breathless with pleasure. Listening to Jamie play the fiddle always brightened her spirits.

Darroch's weapon was a gentle affectionate teasing that never failed to leave her pink-faced and smiling. Somehow he could always make her feel special, liked and respected, even as she was laughing at herself.

The two of them put protective, metaphorical, arms around her and tried to cushion the worst of the bumps, knowing she had to experience them. Jean only half realized what they were doing but she knew that she had made friends here, good friends.

She was working through the dilemma of her crashed marriage, realizing that she never could have dealt with it back in Milwaukee where past, present and future would have overwhelmed her. On Eilean Dubh she'd found the courage to step into an entirely new future. And if she could make a new life for herself on a tiny Scottish island she could do it anywhere.

The truth was she had absolutely no interest in going back to Milwaukee: rattling around that big empty house, waiting for Russ and Sally to come home to give her life meaning, taking more adult ed classes, becoming expert at macramé, decoupage, shell art.

If she still loved Russ she might have been able to make it work. But she was beginning to realize she didn't love him any more. It all boiled down to the question of what could be done with a man who'd wreck a marriage for a bit of sex on the side when he could have had plenty at home. A man who having betrayed once would certainly betray again because he had lost sight of the essential loyalty of marriage.

He had tossed away twenty years of loving and sharing. His wife no longer had all his attention: she was in one compartment of his life and another one had been created for his lovers.

Something had gone wrong with Russ. Perhaps the flaw had always been there beneath the facade, submerged by the challenges of raising children and building a business. Jean knew Russ thrived on challenge, rose brilliantly to the occasion when courage and cunning were needed.

Perhaps there were no more challenges left within their marriage and he'd had to look elsewhere for stimulation. The major hurdles of life having been leaped, he'd succumbed to the worst, the most insidious enemy, one to which men were particularly vulnerable: boredom.

In some men it might have led to alcoholism. Jamie had said that was what sometimes happened to men on Eilean Dubh in the inactivity of long winter months. In Russ it had led to adultery.

Having reached this understanding she came to a conclusion: a man who could wreck a marriage out of boredom was not worth keeping. After all, *he* could have taken up macramé. Or decoupage.

And she couldn't live with a man she couldn't trust. Her marriage was over.

The realization sent shock waves of terror through her, mingled with a heady new sense of freedom. She wrote a letter to their family lawyers, stating her intention of divorcing her husband, typing it on the hotel's ancient typewriter. She put the letter in an envelope, sealed and stamped it and left it on her window seat for twenty-four hours.

Then, having experienced no change of heart, she mailed it.

Infidelity was rare on Eilean Dubh, Darroch said. It was not because of the certainty of swift and furious denunciation from the pulpit, although that played a part. Nor was it the lack of private trysting places and the inability of anyone to keep anything secret from the curiosity of their fellow *Eilean Dubhannaich*, who would have ferreted out the hiding place of the Holy Grail if it had been on their Island.

Few people had the time to fool around. Life on Eilean Dubh was constant hard work and men and women needed each other for survival. A crofter needed a partner because there was too much work for one person. If a spouse died, unless a new spouse was found or there were children old enough to do adults' work, crofting would have to be abandoned for another means of making a living. It was very much like the American frontier: no one could go it alone.

So adultery or anything that might destroy a marriage was seldom risked because it was not a risk worth taking. If you had marriage problems you made the best of it.

That didn't mean marriages on the Island were idyllic. Even Jamie and Màiri and Ian the Post and his Catrìona had their off days. But by and large, most people managed to rub along quite contentedly with their partners.

It gave the Island stability. The *Eilean Dubhannaich*, faced daily with the uncertainties of weather, the problematical state of their animals' health, the falling prices of livestock and the rising prices of everything else, prized the stability of marriage.

Jamie and Darroch loved to talk, even after an evening of singing. While Màiri was resting her fingers and Jean her voice, the two of them would chat on indefatigably. When they ran out of things to talk about they told stories, each trying to top the other. It was mainly fairy stories they told, elaborate concoctions of the impossible and the improbable, each man trying to add more convincing details and told so straight-faced that Jean half believed them. Then Màiri would say briskly, "What nonsense!" And Jamie would say, "Well, it could have happened that way," and Darroch would nod solemnly.

The stories had the usual components of shape-shifting and baby-swapping of fairy stories the world over. There was also a strong element of unrequited love and lust fulfilled and unfulfilled and the consequences of both. The stories and the storytellers wove a spell around Jean, wrapped her in a blanket of belief and knowledge quite beyond anything she'd ever experienced.

The stories were very old, Darroch said, originally told by *sgeulaichean* around the fires, and intended to teach morality and proper behavior, more effectively than the distant, formal Latin abstractions of the still-new Christian church.

Jean loved them. Nights when she could not sleep she started writing them down, trying to capture the rhythms and nuances of Jamie and Darroch's voices. The stories spoke directly to her and distracted her from the problems of her life.

Darroch said they'd never been written down, in the Gaelic or English. Jean thought that was something she could do: compile them into something that Isabel could put in the library. That would be a solid, enduring contribution to Eilean Dubh. Perhaps someday they could be published.

She'd once harbored dreams of being a writer and she knew she had talent. In high school her essays were always the ones picked by the teachers to be read aloud. In college her papers had gotten As and her contributions to the school literary magazine were welcomed with enthusiasm.

But there'd been no time to write with a young family's demands. Now she wondered why she hadn't gone back to writing once the kids were grown up and she had the luxury of long afternoons. Why had she spent all her time on volunteering, gardening and book clubs?

Because she hadn't had anything to inspire her before she came to the Island. Now she was experiencing an awakening of the spirit and the imagination. Now words came into her head, phrases, sentences. Now ideas woke her in the middle of the night, not the numbing depression of earlier weeks.

She began to spend a few minutes every night looking over the stories, revising, rewriting, and the minutes lengthened into an hour or more. If she woke up the next day with dark circles it was no longer from crying all night; it was from writing too late.

Darroch knew something had changed in her but he didn't know what until she found the courage to show her first finished story to him. He read it slowly, with mounting enthusiasm. He thought it was beautifully written and captured the spirit of the fairy tale perfectly, but he'd never been a gusher, so when he finished reading he put down the pages and smiled at her. "Very nice, Jean."

"I made a few changes so the story would flow better but I tried to keep the feeling . . . the Eilean Dubh feeling . . . the way you and Jamie tell the stories . . . " she stammered anxiously.

To hell with not being a gusher, it was *miorbhuileach* and he told her so. She glowed with pleasure. "Do you have any more?" he asked.

"I have another nearly done. I hope to put together a collection for the library. A contribution that will last after I'm gone."

Gone. The word fell between them and lay there.

Darroch was astonished at the wave of emotion that swept over him. Jean, gone? He took her hand and held it. "Don't talk about leaving, Jean. If you're happy here, why think about leaving?"

"Umm . . . well, I don't, most of the time." It was true. Whenever the idea of going back to Milwaukee came into her mind she repressed it firmly. She squeezed his hand. "I like it here."

"Good. We like having you here." Then he blurted, "I like having you here."

How sweet, she thought, and her answering smile was so wide that he was warmed. He grinned back. "Sing something, Jean," he said.

Her days fell into a pleasantly crowded routine. Three mornings at the Playschool, Fridays riding with Ian the Post to Airgead to work with fifteen-year-old Flòraidh, her translator. Wednesday afternoons with Jamie and Gordon. Other afternoons were spent reading, working in the cemetery, shopping (which always involved lots of friendly conversation in her halting Gaelic with the amused shopkeepers), and listening to her language tapes. Music on Thursday nights in the residents' bar, and more music at the *cèilidh-ean* and after dinners with Darroch and the MacDonalds.

Sometimes she walked up into the dark mysterious hills. She discovered a secret field of wildflowers that astonished her because it changed weekly. One week the flowers were white and waist-high, the next yellow with blue underpinnings and the next they became a carpet of blue stretching to the horizon.

She hiked each time towards that horizon, knowing the sea was there and longing for a glimpse of it. Often the landscape fooled her, promising a sea sighting but over so many hills that she'd give up, afraid dusk would catch her far from town.

But sometimes she would come all unsuspecting to the top of a cove carved into the cliffs, at its base a pure white beach caressed by waves. She'd stand and stare until she had to turn away, dizzy with the ocean's possibilities.

One day she walked the hills with Darroch, their long-legged strides matching, alternating words and peaceful silence. They enjoyed each other's company so much that they began spending time together in his cottage making music and talking.

One day, settled on his sofa with tea, they drifted into a conversation about their marriages. It dawned on Darroch that he'd talked a lot but hadn't heard much from her.

"Tell me about your life in Milwaukee," he said. In reality he wanted to hear about Russ and decided to be forthright about it. "How did you meet your husband?"

Her eyes were suddenly far away. "High school. He was a BMOC . . . Big Man on Campus. Captain of the football team, class president, good student but lazy. Tall, handsome, self-assured. I was the editor of the school paper, a radical, wrote fiery editorials about social injustices. Studied hard and got straight As, except in geometry. One day after French class . . . Madame had given him a hard time about the *passé simple* . . . he asked me if I'd help him with French. I said sure, if he'd explain to me about squaring the hypotenuse."

She set down her cup. "We became friends. Everybody thought we were an odd combination and when he asked me to the Senior Prom the other girls seethed with envy. But he was really sharp, you know, smart, quick. It just wasn't cool to let people know that. With me he could let it show and we had great conversations about the meaning of life, that sort of thing. I was a challenge. None of his other friends were intellectuals and I considered myself very much an intellectual.

"The night of the Prom we went up to the Point, where everyone went with their steadies to neck. We petted . . . it was the farthest I'd ever gone sexually. I wasn't ready for the rest of it, if you know what I mean. And he stopped and respected that. He was really gentle and considerate with me. We discovered we were in love. I thought he was the most wonderful guy in the world."

She sighed deeply. "He went off to college and we wrote letters . . . well, I did. He wasn't much of a letter writer. I figured he'd find someone else and forget me. But he came back to Milwaukee because his father had health problems and needed Russ at home. We both ended up at the U in Madison. I hung out with the hippie folksinger crowd and he was majoring in business so we didn't move in the same circles.

"But one day he called me and we went out. He was as charming as ever and I fell for him all over again. We started going steady the year I was a sophomore and he was a junior. We became lovers in November.

"He really wanted to make love, the way experienced guys do, I guess, and I thought I'd been a virgin long enough."

She picked up her teacup and leaned forward, hiding her face behind her hair. "I found I liked it . . . sex, I mean. We were very compatible but we weren't always careful. I got pregnant in March.

"Our parents were furious. His mother said what would she tell the relatives, my father wanted to thrash Russ, but my mother's reaction was the worst. All she said was, 'Oh, Jean.' And I knew right away how disappointed she was. She thought I'd been caught in the housewife trap, babies, housework, no more education. She'd wanted me to go to grad school, study for a profession.

"We got married quickly, no fancy wedding. I finished my sophomore year and Rod was born that winter. Russ' Dad gave him a part-time job and both families helped us financially so Russ could finish his degree."

She shook her head. "It was kind of humiliating but it worked out because both sets of grandparents adored Rod. He was the cutest baby imaginable and very smart. I had Sally a year and a half after Rod and she was so sweet and smiley everyone loved her too.

"And it was okay, our marriage was fine. We had lots of fun, the four of us. Doing simple things that didn't take money, like biking and camping.

"Russ wanted to go to grad school in business administration but his father had a serious heart attack. He needed to retire and he wanted Russ to take over the business. So he did, he owed it to his dad.

"He was great. He realized computers were the future and took the firm into them, phasing out typewriters and adding machines. He taught himself all about them, took night school classes, got in on the ground floor with people designing and building them. He discovered his real gift was for creating software for special applications. He took the firm out of sales and into designing software and never looked back. He's a huge success, nation-wide reputation. Specializes in quick fixes for very important small jobs.

"I did the housewife and mother thing and helped in the kids' school. I enjoyed that but then a recession came and I had to work in the business so Russ could cut staff. When we were financially sound again Russ didn't want me to work. I was at loose ends so I went back to the U and finished my degree. Filled my life with everyday things . . .

"I thought we were happy." She was crying now, remembering Russ' betrayal and her sudden realization that the life he was leading was not the one she thought they'd been leading together.

Once she'd let her guard down she couldn't stop crying. She trembled and wept as all the misery of the last few months poured out. Such a torrent of tears would have intimidated a lesser man than Darroch. But he'd never been afraid of genuine emotion, it was part of his professional life as an actor.

"Let it go, let it all go," he whispered. He lifted her legs over his so she was half sitting on his lap and tightened his arms around her, holding and rocking her as though she were a child, crooning incomprehensibly in the Gaelic.

She was an innocent, Darroch thought, married too young and a mother too young, seduced into thinking marriage would solve all her problems forever. Always protected and cared for until she'd had the rug pulled from under her feet. How tender she was, how vulnerable. There was something to having had a lot of experience in love, he decided, remembering his own failed romances. Exquisitely painful but he didn't regret one of them. They'd made him what he was today, made him able to understand her heartbreak and able to help her.

She gasped, "I want to know why he did it."

"There is no why, it just happened," said Darroch, his voice harsher than he'd intended. "The sooner you realize that the sooner you'll get over it."

She stilled, looking at him, and he could tell what he'd said was an entirely new thought. Maybe it really wasn't some deficiency of hers that had caused Russ to stray. "I thought it was something I'd done wrong. That I wasn't exciting enough . . . or pretty enough . . . or no good in bed . . . " Her voice trailed off once she'd managed to voice her deepest fear: that after twenty years of marriage the lovemaking she enjoyed so much was not adequate for her husband. *She* was not adequate.

"None of that is true," he said. "You're a fine person."

Presently he mused, "Màiri and I were best friends, soul mates, from childhood. Became lovers on her seventeenth birthday, planned to marry.

Then I won a scholarship to the Academy and wanted her to come to London with me while I learned to be an actor. She was appalled at the idea and said no, that city life and city people would kill her, that her place was on Eilean Dubh. I'd always known of her devotion to the Island and I realized then what that meant: she intended to spend her life here, working for our community.

"We were at an impasse. I couldn't give up acting and she couldn't give up Eilean Dubh. Then Jamie came along and made her happy again. I couldn't believe, at first, that she'd fallen in love with another man; I was still in love with her and miserable without her.

"By rights I should have hated him, thinking about him making love to her, making music with her. Some nights I woke up in a cold sweat, imagining them together. But no one could hate Jamie and finally I came to love him too, knowing how happy he made her and how right they were for each other."

But it still hurts, he thought, that I lost her. He'd tried to deny it to himself but it still hurt, resonated inside him as a deep enduring ache. He wanted to share that with Jean but he couldn't, not yet. She had enough to handle without his problems.

"Now 'Rienne . . . " he paused. "Maybe you don't want to hear this . . . " She nodded, sniffling. "I'd met Adrienne before she came to *The Magician*. Everyone in theatrical circles knew her. The adorable ingenue, full of fun, dressed like a model, not at all my usual type of woman. 'The Blonde Bubble,' people called her. She made me laugh at a time when I needed to laugh. We were married six months after she came on the program. The producers loved it, the Beeb loved it, the public loved it. I loved it too. It seemed as though we were always having a good time.

"But she wouldn't see the other side of me, the serious part. She refused to come to Eilean Dubh, not once, not even to meet my family. 'I wouldn't know what to wear, darling,' she said. 'What does one wear on a tiny Scottish island?'

"I managed to sneak home a couple of weeks a year. Then I'd catch hell from Màiri, who wanted to know why I didn't come more often. My father had died and people wanted me here to be the laird. She'd say, 'We need you. Don't you care about us any more?' Jamie tried to make her understand but she wouldn't let it go.

"My heart twisted into a knot every time I came to the Island and every time I left. Then Adrienne came back from a film job in France and told me she'd had an affair with her leading man. I remember looking at her when she said that . . . "

He paused.

"It was the most curious feeling imaginable. I thought, I don't love you any more. And it was if it had all been a fairy tale. I'd been bewitched by someone I'd thought was a princess and she was instead a wicked fairy. We have stories like that on Eilean Dubh, about enchantresses and shape-changers, and here I'd been living in one of them.

"I got up and walked out.

"We met, we even made love once more. Then we arranged the divorce. I asked what she wanted for alimony and she laughed at me. 'Keep it, darling,' she said. 'Give it to the kiddies on your little Island.' So she'd listened to that much about Eilean Dubh.

"She didn't need or want money from me. Her father's an earl, one of the richest men in England. His country place is a stately home called Hammond's Court, a tourist attraction. The Queen came to visit him there and I was presented to her. Adrienne is Lady Adrienne. She doesn't need to work as an actress; it's all a game to her.

"That's the story of my marriage. Three years, that's all. Most of it was fun and the end was like running into a brick wall at high speed."

"Yes. Me too." They were quiet for a few minutes. Then Jean realized how much she'd told him, and that his arms were still around her and her legs were draped across his. Embarrassed, she sat up and moved to detach herself.

"All right now?" he said.

"Yes, thanks." She sniffled and he fished in a pocket and handed her his handkerchief. She wiped her eyes. "You know, you're a really nice guy," she said, and was immediately sorry because she sounded like a gusher.

But he was pleased. The high cheekbones turned pink and the warmth moved into his eyes. "We have to look after each other in this world," he said solemnly.

She said, "Your ex-wife is a fool."

"So is your husband."

Their glances met and held for a long moment and something passed between them: intimacy, shared secrets and a deepening friendship. Then Jean caught a glimpse of the clock. "Good heavens, look at the time. I haven't even begun to think about cooking supper," she exclaimed.

"To hell with cooking. We've had a good wallow in misery, now let's have a night out. May I take you to the Rose for dinner?"

"Oh . . . no, I can't. My eyes must be red. Everyone will know I've been crying."

"We'll tell them you were helping me rehearse a new part and it is very sad. Maybe *Romeo and Juliet*. There are advantages to being an actor, you know."

Sheilah and Gordon joined them for after-dinner coffee. Darroch's request in the Gaelic to Gordon caused raised eyebrows and produced a bottle of champagne. "This is special, my very last bottle of this vintage," said Gordon, pouring with pride for Darroch to sample.

"You'll join us?" asked Darroch.

"The dishes . . . " began Sheilah but Gordon said in horror, "Miss a glass of that champagne? Grounds for divorce, Shee!" Jean said, "We'll all help with the dishes, lovie. Sit down."

Sheila's dessert was served in tall sorbet glasses and consisted of golden meringues filled with whipped cream, shot through with slivers of bitter-sweet chocolate and drizzled with caramel sauce.

Jean and Darroch were speechless with awe. "She calls it 'Eilean Dubh Sunset,'" said Gordon. "The chocolate pieces represent little thunderclouds on the horizon."

"No thunderclouds on our horizon," said Darroch. "A toast to the world's finest chef." And the three raised their glasses to Sheilah.

Dessert was quickly devoured. Then Darroch leaned forward and took Jean's chin in one hand. "Hold still," he ordered, then whisked one long finger around the corner of her mouth. He put that finger between his lips and sucked it clean. "A wee bit of caramel sauce lurking there," he said. "Couldn't let it go to waste."

Jean's pale skin flushed with color. "Greedy," she murmured. "Aye," he said. They smiled at each other, a smile of perfect understanding.

Sheilah and Gordon exchanged glances. Something had happened between these two and they couldn't help wondering what it was.

When Jean was hanging up her clothes that evening she found Darroch's handkerchief in her pocket and realized that she should wash it and give it back. She remembered his beautiful voice murmuring incomprehensible, comforting, words in her ear. No, she thought, I believe I'll just keep it. On impulse she put it beneath her pillow.

I've led a very ordinary life so far, she said to herself, and now I want something different. Adventure and excitement. New projects. New friends. And Eilean Dubh is giving it all to me. I think I'll stay a while longer.

PART III

Darroch

Far an d'fhuair mi m'arach òg,
Fanaidh mi le toil 's le deoin;
Air cho fad 's gu'm bi mi beo,
Cha dean an t-or mo mhealladh as.
Where I was reared as a boy,
there I shall stay with delight and pleasure;
as long as I am living, gold will not tempt me away.

Jonathan MacKinnon

𝒟arroch's first good television role was as a murderer.

His second was a supporting role in a new Britcom and it had been written as a typically BBC comic Scotsman part. He almost declined it for that reason. His agent said, "Darroch, you need the money and the work. Remember, the part doesn't have to stay the way it's written for the pilot. Why don't you see what you can do with it?"

Her advice was good. He found that he could turn the part around, taking dialogue intended to establish him as an ignorant rustic and using it to make the character into a shrewd, sly country man who often had the last word. And he was funny; he had a knack for playing comedy. He began to get fan mail and the writers began to slant the program his way.

It would have run several years had not its lead, an overbearing actor who considered himself God's gift to the theatre, decided to return to the stage in a Shakespearean production. It was widely snickered about in television circles that he was tired of being upstaged by a comic Scotsman.

Darroch was out of work only briefly. His work in the comedy led to him being invited to audition for the title role in a new adventure program for children called *The Magician*. It was the BBC's answer to criticism that too many children's programs were imported from America.

Reading the first script Darroch saw its potential at once. He worked hard to get the role, taking a crash course in magic and acquiring a repertoire of simple but impressive illusions. Before he read at the audition he plucked coins from behind the director's ear, made the producer's wallet disappear and produced a live white rabbit from his pocket, a detail that so delighted the show's writers that it became the Magician's signature. He got the part.

The Magician and Darroch were a smash hit. Seeing their children's fascination with the program, parents sat down to watch with them. Viewers were charmed by its cheerfully unpredictable hero and ratings soared.

Darroch was so good with both magic and magician's patter that little in the way of electronic enhancement of the illusions had to be done, that first year. And his engaging grin delighted both children and adults.

His fan mail rose steadily and contained a fair proportion of love notes from stricken women. Some of the notes made him raise his eyebrows and a few actually made him blush. "What in the world are these lassies thinking, to write such stuff to someone they don't know?" he wondered aloud and the jaded secretaries smiled at his innocence.

By the second year the show began to acquire cult status. The perks of a successful television program surfaced: personal appearances, endorsements, and syndication abroad, Australia first, then North America. Darroch found himself possessed of immense popularity, widespread recognition and at the end of the year a lucrative new contract. And more money than he'd ever had, more than his parents had earned in a lifetime, and promise of more to come.

He was grateful but baffled. He had no idea what to do with the money or how to manage it. He bought himself a handsome apartment in a remodeled warehouse on the Thames. It was grand to have his own place to retreat to at day's end and his thrifty soul was pleased he could rent it to other theatricals when he was on Eilean Dubh.

He splurged on a beautiful Bentley motorcar, ten years old, in such perfect condition that he dared not drive it in London. He took it to the Island and weathered the gossip that the Laird's son was getting above himself.

But he remained as friendly and approachable as ever and the *Eilean Dubhannaich* accepted the fact that Darroch was making his way handsomely in the world. They became very proud of him.

He still had money left, more coming in and more questions than answers. He asked his agent Liz what to do.

She said, "You need a good accountant. I know one who's an absolute genius. Her clients rave about her. She's great on taxes and investments and everybody swears she's psychic about the market. We call her the Welsh Wizard. Truth is, none of us can pronounce her name."

"Welsh, eh. A fellow Celt. Sounds good."

"Right, I'll try to get her to see you. She hasn't accepted new clients for a year but I'll see what I can do."

It was *The Magician* that got Darroch in to see the Welsh Wizard. Her ten-year-old daughter Ceridwen was besotted with the show and the prospect of securing an autograph for her was too tempting to resist.

Blodwen Llywarch was tiny, just over five feet tall, with jet black hair to rival Darroch's and snapping black eyes, the very picture of Welsh womanhood, shrewd intelligence in her face. She eyed Darroch over the expanse of her huge walnut desk. His earnings did not put him in the class of her top clients but he interested her.

"How may I be of service to you, Mr. Mac an Rìgh?" she asked.

He had been eyeing the nameplate on her desk. "First, teach me how to pronounce your name."

She thought at first he was making fun of her but decided to take him at face value. "To pronounce the double l, put your tongue behind your top front teeth and blow." She took him through her name syllable by syllable and he repeated it until he got it right. She nodded a regal approval.

"Are you a native Welsh speaker?" he asked. She nodded again. "*Glé mhath*," said Darroch, "I'm a native Gaelic speaker. I admire how successful you are at keeping your language alive. I wish we could do as well with ours."

Blodwen was a passionate Welsh nationalist and language advocate; she'd gone to jail for it in the protests a few years before. She warmed to him.

She said, "We're trying a variety of things. Some work, some don't. Fighting the government is the biggest problem. The damned Tories would be happy if the language disappeared overnight. We're a real thorn in their side, always wanting road signs in Welsh and other troublesome and expensive things."

"Good. Keep the pressure on. Government indifference is our biggest problem. We've much we want to do to keep our children speaking the Gaelic. We think we've got to target the youngest ones but we can't get funding. That's one reason I'm here. My friend wants to set up a Gaelic playschool on our Island and I want to donate the money but I gather it's more complicated than writing out a check."

She considered him carefully. "What else do you want to do?"

"Tons. We need housing improvements, services for the elderly, hospital equipment, books for the library."

She said, "Have you thought of becoming a trust?"

He choked on his tea. "Me? A trust?"

"*Wrth grws*, of course. It's the way to accomplish what you want to do. Keep enough for your needs and to invest for your future and put the rest in a charitable trust. It'll be a tremendous tax help as well. Without it you'll lose a lot to the Inland Revenue."

Darroch had never had enough income, as crofter or as actor, to be concerned about sheltering it from the taxman. But he'd participated in enough discussions with Island social activists to share their opinion that the bulk of tax money went to London and the Home Counties, much of it to build roads so that the Hooray Henries could commute to their jobs in the City. Not enough money went to education, housing, health services or the poor, the activists thought.

He liked the trust idea and said so.

"Right. We'll set you up with our staff and we'll get going straightaway."

He grinned at her. "What's the Welsh for 'okay'?"

She grinned back. "*Da iawn*. What's the Gaelic?"

"*Ceart math*." He stood up and extended his hand. "I will await your commands, *a charaid*."

After he left Blodwen remembered that she'd forgotten to get his autograph. Oh, well, she thought, plenty of time. Apparently they'd be working together. Ceridwen would be pleased.

All through the next year Darroch worked harder than he'd ever worked before. He took every job offered him, from commercials to a night club act, anything that the BBC approved as not detrimental to the image of their precious Magician. He opened supermarkets. He played in Christmas pantomimes. He did magazine advertisements.

The Welsh Wizard worked hard too, managing his portfolio herself. Still there was not enough money to set up the Trust, since only the interest from the Trust's funds could be spent, never the principal, and an astonishingly large principal was required to produce spendable income.

A break came when his rising profile as an actor brought an offer of a part in a mini-series to be filmed in Los Angeles, British actors being fashionable in American television that year. The money was excellent and he saved even more by taking the per diem offered him and finding an inexpensive apartment instead of luxury hotel digs. It was cozy, with a private patio where he could work on acquiring a California tan. He cooked his own meals, which saved more money.

One of the mini-series writers was an Englishwoman who always took under her wing visiting Brits. When she learned of the trust she told him about the "California Scots," Americans of Scottish descent who worked for the welfare of what they staunchly regarded as their homeland. "They've deep pockets," she said, "and they're passionate about Scotland. If you could get them interested they could do you a lot of good."

She got Darroch invited to the home of one Robert Burns MacDonald for dinner, and his jaw dropped when he arrived at the mansion and saw the elaborate Scottish outfits of the men who were his fellow diners. When his host introduced him one man asked accusingly, "Where's your kilt, laddie?"

"At home. I never thought to have a reason to wear it here." He shook his head, astonished, at their kilts of the finest wool, sporrans trimmed with elaborate silver Celtic knotwork, gem-adorned *sgianan dubha* thrust into hand-knitted hose, hand-tailored Prince Charlie coatees. I've nothing so fine as theirs, he thought, remembering his well-worn kilt. Outfits like these were so expensive only Americans could afford them.

Over a meal of roast beef and haggis, neeps and tatties, served with fine wines and finished with a selection of whiskies, Darroch answered question after question about Eilean Dubh, and found that his companions were amazingly sympathetic to its problems. Any of one of them, he realized, could buy and sell the Island, but they seemed more interested in preserving it.

When he told them about his proposed trust, they listened politely, but when he mentioned Eilean Dubh's traditional music there was sudden marked interest. "Real Gaelic music, is it?" Darroch explained that the Island's isolation had kept its music in a near-pristine state and there was a general sigh of pleasure. "Give us a tune or two," said one man. "You have the Gaelic, of course?"

"Of course," he replied, and began to sing. He was hoarse by the time they let him quit.

"Well, now," said Robert Burns MacDonald. "That's worth saving, lads. I'll open with twenty-five thousand for Darroch's trust."

"I'll see your twenty-five, and raise you ten," said another.

"Too rich for my blood but I'll put fifteen in the pot," said a third. "Maybe more next year."

By the end of the evening the trust was over one hundred thousand dollars richer, with the promise of more to come at the beginning of the next tax year. The men smiled in satisfaction at each other. Robert Burns produced a tray of fine cigars. "Good lads," he said. "I knew the homeland could rely on you."

"Come have a few rounds of golf with us tomorrow, Darroch," invited a man named Scott MacDuff.

Darroch was reluctant to admit that he didn't know one end of a golf club from another and took refuge in the excuse he would be filming the next day.

"Any golf courses on your Island?"

"No," said Darroch, stifling a chuckle at the thought.

Scott said, "There's an investment possibility. Build a good course, get Ronald Steele to design it. Wonderful tourist attraction, Darroch. A challenging course would bring in the money boys, generate income for your people. Golfers are big spenders and they're always on the lookout for exciting new courses."

Darroch barely concealed a shudder, thinking of Eilean Dubh overrun with rich golfers, frightening the sheep with the put-put of their little mechanized carts. "I'm sorry," he said, "but I don't think there's a spot of land on the Island big enough . . . or flat enough . . . for a golf course."

"Not true. You can put a golf course just about anywhere you want. I've seen fairways less than fifty yards wide and I've played courses where you don't get a flat lie to save your life. It makes you a better golfer to play under these conditions, because depending on the lie you get . . . uphill, downhill, sidehill . . . it changes where you put the ball in your stance, and it changes the direction and loft of the shot. It's all very tricky." Scott sighed happily, thinking of his beloved game.

Robert Burns watched Darroch's expression with amusement. "I'll bet that's more than you ever wanted to know about golf, Darroch. Relax, Scotty, there doesn't have to be a golf course in every square inch of Scotland."

Darroch said hastily, "Our tourist attractions are bird-watching and *cèilidh-ean*, if any of you are interested. We'd be delighted if you'd pay us a visit."

Robert said, "I'll take you up on that one of these days. Good hotel there?"

"*Miorbhuileach*," Darroch replied and spent the next few minutes rhapsodizing over Sheila's cooking. By the end of the evening there was considerable sentiment for a visit en masse to Eilean Dubh.

Robert Burns MacDonald took Darroch in charge and trotted him around to St. Andrews and Caledonian Society meetings, clan gatherings and Highland games and the astonishing generosity of the California Scots made him almost tearful.

When the mini-series was finished Darroch returned to London, his pockets bulging with American largesse. He strode into Blodwen's office. "Blod, you'll never guess what I've got . . . " he began, at the same time as she said, "We've had a brilliant run in the market, Darroch, good luck with a couple of little stocks that went through the ceiling . . . "

When they'd counted their pennies Blodwen announced triumphantly that they'd enough to set up the trust. She took him home to her family and they celebrated with champagne and roast lamb.

It gave Darroch great satisfaction to tell Màiri about his Trust. He'd proved he could leave Eilean Dubh and still contribute to its welfare. He asked her to serve with him on the Trust's Committee of Management and together they chose the rest: a minister, a teacher, a doctor, a retired nurse, a merchant, a hotel owner, a housewife and two of the Island's most vocal activists, who held diametrically opposed views.

He swore Màiri to secrecy about the origin of the funds. It was a secret that could not last long, the *Eilean Dubhannaich* having their ways of finding out what they wanted to know, but he gained enough time to get the Trust up and running before everyone on the Island formed an opinion about it.

The first grant made by the Trust was for the Playschool and Màiri had it in operation in three months. She took over an abandoned school building and an army of Islanders cleaned, painted, plumbed, repaired and sewed. She ordered books and materials for her teachers and after much goading accepted a computer from Darroch, an ardent advocate of the new technology.

The school opened to full enrollment. The children loved it and flourished in a Gaelic-speaking environment, the temptations of English forgotten for three hours each morning.

Thus launched, the Trust sailed aggressively into new waters. It restructured the Co-Op. It provided money for materials to enlarge the Citizens Hall, with the *Eilean Dubhannaich* contributing the labor. It bought a van for the Old Age Pensioners Home which was rechristened with the more dignified name of the Seniors' Residence. It established scholarships for young people who wanted to study on the mainland.

The Trust flourished. Eilean Dubh flourished. Darroch's career flourished. He was happy about all of that, but it did little to assuage the loneliness that haunted him.

Màiri was always in his mind. Though he knew that she was lost to him forever, though he rejoiced at her happiness with Jamie, he missed her desperately. He found himself talking to her, sometimes, because she was always with him and so real that he could feel her presence.

There were other women for him, of course; a man as attractive and charming as Darroch would always attract women.

He and a pretty, brown-eyed young actress named Morgan Jenkins fell in love and he moved in with her in the third month they were together. But it was inevitable that their careers would part them. She wanted to be a director and accepted a job in Australia in a theatre in a medium-sized town called Kookaburra Springs.

Darroch had known their relationship was over when she left but he still hungered for her. She was having trouble accepting it too. Tearful phone calls from Australia always came at a time when he was feeling low.

"Sweetie, I miss you so much," she mourned. And one night . . . midnight in London and sometime the next day in Australia . . . she talked in vivid detail about their life together. "Remember," she said, over and over.

Agonized, Darroch said, "Morgan, I remember and it does no good. It's gone, it's over."

"I could come back, I'm not a convict sentenced to life in Australia. I don't have to stay."

"Morgan, *mo ghràdh*, why do you torment me?"

Finally in one call she started to tell him about Matt, the millionaire financing the theatre in Kookaburra Springs. "He's sweet. I think he fancies me."

In the end she got both the director's job and the millionaire. He'd taken one look at Morgan and fallen in love. It took him a year to win her. Darroch was just starting to film *The Magician* and he could not go to their wedding.

Morgan's going left him absolutely bereft. Loneliness tormented him again.

He missed sex, too. Morgan had been so passionate, so giving, that wonderful sex had grown to be a cherished part of his life. He dreamed about sex. Sometimes it was with Morgan, sometimes with Màiri, sometimes with a composite who had masses of red-gold hair, brown eyes and a sumptuous figure, a stubborn streak and a lovely giggle who called him "sweetie."

Màiri and Morgan, Morgan and Màiri. Over and over in his head they warred for attention. Passionate, loving, intelligent, they'd spoiled him for other women.

He could not bring himself to begin a new sexual relationship, however much he craved it. He needed companionship as well as sex and he got neither.

There were, of course, women who were more than interested in sleeping with him. Françoise, a French actress starring in an Anouilh revival in London, went out of her way to seduce him. She was lonely for her lover and she found Darroch very attractive when she met him at a party. She invited him home with her that evening and he accepted, much to his surprise. She was the kind of woman his lonely soul craved, sexy and companionable.

She made those months bearable. They could call each other without reservation. "I'm lonely, can we get together?" "*Mais oui, chéri.*" "*Thà gu dearbh, m'eudail.*"

She gave him sound advice about his career, too. "You are a good actor but the stage is not the place for you. You are not handsome but your face, your expressions, are compelling, made for television. When you're in a scene the audience's eyes and ears are always drawn to you, to see how you react as well as to hear what you're saying. Television is your future." He took her advice and asked his agent to concentrate on finding him television roles.

From her ten-year age superiority she tended to dominate their relationship. It was she who said if he could stay the night and she who sent him home on other occasions. Her determination of their sexual encounters he accepted until one night when she said no and he wanted her badly. He lifted her in his arms, carried her to bed and kissed her until she became, all at once, eager. Afterwards she said to him, her face straight but her mouth quirked up, "You are not a bad lover, *mon brave,* for an Englishman."

Insulted, he lifted himself on his elbow, put his hand under her chin and turned her face to him. In his curious mixture of English, French and Gaelic he said, "*Écoute-moi, m'eudail.* I am not, I never have been, and I never will be an Englishman. *Comprends-tu?* I am a Scot."

She said teasingly, "There is a difference, *n'est-ce pas?*"

"*Mais oui, une grande différence, ma petite.*"

"*Alors. Vive la différence, chéri!*"

But when the play's run was over she went back to Paris and Henri.

It was the Island that saved him. He woke one morning and realized that he'd been dreaming about wide skies and mountains and the odor of peat fires. I'll go home to Eilean Dubh, he thought, then laughed at himself for sounding like Scarlett O'Hara.

The post that morning brought a letter from Màiri. "Your father's not well. You must come home," she wrote.

It was a good time to get away; all the theatricals were on vacation. And it was time to make his peace with Eilean Dubh. He'd been away too long.

He was on the Island when his father died and when Màiri and Jamie's twins were born, a red-haired girl named Eilidh and a blond boy named Ian.

He was accepted back with love and he was an *Eilean Dubhannach* once more and for the rest of his life. And he was now, with his father's death, the Laird.

Fàilte Gu Eilean Dubh

(Welcome to the Dark Island)

Scottish country dance, medley for 4 couples in a longwise set
Devised by Lara Friedman-Shedlov, Summer 2001

Tune: "Audrey McClellan/Thistleonia" by Sherry Wohlers Ladig

STRATHSPEY:

1-8   1st couple lead down the middle and up, finishing facing 1st
       corners (2nd couple step up on bars 3-4).

9-16   1st couple set to corners and partner. On bars 15-16, 1st couple
       set advancing to pass each other by the left shoulder and end
       back-to-back in the middle of the set, 1st woman facing up and
       1st man facing down.

17-20 1st woman with 2nd couple, 1st man with 3rd couple dance right
       hands across.

21-24 1st couple dance half reels of 3 on the sides with their two
       corners, passing 1st corner right shoulder to begin. At the end of
       the half reel, 1C pass each other by the right shoulder in the
       center of the set to flow into . . .

25-28 1st man with 3rd couple (now at the top) and 1st woman with
       2nd couple (now in 3rd place) dance left hands across.

29-32 1st couple dance half reels of 3 on the sides with their two
       corners, passing 1st corner person (who is in 2nd corner's posi-
       tion) left shoulder to begin. At the end of the half reel, 1st couple
       pass each other left shoulder to end on own sides in 2nd place.

REEL:

1-32   Repeat bars 1-32 of the strathspey from 2nd place in reel time.
       1st couple finishes in 3rd place and then steps down to the
       bottom of the set as a new top couple begins the strathspey.

Note: At the end of each of the hands across figures (bars 17-20
and bars 25-28), 1st couple will already be holding hands with
their corner. They may retain hands with the corner person
momentarily as they flow into the half reels.

PART IV

Jean and Darroch

Seventeen

Thigh crioch air an t-saoghal, ach mairidh ceol agus gaol.
An end will come to the world, but music and love will endure.

Gaelic proverb

*J*ean dressed carefully for her debut at the *cèilidh*. She knew she'd have more self-confidence if she looked good and she needed all the self-confidence she could muster. She made up carefully, put on an emerald-green dress that brought out her eyes and matching rhinestone earrings. When she was ready she went down to the lobby to meet Darroch.

He was there with Gordon. "*Feasgar math, a Shìne*, and don't you look grand. Off we go, then. See you later, Gordon?"

"As soon as I close up the bar. Sheila's already gone down with food."

The *cèilidh* began with tunes by the black-haired piper, Fearchar MacShennach. He was followed by the school pipe and drum band and the young Highland dancers. Then it was their turn. Jean took a chair by the piano while Darroch introduced them. He came and sat by her while Jamie took center stage.

He said, "Bonnie Prince Jamie always goes first."

"Bonnie Prince . . . Jamie?" said Jean.

"Look at him. As regal as the Queen."

Indeed he was both regal and elegant, cornsilk hair glowing like a halo, far more royal and handsome than the Prince of similar nickname. His blue shirt, the exact color of his eyes, complemented the MacDonald tartan of his kilt. Jean stared in admiration.

No one ever knew what Jamie would play; sometimes they doubted he himself knew until he put bow to fiddle. Màiri sat, resigned, on her piano bench, ready to accompany whatever he came up with.

Tonight, though, he was soloing. Màiri turned around to watch and they all listened to a brilliant cascade of notes showering from the fiddle like a torrent of rain from the heavens. He took a simple Gaelic tune, tore it to shreds and reassembled it bright and shining in three minutes. He finished triumphantly and paused for seconds, not long enough for the stunned audience to react, threw a glance over his shoulder and began to play the intro to Darroch's first song.

Darroch, taken by surprise, blinked and then jumped up to stride to the microphone. He said something indignant to Jamie who smiled angelically.

Darroch's voice rolled out over the room. As was traditional at an Eilean Dubh *cèilidh*, he began with the chorus, then alternated verse and chorus so the audience could join in.

My, but these people were good. Jean hoped she could measure up. She had given careful consideration to her choice of song for her debut. Once she had decided, she asked Gordon for his opinion and received his approval. He taught her two Gaelic phrases with which she could introduce herself.

Now she wondered if she had nerve enough to go through with it. She stared out at the sea of curious faces and shivered. Darroch, sensing her stage fright, whispered in her ear, "*Misneach, a charaid*. Courage," and introduced her as a visitor from America.

She took a deep breath and said slowly and distinctly to the audience, "*Tha mi duilich, chan'eil Gàidhlig agam.*" I am sorry, I don't have the Gaelic.

The effect was electrifying. Every head in the room turned to look at her, one hundred pair of eyes stared. The drinkers at the makeshift bar turned around and the sandwich ladies paused, teapots in air. The room went absolutely silent.

She heard Darroch's surprised intake of breath, felt rather than saw Jamie's smile. In the front row Gordon gazed up at her and gave her the thumbs-up sign. Elsewhere in the audience she spotted several Thursday night regulars, grinning at her.

Encouraged, she said, "My ancestor left Eilean Dubh for America two hundred years ago, leaving behind the woman he loved. They never met again. This song makes me think of them." She held the guitar close for comfort but sang, unaccompanied, the Irish song "Kathleen Mavourneen." Her voice soared, pure and unadorned.

Oh, hast thou forgotten how soon we must sever,
Oh, hast thou forgotten this day we must part.
It may be for years and it may be forever.
Then why art thou silent, thou voice of my heart . . .

There was no applause when she finished, just that same unnerving silence. Darroch came to stand by her and she looked at him in despair. She had failed, they didn't like her. But he smiled encouragingly just as the room came alive. People murmured excitedly to each other and someone called out something in Gaelic, which others enthusiastically seconded.

"They want you to sing something else," said Darroch.

"What shall I sing?"

"'Hard Times,'" said Jamie, appearing at her elbow. He tucked his fiddle under his chin and began to play.

'Tis the song, the sigh of the weary,
Hard times, hard times, come again no more . . .

This time there was no silence when the song ended. Comments and murmurs rose enthusiastically. Darroch smiled in triumph. "'*Fear a' bhàta*' now, I think."

They sang beautifully together and the rosewood guitar rang out sweet and true. At the end, as Darroch took her hand for a bow, he whispered, "I'm sorry, Jean, I forgot to warn you. On the Island, people don't usually applaud. Silence is a sign of approval."

He escorted her to her chair. She felt the curious looks but they no longer bothered her. She sat back and enjoyed the rest of their set.

The dance band filed on stage and Jamie and Jean packed up their instruments. She patted the precious guitar lovingly and put it beside Jamie's fiddle under the stage. As they walked through the crowd people smiled and spoke to Jean, nodding approval.

"Now we eat," ·said Jamie, rubbing his hands together. He led them to the dining hall, found a table and headed off.

"Sit you, ladies, I'll get your plates," Darroch offered. "What will you have?"

Màiri, who never ate before performing, was starved. She said eagerly, "Some of Barabal's crab sandwiches. And cucumber sandwiches, Liz

Thomas promised to save some for me. And Sheila's chocolate cake, Darroch. And a big pot of tea."

"*Agus uisge-beatha*," said Jamie, reappearing with four little glasses of a pale golden liquid.

Darroch smiled at Jean. "What may I get for you?"

"What Màiri's having sounds wonderful." Terror had kept her from eating before the *cèilidh* and performance adrenaline had kicked in to sharpen her appetite.

"Best come help me carry, *a Sheumais*. Sounds like the lassies plan on making a meal of it."

They feasted on Island home cooking until Jean, for one, was stuffed. She pushed her chair away from the table and sighed happily. "I'm glad we don't have to sing any more," she said. "I'd pop a button off in someone's face."

Islanders began to drift by their table. Several Thursday night regulars drew up chairs. Others stopped for a few words and to be introduced to Jean. The Thursday nighters preened; they were already the newcomer's friends.

Jean joined in the dancing with enthusiasm, if not skill, and Darroch let her try some of the harder dances. She danced "Màiri's Wedding" with him in terror and delight. All the dancers coached her through it. "Right shoulder . . . no, the other right!" "Face me." "You're doing grand!" The dance ended with an eight-person circle to the left and back. All the dancers whooped, Jean along with them.

Walking off the dance floor Jean glowed with pride. She had actually gotten through a difficult dance without embarrassing herself or running into anyone. And it was the closest thing to flying she'd ever experienced outside of an airplane.

Darroch said approvingly, "We'll have to teach you the Scottish country dance footwork. I think you could do quite well." She turned pink with pleasure.

At the evening's end he walked her to the Hotel. She said very little and he commented on her silence. "I'm still trying to absorb it all. This was one of the most satisfying nights of my life."

"*Miorbhuileach!*" he exclaimed, delighted. "So you enjoyed yourself."

"Oh, yes. Now there's just two more things I want."

"And what might they be?"

"Mastery of Gaelic . . . the Gaelic . . . and my own little place to live."

"Neither is impossible," he said, "but both will take a bit of time."

At the Hotel door he paused. "I think Ùisdean's spirit would be pleased tonight, don't you? One of his descendants finally coming home." His mouth was warm against her skin as he kissed each cheek.

They stared into each other's eyes for several long minutes. When Jean finally turned to go inside, her legs felt distinctly unsteady. Perhaps there was a third thing she wanted, after all. She held onto the railing as she climbed the stairs.

Jean was rapidly integrating herself into Island life. She joined in the monthly cleaning of the Citizens Hall organized by Màiri and staffed mainly by OAPs, old-age pensioners, and young mothers whose children played in the Hall while they worked. Everyone dusted, swept and washed windows.

Darroch was there too. She realized his part in Eilean Dubh's social fabric when she became aware that wherever he sat down an audience collected, attentive and talkative.

Màiri set out the tea urn and plates of biscuits for afternoon break. Darroch was sitting across the room from the tea table. Filling her cup, Jean glanced over and noticed people pulling up chairs around him. Jamie, noticing the direction of her look, said, nudging her, "Darroch and his *eun-laith.*"

"What?" she asked, puzzled. Then she noticed that nearly all those around him were women, a couple of elderly men on the fringe. Red hair, black hair and an occasional blonde, and all the heads shining like birds' plumage in the sunlight pouring through the windows. She raised her eyebrows at Jamie.

"His birdlings. The women. They settle around him as naturally as a flock of birds settles in an oak tree."

She still was puzzled so he added, "Darroch draws the Island women to him like a magnet draws iron. They like talking to him and he likes listening to them. He gets most of his information about what's going on here from them. They tell him things he needs to know to be a good laird."

"But I thought . . . "

Jamie read her thought. "It's just the title he denies, not the role. He takes the duties of his position very seriously."

Jean thought, will I ever understand this place? She watched the group.

An elderly lady sat in the position of honor at Darroch's right and she was expounding at length on some point. Darroch and the rest were listening respectfully.

At Darroch's left sat Barabal Mac-a-Phi, bright-eyed, alert. Next to her sat Ian's Catrìona and beyond her several women Jean recognized from excursions into town: Beathag the Bread, Cailean the Crab's wife and the two who worked in the Co-Op.

In other chairs sat women whose fingers were flying over wool and needles. Jean realized they must be members of *Co-Op nan Figheadairean*, the Knitters' Cooperative.

Màiri had told her about the phenomenal success of the knitting project. Darroch had presented a hand-knit sweater from Eilean Dubh to a trendy theatrical lady of his acquaintance. She had worn it on stage in a hit play and credited its source in the program. Another actress, not to be outdone, had coaxed a sweater from him with the promise of wearing it on a popular Britcom.

A little more work by Darroch and an elegant London shop accepted a small consignment of sweaters. They sold quickly and the shop became a regular outlet. Soon special orders were being taken and rumor had it that a certain Royal lady had ordered one. When it was glimpsed on her in a fashion magazine that was all it took. The sweaters caught on. Each sold at a handsome price and the sale of even one a month meant a substantial boost to the knitters' income.

Watching the group, Jean too felt lured to Darroch's side. Resisting the pull, she said to Jamie, "Why isn't Màiri one of the birdies?"

He grinned. "Ach, you know Màiri. She hates being one of the crowd. She prefers to be in charge of it."

Aye, thought, Jean, slipping unconsciously into Island speech, and she already has Darroch's ear on everything. She looked wistfully at the *eunlaith*. The youngest women, in T-shirts and jeans, were sitting on the floor. One began to talk and was accorded the same respect the elderly woman received. She gestured emphatically and heads nodded in agreement.

"What are they talking about?" wondered Jean.

"Anything," said Jamie. "The Playschool, save the wildflowers, computers for the High School. They'll tell him what he should know." He smiled at her. "Will we join them?"

"Oh, yes," said Jean before she thought. Then, trying to be cool, she said, "If you want to, Jamie."

He smiled. "Come on, then."

She followed him to the group. The young woman had finished and everyone began to respond. Darroch was listening to the older woman and when she finished he turned and saw them. His face lit up. Automatically he switched to English. "Here's our Jamie and Jean with him." His voice softened on the last name.

Barabal gave Ian's Catrìona an I-told-you-so look. Several others caught the change in his voice and glanced at each other in surprise, then turned to stare at Jean.

Jamie thought, why don't you take out an ad in the newspaper, Darroch. It could hardly be more obvious.

"Come sit with us," said Darroch, his eyes on Jean. Barabal moved over. "Sit here, Jean," she said, opening a space between herself and him. Awkwardly, Jean maneuvered her way through the women on the floor to the couch. "Hi," she whispered, glancing shyly around.

"Do you know everyone, Jean?" he asked and she shook her head.

"I don't know her," said the elderly woman and Darroch said, "Jean Abbott, from the United States. Lady Margaret Morrison."

"Never mind the lady business," she said impatiently. "An American won't care about that. It's just useful to impress the *Sasannach*."

"Margaret, *mo luaidh*, you are a *Sasannach*. Remember?" said Darroch gently.

"Nonsense, just an accident of birth. In my heart I'm an *Eilean Dubhannach*." She said something sharp in the Gaelic and everyone chuckled.

Jean was impressed. Lady plus a first name, she remembered from Regency novels, was an earl's daughter or higher. An aristocrat, an Englishwoman and she had the Gaelic, Jean thought in wonder. Whatever next? "Don't let us interrupt," she said, but Lady Margaret's curiosity had been aroused.

"What's an American doing on Eilean Dubh?" she demanded.

"Her ancestor's from here, *a Mhairead*, and she's come to visit the homeland."

"Ha," said Lady Margaret. "Like me, my dear. My grandmother was born on the Island. She married an Englishman, though, and they had the poor judgment to settle in England. But love of Eilean Dubh will out, even in a third generation, or later." She leaned forward and recited:

From the lone shieling of the misty island
Mountains divide us, and the waste of seas.
But still the blood is strong, the heart is Highland
And we in dreams behold the Hebrides.

Her voice trembled with emotion. Jean stared at her and breathed, "Yes, I've felt that. More and more, the longer I stay."

For a moment the two women looked at each other. "Be careful, my dear," said Lady Margaret quietly. "It will be hard to leave, when the time comes."

"If the time comes," said Darroch under his breath. Aloud, he said, "Jean's learning our music, Margaret. You'll hear her sing at the *cèilidh* Friday."

Jamie had pulled up a chair next to Beathag the Bread and he thought it wise to steer the conversation in another direction. Jean was looking distinctly uncomfortable at the attention being shown her and he could tell that gossip was beginning to percolate in several heads. Moreover, though *Eilean Dubhannaich* loved their Island, what they considered "tartan sentimentality" made them uncomfortable and he feared someone would say something that would hurt Margaret's feelings. So he changed the subject. "Margaret, how long are you with us this time?"

"Not nearly long enough," she said crossly. "I'm due at Balmoral in September to dance attendance on the Royals." One of the younger women said, "How can you stand it, Margaret? Hanging around that lot, and you a staunch republican."

"We've not got a republic yet and an ear at Court is always useful," Margaret said sharply. "Besides, I quite like HM. She's got a good head and a good heart. She's interested in what I've told her about our Playschool and that might be useful."

"Maybe, but how's that going to get a new roof for the Playschool?" the younger woman retorted and they were off and running. Glad to be out of the spotlight, Jean sat back and let the talk swell around her. It was, in unconscious courtesy, in English.

When Màiri signaled by packing up the tea urn that the break was over Jean stood up with the others, intending to help in the kitchen.

Lady Margaret said, "Stay a moment, my dear."

It was a gentle but regal command. Jean sat down again. She felt Margaret looking at her with curiosity.

"So you have an Eilean Dubh ancestor. Who was it?"

Jean explained she was researching that question but it was slow going. "The language is the problem. I can't learn the Gaelic fast enough, especially the old-fashioned kind, and my translator hasn't got a lot of time this month. She's helping her father whitewash their cottage. I envy your fluency, Lady Margaret."

"My childhood nurse was an *Eilean Dubhannach*. She . . . and my mother . . . were determined I should have the Gaelic. My father disapproved so we kept it secret. I learned even faster that way. Tell a child she shouldn't do something and watch her do it with enthusiasm.

"And my mother brought me to the Island for visits every summer and I had to be fluent or I wouldn't have had playmates. Tell me, my dear, how you discovered your ancestor came from here?"

Jean explained about the letters. "They're faded, the handwriting is difficult and the Gaelic is eighteenth-century. Even Darroch is having trouble with it."

Lady Margaret noticed how Jean's voice had softened on Darroch's name, as his had on hers. "Are you married?" she demanded abruptly.

Flustered by the unexpected question, she said, "Yes."

"Where is your husband?"

Jean recovered her self-possession and her voice turned cool. "In Milwaukee."

"Will he be coming to visit the Island?"

"No," said Jean abruptly. She turned to the activity that had resumed around her. "If you'll excuse me, Lady Margaret, I should help with the work."

The other woman was suddenly comfortable and reassuring. "Call me Margaret, my dear, all my friends do. Now, if you'd like, I could help you with your letters. I have some experience in reading and translating our older Island written materials. I could perhaps work more quickly than Darroch." She paused. "Unless, of course, you prefer to keep the contents private."

Jean was delighted. "No, no, it was all two hundred years ago, that's not an issue."

"You'd be surprised," said Margaret wryly, but Jean continued, "I'd love your help. Darroch's so busy. I hate to take up his time."

"I'm sure he doesn't mind," Margaret commented and noted with interest that Jean's cheeks turned pink. *Whatever is going on between these two it seems to be mutual,* she thought.

Like most Eilean Dubh women over the age of ten she was a wee bit in love with Darroch herself. She turned and looked around the room for him. He was high on a ladder steadied by Jamie. His lean body reaching upward, one long arm stretched to the limit, he was replacing a light bulb in the ceiling.

"He's the only one tall enough to reach those bulbs," said Margaret fondly. "What a job of work for the Laird. An English lord wouldn't be caught dead doing that."

"Ah, but he's different, isn't he." Jean's voice was soft with admiration.

Be careful, my dear, thought Margaret again, *you're on dangerous ground.* "Aye, he is. Now run along and help. We'll talk later and arrange a time to work on your letters. I'm quite looking forward to it."

Jean thanked her and, dismissed, got up and went into the kitchen to wash dishes.

Audrey McClellan

moderate tempo　　　　　　　　　　　　　　　　　　　　　　　　*strathspey*

Thistleonia

fast tempo　　　　　　　　　　　　　　　　　　　　　　　　　　*reel*

Eighteen

Beloved Mòrag, my heart,

I write to tell you of my safe arrival in the Town of Baltimore after an arduous sea-journey, the details of which are too harrowing to commit to paper.

This Town is far beyond your imagining, it is a-bustle with people, horses, carriages and wagons, none of which seem ever to be still. Here in the Inn where I lodge there are comings and goings all night, footsteps on the stairs and men's voices in the halls. I hear them even in the attic room where I sleep, being able to afford no better.

But at last a measure of quiet reigns and I lie in my bed and let my mind roam to the peace of our Island and the day's noise is replaced with the sound of an Eilean Dubh wind sighing in my ears. The scent of peat fires and heather comes to my nostrils and the raw odors of town are gone.

It is then I let myself think on you and I behold as if in a dream your dear lovely shape. I pull you close and let my mouth feast on yours and taste the honey of a thousand Eilean Dubh bees . . .

Ùisdean's first letter to Mòrag, translated by Darroch Mac an Rìgh

*J*ean was working in the cemetery. She'd reached the point where Lady Eilidh's grave was almost finished and what was left was pure slogging on hands and knees. The afternoon sun was hot on her face and a few languid flies buzzed around.

She sat back and wiped the sweat from her forehead, leaving a smear of dirt behind. A prickle lodged in her glove scratched her cheek and she winced. She was suddenly aware she was very hungry. She had skipped lunch in order to catch a ride up to the cemetery with Màiri who'd left Playschool early for a doctor's appointment.

She sat on the cold ground and wondered what to do. Ian the Post would not be by for two hours and a walk to town would take at least an hour.

When the Bentley pulled into the parking space below she stared in surprise. The answer to a maiden's prayer, she thought, when the tall figure got out, waved and headed up hill.

Darroch couldn't help smiling at the picture she made, hair disheveled, face dirty. She had torn a hole in one knee of her jeans and her sweater was muddy.

"Hello, glamour girl," he said, grinning.

She said, "Hi. You don't have a candy bar on you, I suppose?"

"Even better. It's such a beautiful day I'd a mind for a picnic. Care to join me?"

"You bet," she said with alacrity. He extended a hand to her as she scrambled up.

"Sheilah packed a basket. Come help me carry." At the car he held out a tartan blanket. "You take the rug and I'll bring the basket."

She said, looking at her hands, "I'm too dirty to eat."

He took a plastic bottle out of the car. "Sheilah thinks of everything when she packs a picnic. Hold out your hands." He poured water over them. "She put soap in it. Don't lick your fingers after you eat." He pulled out his handkerchief, wetting it from the bottle. "You've had your nose in your work," he said, dabbing the dirt from her face.

The picnic was no accident. He'd run into Màiri in the village and she'd mentioned she'd taken Jean to the cemetery before lunch. He'd sprinted to the Hotel and coaxed food from Sheilah.

On the hilltop he spread out the rug and unpacked the basket. He set out fruit, sandwiches of crab and smoked salmon and a bottle of wine, pouring two glasses. "*Slàinte*," he said, handing her one.

"*Tapadh leat*," she answered. "Bless you and bless Sheilah."

Afterwards she lay down on the blanket. "I have to rest for a bit," she said and closed her eyes. "This sunlight makes me want to curl up like a cat and take a nap." She stretched luxuriously and arched her back to relieve the gardening twinges.

"You learn to take advantage of sunshine in Scotland," he said, leaning back against the bench and folding his long legs in front of him. He poured wine into his glass and sat relaxed, enjoying the view of the ocean below the cliff.

Then he glanced down at Jean and was suddenly aware of the swell of her breasts against the sweater, of the way her slender waist tapered into hips that were rounded and voluptuous. A wave of desire swept over him and left him hard and trembling. He could not tear his eyes from her.

He set his glass down carefully, so unprepared for what he felt that he could scarcely breathe.

Jean turned onto her side facing him, head pillowed on her hands, eyes closed. Darroch swallowed hard. He drew his legs up, folded his arms and put his head down on them, turning away from her.

I have been too long without a woman, he told himself, then realized that it was not just any woman he wanted, it was Jean. Sweet, smart, funny Jean. A voice like an angel and a heart big enough to take in all of Eilean Dubh. He wanted her, only her. He thought hungrily of running his hands over her, coaxing her mouth open with kisses. He imagined her sun-glittered hair slipping through his fingers, the shape of her breast curving under his hand.

The lust he felt was astonishing. He'd given up sex after his divorce, tired of the whole game. He'd indulged himself freely as a young man in London and he thought it wouldn't hurt him to lay off until the right woman came along. He'd about given up hope of that and suddenly here she was.

Stop it, he told himself. She's a friend and she's married. You mustn't think about her this way. But his body was not responding to reason.

Jean opened her eyes and looked at his bowed head. "Are you all right, Darroch?"

"Aye," he said. No, I am not all right, he thought, and that's the first lie I've ever told you. See how sex leads to lies? "The sunlight on the water blinded me for a moment." Another lie.

She sat up reluctantly. "It's so lovely I could stay all day. But I'd like to finish Lady Eilidh's grave this afternoon. I'm so close."

He knew he should leave, that he'd be further tormented if he stayed within reach of her. But he said, "I'll stay and help if you'd like."

"Wonderful . . . um . . . *miorbhuileach*!"

"I'll pack up the picnic if you want to go down and get yourself sorted."

"Damn, I've forgotten where I left my gloves."

"On top of the Bentley."

Alone on the hilltop he talked seriously to himself. So sex has reared its ugly head. Not surprising, she's a very desirable woman. You, on the other hand, are a very sensible man. Will you risk destroying your friendship by giving into these lustful feelings? She might be offended, shocked, if you let her know what's in your mind. And it was lust: he knew exactly what he wanted to do with her and to her.

He was still enough of a Presbyterian to be alarmed at that lust, and ashamed, because it was directed not at a willing, unattached, definitely interested woman, but at a dear friend. Who was married.

A Dhia, he thought, she might be afraid to be alone with me if she thinks I might make a pass at her. He shivered. He did not want to jeopardize their present relationship and anything beyond that seemed unlikely. No one understood better than he how she felt about betraying marriage vows.

When he had gained enough control to meet her by the Bentley he was almost undone when she smiled up at him, green eyes flashing golden in the sunlight. She said, "The hardest part of gardening for me is keeping my gloves on. But I learned my lesson after I grabbed a handful of nettles hidden in that tall grass."

She had gone back to the Hotel, chagrined, with a swollen left hand. Sheilah had made an herbal bath for her hand that had soothed it by next morning but she'd been cautious ever since.

He nodded agreement and fished work gloves out of the car. "What shall I do?"

"There's weeds left in the border around the tomb." She said doubtfully, "It means crawling around on your hands and knees. Your clothes . . . "

"Old." He knelt and began working.

She finished first and straightened up with a hand on her aching back. Darroch was pulling weeds furiously. She let her eyes wander over him, enjoying the broad shoulders, the long lean line of his back, the slim hips culminating in the beautiful trim bottom. His old jeans had memorized every curve and angle and molded themselves to him. What a lovely man, she thought dreamily, and how magical it was to be with him, on this hill, on this Island, in Scotland.

A final weed defied him and he pulled off his glove impatiently, gripped it between thumb and forefinger and yanked it out. Like some ancient warrior Celt with the head of an enemy, he flourished the weed in the air, then turned and laid it at her feet. "For you, *mo leadaidh*," he said triumphantly. "So perish all your enemies."

Bemused, Jean stood staring down at his dramatically bowed head. His hair was wholly without red or brown undertones; it was black, jet black, raven black, the color of polished onyx, highlighted by an occasional silver thread. She imagined running her hand through it, wondering if it would be silky to the touch.

"You've done a good job," she said.

"Not a patch on what you've done. You've rejuvenated Lady Eilidh's grave."

Embarrassed, she said, "I enjoyed doing it. Lady Eilidh deserves it."

They exchanged smiles.

"Darroch," Jean said suddenly, "are there fairies on Cemetery Hill?"

"Oh, aye," he answered, surprised by the question. "Here's where they hold their most important ceremonies: marriages, drummings-out, pixie-hurling, all that sort of thing. On Midsummer's Eve it's wall-to-wall with the People. There's not a mortal on the Island dares go near the place that night."

"I thought so," she said, her eyes soft and mysterious.

Darroch thought of putting his hands on her hips, pulling her into his arms and kissing her till she gasped for breath. He could almost taste her mouth. He stood up hastily and nearly fell over a tombstone. Furious with himself, he said gruffly, "Are you ready to go home?"

"Yes, please." She surveyed the grave. "I'd like to clean the lettering on the stone next. Perhaps a toothbrush? But how do I get water up here?"

"I'll help you sort it, but not a toothbrush. You'd be at it for years."

"I have plenty of time," she said, smiling.

Time. Time on Eilean Dubh. The pleasure of that thought glowed in both minds.

When they entered the Rose, she asked, "Will you stay and have dinner with me?"

But he was being firm with himself. "I'd like to but I have a report to write. I've been putting it off for a week. I'll see you tomorrow night, Jean. Supper with Jamie and Màiri, don't forget."

"I won't," she said. She couldn't conceal her disappointment that he wasn't staying. She looked wistfully at him. He hesitated about his customary kisses . . . it was daylight, after all . . . but then he thought, the hell with it. He bent and kissed each cheek and was rewarded with a wide warm smile.

Home, he fixed supper, mind working through his new problem. He knew he'd the right of it when he realized he'd been too long without a woman. He'd always needed a loving, intimate relationship with a woman. When he'd been without one . . . after Màiri, after Morgan, after Adrienne . . . he'd been lost and empty.

Or perhaps it was the influence of Ùisdean's letters, which were growing more erotic with each one he read. Perhaps they were rousing in him emotions he'd sensibly buried three years ago. The night before last he'd translated the third letter and found that he could not bear to sit still while he read it to Jean, seated at his computer, taking down the English as he spoke it. Ùisdean wrote of his longing for Mòrag, reminiscing in vivid detail of how they'd made love on a summer day by a loch.

When he'd finished the translation there'd been a short silence. Jean's fingers had stopped flying over the keyboard and she'd sat motionless. He'd thought she was overcome with embarrassment until she said, "How wonderful, to love each other so much." He'd had an absurd desire to kneel beside her and kiss away the tears rolling down her cheeks.

He realized now that he knew very little about Jean's feelings. She'd not been forthcoming about her life in America. She'd not said much about it after her two anguished outpourings, except for talking about Sally, which she did regularly and with enthusiasm. Otherwise, he thought ruefully, she listens to me talk.

For all he knew she was still in love with her husband. Or missing her comfortable American life. Or her family. She might be planning to go back any day. The thought was like a knife in his heart.

Out of his musings grew a firm resolve to keep her on Eilean Dubh, and he knew just how to do it. With that decided he turned purposefully to his computer and began to write his report.

That, at least, would not be a lie.

Sheila's eyebrows rose as she surveyed the collection of dirt smears on Jean's clothes. "Had a good day in the cemetery, I see."

"Yep. Finished Lady Eilidh's grave, with Darroch's help."

"Where is he? Isn't he staying for dinner?"

"No, he had something to do tonight." Jean looked down at herself. "I'd better go clean up."

"You got a letter today." Sheilah stepped behind the desk and handed Jean an envelope.

She looked at the letter, expecting it to be from Sally. She recognized her husband's writing and her heart sank. She stuffed the envelope in her pocket and hurried upstairs. In her room she pulled out the letter and grimaced, then tossed it on the bed. Time enough for that later, she thought.

She came back from a wonderful dinner and a whisky shared with Sheilah and Gordon, feeling delightfully relaxed. That lasted until she discovered the neglected envelope. She felt better able to deal with it now. She sank down onto the window seat and began to read in the early evening light reflected from the sea.

Russ had finally snapped. Full of hurt pride, he'd resolved when Jean left that he wouldn't write or call begging her to come home, and she'd stopped writing to him, unable to keep up a friendly façade when she'd had no response.

Now, overwhelmed by anger and frustration and even fear . . . what if she decided not to come back . . . he'd convinced himself he was the injured party and written her an indignant letter.

Dear Jean,

You're probably surprised to get a letter from me as you always complained I never wrote to you when I went out of town. But I have something important to say.

When are you coming home? I need you and Sally needs you. You can't just walk out on us. Our friends are asking questions and I don't know what to tell them. It's embarrassing. And Sally's really upset. She misses her mother.

I can't imagine what you're doing over there anyway. You're an American, what business do you have in Scotland? Sally says you're back to singing folk music. For God's sake, Jean, I thought you outgrew that years ago.

Your lawyer tells me that you've signed papers to begin divorce proceedings. You know that's ridiculous. I admit I made a mistake and I'm sorry. There's no reason to end our marriage. We've been together twenty years and we have lots of good years ahead of us.

Please write or call to tell me you're coming home. If you'll forgive me for having an affair I'll forgive you for running off and we can start again.

That's all I have to say and I hope to see you soon.
Love, Russ.

She threw the letter down and it drifted off the window seat to the floor. She was astonished at the guilt that overwhelmed her. Her family needed her.

How could she think of staying away, how could she think of divorce? Why couldn't she give Russ another chance? She owed it to him for giving her a good life and two great kids. And now he'd finally admitted he'd made a mistake and said he was sorry.

And she hadn't even written to ask him for a divorce; she'd taken the coward's way out and let her lawyer do the talking. That had not been fair to Russ, no matter what he'd done.

She rubbed her scratched cheek and looked at her scraped hands and broken fingernails. What was she doing here anyway? Weeding an old deserted cemetery on a tiny Scottish island, how crazy. Wasting her time chasing ancestors and playing folk music. Learning an obscure language. Running after an actor.

She turned red at the last thought. Was that how it appeared to the *Eilean Dubhannaich*? That she was setting her cap, or whatever they'd call it, at Darroch? Had she been taking up too much of his time, taken advantage of his friendly nature? Maybe he was just nice to her because she was a visitor, and so were Màiri and Jamie and everyone else. Maybe they'd be just as happy if she went home.

Her carefully constructed and cherished life on Eilean Dubh was dissolving into dust around her. She didn't belong here, she'd never belong here. She belonged in Milwaukee, Russ' wife and Sally's mother.

Russ was right, it was ridiculous to stay on Eilean Dubh. But she loved it, she'd never felt more at home in her life. She loved the Island, she loved the music and the language, she loved . . .

Stop it, she told herself, but she couldn't. The choked feeling in her throat turned into a sob. She yanked on her nightgown, washed up, weeping, and went to bed to cry herself to sleep.

Damn it, she thought, Russ has done it to me again.

Nineteen

The heart is gone from me that I am leaving my Island
And the longing to return will never end.

"Leaving Eilean Dubh." Island folk song

$\mathcal{S}$he awakened next morning with swollen eyes, a red nose and a black cloud that materialized over her head when she remembered Russ' letter. The obvious symptoms had disappeared by the time she got to the Playschool and she greeted everyone with determined cheerfulness. She scurried into the office, avoiding the usual morning chat, worked feverishly at the computer, and was done with everything she had to do by eleven.

She stared at the screen, then decided she was either going to have to start writing her memoirs or get up and do something else. She opted for the latter. "I'm all done so I'm off," she told Màiri.

"See you tonight," said Màiri. "Will you pick up the wine or shall I?"

She'd forgotten that tonight was supper at *Taigh Rois* and rehearsal for next week's *cèilidh*. She thought about making an excuse but then told herself, why not enjoy it while you can? You'll be gone soon enough. "I'll get it," she said and left. The black cloud came back and trailed over her head as she walked into town.

It stayed with her until lunch and only disappeared when she wandered into the kitchen and offered to help Sheilah. Since a large party had shown up unexpectedly in the dining room, hungry and hopeful, her offer was gratefully accepted. She got hot and sweaty stirring soup and was tired enough afterwards to lie down for a nap. She actually slept and her troubles seemed less formidable when she woke.

So she was able to be bright with Darroch when he picked her up, lively through supper and cheerful while they made music together. But it all fell apart when Darroch pulled out a new song.

"I thought you'd like this one, Jean; it's an emigrant's lament. 'Leaving Eilean Dubh' it's called in English," he said.

Jean glanced across the table at the others. Abruptly her eyes filled with tears. She rose, murmured, "Excuse me," and made her way blindly to the door and outside.

The three looked at each other, baffled. Màiri was on her feet following Jean before the men could react.

"What's amiss with the lassie?" wondered Jamie.

Darroch shook his head. "She was fine when I picked her up."

Màiri stood in the doorway until her eyes adjusted to the dark and she spotted Jean sitting on the garden bench. "What's wrong, *mo phiuthar?*"

Jean said, "I had a letter from Milwaukee. Russ wants me to come back."

"Ah." A cold breeze blew across the back of Màiri's neck and she shivered. "What will you do?"

"I keep thinking about my children . . . especially Sally. I walked out on her, Màiri. And what about Russ? God knows, he only did what a lot of men . . . and women . . . have done. Don't I owe him forgiveness?"

Màiri, who knew nothing of Jean's marital problems, shook her head, uncomprehending.

Jean said desperately, "I always meant to go back to America. I never thought I'd stay here." She turned to look at the other woman and the light from inside reflected in her eyes like sparks from a fire. "But I talk with the three of you and sing and it's as if I never lived anywhere else . . . never had another life. I feel I belong here."

Her voice softened. "And Darroch . . . to sing with him is so deeply pleasing. It feels like we're the two halves of one voice."

Màiri was aware of all that was deeply pleasing about Darroch and she understood the unconscious yearning in Jean's voice even if Jean did not. She sighed and nodded.

Jean stared out into the night. "I'm afraid of what's happening, Màiri. I'll be so dissatisfied in Milwaukee. I'm afraid I'll end up not belonging anywhere."

Màiri said, "Where do you want to belong?"

Jean's voice was a whisper. "Here. And that is terribly wrong."

"Why?"

"Because this isn't my home. I'm American, I'm married and I should be in Milwaukee with my husband . . . " She stopped, biting her lip to keep the tears back. "You and I don't even speak the same language. But how can I bear to leave?"

She gave up the struggle and began to cry. "It's those damned sunsets. Sheilah said the sunsets would get me if I stayed long enough."

Intimacy did not come easily to Màiri. She put an awkward arm around Jean.

Behind them, Darroch said, "I brought coats. I thought you might be getting cold."

Màiri stood up. "Sit with her, Darroch. I'll make tea." In her experience tea was a sure cure for almost any problem.

Darroch moved with alacrity to wrap his coat around Jean as he sat down. "Can I help, *mo charaid?*" He put his arms around her and wiped a tear from her cheek with his finger. There was an odd pain in his chest to see her distress.

"It's nothing," said Jean. "I'm being foolish. Sometimes those songs get to me."

He studied her. "Is that all?"

"I had a letter from my husband. I can handle it. I just need time to think."

That damned Yank was making her unhappy again, he thought. I'd like to wring his neck. "Relax then, and look at the stars. They have a profoundly soothing influence." He tightened his grip and murmured something in the Gaelic in her ear, something rhythmic and soothing.

Caught as always by the language, she asked, "What are you saying?"

"It's a traditional Island prayer for peace of mind."

She had not imagined him to be of a religious bent. "To whom is the prayer addressed?"

"To the One Who Listens, of course." He squeezed her shoulder. "Better now? Come in and have a cuppa." He would have liked to stay there but her body pressed so closely was giving his body ideas.

He rose, lifting her up. She hugged his coat to her, wishing she never had to take it off, but surrendered it when they were inside.

Màiri poured her a cup of tea and Jamie took down the whisky and poured them each a dram. Then he picked up his fiddle. He played a melody so hauntingly beautiful and sad that they were struck to silence. Tears appeared again in Jean's eyes when she recognized the Island's beloved "Emigrant's Lament," yet another song about parting. She knew the English words:

Away, away, over the steel-gray sea,
Away, from the beloved Island . . .

"Jamie, dear boy . . . " began Darroch but Jean shook her head. "*Tapadh leat, a Sheumais, mo charaid*, that was lovely." She smiled weepily. "I'd like to go home now, Darroch, if you don't mind."

"Aye." He got his coat and helped her into it. At her protest he shook his head. "We can't have you getting cold." He buttoned her into it. The coat draped down to her ankles, the sleeves covered her hands and it was deliciously warm.

Màiri said in her abrupt way, "You're tired, you've been at your projects tooth and nail. Don't come into Playschool tomorrow." As Jean opened her mouth to protest Màiri added, "You said you were caught up and I don't have anything ready. Sleep late, then do something just for fun."

"And don't go near the cemetery," Darroch added firmly. "Take the day off."

"*Oidhche mhath*," said Màiri. She squeezed Jean's hand in an unusual display of affection. "Don't worry, *mo Shìne*," whispered Jamie, kissing her cheek. "It'll all come right, in time."

Darroch and Jean drove slowly through the starry night back to the village. The moon went behind the clouds and it grew very dark. Along the road little bright eyes gleamed in the headlights and once Jean caught sight of a fully-grown fox darting along the verge.

They reached the Hotel earlier than usual and Gordon was still puttering in the lobby. He smiled. "I'm off to bed. Turn off the lights when you come up, please, Jean," he said and left.

She slipped off Darroch's coat and held it for him. He could feel the warmth of her body still in it.

She smiled at him, expecting his customary nighttime salute but tonight he kissed both cheeks and then brushed her lips in a fleeting touch that seared like a flame. Without conscious thought she kissed his cheek. He captured her hands.

They held hands for a long moment, looking at each other. "Better now?" he said.

She nodded. "It must have been that prayer," she said.

He said, "If you go for a walk tomorrow, tell Sheilah where you're going. Maybe I'll catch you up." He smiled and was gone.

After he left she went up to her room, read Russ' letter again and wept again. "You're getting to be a real crybaby," was her last thought before she fell asleep.

Twenty

Oh, Mòrag! If only I were with you!
In our own wee cottage by the sea. . .

Ùisdean's second letter to Mòrag, translated by Lady Margaret Morrison

*J*ean awoke with the feeling she'd barely slept. Odd, disjointed bits of dreams flitted through her mind. Downstairs, Sheilah scolded, "Too many late nights! You'll wear yourself out."

"Well, I have today off for rest and recreation, the powers that be have ordered it. I'm going to take a walk after breakfast."

"Go up the hill. A good climb and today the view will be grand, not a cloud about."

Gordon added, "You might be able to see as far as Islay. Maybe even the Paps of Jura."

"Dress warmly. There's always a stiff wind blowing up there," advised Sheilah.

Forewarned, Jean put on her hooded sweater and draped a wool shawl over her arm. The climb was challenging and when she finally rounded the last curve to arrive at the top she was too exhausted to take in the view at first. She headed for the bench.

Sitting down, turning to face the ocean, she was transfixed. The sea was busy and sunlight played across white-topped waves and shattered into a myriad of colors. She felt her tension drain away as she stared out at it. She'd thought private quiet time would help her sort out her feelings but the view was so relaxing her mind emptied and she sat looking at the water, thinking of nothing.

When she saw a figure in a black coat working his way up the hill she knew immediately who it was. She watched him on the winding path, now hidden by a rock outcropping, now visible. When he rounded the final curve Jean could see the sudden pleasure on his face and feel it reflected on hers.

"Looking for someone?" she said. "Or just passing through."

He grinned. "Looking for someone. Found her. May I?" he said, gesturing at the bench.

"Of course. That's quite a climb. Wore me out."

Seated, he turned his attention to the sea. "Worth it, though, for the view," and he looked back at her, liking the way the wind turned her cheeks and the tip of her nose pink.

She wasn't sure which view he was referring to. Darroch, watching the sunlight play on her hair, knew exactly what he meant.

He draped one long arm across the bench behind her. The wind blew a lock of her hair toward him and he captured it with his hand, feeling a curl wrap itself around a finger. He felt he could sit there forever. "How are you today?" he said.

"Bewitched, bothered and bewildered. Tell me, Darroch," she said, gesturing out at the sunwashed sea, "how could anyone bear to leave this?"

He felt a tremor of alarm but said lightly, "Wait till you've experienced a Force 9 gale in December." The wind picked up and she pulled the sweater together and buttoned it. He unfolded her shawl and draped it around her shoulders, then put his arm back on the bench behind her. She felt cocooned in warmth.

Jean said, "Weather is irrelevant. California has wonderful weather and terrible earthquakes. Florida has wonderful weather and spiders the size of dinner plates. Weather isn't what counts."

"What does count?"

"Family, friends, music, the sea . . . or Lake Michigan, that's nice too." She shrugged restlessly.

"*Mo charaid* . . . is there anything I can do? I don't like you to be unhappy." He leaned toward her and their glances locked and held for a long moment.

Jean thought, careful, careful, this is tricky. You could really get lost in this man; he's easily the nicest guy you've ever met. She was mesmerized by his eyes, so deeply blue. Today they were the color of an Eilean Dubh sky just before a thunderstorm.

When he leaned closer she felt herself drawn to him. He's a friend, a good friend, and just that until I sort out the relationship with Russ, she thought, but the possibility of something more than friendship had abruptly become very real. She swallowed and turned her head away.

"I have two things to tell you, Jean," he said, accepting her withdrawal. "First, I'm leaving the Island for a while."

"How long?"

"Around six weeks. I've a job with the Beeb. We're starting our next *Classic Theatre*." He grinned. "Do you fancy me as Heathcliff?"

"What! You're doing *Wuthering Heights*? My favorite book." Then it dawned on her. "That's a long time to be gone." No singing together, no talking together, no laughter. No Darroch. Suddenly she felt lonely and depressed again.

He said softly, "Will you be here when I return, *mo Shìne?*"

"I don't know," she said. She turned her head to the sea. "I'd like to be."

"You want to stay, don't you? Can you not follow your heart?" And how can I go to London, not knowing if you'll be here when I come home, he thought.

"People have commitments," she said, her head bowed. "Can't always do what you want, you know."

Darroch was suddenly aware that what he wanted was to kiss her, really kiss her, not just a friendly kiss. Her mouth, half hidden by the hair that the wind was whipping around her face, lured him. What would she be like in his arms, he wondered. Warm and yielding? Or vibrant and aroused? His hand reached for a strand of her hair, wanting to feel once again the curl take possession of his finger.

Simultaneously they heard a chattering of girls' voices below on the path and advancing rapidly. They moved apart just as the first three of a troop of Girl Guides spilled from the path onto the cliff. The girls swarmed to Darroch, chattering in the Gaelic. They were followed by more girls and farther behind them the Guide leader.

They were shy with Jean, shaking hands formally when Darroch introduced them. He knew all the girls' names and was clearly a favorite. They giggled when he said solemnly, "Now we need to speak English, ladies. Our visitor is just learning our language."

When they switched languages, Jean was relieved but disappointed. "Don't speak English just for me. How will I ever learn?" she said.

Guide leader Elizabeth Thomas, the friendly English schoolteacher, came puffing up the cliff, red-faced from the climb. "Hullo, you two. Isn't this a glorious day? The view is so splendid I could hardly watch where I was walking from wanting to look at the sea."

"Come and sit down, Liz." Darroch stood up politely.

"Thanks. If I catch a bit of rest now and again it's easier to keep up with this lot," she said. The girls had lost interest in the adults' chat and were rummaging in the grass, looking for wildflowers.

Darroch said, "We're on our way back down. Much easier than going up."

Liz smiled as they left. "Don't get going too fast and fall off the cliff!"

The path seemed steeper going down than it had coming up. "Take my hand, we'll brake each other," he said. His long fingers closed warmly around hers.

He stopped for a moment. "I've something else to tell you . . . to show you, really."

"Okay." She concentrated on keeping her footing as they went down the path much too fast. When they reached the bottom he headed for the Bentley parked across the road from the Hotel. He kept her hand and drew her with him.

"Where are we going?"

"For a wee ride."

Jean was surprised when the Bentley stopped by the cottage at the top of the road leading to Darroch's home and *Taigh Rois*. It was a tiny one-story house nestled behind a stone wall that made it barely visible from the road. It was in the usual Island style, wide and low with thick white stone walls.

The golden-brown thatch of the roof was tightly packed, sharply cropped at the bottom edges and covered with a net weighed down with large rocks dangling from ropes.

Darroch said, "There's only a few thatched houses left on the Island. They're too expensive to maintain." She followed him as he unlocked the door and went in. How odd, she thought. She'd understood that Eilean Dubh houses were never locked.

Reading her thought, he said, "I've kept the door locked because the cottage has been repainted and there's been construction work done. I didn't want any exploring children wandering in."

It was very much like Darroch's home, only smaller, with whitewashed walls and beautiful wood floors. As in his, the walls had been knocked out to make one room.

She was drawn to the large window over the sink, to a spectacular view of the sea off the cliff behind the cottage. Waves crashed against the rocks, sending a salt shower over the shingle beach not far below. She leaned into the view, entranced.

"I knew you'd like that window," Darroch said. "I had it put in because you enjoy mine so much."

She turned to look at him. He was standing nearby, leaning against the sink, arms folded, watching her. "What do you mean? Darroch, who lives here?"

He said, "You do. If you want to."

"Me? It's for me?"

"It's very small but the plumbing's good and so is the wiring. The bedroom and bath are in the addition on the back." He watched her anxiously. "Do you like it?"

Jean turned again to stare at the sea. She was overwhelmed but she was determined not to be a gusher. "I do. You'll tell me what the rent is."

"*Ceart mhath.*"

"And it will have to be a short-term lease. Month-to-month."

"*Ceart mhath.*"

She looked around at the cottage, took several impulsive steps forward and stood in the middle of the room. "I love it," she said simply.

He felt he'd won a victory. The cottage would hold her until he returned; he was sure of it. Perhaps it was fighting dirty but he didn't care. He needed to keep her here. He had known without conscious thought that it would come to this when he'd started remodeling the cottage with her in mind. It had tormented him that she might decide to leave before he got it ready.

In a nearly normal voice he said, "It will be a wee bit hard for you because you have no transport. You can ride into town with Màiri to the Playschool and for shopping. When I'm back it will be no problem. I'll take you where you want to go."

"It's only a mile or two. I can walk." Joy filled her. "Oh, Darroch! How is this possible?"

"I own this cottage. I inherited it from my mother; she was born here. We've been using it to house the man we hire to help with the crofting work. It helps pay my way because I've often got to go away from the Island so I can't do my share of the physical work. Our man left last July. He's marrying a woman in Glasgow and moving there." He shook his head at the idea of this terrible fate.

"Now we've hired Somhairle Mac-a-Phi *as òige*, Barabal's oldest, and he's content to live at home. He'll be paid extra if we don't give him housing and he's saving to buy a truck. Besides, Barabal thinks he's too young to live alone, only eighteen, and what she says goes. So the cottage isn't needed and your rent will help pay his wages."

"But Darroch, you said housing was scarce. Isn't there an Islander who needs the cottage?"

He shook his head. "I did make inquiries, I had to. The cottage is too small for a family. Family housing is what's needed, so it's yours with a clear conscience. Would you like to start moving in, so I can help you settle before I leave?"

"Shouldn't I give Gordon notice?"

"I've already done that, last week." At her look of surprise he said, "Cheeky of me, but he knew you were looking for a place. I told him there was a cottage vacant you might want but that it was up to you."

"So I can move in right away?"

"Tonight, if you wish."

She shook her head. "No, one more night at the Hotel, to say goodbye to Gordon and Sheilah and to get used to the idea of having my own space. I've not had such a luxury since I was nineteen and had my own apartment and that only lasted nine months. I feel like twirling around and throwing my hat in the air like Mary Tyler Moore."

"Or dancing on the ceiling like Fred Astaire?"

"Yes, that too. Thank you, Darroch."

"My pleasure. Now, shall we get your things or would you rather go grocery shopping?" He felt a childlike eagerness to see her installed in the cottage.

"Let's go shopping, I want to cook tomorrow. What would you like for supper?"

"I'm invited to dine with you, am I." He smiled. "I'd like whatever you want to cook."

Jean was running through her mind all the delicious American dishes she'd been missing and came up with fried chicken. "I know something you'll like."

"Do you," he murmured, leaning closer. I know something else I'd like, he thought, looking at her mouth longingly. But he was reluctant to make advances to her the first minutes they were alone in the cottage.

Making up a grocery list in her mind Jean didn't notice. "Where do we go to shop for the basics? Is there a supermarket on the Island somewhere?"

He smiled at the idea. "That's the Co-Op. Sainsbury's it's not."

"What's Sainsbury's? Anyway, I was joking. I want to take a basket and go from shop to shop like the women in British mystery novels."

"We'll stop at the basketmaker's first, then." He took her sweater by the lapels and began to button it. "I wish I could be here to help you settle in. It's going to be a long four weeks alone in London."

"I thought you said six weeks."

"I'll do my acting fast. Maybe I can cut it down to four." He hesitated, looking at her, his hands still on her sweater. "You're happy, then?"

Warmth glowed between them; she could feel it down to her toes. "Very happy, thanks to you," she managed to say. "Let's get those groceries before the shops close."

He let her go, then felt in his pocket. "Your keys, madam. Don't leave home without them." He handed her a ring with two large old-fashioned keys attached.

"Shall I lock the doors?"

"Well, people will consider it showing off if you do. Who does she think she is, why does she think we'd steal her old rubbish, that sort of thing."

"So why do I need keys?"

"Just for the fun of having them jingle in your pocket," he said.

At the Co-Op, Jean was introduced to British groceries. They wandered the aisles while he explained. "Demarara sugar is brown. Good in coffee and on porridge, if you prefer sugar to salt. Mince is hamburger. The Co-Op always has a pound in the freezer for emergencies but you're best off buying it from Murray the Meat; he grinds it fresh every day. Murray also has streaky, what you'd call bacon, and gammon . . . that's ham."

"It's a whole different language. And I thought the Gaelic was hard!"

"Fish you should get from Cailean the Crab; his is freshest. He has crab and prawns too, and sometimes lobster but that's too expensive for us ordinary folk. The lobsters our fishermen catch are flown to London and Paris for posh restaurants."

He led her down the prepared foods aisle, gesturing with his long slim fingers. "Sausage rolls, children like them. Potted prawns, quite nasty. Pork pies, depraved things to eat! Crisps are potato chips, you'd always have them with that lot. Tinned drinks and beer. And shandy, that's lemonade and beer mixed. And Bovril and Marmite, both unspeakable." He shuddered.

She laughed. "You're a food snob, aren't you? So am I."

"I knew there was a reason why we get on so well," he answered, grinning.

They took the groceries back to the cottage. When they had put everything away he drove her to the Hotel. "I can't begin to tell you how happy I am," she said.

"*Miorbhuileach*," he said in satisfaction and his kiss on each cheek was lingering. They smiled into each other's eyes until she turned reluctantly to go inside. "*Oidhche mhath*," she said.

"*Oidhche mhath, mo leannan*. I'm looking forward to supper tomorrow night."

"Me too . . . lovie." The last was said so softly he wasn't sure he'd heard her correctly, but she was gone.

When she told Sheilah and Gordon her news Sheilah hugged her. "I'm glad you've got a cottage but I will miss you."

"Call me any time you need potatoes peeled," Jean said.

Twenty-one

My angel, I remember the first kiss you gave me,
and every one of the thousand since the first.
Some were gentle, some were wild and I prize them all.
But the ones I prize the most were when you
opened your mouth to me and let me taste you . . .

Ùisdean's third letter to Mòrag, translated by Darroch Mac an Rìgh

The next day Darroch helped her move to the cottage, then left. When he returned there was ample evidence of her work: sofa pillows fluffed, kitchen table scrubbed and sink drainer full of clean dishes.

"Are you sorted, Jean?" he asked.

"What?" she said, looking on the shelves for mixing bowls. She opened a cupboard below the sink. "Oh, here's lots more stuff."

"My mother had every kitchen gadget you could imagine. I left that batch you've just found for Fergal. But I don't think he did much cooking so they've probably not been used for years."

"Yes." She touched a bowl's dusty rim, then handed it to him. He ran hot water into the sink and began washing what she gave him. Pleased, she said, "You're quite domestic, aren't you."

He said, "Well, I've spent a lot of my life living alone. I had to learn."

Jean sat back on her heels, watching him. Why alone, she wondered. Such a nice man, why hadn't someone snapped him up? Perhaps he hadn't wanted to be snapped up, after the unhappiness of his divorce. "Do you mind living alone?" she said.

He shot her a quick veiled glance. "It's preferable to some other situations."

"Yes." She stuck her head into the cupboard. "Ah, dish towels." She brought them out. "I'd better start supper. I've invited Màiri and Jamie at six-thirty."

He was disappointed that they weren't to dine *a deux* but he understood her need to celebrate her new home and repay past hospitality. "What shall I do?"

"Peel potatoes?"

"Aye." He took the bowl he'd washed, potatoes and a knife and sat down at the table where he could watch while she prepared chicken pieces, skinning them, dipping them in egg and water, then in seasoned flour. She put them into a skillet of hot fat where they sizzled merrily.

Watching her, Darroch got careless with the knife and slit his finger. She turned at his yelp of pain. She knew just where her first aid kit was; she'd unpacked it an hour ago. She smoothed antiseptic ointment on the cut, then put on a bandage. On impulse she kissed the cut finger. "There, a kiss to make it better," she said.

She smiled up at him and surprised a curious look on his face. The air between them shimmered as though in a heat wave. She could not take her eyes from his.

His hard-won, rigidly-maintained restraint was slipping away like the tide in Ros Mór harbor. "What a wonderful mouth you have," he said softly.

"No, I don't," she blurted. "It's too big."

He put his hand under her chin and turned her face from left to right, looking at her carefully. She went still with shock at his touch. "No, it's not, it's just the right size." He said, "Jean, I want very much to kiss you. Would you mind?"

"Umm . . . no, I . . . I mean, yes, I wouldn't mind . . . I mean . . . " She turned her face up. His mouth touched hers gently, then firmly.

The kiss was as warm and sweet as a bowl of ice cream melting in the sun. Waves of the most exquisite desire washed over him. He lifted his head and murmured, "Just the right size. And delicious. Soft as a peach."

Dazed, she said, "But not as fuzzy, I hope. You know, your eyes are the bluest I've ever seen." They were at this moment a deep glowing sapphire, as bottomless as Airgead Harbor.

"Eilean Dubh eyes and the bluest on the Island belong to Mac an Rìghs. Yours on the other hand are the exact shade of the tidal pool just off Airgead Point." He put his hands on her shoulders and smiled at her. "Or the color of a Coke bottle."

"Peridot, from my dad's side of the family. His were the same as mine."

"Is that the Eilean Dubh side? I can't think of any Islanders with eyes so green."

"Yes, Ùisdean's descendants. My husband says my eyes are the color of seaweed. I hate that."

Your husband is a damned fool, he thought, and said aloud, "He's never seen seaweed, it's a horrible yellow-brown. Your eyes . . . " One hand left her shoulder and moved to her throat. Jean froze, unwilling to break the spell.

"Your eyes are lovely; they're clear and honest. I want . . . no, I need . . . to kiss you again." He kissed her lingeringly, sucked her lower lip between his and nibbled it. Then his tongue slipped gently into her mouth and caressed it.

Her eyes went wide with surprise. She'd never experienced such a kiss. Russ's kisses were brusque and perfunctory, as though he'd no time to waste on such foolishness. He'd told her once that he didn't like kissing. Clearly, Darroch did. And he was very good at it.

She pulled herself back to reality with difficulty. "I don't think we should do this. I like it too much."

"Me too. I wish I didn't have to go to London on Monday." He hesitated, then said, "I suppose you wouldn't want to come with me. My flat has two bedrooms. We could be perfectly proper."

"Yes, but would we be. I've heard London nights are long and cold and people have to huddle together for warmth."

"Is that the reason they're giving now?" he said. "You'd like London. All day for museums, parks and shopping and in the evening theatre, music, ballet. We'd take the guitar, we could sit on my balcony and make music at night. And talk. Imagine all the time we'd have to talk."

"Darroch, it sounds wonderful but it would be a little hard to explain that I'd run off to London with you to sit on your balcony, even if you do have two bedrooms. I am married, after all. And I like kissing you too much to try it."

"And you've a new cottage to play house in," he said regretfully. "I thought you'd say no."

She heard splattering. "Oh, the chicken!" She pulled away and turned to lift the lid and peer inside. He watched her sniff and probe and adjust the fire under the pan.

She put the lid back and turned to him. "Listen, Darroch," she said hesitantly, "I want you to know something. I have been married to Russ for at least two hundred years and I don't go around kissing strange men."

He grinned and opened his mouth to reply but she laid her finger across his lips. "Yes, I know, you're going to say you're not so strange. You are, you know. Nothing in my life has prepared me to deal with a folksinging actor who's the no-I'm-not-really laird of a tiny Scottish island where everybody speaks an obscure language and nobody has any interest whatsoever in owning a microwave oven."

He said, stung, "That's not true, Jean. I myself have a microwave oven. It's in my London flat."

She seized his hair with both hands. It was, as she'd expected, silky to the touch. "I'm trying to make a point. In all my twenty years of marriage I have not kissed any man but my husband. Unless you count Brad Johnson and that's not really fair."

"Why not?"

"He chased me around our kitchen table at a New Year's Eve party and when he caught me he kissed me. I don't think that should count because I didn't enjoy it."

"Not at all?"

"No, I slapped his face."

"I'm certainly glad I asked permission first."

"So the fact that I kissed you . . . "

"Twice."

" . . . is something special. To me, anyway. And I have to think about it. Why it happened and that sort of thing."

"*Thà gu dearbh*, aye, of course. I feel the same way. It's very special. But just in the interests of research . . . " He cupped her face between his hands and kissed her again, his mouth soft and coaxing on hers, inviting her response.

When they came to, her hands were fisted in his hair and he was leaning her back against the counter, careful not to let his pelvis touch hers so she wouldn't realize the extent of his arousal.

"You're making my heart pound," she gasped.

"Let me feel." He put his hand over her heart and felt the wild reverberations. Just a few inches lower and he'd have her breast under his fingers, he thought, and forced himself to move his hands up to her shoulders again. Funny how breasts were forbidden erotic objects and shoulders were not. But he realized that touching any part of Jean was going to light him up like Piccadilly Circus.

He read three emotions warring in her. Yielding, which he recognized from years of experience in making love to willing women. Trust, which touched him deeply. And a surprising innocence. He decided to ignore the innocence and go with the yielding.

He bent to her mouth again, greedily this time, and her toes curled from sheer pleasure. This really has to stop, Jean thought. Another kiss and I might follow him to London or Timbuktu or wherever. "It's a good thing you're going to London. This is pretty intense," she gasped.

"I wonder if we could be done with filming in three weeks," he said wistfully.

"We'd better pull ourselves together. Company will be here any minute."

"All right, you're the boss, it's your house. What would you like me to do?"

What I'd like you to do, she thought, is unbutton my blouse and run your fingers down my throat and lower . . . She blushed scarlet, the color flaming in her face and sweeping over her body, disappearing under her clothes.

He watched, fascinated. "Now I wonder," he said softly, "what's going on in your head to turn you that lovely color."

They stared at each other. He took a step forward and she was suddenly terrified that he was going to kiss her again and she would lose all control. She backed up against the counter, seized the bowl of potatoes for protection and stammered, "Ummm . . . please set the table. And . . . umm . . . Darroch. I really liked it. Kissing you, I mean."

He grinned at her triumphantly. "I'd hoped you would," he said. "I liked it too. Kissing you is like having a mouthful of honey." Jean almost dropped the bowl.

When Màiri arrived she exclaimed, "The old cottage looks so homely! I always thought this was a lovely little place, especially after Darroch fixed it up for his mother."

"Not that she cared," Darroch said ruefully. "I think she'd rather I'd left it as a *taigh dubh*."

"Nonsense," said Màiri briskly. "She talked about it often, how pretty it was and so easy to care for. And how thoughtful her son was to make it so comfortable for her."

"Is that so?" Darroch was absurdly pleased. He'd never suspected. His mother had not been what the Island called a gusher, one free with compliments and praise, and he'd always been a bit afraid she'd not liked the cottage when it no longer resembled the one of her youth.

Jean was finishing up dinner and Jamie, sitting at the table, watched happily. It felt right to him, this combination of people and place; there was something good and natural about it. And he sensed the change in Jean and Darroch's relationship. Jean looked dazed and Darroch looked . . . hungry. Jamie knew that hunger well and felt intense sympathy for his friend. The air snapped and crackled with sex and he loved it, and thought about the pleasure he'd have with his wife when he got her home.

The dinner was a success. "American fried chicken! *Miorbhuileach*," said Màiri.

"My mother's recipe," said Jean.

"Here's to your mother, Jean," said Jamie, raising his glass.

After dinner Darroch washed dishes and Jean dried. She liked that job. It meant she could stand by him at the sink and look at his profile.

He was enjoying looking at her too. He said softly, "You are beautiful, Jean. I want to kiss you again."

"I'm not in the least beautiful." She was blushing, her face so rosy that Jamie, across the room by the fireplace, could see it.

"Are you always going to contradict me? You are beautiful. You are my favorite shade of pink." He grinned at her.

"Damn it, I hate blushing. Anybody can tell what I'm thinking."

"What are you thinking?" His voice was a whisper.

She whispered back, "I'm thinking about kissing you."

"Ahhh," he said in deep satisfaction. He bent suddenly and brushed his lips across hers. "That's the fifth time. Do you still like it?"

"Oh, yes. Far too much." She smiled at him, completely besotted.

Jamie was working Màiri like a sheepdog works a restless ewe, keeping her cornered by the fireplace. Every time she tried to get away he handed her music to sort. Finally she eluded him and marched into the kitchen.

"Give me the towel, Jean. I'll dry and you put away. Then we'll get done in time for some music."

With a sigh Jean relinquished the towel. She had been enjoying the flirtation . . . if it could be called that . . . very much and she was so absorbed in Darroch she could barely bring herself back to reality.

When the dishes were done they got out instruments. Màiri was teaching Jean a song called "*O till, a Leannain*," return, my darling. Jean had no trouble with the chorus and the first verse but halfway through the second she lost the Gaelic. Darroch lined it out for her and she sang it, then they harmonized. On the third verse she broke down entirely. "I'm sorry, this one is hard. What does it mean, anyway?"

Darroch said softly, "I am going far from my dearest lass but never shall I forget the touch of her sweet lips on mine. I pray she waits for me and keeps me in her heart." He smiled into Jean's dazzled eyes.

"My goodness," she said. Her heart jumped and fluttered.

Jamie raised his eyebrows. "A . . . free . . . translation," he murmured.

Màiri's attention had wandered as usual when it came to English translations. "Look at the time!" she exclaimed. "It's getting on to midnight."

"I should go," said Darroch reluctantly. "I've still got some packing."

"We'll all go. Darroch, I'll pick you up at eight tomorrow, *ceart math?*"

"*Tapadh leat, a Mhàiri.*" They were putting on their coats and gathering up music and Jamie's fiddle. Darroch said, "Jean, I hate to think of you here without transport. Shall I leave the Bentley for you? Could you drive it?"

Jean shuddered. "No thanks. A stick shift, driving on the left, single lane roads and a classic car. It makes my stomach hurt just thinking about it. I appreciate the offer but I'd rather walk and live."

"Well, stay off the roads when it gets dark. There's no street lights and it's very hard to see pedestrians. Jamie, you'll look after her?"

Jamie and Màiri exchanged glances. Jean went blank, bemused by the idea of someone being asked to look after her.

"Not to worry. Jean knows she can call on us if she needs anything," Jamie said.

He took Màiri's arm and steered her to the door. Darroch went with them, looking over his shoulder thoughtfully. A minute or two later he was back, stepping inside the door and calling to the other two, "Go ahead, I'll catch you up."

"We'll wait for you . . . " Màiri began.

"No, we won't," said Jamie firmly, tucking Màiri's arm in his and pulling her down the path.

Darroch said, "I couldn't leave without kissing you goodnight and goodbye."

"Is that one kiss or two?" said Jean and stepped forward into his arms.

He pulled her close inside his coat, ending up with one of his arms wrapped around her shoulders and one around her hips. She got one arm about his waist, the other was crushed against his chest. Her face was next to his coat and her nose was filled with the odors of wool, peat smoke and the faint wisp of their goodnight whisky on his breath. It was his heart that was pounding now, under her hand. She felt more than a little dizzy.

He said in her ear, "I'll call you from London. No, wait, you don't have a phone. I'll leave messages for you on my machine. Or if we can pick a mutually agreeable time I'll call you at my cottage. And Jean, have Jamie . . . no, Màiri, that's better . . . call Murdoch and get him to speed up installing a phone for you."

"Um . . . which Murdoch would that be?"

"Murdoch the . . . let me think now, how to say it in English . . . that would be Murdoch the Arranger."

"I don't think I've met him," she murmured.

"Well, he's a busy man, doesn't have much of a social life. We have maybe thirty seconds left together, Jean. Why the hell are we talking about Murdoch?"

"Who?" Jean worked her arm free from his chest and put it around his neck to draw his head down.

Afterwards neither was sure if it was seconds, minutes or hours that they were in each other's arms before he said, "I'll go now, while I still can. *Mar sin leat, mo Shine.*"

"I'm really going to miss you," she whispered. "Mar shin lot . . . what does that mean?'

"Bye for now," he said and walked out the door. She stood still for a moment, then ran to the kitchen window so she could watch the tall figure go down the hill.

She sighed. It was going to be a long three, or four, or six weeks.

Darroch walked across the tarmac to the helicopter, a suitcase in each hand. Murdoch the Chopper said, "Off to London, is it?"

"Aye."

"Staying long?"

"Six weeks or so."

"Pity." Murdoch shook his head. "You'll miss autumn. I always think October is our finest month."

"Don't rub it in, Murdoch, I hate like hell to go. Have to put bread on the table, though."

"Good part?" Murdoch, like the other Islanders, had become television experts since Darroch's success and took a proprietorial interest in his career.

"Aye. Heathcliff in *Wuthering Heights* on *Classic Theatre.*"

The other man nodded authoritatively. "A fine program. The family and I enjoyed *Jane Eyre.*"

Darroch, used to having his theatrical efforts carefully scrutinized by his fellow Islanders, smiled his thanks and changed the subject. "Is it just me today?"

"You and a couple of birdwatchers heading home and Beathag MacShennach's prize pig, going to a farm just outside Edinburgh to be inseminated."

"What, all by herself, no escort?"

"I'm her escort. Her limousine is waiting at the other end."

"Give us a lift to Edinburgh, then? I hate that Inverness train connection."

"*Thà gu dearbh*, room for both you and Lady Elspeth MacGonnigal in the truck."

"Lady Elspeth . . . ?"

"The pig. Daft name for a porker, *nach*?"

The helicopter headed north over *Cladh a' Chnuic* as it left the Island and Darroch stared down at Jean's cottage.

Yesterday had affected him deeply, had awakened emotions and desires he'd trained himself to forget. At forty he'd resigned himself to being alone the rest of his life. Could he bear to become involved with a woman again? His track record wasn't wonderful, he thought ruefully. Jilted once, left once, betrayed once. The pleasures of those three loves were muted by the remembrances of their endings.

His women hadn't fared well, either. He remembered all too vividly Màiri's suffering after their parting, until Jamie'd appeared to rescue her. And Morgan's tearful middle-of-the night calls from Australia. And Adrienne's despairing face when he'd asked her for a divorce. Poor Adrienne, he still felt guilty about her.

Face it, Mac an Rìgh, you're a jinx to women, he thought glumly. Are you going to expose another one to your tender mercies?

And Jean was high risk. Not only was she American, a foreigner, but she was, he forced himself to remember, married. What were the odds she would be willing to commit to a relationship with him and an obscure and backward Scottish island? For he was a package, himself and Eilean Dubh.

And what kind of a relationship could it be? If she wasn't married he'd have whisked her off to London and he'd have her in his bed tonight; he was that confident of his powers of seduction and of her response. But she was married, and adultery was unthinkable . . . wasn't it?

He sighed. Lusting after another married woman. Isn't Màiri torment enough for you?

With a tremendous effort he forced lust out of his mind, reached into a pocket and took out a cassette tape. He'd recorded Jean singing three new songs with the idea that he'd work on the harmonies in London. Now, however, he just wanted to hear her sing. He rummaged in the other pocket, found his tape player and put on headphones. He popped the cassette in and settled back to listen.

Still tentative on the Gaelic, but getting better, and hesitant at times because the songs were still unfamiliar, but always the same sweet, warm voice. In his mind he could see her, head bent over the guitar, soft hair falling over her cheek.

And he realized that if Jean was the question, yes was the answer.

Twenty-two

*An Eilean Dubh house is typical of the Hebrides. It is divided into three
compartments. One end is the cow-byre, a refuge for the beasts in bad
weather. The other end is the sleeping area. In the middle is the main room,
with its fireplace of flat stones in the middle of the floor, no chimney, merely
an opening in the roof for the egress of peat smoke. The inside becomes
thoroughly blackened by the smoke; hence the name Taigh Dubh,
or black house . . .*

Robertson's Relics

In the end it was closer to seven weeks that Darroch was gone.

Jean was enjoying being a housewife again. She didn't fool herself about
the simplicity of her lifestyle, though. The little house was easy to care for
because there were no drawers stuffed with bills, no mail to answer, no
phone calls to return.

She knew if she stayed on the Island for any length of time the table
would pile up with mail, she'd have to start a phone number file, get a calendar and stock her kitchen with more than the basics.

For now she was content. She had time to cook, read, practice music,
study the Gaelic. She was beginning to entertain serious doubts about ever
attaining much proficiency in that subtle and elusive tongue but she plowed
on diligently. At least she could now sing in it without Màiri and Jamie
wincing. And she was giving the shopkeepers a good chuckle whenever she
talked to them in their language. A few were even starting to take her seriously, offering helpful corrections and supplying words when she ran dry.

She worked in the tiny cottage garden when the weather was not too
cold. She'd discovered an ancient climbing rose growing up the northwest
corner of the house and was slowly pruning it into a semblance of order. It
had the biggest thorns she'd ever seen. She had no trouble remembering to
wear gloves.

Her work in the library was going slowly. Although she had learned a great deal about Eilean Dubh history, no clues were emerging to the identity of Ùisdean and Mòrag. If it weren't all so interesting she would have given up long ago.

It was all interesting, on Eilean Dubh. Everything was so different from life in Milwaukee that sometimes she felt she'd landed on an entirely new planet. Why aren't I homesick any more, she asked herself, and had no answer.

One day, looking out her window at the sea dashing itself against the rocks, she began to wonder how hard it would be to get to the shore. She bundled up against the October wind and went outside.

Beside the storehouse she found the path. It was overgrown with brambles but she hacked out a passage down the steep hill and burst out, panting with exertion, upon the pebble beach called the shingle. Before her the ocean stretched endlessly to the sky.

The sun came out suddenly, a welcome sight after several cloudy days, and its rays rippled over the waves and splintered into blue-dominated rainbows. She stood, eyes wide, an irrational happiness filling her. Negative ions, she thought. Isn't that what sun and sea spray produce, and don't they improve a person's outlook? Whatever it was it was working. She couldn't remember ever feeling so good.

Except that she missed Darroch desperately.

She wasn't as innocent as he thought. She might not have a lot of experience with a lot of men but she had twenty years experience with one. She knew when a man desired her, recognized it in Darroch from the way his eyes had darkened and his hands had trembled on her shoulders. He'd been careful to keep their encounter funny and sweet but instinct told her their relationship had changed. He wanted more than kisses.

And maybe she did too. Without effort she could remember the imprint of his mouth on hers. What if he made love as beautifully as he kissed? She had a sudden, hot awareness of what it might be like to be intimate with him.

Her knees weakened and she sat down abruptly on a large rock. Its sharp edge cutting into her bottom brought her back to reality. She was amazed at herself. She'd never felt an intense physical attraction to a man other than her husband, never even thought about it except in the abstract. No brownie points there, she thought. It doesn't count that you've never succumbed if you've never been tempted. And she'd never been tempted, until now.

She had an unwanted pang of understanding for Russ but immediately shoved it out of her mind. She wasn't contemplating serial adultery, after all.

Stop it, she told herself. You're not going to fall into Darroch's arms like a besotted teenager just because he's the sweetest man you've ever met, and the sexiest. You're married, you're emotionally vulnerable and you're going to be very, very careful. You're going to take it one step at a time and see what happens.

She just hoped she had the self-restraint to follow her own advice.

She walked to his cottage every day, supposedly to check it over, but in reality because she could feel his presence there. There was always a message for her on his ansaphone and his mellow actor's voice warmed her heart and body.

By the second week neither could bear any longer the loss of their daily Island conversations and they fell into a routine of talking every night, Jean on his cottage phone. She told him about Eilean Dubh events and he told her stories about television and his theatrical friends. His stories were funny but they made her long for him and some nights she went home sad and lonely. It was some consolation that he sounded lonely too.

A *Dhia beannaich mi*, acting is hard work, Darroch thought as he left the BBC's Television Centre in Wood Green after a tough day. It had been topped off with a brief, intense discussion with the director who'd reminded the cast that a key scene was to be shot the next day: Heathcliff's passionate encounter with the dying Cathy.

He stood for a moment deciding whether to pick up food or eat leftovers because he was definitely too tired to cook. He decided on Indian takeaway and rode home on the Tube with a hot package on his lap and the spicy odor of vindaloo rising around him.

It was five minutes walk to his flat from the Tube and he moved briskly, looking forward to his nightly chat with Jean. Still he found time to enjoy the Thames flowing beside the embankment. The river always reminded him of home and the sea even though the only thing the burbling Thames and the riotous ocean had in common was that both were wet.

Màiri'd called last night with the news that Co-Op third quarter earnings were down which meant a smaller dividend check for everyone, which meant belt-tightening all around. Which meant people would have less to spend in the Co-Op. Which meant fourth quarter earnings would also be down. He sighed in resignation. Eilean Dubh, he thought: Gaelic for always something to worry about.

He glanced at his watch when he let himself into the flat and realized he had missed Jean's call. The Indian restaurant had taken longer than he'd realized.

The message light on the answering machine was blinking. It was Jean. She said she was sorry she'd missed him, that there wasn't much happening on the Island, that it had rained that morning but the afternoon had been brilliantly sunny. He closed his eyes for a moment, thinking about a brilliantly sunny day on Eilean Dubh.

He replayed the message just to listen to Jean's soft sexy voice. She spoke into his answering machine as shyly as though she feared someone was overhearing her most intimate thoughts and she sounded like Marilyn Monroe. He didn't understand the last word she'd said. He played it a third time and put his head down by the machine.

Lovie. That was it. She'd said, "Good night . . . I mean, *feasgar math* . . . lovie."

Lovie. Damn. He was definitely going to be home on time tomorrow night.

So the days passed for them both, and October turned into a November that grew grayer each day. Winter was coming.

Twenty-three

Some roads (often called single-track roads)
are only wide enough for one vehicle.
They may have special passing places.
Pull into a passing place on your left,
or wait opposite one on your right,
when you see a vehicle coming towards you
or the driver behind you wants to overtake.
Do not park in passing places.

The Highway Code

*J*ean reserved Fridays for work in the library, riding up to Airgead and back with Ian the Post in the post bus.

The rides were for the most part quiet. Used to the friendly garrulousness of most Islanders it puzzled Jean that Ian did not chat with her. She started to worry that she had offended him in some way.

She decided to make an effort to talk to him in her fledgling Gaelic. One morning she picked a phrase out of her exercise book. "'*Se là brèagha a th' ann,*" she began. It's a beautiful day.

He sent a quick look over his shoulder. "'*Se,*" he said noncommittally.

Jean sneaked her textbook out of her purse. "*Tha e nas blàithe na bha e 'n-dè,*" she read. It's warmer than yesterday.

He mumbled something.

"I'm sorry? I mean, *tha mi duilich?*"

"Blah-yuh. Warmer is blah-yuh. Not what you said."

"Thank you for telling me. *Tapadh leat,*" said Jean. "Is that right?"

"It is britty goot."

"Pre-tee," said Jean before she thought.

"Pre-tee," he said carefully and in the mirror she saw his lips move as he repeated the word under his breath several times.

A silence fell. Jean could not think of any other phrases to try on him. None of her other weather sentences were appropriate, as it was not raining, there was not a high wind blowing and it was unlikely to freeze that summer evening.

Ian pulled over in front of a cottage and got out to drop off the mail. When he returned Jean decided to try again. She'd found another phrase in her book.

"*Co a tha a' fuireach anns an taigh seo?*" she said. Who lives in this house?

Ian turned in his seat and looked at her steadily. She realized suddenly that he was offended. "Mrs. Abbott, I know my English is not good. But I can understand it. It is not necessary for you to be speaking the Gaelic to me."

Astounded and embarrassed, Jean stammered, "Ian, I'm sorry. I didn't mean . . . it's just that I'm trying to learn the Gaelic and the only way to learn is to speak it to people." Then she realized what he'd said. "And your English is fine. I don't know what you mean."

"I know I do not have the English well, you do not need to be nice with me. I was ill with the asthma the first year we studied it and I am missing much. Since then I was not able to catch up. It is making me unhappy because it will be hurting my chances for . . . moving forward, is that right? . . . with *Am Post Rìoghal.*"

Listening to this passionate speech Jean realized why he had been unwilling to talk to her. She said, "You have to speak really good English to get promoted, is that it?"

"*Tha, tha*, it is a large problem with me. The *Àrd-fhear a'Phuist* MacLeoid is for retirement in the next year and the examiners will be coming from London to test for his . . . the person who is . . . I am sorry, I am not good with the future."

"His successor, you mean."

"That is it," he said eagerly. "They will be from England, they will be wanting someone who can speak good English and write it too; the Postmaster is having lots of letters to write. And they will not be wanting me. They will pick some young body out of school or bring up a *Sasannach.*" He shuddered. "That person will be my . . . chief . . . and I will not be enjoying it at all."

Jean was silent, thinking. Ian drove on, his shoulders hunched in unhappiness.

After a pause she said tentatively, "Ian, what if we make a deal?"

"What is that, to make a deal?" he said, puzzled.

"I want to learn the Gaelic, you want to improve your English. Why don't we help each other?" He stared at her. "I've done English as a second language tutoring, I majored in English in college and my grammar and spelling are excellent.

"We could speak English going to Airgead and the Gaelic on the way home. Or speak each other's language as we go along. And if you wanted to write essays or practice letters I could correct them and tell you what was wrong. You could write samples for the Post Office test."

As he hesitated, she went on eagerly, "What do you say? I ride up to Airgead with you once a week so we'd have regular practice sessions."

"I don't know," he said slowly. "I do not wish to be a difficulty."

"Ian, you would be helping me. I hate bothering Màiri and Darroch with my questions and they usually end up speaking English to me because it's easier."

He considered very carefully. The silence lengthened. Jean waited. Finally he said, "If it is not an imposition to you, I would like to do it." He turned and smiled.

"Dynamite!" she exclaimed and saw his puzzled look. "That is to blow up, is it not?" he said.

So Jean began her first lesson.

It was inevitable, on Eilean Dubh, that there would be talk about the fact that Mrs. Abbott and Ian the Post were having regular assignations on Fridays on the road to Airgead. Passersby noticed that they seemed to be deep in conversation. Sometimes they stayed parked on the verge for what seemed an unduly long time as they carefully sorted out a point of grammar. The gossip mill began to grind.

It was inevitable that those who talked would make sure that the talk reached the ears of Ian's Catrìona, his wife of two years and a woman as smart as she was beautiful. She had long blonde hair, a beautiful face and figure and she had been first in her class the year she graduated.

Catrìona simply didn't believe her husband and the American woman could be involved in a romance. There was, for one thing, a fifteen-year difference in their ages. And then there were Barabal's insights.

She and Barabal were close friends and Barabal had confided the observations she'd made regarding Jean. "Our Laird has his eye on her," Barabal had said. "And she is doing her share of looking right back."

"Do you think so?" said Catrìona, surprised.

"Aye, it's so, and a fine match to my way of thinking. She's a good-hearted, sensible lass, just the sort he needs. And aren't they the beautiful singers together! What a pity she's married, but I have heard she has left her husband so maybe there's hope for our Darroch." She smiled wisely. "In America, marriage is not always forever."

Catrìona considered all this. She began to observe the two carefully. She noticed that Darroch called in at Playschool nearly every day, more often than before, and that he always said casually as he was leaving, "May I give you a lift, Jean?"

And Jean always replied, "Oh, yes, if it's not out of your way."

"Not out of the way at all," he'd say. "I'm going right by the Hotel."

And the two of them would smile at each other. It dawned on Catrìona that they were playing a little game, perhaps unconsciously, for the benefit of onlookers. She noticed that Jean would turn a becoming shade of pink and that Darroch's smile for her was especially warm. Catrìona was not sure they realized what was happening to them.

She watched them at each *cèilidh* as they sang together, looking into each other's eyes. Barabal has the right of it, she decided. There is love growing there.

Like every other Island female Catrìona was very aware of Darroch's considerable presence and charm. She could not believe that Jean, a woman she liked and respected, could handle a husband in America and the attentions of dashing Darroch and still have time to seduce her Ian.

Catrìona's knowledge of her husband also kept jealousy out of her heart. No one would have guessed it of quiet, serious Ian, but he was an ardent and inventive lover. They kept each other so busy in bed she was sure he'd no interest and no energy left for another woman. But she was curious so she said to him one night, "Ian, *mo ghràdh*, you are making a good friend of Mrs. Jean, are you not."

He hesitated. "*Mo Chatrìona*, I have something to confess." And for one awful moment Catrìona thought she'd made a mistake. Then he said, "We have made the deal. She is improving my English and I am helping her to learn the Gaelic. Please do not tell anyone. I am afraid they will make fun at me."

Catrìona almost laughed with relief but realized that would hurt him. He was very sensitive about the deficiencies he perceived in his English. She said, "Is it the promotion you are thinking of?" When he nodded, she put her arms around him. "You are always looking out for us, *m'eudail*. Tell me if I can help; it is a fine thing you are both doing. I will give my thanks to Jean when I see her next. She is a good woman."

"Oh, she is *miorbhuileach*! I hope she never leaves the Island."

Catrìona, thinking of Darroch's rapt and tender expression when he looked at the American woman, agreed heartily.

Jean and Ian soon became good friends. She learned his mail route and offered to help by sorting mail as they drove along. "My thanks, Jean"—she had finally gotten him on a first name basis—"but that would be against the rules of *Am Post*. You are not a member . . . an employee, I mean . . . so you may not handle the mail."

"Oh, sure," she said. "What else could I do? I know, I can fold newspapers so you don't have to do it when you put them in the letterboxes. I'm a good folder, I used to do it for my kids when they had paper routes. Fold them tight so they can be flung up on people's steps and the route goes twice as fast."

So they bounced along, speaking English in one direction and the Gaelic in the other, Jean's fingers flying over the papers. Prefolding them cut a few minutes off the route so they had time to stop at a scenic overlook to share sandwiches. By unspoken agreement, lessons were dispensed with then and they chatted for fun. Ian liked hearing about America and she discovered he was a gold mine of information about the Islanders. She especially enjoyed listening to him talk about Darroch, whom he admired greatly.

"He makes much money from *The Magician*; it is shown all over the world. He gives his money to the Trust and it provides scholarships and grants to help everyone." That was news to Jean, that Darroch's earnings funded the Trust.

And, "The seniors at the OAP home love him. He visits and talks and listens to everyone."

And, "It is a great sadness to us all that he has not found a wife. We would like an heir from him. His is a fine family, a very old one, and should not die with him."

That bloody laird business, Jean thought, but she couldn't blame the Islanders for how they felt. She realized Darroch understood their feelings too, even if he didn't approve.

One day as they drove along Jean said, "Ian, I wish I could learn to drive your way, on the wrong, that is, the left side of the road. Then maybe I could get a little car and be more independent."

"Perhaps I could be teaching you."

"How?"

"You could drive the post bus."

"But isn't it the property of . . . um . . . *Am Post?*"

"Oh, no. It is mine. I use it for the post and I am given . . . re-im-burse-ment . . . for that. It is for me to decide who drives it. And I always drive slowly and everyone knows my route and watches for me. So there would not be high speeds and many cars to worry you while you are learning."

Jean said hesitantly, "I don't know. I haven't driven a stick shift for twenty years."

"There is no hurry. When you are ready we will drive. But we should start while the weather is fine."

She said, "Okay, if you're willing I'll try. Do I need a learner's permit?"

"You may apply for one today in Airgead."

She did and after her permit was issued, she slipped timidly into Ian's seat in the most deserted part of his route. He affixed a large letter "L" to the license plate, indicating that a learner was at the wheel.

The stick shift was not easy to get the hang of and they lurched along until Jean, in despair, said, "Ian, I'll never remember how to do this. Maybe I should give it up."

Ian was extremely prone to motion sickness and the drive had been quite a trial for him. He said valiantly, "But you are getting better already. And it is not so hard as learning to conjugate the verb 'to be', *nach?*"

She noticed the greenish tinge to his face and resolved to try harder. By sheer concentration and determination her driving began to improve. Then one day she felt "the click" and the ability to drive a stick shift was back.

For the next lessons they turned off the main road and Jean practiced driving on single-track roads. She learned to spot the passing places and not to freeze in terror when another car approached. Backing up was another hurdle: she had to figure out which shoulder to look over.

From then on, she needed just to concentrate on driving on the left and learning about roundabouts—there were two, one in each village—and how to interpret signs, which, of course, were all in the Gaelic. The Islanders had fought for Gaelic signs years ago and systematically destroyed any English ones put up. "What does that one mean?"

"Umm . . . " he searched his mind for the English. "It means . . . adverse camber."

"I've never heard of an . . . adverse camber. Is it some kind of animal?"

"If we are telling the absolute truth . . . I don't know what it means either. Perhaps it suffers in the translation."

Twenty-four

He felt as if golden harps were singing in the air,
and fairies were tickling him down the back with peacock's feathers.

Neil Munro

$\mathcal{D}$arroch awoke joyful and eager, as he always did on a day when he was going home. His usual routine was to eat a quick breakfast, pack his shaving gear, lock the flat and take a cab to King's Cross to catch the 10:30 Flying Scot, the fast train to Scotland.

When the Flying Scot limped into Edinburgh two hours late, it had encountered nearly every obstacle fate could throw in the way of a hard-working BritRail train, everything from a broken junction box to a cow on the tracks.

He missed the connection to Inverness by five minutes. He hoped the next one would be in time to catch Murdoch's flight to the Island, but knew it would be close.

The Inverness train had its own troubles and slid into the station well after all hope had died of making the chopper. He stood in the station, wondering what to do. At last he grabbed his bags and made his way downhill to the Tourist Information Office to find out about buses to Oban. He might find a boat to the Hebrides from there.

The Oban bus's meandering route and leisurely pace was relaxing. He felt the tensions of London ebb away under the peaceful influence of the rural Scottish landscape. Finally he fell asleep, head against the window.

Waking in Oban with a crick in his neck and cursing his suitcases that seemed to have grown much heavier since his enthusiastic departure, he went from the train station to the adjoining docks to inquire about getting to Eilean Dubh. Perhaps he could charter a fishing boat. Or steal a rowboat, he thought grimly.

He knew better than to ask at Caledonian-MacBrayne. Their thrice-a-week ferry schedule was as implacable as it had been for twenty years, and the next ferry would leave in two days, no sooner. He was beginning to think he should have stayed in Inverness to catch Murdoch tomorrow.

He got lucky at a small charter office. Everyone there had the Gaelic and they were friendly in the matter-of-fact way of seamen. Yes, they had a boat going out to the Hebrides, taking tourists to bird-watch on the Isle of Rhum. For a fee he could go along and they'd drop him at Eilean Dubh after the tourists were decanted. One of the crew knew the Ros Mór harbor, having worked on an Island fishing boat.

The only catch was that the tourists were coming by bus from Fort William and wouldn't arrive until six. That meant he'd get to Eilean Dubh no sooner than nine.

He didn't care. He'd sleep in his cottage tonight and he'd see Jean if he got home before the *cèilidh* ended. Suddenly light of heart, he left his bags at the charter office and wandered off into Oban. He had time to call in at the Scottish Nationalist Party office for a chat, browse the antique shops for a present for Jean, and have a prawn sandwich and a cup of tea before the boat left.

It was a small boat and the waves, though mild, were vigorous enough to discomfort some of the birdwatchers. The sea never bothered Darroch and he made himself inconspicuous in a corner of the deck, watched the stars come out, and thought in delicious anticipation of seeing Jean.

The birdwatchers disembarked hastily at Kinloch on Rhum, eager to get the boat's pitching motion out of their heads. The boat turned to Eilean Dubh and arrived at nine-thirty. He stored his bags at the harbormaster's office and headed for the Citizens Hall.

Walking in, he realized why he'd not heard the usual *cèilidh* noises from outside. The room was deathly quiet and everyone's attention was riveted on the stage. Even the children still awake were quiet. He slipped into the back and leaned against the wall.

Jean and Jamie were dueting on "The Foggy Dew," an Irish song about the 1916 Easter Rebellion. Jamie was not accompanying her; he was per-forming a fiddle routine of his own devising. Sometimes he harmonized, sometimes he improvised and sometimes he stood and listened as she sang. Their eyes were fixed on each other. There might have been no one else there, so complete was their concentration. Darroch, watching, felt a stab of what would have been jealousy had the man not been Jamie.

I ran through the glen, I rode again
And my heart with grief was sore
For I parted then with valiant men
Whom I never shall see more.
But to and fro in my dreams I go
And I kneel and pray for you.
For slavery fled, oh, glorious dead,
When you fell in the foggy dew.

The song ended. There was a long respectful silence before the Eilean Dubh murmur of approval started. It grew until Somhairle Mac-a-Phi stood up in the center of the hall and began to clap. Others joined him until the whole room, except for parents holding sleeping children, was on its feet, united in approval.

Darroch's heart was filled with pride in Jean. Watching the audience pay tribute to her and to Jamie, her glorious voice still in his ears, he wanted to kneel and kiss her hand. Or her sweet lips, where the music lingered. That seemed a very desirable option, and one he hoped to implement before much longer.

A small hand tugged at his sleeve. "*Gabh mo leisgeul, a Dharroch mhòr.*"

He glanced down at a child he recognized as one of Barabal Mac-a-Phi's.

"*Feasgar math, a Chailean bheag.* What can I do for you?"

"He says he wants you to come on stage."

"Who says?"

"Jamie. He says for you to join them on stage."

Automatically Darroch headed down the adjacent corridor and circled around to back stage, head spinning. How had Jamie known he was there? It was too dark in the hall for him to be seen. Once again his friend's pre-science sent chills down his spine. Every time he managed to convince himself there was no such thing as the Sight, Jamie did it again.

The three were playing a rollicking medley of jigs and reels. He stood listening, tapping his foot. When the tunes ended Jamie said, "We've a friend joining us, *a Shine*," and jerked his chin toward the back of the stage.

Jean swung around and saw Darroch. She was glad she'd turned away from the audience for she felt herself grow pink with pleasure as their eyes met and he smiled.

His name spread from row to row. "Look you now, Darroch's back."

Jean thought, oh, my, he's even better than I remembered, the shoulders broader, the smile sweeter, the eyes bluer. His hair was much longer, though. It curled on his collar in back, was tucked behind his ears *à la* Jamie on the sides and fell over his forehead into his eyes in front. Of course, for Heathcliff, she thought.

Darroch ran a quick eye over her from head to toe, then came forward and smiled down at her, wanting very much to kiss her and very conscious of the crowd watching them. How many other lovers, he wondered, had been reunited on a spotlit stage while two hundred people watched? It was like playing *Romeo and Juliet* at the Barbican.

Jamie said to Jean, "'*Fear a Bhàta?*'"

"No," she said. "The new one. Darroch'll know it."

Jamie began to play "*An Gille Dubh Ciar Dubh.*" Her eyes on Darroch, Jean sang:

My dark-haired lad, mo ghille dhubh,
No one can please me like thee, love, like thee.

The message in the song was confirmed in her eyes. He almost growled, so intense was the desire that filled him. Instead, he contented himself with putting his hand deliberately, teasingly, low in the small of her back where no one could see. It pleased him greatly that she trembled when he touched her. Thankful for the concealing folds of the coat he'd not thought to take off, he raised his voice in harmony.

They finished their set to the audience's satisfied murmur and retired to the dining room. Seated at a table, washing down a salmon sandwich with tea, Darroch remembered what had puzzled him. "Jamie, how did you know I was in the hall?"

"You said you were coming tonight."

"I did not. I planned on Saturday, just managed to get away today."

Jamie said vaguely, "I don't know then . . . a lucky guess. Or maybe I caught a glimpse of your coat."

And Darroch could get no more out of him. Jamie never talked about the Sight; even this brief exchange made him uncomfortable. He rose and wandered off to the food tables and stood contemplating the desserts.

Darroch asked Jean, "How many times did you and Jamie rehearse 'The Foggy Dew?'"

She smiled. "Twice."

"What? Only twice?"

"Tonight was the third time we've done it and each time was different. When we rehearsed the other day he said we could practice more if I wanted but he was comfortable. He said we'd be fine."

Darroch shook his head in disbelief. "It was amazing, one of the best pieces I've heard either of you do."

She shrugged. "It's all Bonnie Prince Jamie. I just sing."

Darroch was not so sure of that but he understood how she felt about Jamie.

Màiri and Jean realized simultaneously how tired Darroch was. His speech and reactions were slowing down. Màiri said, "When did you leave London, *mo charaid*?"

He had to concentrate to remember. "Nine-thirty, I think."

She clicked her tongue. "And on the trot nearly all that time. Why don't you break your journey in Inverness?"

"With Eilean Dubh so close, would you stay the night in Inverness?"

She nodded, understanding. "But we should get you home, *m'eudail*. It's not an endurance contest."

"I'm ready to go," said Jean.

Jamie materialized behind her. "And me."

They collected Darroch's bags and Jamie turned the red Austin up the hill. Squashed in the back seat with guitar, suitcases and Jean, Darroch captured her hand. "It's almost worth leaving to have the joy of coming home again," he said into the dark.

He carried the guitar into the cottage for her and said hopefully, "Will I see you tomorrow? Can we have music in the afternoon and fried chicken for supper?"

Jean shook her head. "There's a big Co-Op meeting tomorrow, Darroch, didn't you know?"

He snapped his fingers. "I'd forgotten."

"It's at the Hotel, all day, two meals provided. One of Sheila's workers has a houseful of children with measles and another has a bad cold. I said I'd help."

"You? What are you going to do?"

"Anything Sheilah tells me to. Peel potatoes, wait tables, load dishwashers. I promised to come at nine."

"It's midnight. You'd better get to bed. I'll drive you there tomorrow."

"You will not. I'm quite used to walking it and you need a good long sleep. The meeting doesn't begin till ten-thirty. There's no reason for you to be there sooner."

They looked at each other. Jean said, "I've missed you so much."

He said, "I've missed kissing you. We were just getting the hang of it when I left. We've weeks of kisses to make up."

"That'll be fun," said Jean. She smiled.

Her smile was liquid gold, it was amber, it was sunshine, and he needed to taste that sunshine. He kissed her. When he raised his head to draw breath he saw she was still smiling.

All her resolutions about being cautious flew out of her head when his mouth touched hers. Her fingertips lifted the black hair and brushed the bare skin of his neck, sending little electric sparks down his spine. "Such long hair," she murmured.

"For Heathcliff. I shaved the beard but I didn't have time to go to a barber before I left London. I'll have it cut next week."

"I like it long."

"I won't have it cut next week."

She put her lips on his and offered, shyly, the tip of her tongue. He seized it and pulled it into his mouth and felt, rather than heard, her sigh of pleasure.

A Dhia, he wanted her. Dizzying visions of sweeping her into his arms and carrying her to bed flooded over him. Sweet Jean. My Jean, he thought.

She wriggled against him and for one mad moment he thought she was going to yield herself then and there. But she was leaning back, breaking the contact.

"They're waiting," she murmured.

"Who?"

"Jamie and Màiri . . . in the car." Her arms were still locked around his neck and her mouth was inches from his.

"Oh . . . yes."

Jean had never fancied herself a seductress but she felt like Cleopatra and Circe combined when he looked at her in that dazed way, his eyes dark and fathoms deep.

"Thank you for the lesson," she said softly.

"Lesson?"

"In kissing. It was wonderful."

"So endeth the lesson," he said, brushing his lips against hers. They smiled at each other dreamily. "I'll see you tomorrow, *mo Shine.*"

She said, "*Mar sin leat, agus dean deagh chadal.*" Bye for now, sleep well.

Gaelic on her tongue was so sweet he wanted to kiss the words on her lips as she spoke them. Best to go now, while he still could. "*Feasgar math, m'aingeal,*" he whispered and left.

Jean sighed happily. Darroch is home, she thought. All's well.

Twenty-five

*Over very low heat, dissolve two pounds of sugar
combined with one cup of rum. Melt over a double boiler
two pounds of bitter chocolate. When the chocolate is melted
stir in one and one-quarter cups of heavy cream . . .*

From Sheilah Morrison's recipe for chocolate mousse

*N*ext morning Jean walked to the Rose. Ian's Catrìona, Barabal Mac-a-Phi and several women Jean hadn't met arrived one by one and everyone was put to work.

Sheilah organized her kitchen like a general her army. It was all Jean could do not to snap to attention and shout "Yes, chef!" whenever she was given an order. It was fun to be part of the smoothly running machine and to understand some of the jokes, the ones they remembered to translate for her, that flew around the kitchen.

There was an all-too-brief pause between luncheon and supper. The workers gobbled lunch and drank numerous cups of tea, then pitched again into the fray. Supper was trays of stuffed quail to be baked, then put on plates with tiny new potatoes and buttered peas.

Tea and coffee made the rounds with chocolate mousse for dessert. Then fell at last in the kitchen a blessed silence, broken only by the hum of dishwashers running. The helpers left, taking paychecks and leftovers for their families' evening meals. In the dining room voices droned on.

Jean sat down with Sheilah to enjoy her quail. "Sheilah, your food is wonderful. How do you manage it?"

"Shortcuts. I prepare some dishes ahead and freeze them, like the game pies, and I made the chocolate mousse last night and put it in the coldest part of the fridge. A proper London chef would have fits because each dish isn't made to order but a London chef wouldn't have eighty covers all at one time." She paused, then said, "I want to pay you for helping today, Jean. I'd not have managed without you."

"There's no question of that, Shee. I was glad to do it and I don't want money."

Sheilah insisted until finally Jean suggested, "Tell you what, make a donation to the Playschool roof fund." That was fine with Sheilah and Jean was pleased.

The kitchen doors opened and Darroch came in pushing a cart loaded with cups.

"Oh, damn, I forgot the coffee cups. I thought we were all done." Jean stood up but Sheilah shook her head. "No, there's not a dishwasher free yet. Thank you, Darroch. Coffee for you, *mo charaid*?"

Even Sheilah the Londoner had picked up the customary Island salutation among good friends. Darroch said, "Sit you, Sheilah, I can pour coffee. Ladies, may I warm your cups? Sheilah, *m'eudail*, might there be another chocolate mousse?"

She smiled. "Top shelf of the left hand fridge, Darroch. I saved one for you."

Jean thought, amused, that he had every woman on the Island wrapped around his little finger and why not? There was no question that he'd ever abuse a trust or be unkind. If he was adored Island-wide he deserved it. She thought of his kisses and realized she would not be the exception to the rule.

"Useful meeting, Darroch?" asked Sheilah.

He settled his long frame in a chair, chocolate mousse in hand. "Aye, it's fine to get everyone together to exchange ideas. Tearlach Ross came up with a suggestion about transport that should save the Co-Op money. That's what comes out of meetings. But they're exhausting. No doubt you both have noticed that." He grinned at them.

When the dishwashers stopped there was a sudden noticeable silence. They sprang to their feet to start loading and unloading. Darroch began to hum as he worked, then to sing. Jean sang along on the songs she either knew or could pick up. Even Sheilah joined in on the "ho-ro, ho-ri" parts.

Gordon, pushing through the doors with another cart, said, "Well, I was coming to help with the washing up and here you're having a *cèilidh*. Shall I get the accordion?"

"Only if you can play and load dishwashers at the same time," Sheilah said.

When they were finished Sheilah sighed, "How wonderful, tomorrow's

Sunday. I think the Wee Frees have the right idea about Sunday. I love an excuse not to work."

"Never let Minister Donald hear you say that about the Sabbath," Darroch cautioned, "but I know how you feel. There's wisdom in the old ways. Folk need a day of rest."

After the work was done and the sunset admired, Darroch and Jean walked to her cottage. "*Tha mi duilich, mo fhlùr*, I should have brought the Bentley so I could drive you home. It was such a glorious morning I had to walk to enjoy it and never a thought about your poor tired feet after all that work."

She'd forgotten her poor tired feet in the sheer joy of tramping along with him, their hands clasped together. "You can't see the sky this well from a car," she said, "even one as nice as the Bentley. Look at the color in those clouds! This place is heaven," she said with such conviction that Darroch was touched. She took a joy in the Island he'd seen only in born *Eilean Dubhannaich* and a few incomers like Sheilah and Jamie. He tucked her hand through his arm and they labored up the steep part of the hill.

He hadn't meant to come in but was lured by the cottage's welcoming warmth. "You've done new curtains! And something else is new, what is it?"

"The curtains are off the peg, isn't that what you say here for ready-made? The sofa pillows are new; they're from the Seniors' Craft Fair. The covers are handwoven. Mrs. MacShennach *as óige*, Barabal's grandmother, crocheted those gorgeous doilies. She's nearly ninety-five, Darroch, did you know? Nobody crochets any more and I've forgotten how, but she said she'd teach me. I'm going round to her at the Seniors' Residence Tuesday.

"The spice shelf's from the Fair, and the coat rack. Jamie put that up for me. That's all that's new. I didn't want to clutter up the place." She paused for breath.

Settling in, he thought, pleased. "Very cozy. I hope you are enjoying it."

"Oh, yes." Jean said, "Will you stay a while? Perhaps have a whisky?"

"As nice an invitation as I could ever receive, given that the inviter is dead on her feet. I could stay, *mo Shìne*, and we could plan on talking for hours, for I've lots to say and I want to hear every detail of what you've been up to. But I think you'd be asleep in my arms in five minutes. Not that that wouldn't be pleasant, mind you."

The idea of being in his arms awake or asleep was vastly appealing to Jean, but her feet had begun to ache in earnest. He noticed she was sagging and steeled himself not to subject her to his passionate embraces tonight. "I'll come over tomorrow after kirk and cook you breakfast; would you like that? We can have a lovely day together catching up." Then he remembered something. "Damn, tomorrow's the annual joint kirk service up in Airgead and luncheon afterwards. I won't get back before supper."

"What would you like for supper? I've some terrific fish and chicken too."

"Thoughts of your fried chicken will sustain me through the afternoon."

"Okay, the bird it is." She stared up into his eyes, willing him to kiss her. He obliged with his customary salute to each cheek, intending to stop there but she turned her head so their mouths met. "I dreamed of you while you were away," she whispered against his lips.

"Me too," he said. "In one dream we four were performing in the Albert Hall."

She giggled. "Was the Queen there?"

"The only queen I dream about is you." Right now, good intentions winging away like migrating geese, he was dreaming of kissing some part of her currently covered with clothing, like a shoulder, but he couldn't work out how to do it without alarming her. Her throat, however, was quite available. His mouth left hers and moved slowly downwards. Jean shuddered and leaned back in his arms, boneless with pleasure and fatigue.

Darroch was ridiculously pleased with the effect he was having and couldn't keep himself from wanting more. "Perhaps just one button," he murmured, putting his hand to her collar.

"Mmm. Maybe even two," she said.

With her collar open he could put his mouth in the hollow of her throat and feel her pulse beating strong and hot under his lips, breathe in the fragrance of her skin. He nuzzled and sighed.

Jean sighed. She didn't care if she was a gusher, she had to say it. "You're so sweet. You're the nicest man I've ever met."

No, I'm not, Darroch thought furiously. I'm a right bastard, a vile seducer and I want to get you into bed and do wicked things to your luscious body. He realized he'd reached the point of no return and made a supreme effort to regain control. "No more of that for now," he said hoarsely. "You need to get off your feet." And onto your back and into my arms, added his treacherous mind. As severe with himself as Minister Donald confronting a sinner, he thought, you lustful *diabhol*, can you not leave the poor lassie in peace the night?

Jean's eyes were wide with surrender. "I love it when you kiss me, I never want you to stop," she whispered.

"I would like to kiss you all night," he said, adding under his breath, "and all over."

He was not sure she heard the last but something flickered in her eyes and she realized suddenly that she was holding the key cards in tonight's hand. He wanted her and would take her with the slightest encouragement. If she pressed herself closer, moved her hips against him, wrapped her leg around his and stroked his calf with her toes, they would be goners.

She wondered dizzily if he would pick her up and carry her to bed. She was no lightweight, but his arms and shoulders were hard with muscle and her bedroom was only a few steps away. Would he undress her completely or just pull off the relevant bits?

Was she wearing something sexy from her last Victoria's Secret order, or her white old lady panties?

He was staring at her with a peculiar intensity and she closed her eyes so that he couldn't read what was going on in her mind. He misinterpreted the action and was suffused with shame. For God's sake, leave her alone, she's exhausted, he thought. "*Oidhche mhath, mo nighean ruadh,*" he said firmly.

Jean, on the point of swooning into his arms, sighed with disappointment. "*Oidhche mhath, mo ghille dhubh.*"

He trembled, the words of the song echoing in his mind. *My black-haired lad, no one can please me like thee, love, like thee.* "Tomorrow, Jean. Remember where we left off," he muttered and stumbled out the door, nearly demented with desire and guilt.

Jean stared after him, realizing suddenly the extent of her involvement with this man. She'd said things to him she'd not said to her husband in twenty years of marriage and she'd opened her mouth to him as trustingly as a baby bird to its mother. She'd imagined herself in bed with him; she'd been on the point of yielding.

Things were moving along rapidly and she had a pretty good idea of where they were heading and she was quite sure she would enjoy both journey and destination.

And it was getting harder and harder to remember that she was still married.

Twenty-six

Owing to the favorable aspect of its mountains, Eilean Dubh enjoys
temperate weather the year around. Occasionally in winter, however, the
Island is subject to sudden and unpredictable storms, occurring on average
once every five years. When storm clouds stall over the northwestern
mountain range, heavy sleet changing into dense snow
combined with abrupt temperature decline can result in
blizzards of monumental proportions . . .

Robertson's Relics

The wind had changed directions twice by the time Jean stepped outside next morning with a basket of wet clothes. Clothespins in mouth, she looked searchingly at the sky. In Wisconsin that dull gray cast would mean a snowstorm, probably a big one with lots of wind and rapidly falling temperatures. She shivered as a breeze licked at her shoulders. Definitely, the temperature was headed down.

Inside, she switched on the radio to the BBC noontime news but the weather report was, as usual, inconclusive: "In Scotland, sunny intervals followed by cloud cover and a chance of snow." She turned the radio off, longing for an American station with its minutely detailed forecasts. "Over Brewer Avenue, snow is expected, but in downtown Milwaukee rain will turn to sleet . . . "

Jean's usual response to bad weather was cooking. The coldest temperatures in Milwaukee had inspired some of her best efforts: pork chops with macaroni and cheese, baked ham with sweet potato pie for dessert, meat loaf and garlic mashed potatoes. Today she had chicken to fry and potatoes au gratin to bake but she wasn't going to start supper until Darroch arrived.

A fridge search produced ingredients for vegetable soup and the oatmeal box yielded a bread recipe. With soup simmering, bread rising and the oven pre-heating, the cottage was warm and cozy and she forgot the threatening skies outside. It surprised her, then, when a gust of wind caught a shutter and slammed it vigorously against the cottage. After she secured it she examined the sky again: definitely snow was coming. She stripped the clothes from the line as rain began, not the usual gentle insistent Island rain but a harsh stinging shower that quickly changed to sleet.

The wind changed direction twice as she wrestled clothes into the basket. It ended up blowing from the north, parallel to the ground, wrestling her for control of the door as she struggled to get herself and laundry inside. Through the window she saw the snow begin, giant flakes dancing wildly on the wind.

She glanced at the clock, worried. Surely Darroch would have recognized the severity of the storm and stayed in Airgead. She tried the phone but heard an irritating buzz instead of a dial tone.

A very early night was beginning to fall. The bright morning sun had long since given up and gone to hide behind clouds.

It was getting cold inside. She built up the fire and opened the oven door to let out the residual heat, then put supper on a tray and went to sit by the fire with a book.

The wind rose suddenly to a furious shriek and sleet rattled on the window glass. Alarmed, Jean got up and went to the kitchen window to discover that a ferocious storm was engulfing the Island. I hope Darroch's safe inside, she thought anxiously. Worry made her pick up the phone again and she tried first Darroch's number, then Màiri's, but the phone only buzzed.

She wouldn't get much sleep tonight; she could never sleep during a storm. She wrapped herself in blankets on the sofa and decided to try television. The choices offered included a travelogue about Bulgaria, an acrimonious debate between two members of Parliament and an American hospital drama.

She chose the drama. It was mildly engaging and the actors' American accents brought a faint whiff of homesickness. She turned off the television when the picture began to break up into wavy lines and ghostly images.

The wind, slipping its prying fingers around the windows, had created so much noise during the evening that she'd gotten used to it. But now she became conscious of a new sound, a steady, repeated thudding. She stood still and listened. It was coming from the front door. Was it possible someone was out in this storm and knocking at her door?

Bits and pieces of Darroch's Island folklore about fierce boggles that roamed by night rose all unwanted in her mind.

The hair on the back of her neck prickled.

It was a long drive up the Island to Airgead and it seemed endless to Darroch when he passed Jean's cottage early that morning. He thought the weather was gearing up for a dramatic change. The sky was an eerie shade of blue with large fat clouds that groaned with snow. Perhaps an early winter was upon them.

Why was he going to Airgead? What he really wanted was to join Jean in her cottage for a delightful day of cooking, talking and making music. Making love. Not consummating their relationship; despite his lust he realized in his rational moments that she was still married. But surely there was no harm in cuddling, if he kept his head.

Perhaps she could be cozened into sitting on his lap and letting him kiss her till they were both silly with pleasure. She made wonderful little sounds when he kissed her; perhaps she would expand her repertoire if his hands became more adventurous.

He glanced up from the road and realized he was in Airgead, but his mind and a considerable portion of his anatomy were in a thatched cottage just above Ros Mór.

As he'd planned, he arrived just in time for the beginning of the service at Airgead Kirk. This was a device he'd worked out in self-defense. If he were nearly late, no importunate minister could grab him and insist he sit in the front pew with the dignitaries. He had sat there the years he was on the Council, but he refused to sit there as a private citizen and he certainly would not sit there as part of that bloody laird business. He slipped into the back pew just before the service began.

The yearly joint service was always a trial of patience and this was particularly true when it was at Airgead. That kirk's Minister Tormod was extremely fond of his own voice and his own opinions and lavished both upon the hapless combined congregations. Those from the southern kirk were used to their Minister Donald's sparse, well-honed sermons and to his thinking as well, which meant he did not have to waste his time elaborating. He and his congregation knew each other well.

But Minister Tormod inevitably seized the opportunity to demonstrate to all those of his religious persuasion on the Island his—to his mind—considerable skills as a speaker and theologian. There was always the un-Christian hope that some might desert the southern kirk for his own. Moreover, he liked to throw in plenty of fire and brimstone, a device that Minister Donald scorned except when it was really necessary to stamp out serious wrong-doing.

Secluded in his back pew in the drafty old stone church Darroch relaxed and let the Ministerial thunder and lightning roll over his head. He found it easy to shut out Minister Tormod after the first sentences revealed the gentleman had nothing new to say.

Darroch's thoughts drifted to two nights ago and to Jamie and Jean, on stage. He replayed the entire performance in his mind, hearing their music as though it were taking place before him.

It was clear to Darroch that Jean had freed what he now recognized as Jamie's enormous talent. It was also clear that he and Màiri, in their single-minded dedication to Island folk music, had been a stifling influence. Someone like Jamie needed to be free to roam the entire world of music, incorporating whatever he chose into his own work.

Jean had made that possible. She'd liberated Jamie as the Island had liberated her.

Jean, in her cozy cottage. He conjured up the green eyes and the tangle of whisky-colored hair and suddenly wondered what he was doing in Airgead Kirk, listening to a man he did not like rave on about a religion he did not believe in.

The temptation was strong to get up and walk out. It was respect that kept him in his seat, respect for Minister Donald as a man and as a friend. He would be hurt if Darroch left, shamed in front of both congregations. Every Islander knew that Darroch refused to join the kirk because he did not accept its teachings but attended services because of his regard for Minister Donald. It gave the Minister prestige to have the Laird as a member, even unofficially, of his congregation.

Darroch sighed and settled down on the hard wooden pew, resolved to do his duty. Soon it would be time for the part of the service he did enjoy, the singing. Tòmas Mac-a-Phi was precenting today, lining out the psalms for the congregation. Darroch enjoyed the man's voice and singing helped him endure the morning.

When the service ended at last, Darroch contemplated a hasty getaway, searching his mind for an appropriate excuse. None had come to mind by the time Minister Donald appeared at his side.

"Ah, there you are, *a Dharroch*. I thought you might not have made it. I didn't see you when we were going in." The Minister knew perfectly well why Darroch always arrived just this side of late. "Come along, I've saved you a seat for lunch between Tormod and myself." He smiled slyly, hearing Darroch's barely repressed groan.

Darroch allowed himself to be ushered into the parish hall for luncheon. He was polite to Minister Tormod, charming to the women and girls serving and attentive to the rest of the diners at his table, including two political types from Airgead whose opinions he privately despised and publicly opposed. But the yearly ecumenical luncheon was not an occasion for wrangling and everyone was displaying company manners.

Father Ian MacDonald from Our Lady of the Island Catholic Church and Father Michael Eliot, a retired Englishman who was vicar of the Island's Anglican church (a very small congregation of incomers), were also at the luncheon. Darroch enjoyed both men and the discussion was brisk and lively.

With Jean's fried chicken in mind, he ate sparingly of the beef and creamed new potatoes and accepted a piece of blackberry pie only when it appeared that Mrs. Murdoch the Chopper would break into tears if he refused. But he waved away firmly the pitcher of cream with which she was armed.

Pushing back from the table when the interminable meal had ended, Darroch readied his excuses and his escape but was taken completely by surprise when Minister Donald rose and said, "Now, *mo chàiradean*, if you'll follow us into the meeting room, we have something of importance to discuss."

A meeting on Sunday? And an ecumenical one at that. Whatever next? "*A Mhinistear*," Darroch began, "I really can't stay . . . "

"Ah, but you must. We're discussing something you'll want to hear about." And the Minister took him firmly by the arm. Bemused, Darroch allowed himself to be led into the meeting.

"We are here," began Minister Tormod importantly, "to discuss ways we might raise money to replace the roof on our Gaelic Playschool." Minister Donald looked at Darroch and smiled his frosty smile.

Darroch knew his getaway was doomed. Resigned, he took a seat.

Two hours slipped away, during which a number of schemes were proposed and one, a grand fête involving everything from a jumble sale to a concert, was adopted. They had just come to the point where they had created a planning committee and were nominating useful members when Barabal Mac-a-Phi opened the door and put her head in. "Excuse me, Father."

Two heads swiveled toward her.

"Your wife called." One head swiveled back to the table and Father Eliot gave her his full attention. "She says the weather is appalling and she wants to know when you're leaving for home."

"What's wrong with the weather?" said Father Eliot apprehensively. His years on Eilean Dubh had not accustomed him to its dramatic weather shifts and he viewed any change as a threat. He hated driving on the narrow, twisting Island roads in winter.

Barabal clicked her tongue impatiently. "Have none of you looked outside?"

Darroch got up and walked to the window. It was small, barely big enough to let light into the old stone-walled room. He stared through the tiny panes and realized that what he had taken for the onset of twilight was instead the darkening effect of masses of whirling snow. He gazed at the storm, dismayed.

The meeting broke up immediately. Both Fathers disappeared to their cars and both southerners were pressed to stay the night in Airgead. "Now I'll not take no for an answer," said Minister Tormod heartily. "You'll not driving home in this, *a Dhòmhnall*. Or you, *a Dharroch*."

"*Gabh mo leisgeul,*" said Darroch and walked to the kirk's front door. Snow was billowing over the ground and a clatter on the roof signaled the presence of sleet mixed with the snow. He peered into the whirlwind and tried to evaluate driving conditions.

Both ministers appeared at his side. "Surely you'll not try to drive to Ros Mór."

"May I use a phone?" Darroch asked and was shown to Minister Tormod's study. He dialed Jean's number but heard only a furious buzzing, which on Eilean Dubh indicated a phone out of order. Silently he cursed Murdoch the Arranger's arrangements.

Clearly the phone had not been properly installed. Or . . . perhaps the wires were down, which would indicate that the storm was bad in the south. He tried Màiri's number with the same result.

He made up his mind quickly. Staying here meant sitting by the fire with both Ministers, listening to them wrangle about minute points of theology. He had to get home, he decided. He couldn't bear the idea of being trapped in Airgead for days. He had waited seven weeks to see Jean and the brief, tantalizing encounters of the last two days had whetted his appetite for more, much more. If the Island was going to be buttoned up by a blizzard he wanted to be snowed in with her, not Minister Donald.

He dug in his pocket for car keys, said a firm farewell to the protesting ministers and stepped into the storm.

Darroch was instantly aware he hadn't buttoned his coat or put on his gloves as the gale whipped around him. Jamming his hands deep into his pockets he pushed against the wind to the Bentley and wrestled the door open. The car started on the first try and he took that as a good sign. There was plenty of gas in the oversized tank and a winter survival kit in the back seat. He could make it, he thought confidently.

Airgead Kirk sat exposed on top of a hill. The wind and snow were fierce but he could see the borders of the road and thought that if it was like this on open ground it would surely be all right down below where the road was sheltered by the mountains.

What he had not reckoned on was a particularly vicious wind blowing up from the sea wherever the road dipped close to it.

Heading downhill, he realized that the sides of the road were vanishing under rippling waves of snow, the verges appearing just often enough to keep him centered. He slowed to a crawl, then realized that he would have to move faster if he was to make it home before the storm truly took over. Cautiously he increased his speed.

The snow blew across the road in snake-like waves, polishing it to a sheer satiny shine and covering and uncovering patches of glare ice. He steered carefully, not daring to swerve around them.

The big car hugged the curves of the road and its undercarriage was high enough to sail over the snowdrifts forming in random patterns. Landmarks were increasingly obscured by blowing snow. He cursed under his breath, realizing that he should have noted the mileage before he left so he could tell how close he was to home. Cottages appeared and disappeared on his right but one looked just like another. Never before had it struck him so clearly how similar all Island architecture was.

At last he rounded a corner and passed a road that he was certain led to *Cladh a' Chnuic*. He cheered up and took first one hand, then the other, off the steering wheel to shake out the cramps. If that was Cemetery Hill he was only a mile from home.

Going down the slope from the crossroad the Bentley hit a stretch of road completely covered with ice and swept free of cover by the wind. Startled by the size of the icy patch and alarmed at his speed he braked too hard. The car fishtailed. He fought the steering wheel that had suddenly developed a mind of its own.

Dreamlike, the big car slid slowly sideways across the road. For one terrifying moment Darroch faced the possibility that he might be at the place where there was no guardrail and the road swerved close to the sea and the rock-strewn shore a long, long way below. We should have put up a fence years ago, he thought ruefully as the car turned itself around and drifted backwards, inexorably closer to the edge.

He couldn't jump out, he'd go into the sea. He accelerated, then hit the brakes in one last desperate attempt to influence the car's movement. It spun again, rapidly this time, flew across to the other side of the road and landed hard in the ditch.

Despite his seat belt he was flung against the door and the breath knocked out of him. He lay still, gasping. It dawned on him slowly that he had survived round one but he still had a long way to go.

After a bit he was able to breathe normally and plan his next moves. Reason dictated he stay with the car and wait for rescue that could not come any sooner than tomorrow. But it was getting bitterly cold inside and the wind was forcing its way through every tiny crack. I can walk it, he thought confidently. It's not far.

He pulled the winter kit from the back seat. There was a hat, scarves, two pairs of gloves and, down in the bottom, boots with socks stuffed inside. He put it all on, dressing awkwardly in the confined space, realizing his shoulder had taken a hard hit when the car had gone into the ditch. It hurt and the muscles were growing stiff. He flexed the shoulder gingerly and was reassured that nothing was broken.

At last he felt ready. He wrapped the scarf around his mouth and nose and crawled up the seat of the tipped Bentley. He put his weight against the door to force it open. A gust of wind banged the door off his sore shoulder and he swore with feeling but gathered his strength and hoisted himself up and out.

The first thing he noticed was that the snow by the car was much deeper than he'd realized. It overflowed into his boots as his feet hit the ground. Grateful for the extra pair of socks, he stood up and tried to make sense of his surroundings.

He was desperately afraid he would not know which direction to walk and realized that if he chose the wrong way he might walk directly off the cliff into the sea. Or if he managed to stay on the road and ended up walking north there'd be no cottages for three miles. I can't make it that far, he thought. Best be right the first time.

A brief let-up in snow and wind, as though the storm was catching its breath, let him orient himself by locating the sound of the sea. Right, he thought, turning to what he was sure was south, here we go.

A hundred yards down the road that kept appearing and disappearing in the snow, he began to have second thoughts. The wind pierced his clothing like arrows a target and exposed areas of flesh burned as sleet pelted them. He pushed on a little farther and then stopped as the road vanished.

It occurred to him to go back to the car and he stood irresolute as the shrieking gale tried to blow him into a snow bank.

He turned and saw that the Bentley had disappeared. Before him was a whiteout and, he realized grimly, the unprotected edge of the cliff with its 200-foot drop. He shuddered. He'd take his chances straight ahead. At least the road ahead curved away from the sea and headed inland.

He plodded on. The wind was suddenly determined to take his hat and he had to stop to wrap a scarf around it. Wind scoured his eyes and tears ran into the scarf around his face and froze there in a rim of ice. His shoulder, hunched up against the cold, ached with a persistent dull pain.

He'd lost all sense of time. He had no idea how long he'd been dragging himself forward, one heavy lift of a snow-filled boot after another. Where the hell am I, he thought. It shouldn't take this long to get to our turnoff.

He stopped in his tracks and concentrated, using all his senses. At last a faint whiff of peat smoke came to his nose. Encouraged, he slogged forward. Where there was smoke there was life.

Some time later he realized he had missed the turnoff. He felt the beginning of panic. I am going to die, he thought, shivering with fear. Damn it, I'm not giving up, he told himself. I'd rather die walking than in a snow bank.

He turned and stared in all directions, straining his eyes against the absolute whiteness. The wind stopped abruptly and a shape appeared to his left, a dark peaked roof atop a pale mound.

Jean's cottage. He hurled himself in that direction, willing the break in the storm to last. By some miracle the wind had swept the snow off the macadam just at the point where the road turned downhill. The slope was dramatic and obvious even in the white waste of snow. He staggered down the icy hill and slid heavily against the wall of the cottage's garden. Grabbing at the stones he pulled himself upright with a tremendous effort and groped along the wall, seeking the gate.

He found it, frozen shut and heaped with snow. Frantic now, he bent and shoveled the snow away with his numb hands. When he was at last able to shove the gate open and thrust himself through he felt a new surge of energy. He realized it would be his last. He was exhausted beyond belief.

Forcing one foot in front of the other, he inched his way up the path to the cottage door. His slippery gloves could not turn the knob. With his fading strength he pounded furiously. Please, please, he thought. Please, Jean, open the door.

And the door opened. A vision of heaven itself seared itself across his eyes and he had to shut them from the pain of the light and the flickering fire. An improbable smell of freshly-baked bread made his head spin. He heard a cry of fright, a gasp of "Darroch!" and felt her hands pulling frantically at his coat sleeves. Faint with relief, he staggered in.

Twenty-seven

There are boggles that live on the land, there are boggles that live in the trees, there are boggles that live in the burns. But the most fearsome of all are the snow boggles that come out to play when nights are bitter cold, when the wind howls and snow falls without ceasing. They're the ones that dance in front of travelers in dreadful storms, luring them from the path and into the deepest drifts, where they'll not be found until spring.

Eilean Dubh fairy tale, translated by Darroch Mac an Rìgh

*D*efinitely there was a knocking at her door. She could not ignore it, not in this weather. Gathering her courage she went to the door, braced it with her shoulder against the expected onslaught of wind, and opened it.

A terrifying figure loomed on the doorstep. It was well over six feet tall, covered with snow, encrusted with ice. Jean screamed and took a step back into the cottage.

Then something . . . perhaps a gleam of blue eyes above the frozen scarf . . . struck her. "Darroch!"

She seized his arm and pulled him inside. He staggered and nearly fell but caught himself with a hand against the wall. Jean wrestled the door from the wind's grasp and bolted it shut. Then she turned to him. "What on earth . . . ?"

"Car . . . slid off the road. Down by the cemetery . . . I walked . . . "

"In this storm? Oh, Darroch. Here, let me help."

She eased off his gloves, covering his hands with hers for a moment to warm them. She unwrapped the scarf from around his face. He winced as a piece of snow detached itself and slithered inside the neck of his sweater.

She was briefly back in Milwaukee, helping a child who'd missed a school bus and stood too long outside waiting. "We'll have you dry and warm in a minute." She bundled off his coat and piled his outer garments by the door, snow melting and puddling around them. "Come to the fire."

"Boots," he stammered and tried to bend down to remove them. "Your floor . . . "

"Never mind the floor. Come to the fire and get warmed up."

Her mind was scrolling rapidly through the winter first aid class she'd taken when the children were young. Hypothermia can kill, warm the victim quickly. She shuddered with terror and wrapped a blanket about his shoulders and tucked another across his lap when he collapsed on the sofa.

Remember that the body may be too cold to generate any heat and warm it from the outside in. She turned to the fire and added peats, setting them on the pile carefully so that she would not smother the temperamental flame. Oh for a load of Wisconsin firewood, she thought in exasperation, a good steady blaze, not just a smolder. But at last it flared up and settled to an intense burn.

She dashed to the kitchen and made tea. She turned on the fire under her soup and briefly considered whisky but remembered that alcohol was bad for hypothermia.

Hurrying back to Darroch, she asked, "Can you talk?" He shook his head. She knelt to his boots. The shoestrings were thawing and she was able to get first one, then the other untied.

"So cold," he mumbled and lay back, eyes closed. A violent spasm of shivering shook him.

"Lift your foot, lovie." She eased his boots off. His socks were soaked. She stripped each foot, looking carefully for signs of frostbite, but the toes were reassuringly pink and he winced as her fingers touched him. Feeling, she thought. Good.

She darted up again and seized a handful of kitchen towels. She patted his feet dry and wrapped each in a towel. The tea was ready. She poured a large mugful and added milk and sugar. She put the mug in one of his hands and wrapped the other hand over it. "This will warm you," she said. His lethargy frightened her.

At last he found the energy to lift the mug and drink. Rivulets of water were running down his face from the melting snow in his hair. She took a towel and blotted his hair, then pulled the blankets up around his head.

He had nearly finished the tea, she saw, pleased. "Are you warmer now?"

"Still cold . . . " He shivered again and his teeth chattered.

"Oh, lovie, you're freezing." She wanted to pull him close and warm him with her body but she knew the blankets would do a better job. The only part of him still exposed was his face. "Poor baby," she murmured tenderly and put her arms around his neck and her lips against his cold cheek.

She knew what could have happened to him. Not a Wisconsin winter passed that the newspapers didn't carry a story of someone trapped in a storm, dying in a snowbank steps from shelter. He might have died just outside her door. The thought was terrifying.

"Your nose is so cold," she whispered.

"My mouth is cold, too," he said, finally thawed enough to speak.

"Oh, lovie." She kissed him, caressing the inside of his lips with her tongue. I taught her to kiss like that, he realized, and trembled with desire. A hot current flooded through him down to his prickly thawing toes and something stirred and hardened in his nether regions. *Miorbhuileach*, he thought, that bit's not frozen and fallen off.

"You're still shivering." She pulled back and looked at him worriedly.

"Not from cold. From pleasure. I'm . . . pleasured . . . by you."

She liked the word. "Shall I pleasure you some more?"

"Aye, please." He wanted desperately to throw his arms around her but he was wrapped in blankets like a mummy. He could only lie, helpless with delight, while she kissed him and stroked his cheek.

The odor of boiling soup brought Jean back to her senses. Fool, she thought, he doesn't need cuddling, he needs hot food. She scrambled up and scurried to the kitchen.

Left alone, glowing with an internal fire, Darroch began trying with fierce determination to extract himself from the cocoon of blankets. When she came back he intended to grab her, pull her onto his lap and fill his cold hands with her warm body.

But when she returned she put a tray with steaming soup and bread dripping with butter onto his lap and a spoon in his hand. His attention was immediately diverted and he began to eat hungrily. The hot food was like a furnace in his belly.

At last he put the tray aside and sighed deeply. "Oh, Jean, that was a near thing. If you hadn't heard me knock I would have curled up on your doorstep and died."

"Darroch, what happened?"

"It was my own stupid fault," he said in disgust. "The storm hit Airgead and I thought I could beat it home." He shook his head ruefully. "Lived all my life on this Island and still think I can outrun the *Bodach Sneachda* . . .

the Snowman. We get a storm like this every few years but this is the worst I've seen in some time.

"There was a meeting after lunch and none of us noticed bad weather coming on until Barabal told us. The Ministers wanted me to stay but I was desperate to get home." He pushed the blankets off a little more. "The storm hit me full force just before the cemetery and the Bentley slid into a ditch below the turnoff.

"When I realized I wasn't going any further in the car I decided to get out and walk. I thought I was nearly at our lane and didn't realize my mistake until I'd gotten away from the car. The storm closed in behind me and I knew there was no shelter until your cottage, so I kept going."

He smiled at her. "And here I am."

"Lovie, how awful."

"I was terrified," he admitted frankly. "I've not been in anything like that since I was twelve and missed the school bus one afternoon. The *Bodach Sneachda* can come down in minutes. I made it to the bus shelter and stayed there until my father came looking for me in our old truck." He shuddered. "I had nightmares about it for years."

He held out his tray. "Do you always have hot soup in a blizzard? I must stop here more often. May I have another serving? It's delicious."

"Of course." When she returned she knelt and got the fire blazing again.

"What did you think, to hear a knock on the door on a night like this?" Darroch said. He was beginning to feel drowsy and it was very comfortable being here with her. The firelight shone around her whisky-colored hair like a halo.

Jean curled up on the sofa next to him, leaning her head on her arm. "I thought it was a . . . what do you call it . . . a boggle."

"A snow boggle. Fearsome creature. What a brave lass, to open the door to it." Blue eyes communed with green for a long moment. Curiously, though the wind howled through every tiny chink and the cottage was chilly around them, neither felt cold.

He said, "Jean, *m'aingeal*, I am afraid I must ask you if I may stay the night."

"Darroch! Of course you're going to stay! You can't go back into the storm."

"I had hoped not to. I'll try not to be any more trouble."

"Nonsense," she said, clearing away his tray. "I'm glad of the company."

She was wondering what to do. She wanted to tuck him up in her bed for she thought he must be dreadfully tired and still chilled. "Darroch," she said, "Please let me put you to bed."

"Take your bed? Certainly not, *mo Shine*. Where would you sleep?"

"I'll be fine here on the sofa."

"No, you won't. Jean, listen. I know these storms. When the snow stops the temperature will drop abruptly and it'll get very cold in here. The fire won't help even if you stoke it every hour." He said firmly, "It's too cold to sleep alone. We'll sleep together in your bed to keep warm."

"Darroch, I don't think . . . " she stopped, not knowing what to say.

"We'll be perfectly proper, don't worry. Go on now, get ready for bed."

He bent stiffly to build up the fire. She put his shoes and socks by the fireplace to dry and spread his coat across the sofa. She rounded up every blanket and pillow she had and put them on the bed, then brushed her teeth.

He came into the bedroom. "Which side do you prefer?" he said.

"Umm . . . the left," she said, embarrassed.

He sat on the edge of the bed. When he started to remove his sweater he flinched. "Jean, could you help me take this off? My shoulder's stiffening up. It smashed against the door when I went into the ditch." There were tears of pain in his eyes by the time the sweater was off.

"Let me look at you." She sat down by him and carefully slipped her hands under his shirt and moved them up to his shoulders. "I don't think anything's broken or dislocated or you'd have passed out from pain. But you're probably very bruised.

"I could massage your shoulder but I don't like to do that till I see the bruises in daylight." She moved her hands in gentle circles over his back. "I'm good at massage; I got a certificate in evening school. I thought it might help my son Rod relax after an asthma attack. I'll give you a massage tomorrow."

"I'll look forward to it," he said and trembled, anticipating her fingers on his skin.

"Get under the covers. Do you need anything?"

He shook his head, lifted his long legs into bed and settled himself on the pillow.

Jean could not bring herself to undress and put on a nightgown. She decided to keep on her turtleneck and slip and take off her skirt. She felt very sheepish climbing into bed. She hadn't slept next to a man in months.

Immediately he moved closer. With an effort he settled himself on his good side and draped his arm over her. He was so tall he could rest his chin on top of her hair, curl around her spoon-fashion and settle his knees under hers as though she was sitting on his lap. *In bed with Jean at last and all I can do is sleep,* was his last conscious thought.

Jean snuggled closer and noted with surprise that proximity was having the expected effect on him, exhausted as he was. Evidence of his arousal pressed against her backside. She wriggled experimentally and confirmed her suspicion. She wriggled again and heard a low growl from deep in his throat. She giggled softly. *Let sleeping lions lie,* she thought, and fell asleep in his embrace.

Jean woke once in the middle of the night. It was eerily quiet. She'd experienced this hush in Milwaukee after storms had blown themselves out but there sounds were always to be heard: a car spinning its wheels, plows on the street, even barking dogs. Here it was so quiet she could hear Darroch's soft breathing.

She was disoriented at first, to find someone in bed so close, an arm still around her. Russ slept sprawled out, covers kicked off, taking up two-thirds of the bed.

As Darroch had predicted, the room had become icy cold. She stuck her nose from under the covers, breathed mistily into the absolute darkness and hastily retreated, seeking his reassuring warmth. She fell asleep again, thoughts of remaking the fire abandoned.

Twenty-eight

To lie by the fire on a cold winter's day
With you beside me. Ah, that were rare delight . . .

Songs of Love, Lady Grizel Mac an Rìgh (176?–1826),
translated by Isabel Ross

Jean woke up the next morning to a freezing room brazenly illuminated by sun glaring off snow and realized she'd forgotten to close the curtains last night. After a moment she remembered why she was in bed still dressed and that she was not alone in that bed. Cautiously she eyed the man lying beside her.

He was still asleep. The black hair was hopelessly rumpled and the color of his face matched the white pillowcase. There were lines of pain around his mouth and he was curled in an awkward position, evidence that his shoulder had hurt him during the night.

Jean gathered her courage and slipped out of bed into the icy room. She found her skirt and wool socks and put them on and grabbed her warmest sweater from a drawer. She washed up, then crept, shoes in hand, into the desperately cold sitting room.

She went from window to window, astonished at the storm's effect. Snow covered everything in thick billows sculpted into abstract shapes by the wind. Curiously, the path leading up to her door had been swept clean by the same wind nearly down to the flagstones. Beyond it she could see Darroch's drifted footprints from last night.

She built a fire. Then she made a pot of tea and a plate of toast and carried it into the bedroom. She sat down on the bed and found he was awake, watching her.

"Am I dead and in heaven?" he said. Jean laughed. "Ah, the laughter of an angel. I must be quite, quite dead. Minister Donald was wrong about all this, you know. I wish I could tell him."

"You'll live to tell him a great deal more than that. Cup of tea?"

"Heavenly, *m'aingeal*." Awkwardly, he levered himself up to a sitting position.

"Is your shoulder bad?"

"Aye." She wedged pillows behind his back until he was comfortable, then poured tea. They drank quietly for several moments, watching each other over their teacups.

Jean said, when the toast was gone, "Take off your shirt."

He raised his eyebrows and she smiled. "We'll be perfectly proper, don't worry."

She helped him take off his shirt and turn to lie flat on his belly. She was apprehensive about what she might see when she examined his back, but there was little bruising. The soreness was from when he'd been flung against the car door.

"Tell me if anything I'm doing hurts too much," she said, and put her hands on him, pressing harder each time, kneading deeply. He groaned in pain.

She focused her attention on finding the knots of tension and working them out, closing her eyes so that she could concentrate on what her hands told her. Gradually she felt him relax and heard his groans turn into sighs. Her hands became gentler, the rhythm of their movements slowing. She allowed herself to enjoy touching his firm muscles, warm beneath her fingertips.

She bent down to look at him. His eyes were closed; he was perfectly relaxed. She thought he'd fallen asleep. She could not resist a kiss on the injured shoulder.

"A kiss to make it well?" he murmured and Jean laughed, flustered at being caught. She said, "If you feel like getting up I think a hot shower would help you a lot."

She carried out the tray and returned with a towel and his socks and shoes, then turned her attention to fixing breakfast.

She assembled oatmeal, toast, marmalade, butter from Dùghall the Dairy and a fresh pot of tea. Dùghall had insisted she take a bottle of cream "for your porridge, Mrs. Abbott." Now she had to admit he'd been right. She thought, does he have the Sight too?

The phone rang. Startled, she picked it up.

Màiri's voice said, "Jean, I'm dreadfully worried about Darroch. His phone rings and rings, I'm sure he's not there. I can't reach anyone in Airgead; the lines just buzz. Where could he be?"

Jean said quietly, "He's here, Màiri."

"Here? I mean, there?" Her voice rose to a squeak.

"He spent the night here."

The silence at the other end of the phone was profound. Finally Màiri cleared her throat and said awkwardly, "Well, *miorbhuileach*. He's all right then."

"He was caught in the blizzard, Màiri. His car went off the road and he walked from Cemetery Hill to my cottage. Heaven only knows how long he was out in the storm. He had barely enough strength left to pound on my door."

"*A Dhia*," Màiri said. "Are you sure he's all right?"

"Very tired, stiff and sore, but able to get up."

"We'll come after Jamie's plowed us out. Look after him, Jean," and she rang off.

Oh, I will, said Jean to herself, staring at the phone thoughtfully.

Darroch seemed much better when he came out after his shower, though a day's growth of beard gave him a rough-and-ready look. He moved his shoulder in experimental circles. "I believe it's nearly sorted," he said, which Jean took to mean that it had improved.

He smiled at her as he sat down at the kitchen table. "What a treat this is. I never get to eat breakfast with a lovely woman in her own cottage. I feel quite privileged."

Sometimes smart answers to his teasing eluded her. She said, embarrassed, "Don't you want some sugar for your oatmeal . . . I mean, porridge?"

"No, on the Island we eat it without sweetening, just a bit of salt. It's also traditional to eat it standing up with your back to the fire."

"How odd."

"Not really. When you consider how cold it gets here and that most houses were heated only with a peat fire, and that fire was on a hearthstone in the middle of the room—not in a fireplace—a number of people could gather around it, eat their porridge and warm their backsides at the same time. And people had only one or two chairs in their cottages so they'd eat standing up, especially if it was too cold to sit on a dirt floor."

She considered the poverty-stricken picture his words conjured up. "They wouldn't have had sugar."

"Honey they had but saved for special purposes like baking. I confess I've tried porridge with whisky on it in my wild younger days."

"How was it?"

"As Bonnie Prince Jamie would say, a waste of good whisky. But an acceptable use for bad."

Always interested in anything concerning Jamie, she asked, "How did he get that nickname?"

"My doing, I'm afraid. He was Jamie the *Sgiathanach* at first, Jamie from Skye, then Màiri's Jamie, but we've several of those. Neither Jamie the Fiddle nor Jamie the Tune seemed special enough. Handsome Jamie was vetoed by Màiri; she said he'd go back to Skye if he heard anyone call him that. He hates it when anyone fusses over his looks.

"Then I was watching him play his fiddle one night and it came to me how much he resembled Charles Edward Stewart, you know, Bonnie Prince Charlie. There's a picture in the Scottish National Portrait Gallery of Charlie that put me in mind of Jamie. Both tall and golden-haired and regal, but the difference is that Jamie has intelligence in his face where the Young Pretender merely looks proud and pompous. And of course Jamie could out-royal the Queen herself when he's in the mood. He looks and acts far more like a king than poor Tèarlach ever did.

"The funny thing is that after I first called him Bonnie Prince Jamie, Màiri took me aside and told me there was a legend in his family that Charlie had fathered a bairn on a young lady in Jamie's direct ancestry. The girl was hastily married off but there was no disgrace attached to her.

"And in truth, Tèarlach was a while on Skye during the '45 Rising. It was a MacDonald, Flora, who helped him escape. Perhaps you've heard about it." She nodded. "An old woman in his family told Màiri the baby story but Jamie has always refused to comment on it. Whether he believes it or not I don't know. Anyway, the nickname stuck. If it's ever annoyed him, he's risen above it."

Jean was charmed. She thought she must have a crush on Jamie, she loved talking about him so much.

Darroch pushed back his chair. He was quite contented but still very tired. "Can we take our tea to the sofa?" he said. He wanted so much to sit by her and hold her hand but he needed the comfort of the sofa for his aching body.

"Go ahead. I'll put the porridge pot on to soak. Otherwise it'll be like cement."

He built up the fire. She could tell it was an enormous effort and when it was blazing he sat back on his heels and stared into the flames. She moved to him. "Come rest on the sofa, lovie."

She let him settle himself, then sat down beside him. After a pause he said, "May I put my head in your lap?"

"Yes, of course." He stretched out facing the fire, head pillowed on her thighs. Jean stroked his hair. "How do you feel?"

"Knackered." He closed his eyes and she reached for the blanket and threw it over him. They rested, lulled by the fire's warmth.

Darroch was thinking dreamily of the pleasure to be had by pulling her down for a kiss, of feeling her sweet mouth open under his like a budding lily, the shy touch of her tongue against his. His hand curved involuntarily, imagining the shape of her breast and her nipple rounding and hardening from the pressure of his thumb. He was too exhausted to do anything about it but the thoughts were deeply pleasing.

"*Mo Shìne*, you've taken such good care of me," he murmured. "It was worth being caught in the storm, to be here with you."

"Shhh," she said, pleased. "Relax. Try to sleep."

He didn't have to try. His eyes closed and she felt the tension leave his body as he slept. She leaned back against the sofa and dozed, her hand on his hair.

Pounding on the door woke her. She lifted her head and said fuzzily, "Come in."

"Jean?" called Màiri's voice.

"Here, by the fire."

"Boots, *a Mhàiri*," said Jamie, catching her by the sleeve as she started across the floor. She grumbled but pulled off her snow-covered boots and threw her coat at a chair, missing it entirely. Jamie picked it up.

Màiri was taken aback by the tableau on the sofa. She moved closer and lowered her voice. "How is he?"

"I'm fine," said a sleepy voice from Jean's lap. "Why wouldn't I be?"

"Hush," said Jean. "People are concerned about you, that's all."

Màiri stared from one to the other. "As if staggering miles through a blizzard wasn't something to be concerned about," she said grouchily.

Jamie was kneeling by the fire, stacking peats. "Ach, he's tough as old boots, aren't you, *mo charaid*."

"Aye," Darroch mumbled. "Old boots."

"You'll not make old bones with this kind of goings-on. Whatever possessed you to go out into that storm? I should think you'd have known better," Màiri snapped.

Jamie said mildly, "Don't scold, *mo ghràdh*. I'm sure he'll not do it again."

"Damned right," Darroch said and resigned himself to the effort of sitting up. "It was a fascinating experience but not one I'd care to repeat." He eyed Jean mischievously. "Unless, of course, I could count on the same reception at the end of my walk . . . and hot soup."

Jean smiled. "You were just lucky. It could have been peanut butter and crackers."

The other three looked puzzled. "What is . . . peanut butter?" asked Màiri.

"Where's the poor old Bentley?" asked Jamie.

"Somewhere between here and Airgead, stuck in a ditch full of snow."

"Ach, *am truaghag bhochd*, the poor beastie. Will I pull her out for you? Driveable, is she?"

Darroch shook his head. "Don't know."

"The roads must be a mess," said Jean. "How did you get here so fast up that hill?"

"My old truck will go anywhere and I've got a plow to put on the front. It comes in handy two or three times a year and lives in the shed the rest of the time."

"I'd best see to the car. It will be easier for Murdoch to plow if there's no obstacles in his way and she might be partly on the road," Darroch said wearily.

"I'll do that for you, *a charaid*," began Jamie but Darroch shook his head. "My car, my job," he said.

Màiri opened her mouth to protest but Jamie scowled at her. She subsided but could not stop herself from mumbling, "Ought to be in bed." Jean nodded, in complete agreement. Men, they both thought.

Darroch's outer clothes were damp but wearable. Jean patted the coat anxiously. "Don't stay out in the cold long," she instructed. "Your coat is still quite wet, you'll get chilled again."

"Yes, ma'am," he said, grinning.

"Màiri, make sure he obeys," Jean said and Màiri nodded grimly. "*Thà gu dearbh*," she said.

"It's worth it to be looked after . . . " he began but Jean shook her head at him. "That's enough of that," she said. "Pneumonia is no laughing matter."

"And a bad cold is nothing to sneeze at, right?" He grinned again and bent to kiss her on both cheeks. "My thanks, *mo Shìne*. I'll see you soon."

Twenty-nine

How will I know my Love? Will there be thunder and lightning
when we meet? Or merely
The sound of a small bird, singing.

Songs of Love, Lady Grizel Mac an Rìgh, translated by Isabel Ross

$\mathcal{T}$he three left Jean's cottage and turned onto the main road. The going was very slow. Drifts had been driven across the highway by the fierce wind and in places it was difficult to see where road ended and ditch began. When they came to the spot where Darroch's car had left the road they almost missed it for the Bentley was covered with snow. To their surprise the car was undamaged.

"We can leave her there till Murdoch's done with the rescues," Darroch said. "He'll be plowing all day but I don't think she's in his way."

Jamie said, "With a chain I could pull her out, but I'm not sure how far you'd get till the plowing's done. The drifts are high; even the Bentley won't clear them."

"Leave her," said Darroch. He felt suddenly weary. Snow had gotten into his boots and his feet were cold and wet again.

They tied Darroch's scarf to the antenna for a marker and trudged to the truck. Màiri had been eyeing Darroch curiously since they'd all met that morning. "You must have been exhausted by the time you got to Jean's. Thank God she heard you knocking."

Fatigue made him blunt. "If she hadn't I'd be dead. Fallen asleep in the snow like the Little Match Girl."

Jamie said, "What if the cottage had been vacant? Could you have gotten in?"

Darroch shook his head. "No, I hadn't strength to break the lock."

"Jean saved your life," said Jamie, and Darroch nodded without speaking. Jamie added, not looking at his companions, "It's a blessing to have her here. I wonder how much longer she'll stay?"

Climbing into the truck, Darroch and Màiri exchanged startled glances. "Why do you say that, Jamie?"

"I was just thinking that a woman like that . . . with another life in America . . . why would she stay here?"

They were all silent, thinking about Jean.

Jamie, in his quiet way, had been giving careful thought to the subject of Darroch and Jean. He had decided they were a perfect match. He thought, they suit each other and she fits in here. Like Sheilah and like me . . . she's a born *Eilean Dubhannach*.

Màiri thought, what if Jean leaves? She's a great help with the Playschool. Our music is better with her; she's a fine singer. And she's a good friend. And then she thought, if Jean leaves, who'll help me look after Darroch?

Leave, Darroch thought indignantly. She can't leave. I need her. I want her.

I love her.

Light dawned. The thought blossomed in his mind and it was so simple he wondered why it had eluded him for so long. He loved her, quite madly.

Why had he ever thought it was just lust? Because he'd been a bloody coward, afraid of getting involved with a woman again, eager to write off the symptoms of love as nothing more than simple masculine desire.

He'd been friendly at first by way of asking pardon for the snub in the bar but when they'd begun to spend time together they'd quickly become good friends. They'd talked with the pleasure and understanding he'd found only with Màiri and Morgan.

But the music had been the real catalyst. The clarity and purity of her voice had made the old Island songs glow with new life and it had affected him deeply.

And she handled herself with dignity. He was sure she was just as affected by their kisses as he was but she did not react with embarrassment, just with a sweet shyness and a tendency to stare at him for long moments when she thought he wasn't looking.

What would he do if she left? Losing her would be unbearable.

What will he do if she leaves, thought Jamie and glanced covertly at Màiri, wondering if she was thinking the same thing.

Màiri twisted around in her seat. She said, "What will . . . *a Dhia beannaich mi*, Darroch, what's wrong? You look terrible."

"It's just a chill," he said crossly. He hated being fussed over but he was wondering what was happening to him. He was burning up and freezing cold by turns and his body ached. His chest was congested and his brain felt like it was wrapped in cotton wool. Was it love that made him feel so dreadful?

"It might be the start of pneumonia. You've had it a couple of times, haven't you? Jamie, let's get him home to bed."

By now Darroch did not feel like arguing. This did indeed resemble the attacks of pneumonia he'd suffered, once in London, once on Eilean Dubh. Above his physical discomfort, however, was a small voice whispering, echoing Jamie: why would she stay?

In Milwaukee she has everything she could want: central heating, microwave ovens, huge houses with grand gardens and acres of grassy lawns. Why would she give it all up for life on this backward little Island? It might be a dying Island, too, despite all we do. Our way of life might be finished, he thought glumly, despite all our efforts.

And he loved her. Loved her sharp mind, her keen sense of humor, her angel's voice. Loved the way her mouth tasted, the way her body felt against his. His teeth ached and his bones hurt with the tide of passion that swept through him. Or was it a fever?

Curiously, his rising temperature made everything crystal clear in his mind. He was suddenly desperate to get out of the car and run through the snow to Jean to ask her . . . what? To stay here? With him? Perhaps she was deciding even now to forgive her husband and go home. He gritted his teeth in frustration.

They pulled into Darroch's lane. Màiri said, "We'll get you tucked up, Darroch, but someone should stay with you in case you get really ill. But I've got to have a look at the Playschool. I'm terrified about the roof with all this snow."

Deciding to nudge things along, Jamie said casually, "I wonder if maybe Jean would come and mind him."

"Of course. I'll ring her, then I'll ring Ros and ask him to call round. Jamie, you get him settled in bed."

Jamie bundled Darroch off, ignoring his protests. "Don't bother Jean. I'll be fine. She put up with me all last night . . . " He didn't want Jean to see him ill. He wanted to go to her, strong and well, and pour out his love.

Jean's phone was snatched up at the first ring. She was barely able to hide her disappointment that the caller was Màiri, not Darroch. "Yes, of course, I'll stay with him. I knew he shouldn't go out, yesterday was awful for him. Can Jamie come and get me?"

"He's on his way. And Jean . . . bring your soup."

Thirty

I wake, I turn, sleep may I nocht,
I vexit am with heavy thocht;
This warld all owre I cast about,
And aye the mair I am in doubt,
The mair that I remeid have socht.

William Dunbar (1460?-1520?)

𝒟arroch was asleep by the time Jamie came back with Jean. All three tramped upstairs and made a solemn circle around his bed.

"What do you think, Màiri?" whispered Jean. Darroch was so pale that she was alarmed.

"I think we should wait for Ros's opinion." The other two nodded. They went downstairs and waited uneasily for the doctor. He came within the hour, after they were out of conversation and tea. Jamie escorted him upstairs.

When the doctor came down, zipping his bag, they watched him in silence. He said, "He's had pneumonia before?"

Màiri nodded and Ros said, "It's too soon to know. I'd like to give him an antibiotic shot but I've used my last one and can't get more until Murdoch plows out my office. He shouldn't be left alone. Can someone stay with him?"

Jamie nodded. After Ros had left he said, "Shall we organize a rota?"

Jean blurted, "I'll stay tonight. I'd like to, I feel responsible somehow." As they turned to her, she added, embarrassed, "Unless you think I shouldn't . . . I mean . . . unless you think people would talk."

"Who's to know?" said Jamie. "Everyone's snowed in. They'll be thinking about that instead of gossip. Màiri, we'll go check the Playschool. Then I'll come back and take Jean home so she can nap. She might have a wakeful night, best to be rested."

Jamie brought her back that evening and they had supper together. Jamie took soup upstairs but reported that the patient was too drowsy to eat.

Màiri issued a volley of orders when they parted for the night. "Ring us if he's worse. We'll be right up and Jamie can go for the doctor. Check on him often, take his temperature . . . " Jamie put a firm arm around her shoulders and steered her out.

Alone, Jean snapped on the television but found she couldn't concentrate. She settled down in front of the fire with a book she'd plucked at random from his shelves. When she found she'd read ten pages of an economics book and hadn't understood a word, she tossed it aside. Might as well go to bed, she thought, and headed upstairs to the tiny second bedroom.

She paused by Darroch's bed and touched his forehead. It seemed hotter but she thought that was because of all the blankets Màiri had piled on. She loosened his covers and he sighed and stirred but didn't wake.

She slept lightly, getting up twice to check on him. The third time she was roused from a deeper sleep by noises from the other room. She got up and ran to his bed.

He was moving restlessly and every time he rolled onto his sore shoulder he groaned with pain. She could not understand what he was saying; it was all in the Gaelic. "*Creag*" was the one word she managed to pick out and she remembered from Island placenames that it meant a cliff. Whatever he was dreaming about, it was very distressing.

What should I do now, she thought. Shall I call the doctor? Or Jamie? Deeply worried, she sat on the edge of his bed and stroked his hair. When he grew quieter she went into the bathroom and wet a towel with freezing cold tap water. She hurried back into the room and moved the dampened towel over his face. He sighed and lay still. She bent down to listen to his chest for the dreaded rales of pneumonia and was encouraged to hear him breathing evenly and without signs of distress.

She wet the towel again, opened his shirt and put it at the base of his throat where the jugular vein neared the surface. When he began to shiver she hastily dried him and pulled the covers up.

He was mumbling and growing agitated again. She slipped under the covers, pulled him close and talked reassuringly into his ear. "Darroch, lovie, be still, *a charaid*," she said over and over, wishing she had a better command of the Gaelic. Finally she began to sing quietly some of their favorite songs. When she had exhausted her Gaelic repertoire she moved to English, dredging her mind for lullabies.

It dawned upon her that this was different from when they'd lain together during the snowstorm keeping each other warm. And suddenly she understood. I love him, she thought. Emboldened by the deepness of his slumber she murmured into his ear, "I love you, Darroch," and slipped into sleep.

A voice was whispering urgently in her ear. "Jean, wake up, wake up, *a Shine*."

She turned over drowsily and found herself face to face with Bonnie Prince Jamie, kneeling by the bed, handsome as a god and smiling with some inner amusement. "How was your night, *mo charaid*?" He brushed her hair back from her forehead affectionately.

"Umm . . . Jamie . . . let me think a moment."

"Take your time, get yourself sorted. Your patient seems better. His skin is cool."

Memory came back and with it awareness that she was lying next to Darroch under the covers. "Oh, Jamie, he had a bad night. The fever came and went and he had terrible dreams. He talked about . . . a *creag* . . . I think he was saying."

Jamie thought. "The cliff, perhaps. He said he'd been frightened in the storm that he might stray over the cliff into the sea."

She shuddered. "What an awful thing to dream about." She was suddenly embarrassed to be found in bed with Darroch. She stammered, "When the fever went down he was terribly chilled so I climbed in to keep him warm. My being there seemed to keep the dreams away. He slept pretty well after I lay down by him."

Jamie smiled at her. "You see how right you were to take the night shift. He'd not have been nearly as comforted if I were lying there." Jean turned very red. Jamie took pity. "Get dressed and go down to Màiri. She's fixing breakfast. I'll see to him."

"Yes, Jamie," she said meekly. She washed up in the bathroom, then went to her room and dressed. When she came out Jamie was talking quietly to Darroch who seemed half-awake. She slipped downstairs.

"*Madainn mhath, a Shìne!* How is he?" said Màiri anxiously, turning away from the stove. She poured a cup of tea and set it down in front of Jean.

Jean recounted the night's events. Màiri sat down opposite her, cooking forgotten. "Talking in his sleep, bad dreams, ach, the poor dear. It was well you stayed with him, *mo phiuthar*."

Jean thought of his distress and agreed. Remembering the revelation of the previous night, she avoided looking at Màiri. She was afraid her feelings would show in her face and she wanted to keep that knowledge to herself, to take out when she was alone and think about carefully.

Ros MacPherson came round after they'd finished eating and disappeared upstairs with Jamie. When they came down the doctor said, "It's the start of pneumonia, all right, but I think we've caught it in time. I gave him an antibiotic shot and I'll leave tablets for you to give him. When he wakes, try to get him to eat and drink something."

When the doctor left Jamie said briskly, "I'll take you home, Jean, to rest. I'll pick you up for supper. Do you want the night shift again tonight?" She nodded. "Perhaps I should stay, too, in case he gets worse. I could sleep on the sofa."

"No, we'll be all right. I can phone you if I have a problem."

"I'm a light sleeper. I'll hear if you ring."

She brought books when she came back later, thinking that she'd have several hours with nothing to do, but when Jamie and Màiri left she found herself exhausted and the idea of mindless television was appealing. When she start dozing off in front of the set she switched it off and went upstairs.

She perched cautiously on the edge of his bed and touched his forehead. It seemed cooler. His face on the white pillow was clearly visible, illuminated by the moon's glow drifting through the skylight. Darling Darroch, she thought, what am I going to do about falling in love with you?

She thought about his kindness to her, the way his face always lit up when he saw her, the way they could always make each other laugh. The way he smiled into her eyes when they sang together. The tender, passionate way he had kissed her.

The urge to kiss him was irresistible. She bent and put her lips against his, his two-day growth of beard rough against her skin.

Look at you, she mocked herself. Mooning over the poor man and stealing kisses when he's too sick to resist. What would you say if he were to wake up now?

A strong arm wrapped itself around her suddenly and dragged her close to his chest. Her squeak of surprise was swallowed by his mouth as he kissed her fiercely.

He'd wakened from a fever-induced, deeply sensual dream, crazed with lust, just before her mouth had touched his. He'd had a vision of a female figure bending over him, the light from the bedroom next door turning her hair into a vivid halo. He thought wildly, angel or fairy? Am I dead or enchanted?

Whatever she was, this time she wasn't going to slip away into the mists of his dreams. His hand captured the back of her head so that her mouth couldn't escape. The other hand moved over her, seeking her breast and getting tangled in a mass of fabric. Why was a fairy wearing a cotton gown? asked his addled brain. Why not silk and gossamer?

But he recognized that sweet mouth and luscious body. Jean. Better than an angel, better than a fairy. Was he still dreaming or were his dreams coming true at last?

When their lips parted she gasped, "You're feeling better, then."

He stared at her, dazed. "My shoulder hurts and I'm freezing."

"Oh, lovie. Let me help," she said and scampered around to the other side of the bed to his sore shoulder. She massaged it gently, slipping her hands under his shirt and working at the knotted muscles until he sighed and relaxed.

"Better?" she whispered and he opened his eyes. "Aye, but I'm still cold."

Jean needed no further invitation. She pulled back the covers, climbed in and cuddled him close. He collapsed again into sleep and dreams.

Bright sunshine streaming through the skylight woke her very early the next morning. The combination of sun, the nightgown and his warmth had left her sweaty and disheveled. She rolled out of his bed awkwardly and went to the tiny bedroom next door. She took off the nightgown and decided to shower.

She peeked into the bedroom. He hadn't moved. She grabbed her clothes, holding them strategically around her, and tiptoed into the bathroom, only to discover there was no place to hang her things. She put them on a chair just outside the door and slipped into the shower.

Afterwards, she dried off and then reached outside for her clothes. The chair had tipped over and they were out of reach. She hesitated, then covered herself as best she could with the towel, opened the door and stepped out.

Darroch, sitting up, propped against a pillow, stared at her in astonishment. He'd had a night of crazy dreams, some wildly terrifying and some wildly erotic, and at least half of them involving Jean. Now she was in his bedroom, wearing only a towel. "What are you doing here?" he said in a puzzled voice.

Jean jumped and the towel unfolded itself. She clutched it to her, stammering, "I can explain."

His eyes were on stalks. She blushes all over, he thought, fascinated, as the pink color moved from her face to her shoulders, past the sliver of hip showing beyond the towel and down her legs. "Ummm . . . could you come a little closer while you explain?"

"No! I've got to get dressed. Would you look the other way, please?"

He groaned in disappointment and slowly turned his head, feeling each muscle and vertebrae creak in protest. Remember, she thinks you're a nice guy, he told himself, but could not keep from fantasizing how much more of her would be on display when she bent over.

Jean grabbed her clothes and retreated. Horribly embarrassed, she didn't come out again until she'd taken a few deep, calming breaths. Walking toward the bed, she said in what she hoped was a normal voice, "How are you this morning?"

"Confused." His eyes roamed over her appreciatively. In her agitation she'd missed a button on her blouse, and her hair, tidied with her fingers in lieu of a comb, was a tangled cloud around her flushed face. The effect was astonishingly sexy. He patted the bed and tried not to leer like the Big Bad Wolf. "Sit here and tell me about it."

She sat obediently, wondering why she still felt naked. "You've been ill. Ros thought you were coming down with pneumonia. He said someone should be with you all the time so Jamie, Màiri and I have been changing off. Last night was my turn."

"You were here with me last night?" He stared at her.

"Yes, I slept in the little bedroom." Well, that was partly true, she thought uncomfortably.

"I dreamed someone was with me in bed. Someone who rubbed my shoulder."

She closed her eyes in embarrassment. She hadn't expected him to remember. "I . . . you . . . your shoulder was so sore you couldn't sleep so I massaged it."

He looked down at the shirt he was wearing, then up at her again, a question on his face.

"Jamie undressed you. He couldn't find pajamas so he put an old shirt on when he put you to bed two days ago."

He said, "I don't own pajamas. And I distinctly remember your hands on my skin, not through a shirt."

She whispered, "I pulled it up. You can't massage properly through clothing."

"Ah." He watched her for a long moment, remembering bits and pieces of his dreams. "Perhaps I had a fever."

She put her hand on his forehead. "Yes, but you seem quite normal now."

Normal, with her sitting on his bed and stroking his forehead so tenderly? He must be a better actor than he thought.

Jean said, "Would you like something to eat?"

"Yes, I'm hungry. Ravenous, in fact." Not just for food, he thought. Her hand, unaccountably, was in his. He squeezed it. "Thank you, Jean, for looking after me."

"I . . . I was glad to do it," she stammered, "Um . . . what would you like to eat?"

"Anything. Just lots of it."

"Okay." She got up, reluctant to leave but desperate to put some space between them so that she could collect her wits. "Have a shower, it'll help your shoulder."

"I hope you've left me some hot water," he said, grinning, though he thought an ice-cold shower was what he needed right now.

Jean fled down the stairs.

Thirty-one

O happy love! where love like this is found:
O heart-felt raptures! bliss beyond compare!

Robert Burns

Breakfast was quiet and relaxed. He seemed his old self, laughing and teasing her gently until she felt warm all over. The tenderness in his voice pleased her. Don't read too much into it, she thought; he's just grateful for your help while he was sick. It doesn't mean he feels anything for you but friendship.

Finishing the dishes, she leaned into the kitchen window and stood looking at the aftereffects of the storm. Darroch came to stand by her.

They looked for a long time at the snow mounds the wind had arranged against the cottage. On the far end of the storehouse, snow was piled as high as the roof edge while a few feet closer the wall was exposed down to the foundation. Beyond the cottage the white landscape undulated down to the sea in great breaking waves. A cold wind whistled around the walls and blew in under the door to lick at their ankles and dispel the last warmth of cooking.

"Wisconsin looks just like this after a heavy snow," she said wistfully. "So serene and pure, like the first day of the world."

"Do you miss Wisconsin, Jean?" He did not look at her.

"Oh . . . " She was surprised by the question. "Sometimes I get a little homesick. Mainly it's my kids I miss. And bagels. And Mexican food. And a good cup of coffee. And central heating, especially today."

He was silent so long she glanced at him to see if anything was wrong. He was still pale and he seemed tired. Jean's heart twisted in her breast. I love him a whole lot, she thought.

In a low voice he said, "Jean . . . would you go home and leave us?"

Leave? She felt ill at the very idea. Something moved inside her, stirred and came out of her mouth sweet with truth. "This is my home, Darroch." Something moved her to turn to him, to take a step towards him. She looked at his beautiful blue eyes, his fine elegant nose. The wave of love engulfing her nearly buckled her knees.

Her pride crumbled. Her caution deserted her. She took her heart out of her breast and laid it at his feet.

"Oh, Darroch." She blurted, "How could I bear to leave? Don't you know I love you?" She put her hands on either side of his face and kissed him. His mouth was warm and surprised.

Oh, damn, you've done it now, she thought, aghast at what she'd said. Panicked, she dropped her hands and stepped backward. If all he felt for her was friendship, she realized in terror, she would have to leave the Island. The thought was like being punched in the belly.

Darroch was quite still, staring at her, his expression unreadable.

A pounding on the door interrupted them. As they swung around the door opened and Màiri and Jamie blew in, heads and shoulders white with snow, a gust of wind billowing their coats around them. Jean turned red and leaped away from Darroch.

"Sorry to burst in," gasped Màiri. "The wind blew the door out of my hand."

Jamie's quick eye went to Jean and he understood at once what they'd interrupted. He put a comforting arm around her shoulders and steered her to the sofa. "I need to warm my bones at your fire, Jean. Sit with me."

Màiri put her hand on Darroch's brow. "How are you feeling?" she demanded.

"I am fine," he said. "Màiri, *mo charaid*, please go home."

She stared at him, unsure she'd heard correctly. "Don't you want to hear about the storm damage? We've been all around the Island."

He sighed and said with resigned affection, "Aye. Tell me about it."

"Well, Murdoch's got most of the north plowed. Eideard MacShennach has dug himself out and he's going to plow our village and the south. Everyone's accounted for, no injuries except for Seumas MacQuirter who tried to ski down to the road, slipped and rolled fifty feet and broke his leg when he got tangled up in his skis. Luckily Murdoch was going by on the plow at the time and was able to get him right to hospital.

"The Seniors' Residence has food to last till Friday. Most of the hospital staff has made it in and the fire brigade's plowed out. And the Playschool roof is intact, Darroch!"

"Thank you, Màiri, that's *miorbhuileach*." He smiled at her so sweetly that she was a little dazzled, used as she was to him. He kissed her cheek, then stopped in surprise. It was gone, that faint sensual tremor he always felt when touching Màiri. For twenty years it had tormented him, this whisper of desire.

He said in her ear, "I love you, *mo Mhàiri*, and I love Jamie like a brother. Go home, please, the both of you. Right now."

She felt the change in him, saw him look over her shoulder to where Jean sat. So the wind's in that quarter, she thought.

"*A Mhàiri*," said Jamie gently, "we must go home. You know the twins will be trying to reach us. Eilidh will know about the storm." Eilidh, who shared his gift of the Sight, always knew when something was wrong on the Island.

"Aye." She turned from Darroch after one last intent look. Testing his patience, she said to Jean, "Do you want a ride home?"

Darroch said evenly, "She does not. *Mar sin leat, a Mhàiri. Mar sin leat, a Sheumais*." It was the rarely used Laird's voice, clearly dismissive.

Jamie had been watching Jean, fascinated, as the expressions changed on her face and the color in her cheeks came and went. He said, smiling, "*Sòlas math, a Dharroch*." Good luck.

"*Tapadh leat*," said Darroch briefly and shut the door behind them. He turned back into the room. To his surprise Jean had vanished. As he moved forward he saw her kneeling at the fireplace, crouched in the position of Island women through the centuries.

He thought, she said she loves me. Joy pierced him, sharp as a knife blade.

A peat brick broke in her shaking hand and crumbled to the floor in pieces. She was very aware that he was standing next to her and she kept her eyes resolutely down.

"Jean," said his quiet voice. She refused to look. "*A Shìne*, take my hands and stand up." Mute, she let him draw her to her feet. She knew he was looking at her but she couldn't meet his eyes.

The fire blazed up and the sudden glare illuminated their faces. He lifted her peat-stained hand to his nose and sniffed. "Your hand smells of the Island," he said and kissed her fingers one by one. "Now, Jean. Tell me again, what you said earlier."

She still wouldn't look at him so he gathered her hands into one of his and used his free hand to lift her chin. "I love you," she whispered, eyes closed.

"*Glé mhath*. Now say it like this: *tha gràdh agam ort*."

She said, "Ha . . . gra . . . gh ackum orst . . . " and opened her eyes.

"*A Dharroch . . . tha gràdh agam ort, a Dharroch*."

Jean repeated the phrase carefully.

"Very nice. Now listen: *tha gràdh agam ort, a Shìne*. Do you understand me, Jean?"

She smiled tremulously. "In Milwaukee people say *Ich liebe dich*."

"Aye . . . German is the loving tongue . . . in Milwaukee, anyway. In France it's *je t'aime*. And in America, it's I love you. I love you, Jean." He put his lips against her cheek and murmured, "So now we understand each other, eh, *mo chridhe*?"

"Oh, yes," she sighed. "Um . . . except . . . what does 'mo hree' mean?"

"*Mo chridhe* means 'my heart.' I've never said that to anyone before."

My heart. She swayed toward him, giddy with happiness. When their bodies touched she thought she might swoon. "Please, can we sit down," she begged. "You overwhelm me, Darroch. I can't think straight, let alone stand up."

"*Mìorbhuileach*," he said and pulled her down to the sofa onto his lap. He murmured, "I'm a fool not to have recognized it sooner but I fell in love with you when I first heard you sing. I'd never heard such a lovely voice."

She said, "I fell in love with you at the first *cèilidh*, I know that now. I didn't let myself realize it until you showed up at my door all bedraggled and frozen."

Gradually they slipped down until they were lying side by side on the sofa. His hand moved over the delicate curve of her breast down to the lovely swell of hip and thigh. He remembered when he had first desired her, that afternoon on *Cladh a' Chnuic*, and his mouth on hers was as hot as a living flame. The reality of Jean in his arms was far better than any of his fantasies: sweet lips, lush curves, long legs twined around his. She filled his senses, made him greedy for more.

His lips moved down to where her blouse hindered his exploration. He bared her throat. Then, unable to stop, he unbuttoned the blouse all the way and pulled it out of her skirt. She was trembling and it excited him beyond reason. He wanted to undress her completely, hold her naked in his arms.

"Tell me if you want me to stop," he whispered and she sighed, "Don't stop. More kisses would be nice too." He laughed and covered her mouth with his. He was hard against her, pressed so closely they were almost one.

Jean slipped into a free fall of desire, yielding herself entirely to the sensations evoked by his kisses and his touch. I want him, she thought. Imagine that, she thought. Imagine making love with him. Taking him inside her.

He said, "Last night . . . or perhaps the night before . . . I dreamed someone lay beside me. She was wearing a gown like gossamer, so thin my hand went right through it to her skin . . . I could feel her breast through the fabric . . . " Remembering the delicious eroticism of the dream he cradled her breast in his hand.

"When I moved my hand over her body her skin warmed me everywhere I touched. She wasn't wearing these," he said as his hand pushed her skirt up and tugged gently on her panties. "I remember . . . " His hand covered her and she gasped. "I remember the feel of soft little curls against my hand."

Jean could barely breathe. "Fever dreams. I held you and sang to you, that was all."

"Is this a dream? I can't tell the difference any more." He put his mouth on her throat, moved to her shoulder, then . . . his hands fumbling clumsily with the clasp on her bra . . . to her breasts. He seized a nipple between his lips and it blossomed in his mouth like a flower.

She arched toward him and moaned with pleasure.

"Ah . . . it's good, isn't it, Jean. You have no idea how long I've wanted you, *m'aingeal*. I want to throw you over my shoulder and carry you upstairs to my bed. But I'm afraid we'd get stuck where the stair curves. I wouldn't be able to wait, I'd have to have you right there. You wouldn't like it, with the cold hard iron step pressing against your bare little bottom."

"Bet I would," she muttered. She would love it, for him to want her so much he couldn't wait. She pulled his head down. To her astonishment she was using her tongue, coaxing his mouth open until they were exchanging deep, hot kisses. She'd never done that before, never in twenty years of marriage. But she'd learned more about kissing from him in five minutes than in those twenty years.

She had never felt such intense desire before. She pulled away and lay looking at him, eyes wide. She said in amazement, "I love you. I want you."

"Ah. You've said that before, Jean, but I'm not tired of hearing it. Feel free to say it anytime . . . especially the part about wanting me. Here's something you'll like, I know." He slipped his fingers between her legs in one swift movement and began to stroke. She arched so high against him that she thought her spine would snap, she could feel all the vertebrae groaning and stretching. Then she came apart in pleasure against his hand, his wonderful, practiced, loving hand.

He'd experienced all kinds of passion, from the mindless desire of women who simply wanted sex to Màiri's single-minded need for him alone. Like her, Jean wanted him, only him. He knew from the way she wove her fingers tenderly through his hair, murmured his name, touched him as though he were precious.

"Now we'll go up to my bed," he said happily. "Assuming we can still walk. Perhaps we should settle for the sofa, or even the floor. What do you think, *mo chridhe*? The bed would be best, I believe. You remember my bed, Jean. Under the skylight."

She remembered. She had held him, massaged his shoulders, let her hand stray down his bare back, stopped herself before she went as far as she wanted. "Why are you wearing all those clothes?" she demanded.

He stared at her. Then he began to unbutton his shirt. "I think it's going to be the sofa," he murmured. "I do not believe I can manage all those steps for imagining myself inside you. I'll be as gentle as I can. I think I have some fraction of self control left."

"I don't want you to be gentle. I want all of you, all of you at once."

Three years, he thought, since he'd made love. It was amazing he remembered how it was done, but he supposed it was like riding a bicycle, you never forgot. He pulled off his shirt and reached down to peel off his undershirt. In seconds his naked chest would be pressed against her lovely naked breasts. After that the sky was the limit and he had no doubt they would reach the sky, they would soar together.

But something was wrong. She was frozen with shock, still as a statue. He stared down at himself. Had his chest exploded, was his heart out of his body, quivering, a Mayan sacrifice to his passion for her?

"I can't," she gasped.

"Can't," he said, dragging the word out, testing the nuances. "Not won't . . . or don't want to . . . but can't. Why not, Jean?"

"I'm married," she said.

"Married," he said blankly. "I forgot."

"What?"

"I forgot you were married."

"How could you forget?"

"He doesn't matter, Jean. You belong to me. You've come here to the Island to be mine. Why else would you be here? You were sent to be mine."

"That's that Celtic mystical stuff, right?" she said, smiling so sweetly that he felt his heart expand.

"So what's your explanation?" He nuzzled her shoulder.

"Good clean living. Suffering in a previous life. Dumb luck. Who cares?" She cried, "What am I going to do? I love you and I want you." Her face puckered like a small child's and he thought she was going to cry.

He wanted to make soothing noises but he was wrestling with the implications of what she had said. He had truly forgotten the existence of that damned Yank, her husband, in the storm of his arousal.

She said, "Adultery's wrong, it nearly ruined my life. What we've got is so good. What would adultery do to us?"

"I would like, just once, to ignore my damned conscience and do what I want," he said fiercely. "And what I want to do is to make love to you until we're both daft and we don't give a damn about anything else."

But they both knew the battle was lost. He put his head on her breasts again and she stroked his hair. After a bit he sighed and said, "Once, when I was at the Academy, I played in a French farce that had a plot exactly like this."

"Oh, yes? Was it a comedy or a tragedy?"

" A little of both, if I remember right. Someone died and someone got married."

"Which part was the tragedy?"

He said, shocked, "Jean! Don't be cynical!"

"Did it end happily?"

"It was a farce. Farces always end happily."

She said, "Kiss me some more."

Darroch realized suddenly that he could have her then and there if he exercised his considerable powers of persuasion. She wanted him, she fairly reverberated with need, her eyes were glazed with desire.

The temptation was strong. Why shouldn't they? Her marriage was over and he was free. He was so convinced she belonged to him that he wanted with all his heart to lose himself in her and feel her hot sweetness all around him.

He kissed her long and deep and felt her surrender, felt in her the same urgency overwhelming him. She said, "Darroch . . . " a question in her voice.

He was suddenly, intensely, deeply ashamed of himself.

She loved him and trusted him. How could he think of seducing her? Here on the sofa, of all places, and only the fourth time he'd held her in his arms.

Jean didn't have any experience with this sort of thing, he realized. She'd had but one lover, her husband. She'd not even kissed another man all the years of her marriage. "Unless you count Brad Johnson. He chased me and kissed me when he caught me." She'd said with satisfaction, "I slapped his face."

She was an innocent and his to protect and cherish, not sweep away in illicit passion. He took his mouth from hers reluctantly and tried to think of how to cool his ardor.

Not here, not on the sofa, he thought, we'll wait for the right time and place. My bed, under the skylight, and Jean in a white gossamer nightgown, buttoned down the front, each button opening to new places to kiss. His need flared despite his efforts and he couldn't stop himself from bending and putting his mouth to her breast.

Jean was giddy with desire. A moment more and there would be no turning back from this delicious craving raging through her body. With her last shred of control she put her hands against his chest and gasped, "No. No, I can't." Then she wrapped her arms around his neck and kissed him fiercely.

"Some ambiguity there, *mo chridhe*," he said, laughing down at her. "Tell me that you don't want me."

"I don't want you," she whispered.

"I don't believe you. Tell me what you don't want me to do to you."

"I don't want you to kiss me, yes, there and there too," she cried as his mouth moved to her throat and lower. "I don't want your hands on me . . . everywhere . . . I don't want your hands under me . . . lifting me up so you can come into me . . . " She said desperately, "Oh, God, I love you. I'm daffy with loving you and I want you so much I ache. If I had my druthers we'd be up-stairs in bed . . . but . . . I can't make love with you while I'm still married. It's not honest. I've never cheated, I can't start now. It would spoil things for us."

"Aye," he said mournfully and nibbled her ear. Jean exhaled slowly, her hands clenching into fists so tight her nails scored her palms.

He lifted his head. "Umm . . . what are 'druthers'?"

"Well, it means . . . " Then she laughed out loud and some of the sexual tension dissipated. "What are we going to do?" she said.

"How about this?" he said and suddenly slipped his hand between her legs again to pet her until she twisted and moaned. "You're very wet," he murmured. "I'd like to take you with my mouth, then slide my fingers inside you and open you, make you ready for me. But this will have to do for now. I have the taste of you and the feel of you and I've given you pleasure. You know you're mine." He smiled.

She burned where he had touched her and his sudden deliberate passion had unnerved her. She felt she must be blushing all over, she felt absolutely enslaved by him. She said abruptly, "I don't care about any of it. Let's go to bed."

"Ah, Jean." He sighed and lifted her up on his lap. "There's something I must explain. It's the Island, *mo fhlùr.*"

She lay against his chest, disappointed and frustrated. It was almost too much to bear, that his caresses had stopped. "What about the Island?"

"There are two sexual taboos here, Jean. One is incest, of course. The other is adultery." He felt her stiffen. "This is a small Island and the stock of people to marry is small. We've known for centuries that the mating of close blood can produce birth defects. That's why genealogies are so carefully kept here.

"But besides that, if a man seduced another man's wife it often resulted in a clan war, to say nothing of mucking up the lineage record and the line of inheritance. The taboo persists. It's deeply rooted in us.

"Everyone knows you're married. If we become lovers we're violating that taboo. I might get away with it; men are given more leeway. And I have a certain position," he admitted reluctantly. "They'd forgive me, eventually, because of who I am. But you're still an outsider. They don't really know you.

"There'd be talk, unpleasant talk. You'd be whispered about, perhaps shunned. In time they might forget. Or they might not. You might never regain their respect."

Jean trembled. Inexorably he continued, "We could never hide it if we became lovers. You're so honest, everything shows in your face. And I'd be too proud of having you for my own to lie about it." He smiled. "And I don't think you know how to lie, do you, *mo Shìne?*"

She said obstinately. "No, I'm no good at lying. But I don't care about the talk. If I can get around it in my own mind, accept that it's all right . . . It doesn't make any difference what others think."

"Will you feel that way when Minister Donald preaches a sermon about us?"

"Good heavens!" She was horrified. "He'd never do that, would he?"

"You don't know the conscience of a Free Presbyterian minister, Jean. He'd think it his duty. And I would agree."

"You would . . . agree?"

"It's what holds us together as a community. Accepted standards of behavior, a moral code applying to everyone, the conscience of a minister . . . it won't change just for us. Adultery is wrong, we both know that. We've both been hurt by it.

"When you're free we can be lovers. But only when you're free of your husband."

She leaned against him. "Can we cuddle? Can we lust after each other in our hearts? Isn't that hypocritical?"

"The act itself is all that matters. The Island allows people that much freedom."

"So there's nothing to do but wait," she said.

"There is a way," he said slowly. "We could leave."

"Leave? Leave Eilean Dubh?"

"We could go live in my flat in London until you're free. We could let people think you'd gone back to America to get a divorce. Then we could come back."

"No, no, we can't do that. Leave the Island? No music with Jamie and Màiri, no *cèilidhean*? And Ian the Post's interview is coming up and he's worked so hard on his English; he just needs a little more help. And I haven't taught Màiri how to use the computer. . . " She shook her head. "No, we can't leave." She looked at him keenly. "And you don't want to go, do you? I wouldn't ask that of you."

Darroch tightened his arms around her. "You've become a right little *Eilean Dubhannach, mo Shìne*. The Island's got its hold on you."

"It's those damned sunsets," she said and smiled at him. She sighed, "I don't know how I'm going to endure it, though. I want you like crazy."

"Well . . . on Eilean Dubh we have a traditional remedy for this sort of situation." He lifted her legs from his and buttoned her blouse. "We make a pot of tea and talk about it."

Thirty-two

Bring me, Beloved, words of love as sweet as kisses.
Songs of Love, Lady Grizel Mac an Rìgh, translated by Isabel Ross

Jean got unsteadily to her feet and walked to the kitchen. She took the teapot from the cupboard but when he came up and wrapped his arms around her she said, "Darling Darroch, if you want your tea go sit down. I can't do this with you so close. My knees will give way."

His chuckle tickled her neck but he went obediently to his chair. When she poured their tea he said, "Henry VIII waited eight years for Anne Boleyn. I think that's the record."

"Yes, and didn't he cut her head off a year or so after they got married?"

"Don't make me wait that long, then," he said. "Now . . . am I to fly to Milwaukee and slip my dirk into your husband's ribs? Or do we send a letter dipped in poison?"

"If there's a dirk to be stuck in his ribs it's my right to do it and don't think I didn't consider it. Darroch, over a month ago I wrote our family lawyers telling them to start divorce proceedings. I thought about it a lot before I made my decision. Now I'm committed."

She stared into the distance. "Russ should have been served, or whatever it's called, by now. I should hear something soon."

Darroch said, "I'm sorry this happened to you, but I'm happy you've already made the decision."

"It's because I came here that I got the courage to cut the ties. All my life I've been afraid of being alone. You and Màiri and Jamie and everyone made me realize I could make a life on my own. I don't have to go back to

Milwaukee. I have useful work to do here, friends, music, a place to live. I have all I want." She added shyly, "Well, almost everything. Now I know I want you, too."

"You have me, for what it's worth," he said.

"It's worth the world to me."

He said, "Ah, Jean . . . I need so much to make you mine. How long until you're free?"

"I don't know. Soon, perhaps, if Russ doesn't contest it. If there are property matters to settle it could take longer. I'm going to let him have everything just to get it settled. I don't need his money. I have my inheritances from my mother and my aunt."

"That's not right, Jean. He's the one who destroyed your marriage. He shouldn't walk away with it all."

"I have enough of my own . . . "

"And I have more than enough for the pair of us," he said impatiently. "That's not the point. You deserve an equal share of what you've both worked for in your years together. That's simple justice. And what about your children? Shouldn't you protect their interests, even though you don't need anything?"

"Oh, I'm sure Russ would look after them."

"As he looked after you? What if he marries again and has more children?"

"Oh, dear, I hadn't thought about that. But Darroch, surely he wouldn't . . . and yet, I hadn't expected him to cheat on me and he did.

"Perhaps you're right. Oh, damn. I thought I could just walk away. But I don't want him to have to sell the house or bankrupt the business to settle with me."

"Your lawyer can work something out. You could set up a trust for your children."

"Yes." She was coming to a decidedly unwelcome conclusion. "Do you suppose it would speed things up if I went back to Milwaukee to talk to Russ?" Another thought occurred to her. "I could see Sally. I left in such a hurry I'm sure she was baffled. I could explain to her about the divorce. And Darroch . . . I should tell her about you."

"You should indeed. We'll want her at the wedding, best prepare her now." He'd known instantly that marriage was what he wanted: Jean, his, forever.

"Wedding?"

"*A Dhia, mo Shine*, I've not proposed to you!" He slipped out of his chair and onto his knees in front of her.

Jean said, embarrassed. "Get up, Darroch, that's not necessary."

"Yes, it is, I've always wanted to do this. Now, Jean . . . come, you must be serious . . . stop giggling . . . give me your hands. Darling Jean, *am pòs thu mi?*"

"Oh, my, I hope that means what I think it means. *Thà gu dearbh* . . . yes, I will."

"Be sure, *mo chridhe*," he warned. "I come with a lot of baggage."

"Lovie, if you had the weight of the world on your shoulders I'd still want you. Ummm . . . unless the baggage includes a couple of wives stashed somewhere."

"Like Mr. Rochester? No, no wives, just an Island," he sighed.

"An Island I can handle."

The phone on the table next to them rang. Darroch swore and reached for it.

Jamie's voice said cheerfully, "*Feasgar math, a Dharroch. Ciamar a tha cùisean?*" How are things?

"Jamie, you damned wee *Sgiathanach diabhol*, if you're watching us on that psychic television screen of yours I order you to switch it off. Now."

"*Ceart math, a Mhic an Rìgh.* I've been getting nothing but static and wavy lines the last half-hour anyway. How are you doing?"

"I was doing just fine until the damned telephone rang," he said pointedly. "What the hell do you want?"

Jamie chuckled. "This woman of mine is bound and determined to bring supper up to you two. And short of locking her in the closet . . . or taking her to bed . . . which I may do anyway . . . I've no way to stop her."

Darroch sighed with exasperation. "May God save me from interfering females."

"No luck, *mo charaid*. God's a woman, hadn't you heard? She's on their side."

Darroch said resignedly, "How much longer do we have?"

"I think I can hold her off for an hour. *A Dhia*, how much longer do you need?"

"A lifetime to say it all, but I can outline it in an hour. *Mar sin leat, a Sheumais, agus tapadh leat.*" He clicked the phone off.

It was only when he saw Jean's puzzled face that he realized he had from habit been speaking in the Gaelic to Jamie. "What's going on?" she said.

"We're about to have company."

She felt a pang of disappointment, but brightened. "Màiri and Jamie? At least I'll have a ride home tonight."

"Home? Why would you want to do that? Why can't you stay here? We've lots more to say to each other."

"Darroch, you can't imagine I could stay here with you tonight in that little bedroom knowing you were right next door. It was hard enough when you were sick and now that you're well . . . well, I couldn't stay away, not after this afternoon."

Darroch was charmed. "*Mo chridhe* . . . am I that irresistible? I can see you're going to do wonders for my ego. But you're right. I predict you'd be alone in your bed for as long as it takes me to brush my teeth."

He put his head in her lap and breathed against her thighs, running his hands up under her skirt. Jean squirmed with pleasure. After a bit she said, "What are you thinking about?"

"I'm thinking about making love to you."

"Oh." Then, "Tell me about it."

So he did. In the Gaelic. He spoke eloquently of the many delicious parts of her anatomy: which ones would be stroked, which nibbled, which kissed.

Breathless, Jean said, "That's not fair. I can't follow all that."

"You'll have to work harder on the language then, won't you." He edged her dress up and nuzzled her thigh. "Maybe you need some private tutoring."

"Stay after school, perhaps?" She tugged on his hair.

"Ow. And lots of homework."

"I've always been a willing student, eager to learn."

She put her arms around his neck and urged him up so she could kiss him, touching his mouth lightly with her tongue, then biting his lower lip. An overwhelming desire raced through him to pull her down on the polished wood floor and have her without any further ado.

"No one should have to endure this torment," he growled.

Jean urged, "Think about going to the dentist."

"No good, my dentist's a woman. I quite fancy her."

"Your dentist's a woman, your agent's a woman, your accountant's a woman? There's a pattern there."

"I like women, especially smart ones. Especially smart, beautiful ones, like you."

She pulled away. "Lovie, I've got to tidy myself before they come."

He grinned. "I like you fine the way you are."

"Nonsense, I must be all rumpled." She glanced at her blouse and discovered he'd buttoned it quite wrong after the session on the sofa. She started to unbutton it, then blushed and turned away from him.

His resolve was sorely tested. He thought with longing of the floor, her body warm and willing under his. "I think I'm going to have to go jump in the snow," he said.

"I'll come with you. We'll make snow angels." She smiled at him. "Won't Jamie and Màiri be surprised?"

"Nothing much surprises Jamie and Màiri will only scold. We may as well please ourselves." He reached for her but she stepped nimbly backwards. "Snow angels," she said. "Cool and chaste." And she laughed.

Thirty-three

*J*ean had never before looked forward to the ending of an evening with Jamie and Màiri, but now it meant that she and Darroch would end up cuddling on the sofa at her cottage. At last they would force themselves apart and he would float back home, dizzy with love and aching with frustration. Jean would crawl into bed, hugging to herself the feeling of his arms around her.

It was hard to keep their happiness to themselves and with Jamie and Màiri, kindred spirits, they didn't even try. After dinner one evening when they all sat down in front of the fire, Jean parked herself in her usual place at one end of the couch. Darroch, at the other end, said, "No, not there, Jean. Sit here," and he'd patted the space by him.

Jean, blushing, had moved obediently to his side. He'd wrapped an arm around her and squeezed her shoulder. "That's better," he'd said and they'd smiled into each other's eyes.

And Màiri and Jamie realized that the relationship between Darroch and Jean had indeed changed. Good, thought Màiri. At last, thought Jamie.

Màiri's thought processes were always linear and naturally she assumed that Jean and Darroch were lovers. They spoke and acted like lovers and it did not occur to her that they were not.

Jamie knew better but he did not know why. Other people's actions and reactions were always so different from his that they made him curious. He said to Darroch one afternoon as they sat together in *Taigh Rois*, "Something's bothering you, *mo charaid*."

Darroch was slumped at the kitchen table, looking grim. "Frustration, pure and simple. I am most damnably frustrated."

Jamie knew immediately what he was talking about. He got the bottle of Laphroaig and two glasses and put them on the table, ready for a little *craic*. "Ahh. . .. you and Jean, is it. You haven't . . . uh . . . "

"Right, mate, we haven't, we don't and we can't. Not while she's still married to that damned Yank."

"Ah." Jamie did not quite understand. In his mind sex was a right and necessary complement to love and Darroch and Jean were as much in love as any two people he'd seen. His own marriage, after twenty years, was a heady mix of loving devotion, deep friendship and passionate sex. He adored Màiri and made no effort to hide it. The smoldering fire in his eyes when he looked at his wife made both men and women weak with envy, for different reasons.

"I haven't your scruples," he said. "My advice is to make love to her. Make her yours." He added abruptly, "I had Màiri a week after we met."

Darroch choked on his whisky. "Jamie . . . "

"Couldn't take the chance she'd get away after I'd lusted after her so long from a distance. Of course she moaned and wept about you the whole time. Verra distracting."

"Jamie, I don't need to know this . . . "

"I knew if she let me make love to her she'd be mine, she wouldn't give her body away. So I had to have her. And I did." He smiled, remembering.

Memory was surfacing in Darroch, too, of an old jealousy. He had never imagined Màiri would surrender to a new lover that fast, and it hurt. "Damn you, Jamie, you mean you seduced her."

"Oh, no. She was quite willing. But she still had you in her head, *a charaid*. I had to get rid of you.

"Women are odd creatures. They keep their attachment to past lovers no matter how the relationship ends. Jean will still have her husband in her mind. Get rid of him. Bind her to you with your words and your music and the pleasure of your cock inside her."

Darroch said, shocked, "Have you no morals?"

"My morals are my own. They're not dictated to me by some minister from something he read in a book. I'd never hurt a woman or a child. I'll never be unfaithful to my wife. I take care of my family. And I give good advice to my friends. Don't let her get away, Darroch."

"I can't have her, Jamie, not while she's still married. You know what this Island is like. One hint of improper goings-on and it'd be Jean who'd pay the price. Me they'd just cluck over. 'Ach, he's chust a man,' they'd say. But they'd think ill of Jean and God knows how long it would take them to forget about it. If they ever did forget. She might spend the rest of her life here stigmatized as the Scarlet Woman." He drained his glass in one gulp.

Jamie, who'd never seen Darroch do more than sip a whisky, was impressed by his misery and poured another dram for him.

"The hell of it is that everyone else can sleep around with no consequences. My wife, Jean's husband . . . "

"What's he like?"

"Good father, hot-shot businessman, selfish to the core and a damned womanizer."

"Oh. Is that why . . . " Jamie paused delicately.

"Got it in one. Cheated on her and told her about it. That's how she ended up here." Darroch picked up his glass. "She was fed up and decided to scarper while she thought things out. Lucky for me, hell on her. I could relate to adultery, one of the first things we had in common." He took a reflective swallow. "Don't let on I told you about Russ, I shouldn't have said anything. She's sensitive about it."

Jamie sipped his whisky thoughtfully. "She's divorcing him?"

"Aye. But he's stalling, probably hoping she'll change her mind. She might go back to the States, see if she can speed things up." He looked even grimmer. "It terrifies me to think of her leaving. Suppose she decides to stay? America offers her so much more, you know. Land of the free, home of the microwave oven and the three-car garage. And if he plays on her guilt feelings about leaving her family . . . " He finished the second whisky in one gulp.

"She's not the kind of woman to care about three-car garages." The Sight told Jamie Darroch had nothing to worry about but as usual he would say nothing about it. "Well, you both have my sympathy. I'm impressed that you're able to . . . what was it the Yank president's wife said? . . . just say no."

"Aye. We're a couple of damned saints," Darroch said bitterly. "God knows why I don't take her to London where people mind their own business. Her marriage is dead and gone. How could it hurt anyone if we became lovers?"

Jamie had no answer for that but to pour a third dram. Darroch said, "Steady on, the women'll not be best pleased if we're roaring drunk when they get home."

"I'll make a pot of tea. That's innocent enough and it'll hide the fumes."

As he was bringing the teapot to the table the door opened. Jean came in, tight-lipped and quiet, behind her Màiri with a face like thunder. The men looked at each other.

"Pleasant shopping, *m'eudail*?" said Jamie in a neutral voice.

Màiri snarled, "Pleasant enough until we met Bridget MacDonough."

"What happened?"

Jean said, "It doesn't matter . . . " Her voice trailed off.

Màiri exploded, "That damned woman always, always gets her knife in! Today she asked about Jean's husband and when was he coming to the Island. She went on and on about how Jean must miss him and wasn't she lonely for her bairns."

Darroch slammed his hand down on the kitchen table. The other three jumped and the whisky bottle rose in the air, swayed back and forth and as though in slow motion began to topple downwards. Jamie grabbed it just in time.

"I've had enough," said Darroch, his voice low, fierce and determined. "I'm moving to London and Jean, you're coming with me."

Màiri was alarmed and even Jamie looked concerned. Only Jean remained calm. "No, I'm not, and neither are you." The other three stared in surprise and Darroch opened his mouth to argue.

Jean said patiently, "I told you, Darroch, this is my home now. No gossipy old bat will drive me away." She smiled. "Let Mrs. MacDonough move to London. I know a nice apartment she could rent. It has a balcony overlooking the Thames."

After a moment of stunned silence Jamie chuckled and said, "*Thà gu dearbh, mo charaid*. You tell 'em."

"Besides," said Jean. "You're forgetting what I said to her."

Màiri began to laugh helplessly. "She told Bridget her bairns were grown and away and that she was divorcing her husband so no, she didn't miss him. You could see Bridget reverberate like an antenna in a high wind. She was so anxious to broadcast the news her feet barely touched the ground when she left us."

"Cat's well and truly out of the bag, *nach*?" Jamie said.

Jean said calmly, "Yep. The kitten's out of the strudel for good, as we say in Milwaukee."

Jamie grinned at Darroch. "Puts you in your place, doesn't it, when the lasses are always right."

Darroch said, "I've often thought the one redeeming trait of my character is my good taste in women." He added, "What in hell is wrong with Bridget MacDonough? Why is she such a torment?"

Màiri said, exasperated, "Really, Darroch, don't be thick. You must know." When he looked baffled, she added, "Her daughter, Elspeth. It's been her life's ambition that Elspeth would catch the Laird, ever since we were all in school."

Darroch turned red with annoyance. "That's daft. Elspeth and Seumas MacQuirter were in love when we were youngsters. I thought they were set to be married, they were so mad about each other. They were always sneaking off together and coming back looking like cats that'd been at the cream. It's a wonder he hadn't got her with child before they were seventeen."

"Aye. But they didn't marry, did they?"

"Well, I always wondered why not," he admitted.

"Because," Màiri explained in tones of infinite patience, "her mother wouldn't allow it. She always had her eye on you for Elspeth. As long as you and I were together she knew Elspeth hadn't a chance and was willing to let Seumas have her.

"After I was out of the picture she was at it again. She forbade Elspeth to marry and made her life hell until Seumas got fed up and courted Beathag MacCorkle and married her. Elspeth's hated her mother ever since, that's why she's so bitter and mean. She's had to stay home with a mother who ruined her life."

"But hasn't Beathag been dead these four or five years? Elspeth never married. Why haven't they gotten back together?"

"I can answer that," said Jamie unexpectedly. "It's her tongue." The others were bewildered. "Seumas got drunk at the cèilidh one night and I went out with him for a breath of air. He was feeling really low, missing Beathag and telling me how lonely he was.

"I asked him why didn't he look out for a new wife and he said he'd thought about courting Elspeth but she'd grown so sharp-tongued he was afraid she'd eat him for breakfast if he tried. Said he couldn't bear the thought of being ridiculed, but Elspeth was the only woman he wanted. So he was at an impasse."

"You know," said Màiri thoughtfully, "I think Elspeth is still soft on Seumas. There'd be a nice match and Bridget MacDonough would get her comeuppance too."

Darroch looked wary and Jamie shuddered. "Women's work, *m'eudail.* I'd not touch that one."

Màiri and Jean exchanged glances. "Hmm," said Jean.

One evening when they were all at *Taigh Rois,* Màiri and Darroch got into a heated argument. Disagreements between the two of them were not uncommon. Màiri's fiery temper escalated them rapidly and tonight they were going at it full speed ahead.

Jean had lost track of the exact focus of the argument . . . something about increasing the number of classes in the High School that were taught in English, she thought. Darroch was arguing, as he always did, that their young people needed to be fluent in English and Màiri was arguing, as she always did, that too much English would lead to mass emigration to the mainland, something all Eilean Dubhannaich worried about where their children were concerned.

The argument had reached the point where they were glaring at each other. Jean glanced at Jamie. He was, predictably, not listening. He usually retreated into his own thoughts when his wife and best friend began wrangling. When the two slipped into the Gaelic, fast and furious, Jean was completely lost and could only stare, dismayed, from one to the other.

Abruptly Darroch stopped talking, leaned back and smiled at Màiri, the gentle intimate smile Jean had come to regard as her personal property. He picked up her hand and began to stroke her palm with his index finger. Her angry voice trailed off and she stared into his eyes as he talked to her softly.

Màiri was blushing, Jean realized in shock. What was Darroch saying to her?

When he lifted her hand to his mouth and kissed the palm Jean felt a sudden overwhelming, disabling surge of jealousy. There's still something between them, she thought, shocked. What a fool I've been.

Jamie smiled and stood up. "That's enough of that for one evening. Stop making love to my wife and give her her hand back, *a Dharroch.* She'll need it for me later," he said. "And *tapadh leat.* Since you've had the rough edge of her tongue tonight perhaps I'll be spared a scolding."

The two looked up at him. Màiri's smile was dreamy. "I never scold you, Jamie, not unless you need it."

"I don't need it tonight. What I need is eight hours of sleep and a cuddle with my wife thrown in at one point or another. Evening, morning, middle of the night, all three, I don't care."

Everyone laughed but Jean.

When she and Darroch got back to her cottage he took off his coat, then slipped hers off her shoulders. He lifted the hair on the back of her neck and kissed her there. She shivered at the flow of intimacy between them. He's not mine, she told herself, he's still Màiri's. Hold onto that thought and try to get through what lies ahead.

When he wrapped his arms around her she was unyielding, as stiff as stone. Puzzled, he asked, "Are you cold, Jean?"

She was cold. She was frozen in despair, her heart was solid ice. "You're in love with her, aren't you," she said. It was a statement, not a question.

He lifted his head from her hair. "What?"

"Màiri. You're still in love with her."

Quietly, he said, "I do love her, yes."

"That's it, then." She pulled away and struck out blindly across the room, not stopping until she ran into a kitchen chair. "Ow," she said pitifully, and burst into tears.

"Jean . . ."

"I can't bear it." She clutched the chair for support. Anguish was pulling her down like gravity and she could barely stand up.

He crossed the floor in one movement and pulled her into his arms but she fought to get away. Tiring of the struggle he picked her up.

"You'll hurt your back," she muttered.

"I'll risk it," he growled.

Out of respect for his back she lay still in his arms, face buried against his jacket. He carried her to the sofa and sat down with her held firmly on his lap.

"Now," he said. "You'll kindly tell me what this is all about."

She stared at him. "You love Màiri."

He said impatiently, "Of course. What's that to do with anything?"

"You're still in love with her." His eyes widened. "I saw how you smiled at her, how you held her hand. I heard how you talked to her. Like a lover. Jamie saw it too."

He said, wonder dawning in his face, "You're jealous."

Her heart was breaking and he was accusing her of jealousy. Now she was angry, a great sweeping wave of frustrated fury that made her pummel his chest with her fists. He caught them and held them easily.

"You love her, you'll always love her, I'm just . . . convenient. You can't have her so you'll settle for me." She said defiantly, "I won't be second best."

A lot of words, some of them angry and some of them indignant, came to his lips but he forced himself to stay quiet for a few moments. Then he lifted her, pulled her astride him so they were face to face.

"Damn it, let me go. Don't do this to me, Darroch." Why were men so much stronger? Her position opened her and she could feel his hard length pressed against her. How dare he be aroused when her heart was breaking? Determined to get away, she wriggled furiously.

He groaned. "*A Dhia*, Jean, have pity and sit still. I'm desperate enough for you as it is without all that squirming. Remember, I'm just a man."

They stared at each other. Then he filled both hands with her hair and urged her face close. He took her with his tongue, filling her mouth, tasting her, stroking the delicate textures inside her lips. Helpless with love she let him have his way.

He said, "Ah, you're delicious, I could devour you. God only knows why you're not flat on your back in your bed with me inside you. You'll take all of me, won't you, Jean. I've never had a woman do that. Every inch, every millimeter will be inside you and my balls snug against your sweet quim."

He slipped his hand down between them and touched her intimately. "You're wet," he whispered in her ear. "All for me, Jean, all for me."

It was unbearable. Even as she arched against his hand she snapped, "All right, you've shown you can seduce me in a minute. That just proves I love you. That was never in doubt."

"So it's my love that's in doubt, is it?" He butterflied his hand against her and she moaned, her body beginning to respond with movements of its own.

"Do you feel what you're doing to me?" He pressed himself against her. "Your bed is so close, your clothes just a minor barrier. Imagine it, Jean. Imagine the pleasure possible, just moments away."

Waves of sensation flooded her body. She collapsed against him and heard, infuriatingly, his chuckle in her ear. He moved both hands behind her, still inside her clothes, to grip her bottom possessively.

"Now, Jean. We've established that you love me. As you say, that was never in doubt. Certainly I've never doubted you. That's part of your enduring charm, that you gave your love so openly. You looked me straight in the eye, that day after the blizzard, and said, 'I love you.' No coyness. Very honest, very American, Jean.

"I should have ravished you that day, just as we both wanted. Made you mine in every sense of the word. You know, I'm not sure self control is all it's cracked up to be."

She said, desperate with need, "You can have me now, if you want."

"Oh, I do want, Jean. Can you not feel what I want?" He pressed up against her in a slow, sensual movement until she gasped. "Now I want you to consider this very carefully, *mo chridhe*. With all this mutual wanting and your undoubted love why are we not in bed right now, wrapped around each other?"

He stared into her eyes and nodded at what he saw dawning in them. "Aye, you've the right of it. Because I love you. I love your conscience, that prickly nuisance. Love you enough not to dishonor you by taking you while you are married. Love you enough to wait until you're free. But the minute you're free I will make love to you until there's no room in your head for anything else.

"Such magnificent self-restraint, Jean. Isn't that proof of my love? Isn't it proof enough for you?"

"But you want Màiri . . . I saw the way you looked at her, how you held her hands."

He sighed. "Time for more honesty, Jean. I wanted Màiri long after our relationship ended, long after she married Jamie. Wanted her with all my heart and soul and body. I fought so hard against it, knowing it was wrong, pretended I felt nothing but friendship. She was someone else's wife, and he my best friend. Jamie knew my love and Màiri knew it and both were kind. So kind, to poor tormented Darroch.

"I dreamed about her and in my dreams she was mine again and we were seventeen with our lives ahead of us. Even when I was with Morgan . . . you don't know about her . . . and Adrienne . . . I dreamed about Màiri. After a while it was just a couple of times a year but it was always the same. I'd wake up happy and then realize it was only a dream. God, it was awful, I'd never believed such misery could be possible.

"Seeing her on the Island . . . most of the time I could handle it but sometimes it came over me in waves, what we'd been to each other, how we'd loved. I knew what I was doing to myself but I couldn't stop."

He sighed. "First love. It's the very devil, isn't it, Jean.

"Then one day a beautiful American woman came on the scene. Do you ever stop to think how close we came to missing each other? If you hadn't thought you knew me, because of *The Magician* . . . hadn't spoken to me . . . our paths might not have crossed and you might have left, gone back to Milwaukee with our never having known each other.

"We became friends right away, remember? Then one day, up in the cemetery, the day you finished Lady Eilidh's grave, I felt such a wave of desire for you I could have taken you right there amidst the tombstones."

He smiled ruefully. "So then I was in a right pickle. Lusting after two women, both married, both unattainable, both my dear friends. What was I, a sex maniac? I would certainly become a maniac of some kind if this kept up."

He took her hand and caressed the palm, just as he had caressed Màiri's an hour ago. Then he grinned unexpectedly. "Shall I go on? I seem to be telling you my deepest secrets. I hope you don't mind."

She whispered, "I don't mind." Just keep touching me, she thought.

He bent closer and said softly, "And then one morning I realized I wasn't dreaming about Màiri any more. I was dreaming about you. Naked in my arms, giving yourself to me, taking me inside you. Now I had only one married woman I was lusting after . . . you. You, Jean. Not Màiri, never again Màiri. I was free. What a gift you gave me, that freedom.

"Fool that I am, it wasn't until the blizzard I realized I loved you. How brave you were, *m'aingeal*, to speak first. I knew then I had to have you for my own. One day it won't be just a dream, you'll be in my bed to kiss and play with and talk to and make wonderful love to forever. My woman. All mine."

She whispered, "But the way you held Màiri's hand, the way you looked in her eyes . . . "

He laughed. "Jamie taught me that. Màiri's hot-tempered; she has terrible rages. I have a temper too and she always brought it out in me when she got angry. We used to have the most dreadful rows, ending up not speaking to each other for days.

"One day I asked Jamie how he dealt with her in her tearaways. He said, 'I let her talk, get it all out. Then I make love to her.' And I understood how to handle her. With tenderness and love, not anger. She still drives me wild at times but I don't fight back anymore, it doesn't work. You don't fight fire with fire. And who cares who wins an argument, as long as love prevails.

"Màiri's a wonderful woman, so full of passion, so caring, so dedicated. I respect her deeply and I love her devotedly. You and Màiri and Jamie are my dearest friends. It's like a cobweb, isn't it . . . these threads that bind the four of us together. Friends and lovers. Jamie and Màiri, Jean and Darroch. Each of us with our heart's desire.

"Now am I forgiven? Is it all clear?"

Jean threw herself into his arms and to her shame burst into tears. "'I'm so sorry! I didn't mean to doubt you. It's just that I love you so much . . . "

"Nothing to forgive, I found your jealousy flattering. A proof of your love, in fact." He took her shoulders in his hands and stared at her. "While we're on the subject of jealousy, let's talk about you and Jamie. I know he's the handsomest man on the face of the planet but must you look at him as though he were a combination of God and a dish of chocolate mousse?"

Blushing, she pulled away. "It's only when he's playing his fiddle. I admire him as a musician."

"You must be the only woman in the world who feels that way, then. Lucky for the rest of us men that he's too in love with Màiri and too terrified of her to stray."

She laughed. He said, "I've seen him undress you with his eyes, the randy *diabhol*. I warn you, Jean, I won't put up with any nonsense from that quarter."

She put her arms around his neck. "Talk to me some more about making love," she said softly.

"Like that, do you? What if I were to tell you how much I enjoy the position in which we now find ourselves, with you astride me, open and inviting, and the warmth of your bottom making me hard. I'm imagining us naked and you very wet, trickles of moisture from your secret spring dribbling over me, bathing my cock in your liquid honey, honey that I shortly expect to taste with my tongue at its source."

It was better than a movie, watching her expression change as his words and his beautiful voice turned her on. First eyes widening, then the expected blush up to her hairline, then her eyes closing in sensual pleasure, then an unexpected, mischievous little smile that did wicked things to him.

He purred, "Do you know, Jean, I haven't seen your feet naked yet. Shall I strip them tonight, pull your shoes and stockings off quite slowly, play with each of your bare little toes?"

Delicious currents of pleasure flowed through her. "You're some talker," she whispered in his ear.

"Aye, well, I can talk about it now because I can't do it. You wait until you're in bed with me. I'll be as silent as a clam."

She laughed. "Darroch Mac an Rìgh, silent? And pigs might fly, and the moon is made of green cheese."

"And women worship Jamie MacDonald because of his fiddle playing. And other great myths of our century."

She peeked up at him from under her lashes, her hand twiddling his shirt button teasingly. "Umm . . . Darroch . . . what's a quim?"

"Allow me to point it out to you," he said, grinning broadly, and his hand began to move slowly down from her shoulders.

It was gradually dawning on the *Eilean Dubhannaich* that there was a special relationship between their laird and the American woman. It may have been because Darroch always seemed to turn up, somehow, wherever Jean was: shopping in the Square, working in the Playschool, weeding in the cemetery.

It may have been the intimate way they stared into each other's eyes when they sang together.

But the obvious tip-off was when they danced the final waltz together at *cèilidhean*. They had danced it together from their earliest acquaintance. Jean loved to waltz; she'd coaxed Russ into taking ballroom dancing lessons one year and she'd become the class's prize pupil. And Darroch waltzed the way he danced the Scottish country dances: confident, graceful, enjoying every minute.

Early in their relationship they'd delighted in big sweeping circles, whirling around the floor. Lately, though, when the lights were dimmed for the last waltz they drew closer and closer until they moved as one, her cheek against his shoulder, his cheek against her hair, holding each other tenderly. It was as though they were able to let down their natural caution when the lights were lowered and the final waltz played.

The *Eilean Dubhannaich*, for the most part, approved. Jean had the stamp of acceptance from Màiri, whose antipathy to foreigners was widely known. Jamie treated her with obvious respect and affection. Barabal, Ian the Post, Ian's Catrìona, Sheilah, Gordon had all become her friends. Even the Minister was known to unbend so far as to smile his frosty smile at her.

And the projects she had undertaken amazed them. She had become

Màiri's right-hand woman in the Playschool. She was not too proud to wait on tables and wash dishes when Sheilah needed help. She had embarked on the study of the Gaelic, which the Islanders recognized with deep pride to be a very difficult language, and she spoke it to them and insisted that they respond in the same way.

And *a Dhia*, she had weeded Lady Eilidh's grave!

It was slower to dawn on them that she might be a candidate for Lady of Eilean Dubh. She was, everyone knew, married.

The Islanders watched and wondered and waited. Stoicism was bred in them, as in all Highlanders, from centuries of poverty and hard times. What would happen would happen.

What mattered now was that Darroch was happy, happier than he had been in years. And because they loved him that was enough for them, for now.

Thirty-four

*I*an the Post always stopped by home on his mail rounds to share a cup of tea with Catrìona, and occasionally, a cuddle, if he was running ahead of schedule. This morning they were having a cozy cup together while Catrìona opened their mail.

"What's this?" she said curiously, pulling a long envelope from the pile. "It does not look like a bill. There is no return on it and the address is hand printed."

"There were a number of those in the post today. I thought perhaps it was an invitation. Do we know anyone who's getting married?"

"It does not look like a wedding invitation," said Catrìona dubiously. She tore open the envelope, unfolded the letter and began to read. Suddenly she gasped and dropped the paper as if it were hot.

Alarmed, Ian said, "Whatever is wrong, *m'eudail?*" He reached for the letter.

She snatched it up. "No, no, you mustn't read it!"

"*A Chatrìona, thoir dhomh-sa an litir,*" he said firmly, holding out his hand.

They stared at each other. Finally she said, "Aye, you're right. You must see it." She handed it to him.

He read aloud, "The wicked American woman seduced your Ian and now she has seduced . . . " He stopped, realizing what he had said. " . . . the

Laird. She is married. The Sixth Commandment says 'Thou shall not commit adultery.'"

Speechless with disbelief he finally managed to say, "*A Chatrìona . . .* " but he could get no further.

She smiled at him. "Well, I know the first part is not true and I don't believe the second part either," she said briskly. "Now, who's playing such a nasty joke?"

He whispered, "You never thought such a thing of me, did you?"

"Of course not, though there were those who tried to make me think it. There were whispers about you and Jean, did you know that?" One look at his aghast face and she had the answer. He hadn't known, he was blushing up to the ears to even think of it.

"I had no idea . . . " he stammered, then grew angry. "How dare anyone say such a thing about Jean?"

"And you, *mo ghràdh*," she said, faintly amused.

He shrugged that off. "It does not matter about me, anyone with a particle of sense knows I am yours entirely. What nonsense, to think I'd play you false." He picked up her hand and kissed it. "But to insult our visitor, my friend and yours . . . you should have told me."

"What would that have done but to make you uncomfortable with each other, you and Jean," she said sensibly. "I took care of it." She smiled with satisfaction.

"What did you do?"

"I made a point of getting to know Jean and I made it perfectly clear to one and all that she was my friend and no one was to say anything bad about her in my presence."

"Ah. I thought you became acquainted very quickly." He was struck suddenly by a thought. "*A Dhia beannaich mi*, there must be a dozen of these letters in the post today!"

She was horrified. "Letters like this? So it is an organized campaign. Who is getting them?" When he shook his head she said, "Yes, I know, you must respect the confidentiality of *Am Post Rìoghal*. But if one is addressed to Jean, I would not like her to open it when she is alone."

"You are right," he said gravely. He stood up. "I must go back on my route or the post will be late. Will you walk out with me, *m'eudail?*"

She followed him to the post bus. He examined the next batch of mail carefully. Then he said, "Were you saying you wished to visit Jean this morning? Fetch a wrap. It's chilly."

She hurried into the house and was back in a moment with purse and jacket. He dropped off mail at several cottages, then pulled into Jean's lane. "I think I will come in with you and say hello to Jean," he said casually.

Jean opened the door. "Hi, Ian, what's this, special delivery? And Catrìona, too, how nice. Come in."

"*Tapadh leat.*" They walked in and stood looking acutely uncomfortable.

Puzzled, Jean said, "Umm. . .. how about a cup of tea? Come into the kitchen." She filled the kettle, put cups and the obligatory plate of biscuits on the table. She made casual conversation, wondering what was going on.

When the tea was ready she brought it to the table and sat down. She noticed that Ian had taken a biscuit and reduced it with nervous fingers to a heap of crumbs. "Is anything wrong, guys?" she asked, looking from one serious face to the other.

Ian said, "There is something in your mail you should read now, *a Shìne.*" He stared pointedly at the letters she had set aside politely until her visitors left.

She flipped through her mail, stopping when she came to a long envelope without a return address. She eyed it curiously. "Is this it?" Ian nodded.

She tore it open and read, "You are an adulteress and will burn in the hottest fires of hell. You seduced Ian and you have lured the Laird into sin. The Lord will wreak His vengeance on evildoers. Beware!"

Ian had never seen anyone turn completely white before. She swayed in her chair and he rose, ready to catch her if she fainted.

Instead, she grasped the edge of the table with both hands, closed her eyes briefly and then opened them. "You both know what this letter says." Horribly embarrassed, she could not look at Ian.

Catrìona said, "Aye, I got one too, *a charaid.*" Then she added, unhappily, "We think there are more although, of course, Ian cannot tell us because the post is confidential."

Jean shook her head. "I don't understand. How could anyone believe this?" Then, struck by the same thought as Ian had been, she gasped, "Catrìona, you don't think Ian and I . . . "

"Of course not. It is not the first time it has been suggested to me, Jean." She smiled. "Your Friday drives did cause some comment."

"What?"

"It seems we paused too long to eat our sandwiches," Ian remarked bitterly, finally able to speak.

Jean said, "And you were still friendly to me, Catrìona?" Then light dawned. "I see. That's why you went out of your way to show that you were my friend." She looked gratefully at the other woman.

"*Tha*, and I thought it had worked. There were no more sly comments for me to overhear 'accidentally.' I never dreamed of something like this." She shook her head.

Remembering Catrìona's earlier words Jean said, "You said there are more of these? Dear God, what am I going to do?"

"No one will believe it," Ian said stoutly.

"Nevertheless, we must get to the bottom of this," Catrìona replied. "You had better finish your route, Ian, and perhaps you could . . . hint . . . to others who get the letter that they should join us here."

"*Thà gu dearbh*, I will do that," he said, nodding and standing up. "I will be discreet but I will let them know we are holding a council of war." He moved to Jean, took her hand and shook it with grave formality. "You are not to worry, *a Shìne*. We will look after you."

He kissed Catrìona and left. When she turned back to the table she saw that Jean was crying quietly. Distressed, she started to move to Jean's side but was waved back.

"I'm all right. It's just that he's so sweet." She brushed the tears away.

"Oh, yes," said Catrìona. "He is a good man, with a kind heart. I am a lucky woman."

"So am I, to have you both as friends," said Jean.

Ian sped through his route in record time. He convinced Barabal to abandon her laundry. After reading her letter she dropped her clothespins and jumped in her little black Austin.

In the square Beathag the Bread and Cailean the Crab were both too busy in their shops to look at their mail and he left it, unhappily, in the usual places. Ros MacPherson was at the hospital, so his mail went through the slot.

The envelope for Sheilah and Gordon he placed in Sheilah's hands.

Sheila said, "It's important?" At his nod she said, "I'm in the middle of making blackberry pies. May Gordon open it?" Ian nodded again and Sheilah went to find him.

Ian's last stop in the village was at the Minister's and here conscience and loyalty hurtled into open warfare. He was sorely, wickedly tempted to take the envelope addressed to the Minister, tear it up and throw the pieces to the far winds but it would be a violation of his duty to *Am Post*.

He stood outside the Minister's door for a long time before sliding the envelope into the slot. His shoulders hunched with unhappiness, he walked back to the post bus.

His final stop was at the Playschool. Màiri also required persuading to read her mail then and there but once she opened it she was like someone on fire. "Do you know what's in this?" she demanded.

He nodded. "Yes, for Catrìona and I also received one. As have several others."

"Who?"

"You know I cannot tell you. It is confidential, the post."

He met her glare bravely. Capitulating, she said, "What are we doing about this?"

"Jean's friends are gathering at her cottage."

Màiri grabbed her jacket and shut off the lights. "Go ahead, I'll follow you."

Màiri was not surprised to find Jean's kitchen table covered with food. It was like a wake. Barabal had brought cookies and Sheilah had sent sandwiches and a blackberry pie hot from the oven. Catrìona had taken over the teamaking and was pouring the third pot of the afternoon.

Màiri took charge the moment she entered the cottage and determined their strategy: any attempt to embarrass Jean would be met with swift action. Offenders would be humiliated and ostracized.

Darroch could take care of himself, they knew. He was, after all, the Laird. But Jean was vulnerable and they would protect her. She was their friend.

Gordon, the only male present, sat, restless, while the women talked earnestly around him. When Jamie arrived, Gordon greeted him with relief.

"What's going on?"

"Come outside and I'll tell you."

When he finished his recital, Gordon was not surprised to see the look of sheer fury on Jamie's face. "Who would dare?" he said when he was able to speak. "*A Dhia*, Darroch will be like an avenging angel, he will come down upon them with fire and sword. I would not be in their shoes when he finds out who they are. And it is all untrue, what the letters say."

He added, "You know they will be wed, those two, after her divorce."

Gordon said, "I had assumed as much. It will be good for the Laird to have a wife."

"Whoever wrote the letter must know that and hopes to prevent it."

"Why?"

Jamie shrugged. "I suspect the jealousy of a woman."

Gordon nodded. "It does not seem the sort of thing a man would do." He moved restlessly. "It is times like this when I wished that I still smoked cigarettes, it keeps the hands busy." He glanced at his watch. "I do not like to leave Jean but Sheilah will be needing help with the evening meals."

Jamie clapped him on the back. "Away, then, *a charaid*. Màiri and I will stay with her." They went inside so Gordon could say goodbye.

Barabal said reluctantly, "I should go too. The children and Tòmas will be expecting supper."

Catrìona said, "We will not leave you if you wish us to stay, *a Shìne*."

Jean got up and hugged her. "I'm fine. Thank you all for your support. I can't tell you what it means to me." She looked at them. She was trying hard to keep her cool and not be a gusher but she was afraid she was going to cry. "This . . . " she waved her hand at the letter resting uneasily on the table by the half-eaten blackberry pie " . . . this doesn't matter any more."

Catrìona too looked on the brink of tears. Barabal took her by the arm and said, "Come along, *mo Chatrìona*, I will take you home. Your Ian has done well today and deserves his supper." To Jean she said, "You are not to be concerned, *a Shìne*. We will see you through this."

Jean was crying when they left, she could not help it. She pulled herself together enough to say, "Shall I make more tea?"

"Not for me, thanks, I'm awash with the stuff," said Jamie. "Do you know when Darroch's coming home from Inverness?"

Jean shook her head. "Maybe tomorrow . . . " She was interrupted by a knock. "Now who is that? Everyone's checked in."

She went to the door. "Darroch! I didn't expect you so soon." She flung her arms around his neck.

He grinned. "If I'd known I'd get that sort of welcome I would have come home sooner. *A Dhia beannaich mi*, Inverness is a tedious sort of place." Then he looked at her more carefully. "Jean, what's the matter? You've been crying. What's happened?"

Behind her he saw Jamie and Màiri. "What's going on?" He looked from one solemn face to another. "Will no one tell me?"

Jamie shook his head. Màiri opened her mouth but could not speak. Baffled, Darroch turned to Jean.

She realized all three were watching her expectantly but she could not bear to put it into words. She said at last, "Come into the bedroom a moment, Darroch."

He followed her with a backward look at the other two. She sat down on the bed and patted the space beside her. He sat obediently. "Well?"

Jean wished she'd brought the letter. It might have been easier just to let him read it, she thought, but the idea of him seeing the awful accusatory words made her cringe.

Darroch said, "Why do I have the feeling you're going to tell me something I don't want to hear?"

She smiled at him ruefully. "Perhaps you have the Sight."

"Shh," he said, putting a finger on her lips. "We don't talk about that." Then he put his arms around her. "If this is going to be unpleasant, welcome me home first." She moved closer and for a few blissful moments forgot her troubles. But when he leaned away and looked at her, waiting, she stalled.

"Ummm . . . how was your meeting in Inverness?"

"Damn the meeting, Jean, what the hell has happened?"

She sighed. "Well, you see, there's this letter going around. It accuses me of . . . umm . . . seducing Ian . . . and . . . leading you into sin . . . and . . . well, it talks about the Sixth Commandment. And burning in hell." She got it all out in a rush.

Bewildered, he said, "What do you mean, going around?"

"We . . . uh . . . think a dozen letters were delivered this morning." She was reluctant to meet his eyes.

"A dozen letters? Accusing you . . . us . . . of adultery? Who got them?"

"Ian can't tell us because the mail is confidential. But he and Catrìona got one, and Barabal and Sheilah and Gordon and Jamie and Màiri . . . and I think, because Ian seemed so concerned . . . the Minister."

Darroch closed his eyes in pain. The Minister. "Who's done this?"

"We don't know. But it explains something that happened Monday."

Jean was remembering with new understanding a puzzling incident. There were two bakeries on the Square and she'd fallen into the habit of going to Beathag the Bread's shop because Beathag made, of all things, croissants. If Jean could not have a bagel a croissant was her next favorite choice for breakfast.

Monday, however, Beathag's shop had been closed so the staff could attend a funeral. Frustrated, Jean headed for the second bakery.

The owner was talking to a woman. Both glanced at Jean. The owner ignored her. The other woman pointedly turned her back.

Jean had never been snubbed on Eilean Dubh and she could not believe it was happening now. Perhaps she'd interrupted a very personal conversation. She waited patiently, then cleared her throat. "Excuse me."

The owner looked at her coldly. "Yes?"

"Umm . . . do you have a loaf of wholemeal bread?"

Behind her a shelf groaned with loaves of bread. "No," she said, and there was ice in her voice.

Jean felt heat rising in her face and she turned away. She fumbled with the door and exited ungracefully.

Out in the fresh air she took deep breaths to steady herself. The slight had been deliberate, intended to hurt and it did. She was what she had never before been on Eilean Dubh: a stranger, an interloper, unwanted. And she had no idea why.

But she still had shopping to do. She summoned up her courage and walked into the fishmonger's. Two women glanced at her and turned their backs. Deliberately one of them prolonged the process of giving her order so Jean would have to wait.

Cailean the Crab had no idea what was going on and he was appalled at what he clearly recognized as an insult. Nor did he intend to be made part of it. "*Gabh mo leisguil*," he told the women and turned to Jean. "Yes, love, what can I do for you?" he said. He always forgot to speak the Gaelic to Jean and he enjoyed showing off his English to her appreciative audience.

Jean breathed a sigh of relief. At least she wasn't going to be snubbed by everyone. She ordered fish and prawns and gave Cailean her most grateful smile. "See you again," he called after her. "*Ceart math*," she responded.

But the two experiences had sapped her energy and she needed time to think about them before she risked any further interaction with the Islanders. After supper tonight she would ask Darroch what he thought was going on.

But she forgot to ask. He'd received a gossipy e-mail from a fellow actor in London, full of sly and acerbic comments about mutual theatrical friends and he shared it with Jean, acting out all the characters involved and adding his own witty sidelights. She laughed so hard the snubs receded to the back of her mind and she thought no more about them. Until now, when they started to make sense. There was more to this than one person sending letters.

Darroch was as speechless as she'd been earlier. Finally he pulled her fiercely to him. "For this to happen when I was not here. For you to face this alone . . . "

She said happily, "But I wasn't, lovie, that's what's so wonderful. Ian and Catrìona came down to make sure I wouldn't open the letter alone. Then Ian got our friends to come and they stayed all afternoon. Everyone's been so kind and supportive."

Gossip did not surprise Darroch, it was Island disease and hobby. Criticism of Jean would have made him angry, for he thought her above reproach. But outright slander in an anonymous letter left him quite livid with rage. All the tightly leashed instincts of the Laird and two hundred years of Mac an Rìgh domination of the Island sprang forth in his cold hard fury. How dare anyone insult his lady? He would find out who was responsible for this outrage and deal with them swiftly and without mercy.

He stood up, pulling Jean with him. "I need to talk to Màiri."

Màiri said as they came in, "Jamie's gone home to fetch chops for our supper." She glanced at Darroch, trying to read his face.

He said, "Màiri, what's this about?"

She heard the controlled anger in his voice and looked at him warily. She was sitting at the table, a pan of potatoes in her lap and a knife in her hand. "I'd guess Bridget MacDonough and her cronies." She jabbed a potato viciously.

"Her again! Whatever for?"

"If you'll recall what I've said before, she does not want you to marry anyone but her daughter. She especially does not want you to marry an outsider." She paused. "I'm sorry, Jean. She is one of the few left who might consider you an outsider."

"The woman is *as a chiall* . . . insane. Elspeth and I have not the slightest interest in each other. We've never had the slightest interest in each other."

Màiri sighed. "As long as you are unwed there is hope, to her way of thinking. She wants her daughter to marry the Laird and she does not care how it happens."

Darroch snarled, "That bloody laird business. I'll rid this Island of that foolishness if it's the last thing I do. The MacDonoughs are going to be very sorry she started this." His face was set in a quiet anger more disturbing than an outburst of rage.

Màiri said, "Darroch, no one cares."

"What?" He looked at her, not understanding.

"We know how it is with you and Jean, that you're waiting for her divorce so you can marry." Jean felt her face turning red. She had not realized their private affairs were so widely known. But it was Eilean Dubh, where everybody knew everything about everybody else. "What we want . . . and need . . . is for Jean to stay here and for the two of you to be happy together. And for her to do what she has been doing ever since she arrived: making herself a part of the Island. She is one of us and we need her.

"Adultery is not the issue. Do you understand me, Jean? Darroch? No one who matters cares if you are lovers."

Darroch said quietly, "Except for Minister Donald."

Màiri sighed again and picked up the knife. "Aye. Except for Minister Donald."

He stood motionless, then headed for the door, calling over his shoulder, "Màiri, please call the Manse. Ask if the Minister can see me in fifteen minutes. And will you wait supper for me? I did not have one good meal in Inverness and I am starved. Especially for chops."

Thirty-five

Speak not evil of one another, brethren.

James 4:11

*T*he Minister's housekeeper ushered him in reverently. "He is working on his sermon for Sunday," she whispered. "He normally would not see anyone but he seemed to be expecting you." And he would always see the Laird, she thought, but did not say it.

The only light in the Minister's study came from the lamp on the old desk behind which he sat. The room's corners were shrouded in shadow and the drapes were tightly drawn to keep out the cold.

When the housekeeper ushered him in Darroch was for a moment back in his childhood. As the Laird's son, he'd been subjected to weekly sessions with the Minister who'd been responsible for teaching the boy about religion and about Island history.

Darroch remembered being frightened, at first, of the imposing man behind the desk though later he came to enjoy their meetings. The Minister had seemed ancient but Darroch realized that he had been only in his early thirties at the time. He had had the gift of making Eilean Dubh's history vivid and exciting and religion majestic and terrifying. The two had forged a bond of respect and trust that still existed. And the Minister's dramatic flair and deep voice had taught Darroch a great deal about acting.

The Minister stood and they shook hands, acknowledging the formality of the meeting. He poured them each a whisky. "*Slàinte,*" he said.

"*Slàinte,*" responded Darroch.

The Minister said, "This is the Bowmore. A sixteen-year-old."

"Very fine," said Darroch. He looked into his glass, then said, "*A Mhinistear,* I have come to ask for your help."

The Minister said, his voice deep and formal, "How may I be of assistance to you, *a Dharroch*?" In his mind Darroch was a curious combination of the student of thirty years ago and the Laird. The Minister was very much in the Island tradition and he regarded the person and position of the Laird with reverence. To be asked for his help was deeply flattering.

"The reputation of a good and gentle lady is being damaged," said Darroch, "and my character is being maligned. I ask your help in stopping this."

The Minister looked at Darroch from under his heavy brows. "I assume you refer to the story being circulated about you and the American woman." Darroch nodded. He looked down at the papers on his desk and said coldly, "I am preparing Sunday's sermon. It is on the Sixth Commandment."

Darroch slammed his whisky glass down on the desk so hard that the Minister jumped. "I suggest a new text for you, *a Mhinistear*: the Eighth Commandment. Thou shalt not bear false witness."

They stared at each other. Finally the Minister said, "Are you telling me that it is untrue, what this says?" He picked up the letter that had caused him so much pain. He was prepared to denounce the Laird's trespasses from the pulpit; it was his duty, but everything he held dear revolted against it. His conscience told him what to do but his heart hurt. To damage the Laird's position on the Island would be very painful for him.

Darroch said, in a deceptively gentle voice, "I am surprised you have to ask me that. I am surprised you should think evil of me, and you knowing me all my life. And you having a hand in my upbringing as well."

The Minister was, for once, at a loss for words. Darroch said quietly, "It is harmful to our Island that the Laird's future wife should be slandered."

"She is divorcing her husband to marry you, then?" The Minister's tone was accusing.

"She is divorcing her husband because he has played her false with more than one woman; she does not know how many. As I divorced my wife for the same reason. You will understand why a charge of adultery is so repugnant to both of us."

The Minister nodded.

Darroch ran his hand through his hair. "I will not say we have not been tempted. The waiting has been very hard for both of us; we are tested sorely whenever we are together. And I want her so much I will be a blithering idiot by the time this is sorted, fit only to sit in a chair and stare into the fire.

"We have shared our passion but we have not made love, we are not lovers. To be accused of that from which we have restrained ourselves with so much pain is intolerable."

The Minister's wife had died over ten years ago but he still dreamed of her, still woke up in a sweat, remembering the sweetness of her mouth and the warmth of her embrace. He nodded somberly. He understood desire. It was one of the qualities that made him a good minister.

"My lady loves the Island, our music and our language and she has made many friends here. It will break her heart if people turn against her when she has committed herself to them and to Eilean Dubh. Rather than have her hurt I will take her away, and once we have left it would be hard to return." Darroch stared into a distant dark corner of the room. "She will not want to go, of course. She thinks of Eilean Dubh as her home."

"A Dharroch . . . what can I do? Slander and lies spread more quickly than weeds in a garden."

"This slander is being spread by one in your congregation, a Mhinistear. It is your duty to stop it."

"Ah. You are sure of this?"

Darroch nodded. "I will not name the name but we have concluded that only one person could be responsible."

The Minister nodded. Then he stood up. "I must ask you to excuse me. I have a sermon to rewrite."

"Of course, a Mhinistear." Darroch rose and held out his hand.

The Minister shook it. "Will I see you in kirk on Sunday?"

"Of course." Darroch turned to leave.

"A Dharroch . . . bring your lady with you." The Minister smiled his frosty smile.

Darroch raised his eyebrows, then nodded and left.

He made the drive back to Jean's cottage with a heart that had been lightened. The three gazed at him expectantly when he entered. "Did you wait supper for me?"

Màiri snarled, "Darroch . . . "

He turned his sweetest smile on her, put his arm around her shoulders and kissed her cheek. Then he put his other arm around Jean. "It is all right. I have spoken to the Minister. He will put a stop to this nonsense." He looked at them. "Now may we have our supper?" he asked politely.

Thirty-six

My bed is narrow and hard and stuffed with pine boughs.
But were you beside me, my angel, it would be scented with roses,
it would be as soft as the clouds in Heaven's sky . . .

Uisdean's fifth letter to Mòrag, translated by Darroch Mac an Rìgh

*M*àiri and Jamie left shortly after supper. Darroch and Jean waved goodbye from the doorway. Then he turned to Jean and pulled her close. She said, "Shut the door, lovie. I don't want any more letters."

He chuckled and reached behind her with one long arm to pull the door shut. "Let's sit by the fire, *mo chridhe*. You've had a hard day."

"I'm all right," she said but she followed him to the sofa and let him pull her onto his lap. Wrapped in his arms, she sighed, "I want you so much. Those damned letters were right about that."

"I had such a dream of you in Inverness," he whispered. "So sensual and loving, I woke up at four o'clock and could not go back to sleep." He had paced the floor till morning, wondering how much longer he could endure it.

"Everybody thinks we're lovers already. Why don't we just go to bed and let them enjoy being right?" she demanded.

"But then I would have to call the Minister and tell him to change his sermon back to denouncing us for adultery. It seems a little hard to ask him to do that. It is late and he will have put his typewriter away."

Jean looked at him and saw that he was trying not to smile. "Nuts," she said and punched his chest lightly with her fist. "So we're back to the French farce business."

"I am afraid so. Now it's time for you to go to bed. You will understand what a sacrifice I am making to Island morality that I do not climb in with you."

"A girl can try," she said and her hand slipped down to touch where he was pressed hard against her thighs.

"*A Shine*, what are you doing to me?"

"I am seducing you. If I am accused of naughtiness I may as well get some fun out of it."

She leaned into him, her eyes wide with invitation. Images of warm chocolate sauce, featherbeds, soft tropical breezes invaded his mind. Her left earlobe assumed a sensual quality quite unexpected in an earlobe. He bit it. Then he put one of her fingers in his mouth and raked it with his teeth.

She moaned.

In spite of his best resolutions he laid her down on the sofa and petted her until she wriggled with need. "I don't know why this is okay and intercourse is not. That's hypocritical," she gasped. "I am absolutely dissolving, I want you so."

"Well, will I call the Minister? He will not have gone to bed yet."

She could not help it, she began to laugh. "All right, you've convinced me. Go home, your virtue is safe for another night."

"Before I leave . . . " He bent to her and they kissed and nibbled until their lips were swollen.

"Ah, Jean . . . how good you taste. Sheilah could not make a dish that was more delicious."

"Not even her chocolate mousse?"

"I would like to cover you in Sheilah's chocolate mousse and lick it all off." He was trying to ignore the ache in his groin. He hoped it was not true, all he had heard about what happened to the male organ when its owner was aroused and frustrated time after time.

She moved against him. "Let me please you with my hands. If I can't take you inside me let me love you that way."

She meant it, too. He had only to consent and she would take him to heaven. And that would be the end of his self control. They would be in bed together in a heartbeat and they would probably stay there forever. While voices rose around them, talking, judging, condemning.

They'd been on their best behavior so long. He could not let it all go now. He sought a distraction and hit upon the worst possible one. "What do you wear to bed?"

"What? Oh, just a plain nightgown."

"Tell me about it." For his sake, he hoped it buttoned up to the neck and was made of steel plate.

"Well . . . it's simple . . . not sexy at all, everything's covered up. Three-quarter length sleeves, round neckline. White, with a pattern of rosebuds."

Rosebuds. His Jean in a bed of rosebuds. Making love to her with the fragrance of crushed roses rising around them. Dear God, he had to stop this; he would be insane in seconds.

But he heard himself saying, "When we make love for the first time I want you in a white nightgown, soft and sheer as gossamer. One that I can strip you of quickly, but first I will want to look at you, have my fill of looking at you. And that will be the last nightgown you'll ever own. You'll come to bed naked with me after that."

"Ummm . . . I don't know . . . I never have . . . there's always been the children, you see. If I had to get up with them . . . "

"Naked, Jean." He nuzzled her cheek.

She laughed deep in her throat and he thought it was the sexiest sound he'd ever heard. "Okay. As long as I don't get cold."

"Do you think I would let you get cold when we are in bed together?"

His wonderful actor's voice whispering in her ear made her quite reckless. She put her arms up to draw him closer. "Call the Minister, lovie."

If he pulled himself together he could stand up and if he could stand up he could make it to the door. And if he made it to the door they would both be safe. Safe and respectable. The Laird and his very respectable, very proper, well-behaved American lady. Who was killing him with desire.

Detaching himself from her was like climbing out of a warm bath into a freezing shower and her arms were twined around him like ivy around an oak tree. He said, "You've got to help me, Jean. You know I can't stay here tonight."

"I do?" She considered him carefully. "Why do I know that?"

He gritted his teeth and prayed for strength. Why, just once in his life, couldn't he fall in love with a biddable woman, one who would do as she was told? "I can't do this by myself, Jean. I can't walk away from you."

Her arms dropped reluctantly from his shoulders. They stared at each other for a long moment. Then she smiled. "You win," she said.

"We both win. And live to win another day. *Oidhche mhath, m'aingeal.* Dream of me." He stood up.

"Oh, I will. Assuming I get any sleep at all."

At the door he paused and turned around. "Don't forget about the nightgown," he said, grinning, and was gone.

Jean sighed and prepared herself for a restless night, heavy with dreams. Life on Eilean Dubh is entirely too exciting, she thought.

Thirty-seven

*Let all bitterness and wrath, and anger, and clamour,
and evil speaking, be put away from you,
with all malice: and be ye kind to one another,
tenderhearted, forgiving one another . . .*

Ephesians 4:30-32

*W*hen Darroch told Jean that he wanted her to accompany him to kirk on Sunday she was taken aback. Part of her feared being snubbed. She realized quickly that Darroch would not expose her to such humiliation. Then she began to worry that she didn't know how to dress appropriately for the strict and somber Free Presbyterian service. "Do I wear a hat, Darroch? Gloves? High heels?" she fretted.

He shrugged his shoulders helplessly. "I don't know, *mo fhlùr*. I have never noticed what the ladies wear. Ask Màiri."

"She doesn't go to your kirk. She doesn't go to church at all." Jean worried and fussed over her wardrobe. One outfit was too brightly colored, another had short sleeves. Were short sleeves proper?

Darroch said, "*Tha mi duilich, a Shìne*, I don't know what to tell you. Is there no one you can ask?"

She thought furiously, then snapped her fingers. "Catrìona! Isn't she one of Minister Donald's congregation?" Catrìona, reached by phone, was flattered to be consulted. No, gloves weren't necessary, a hat was nice if she had one but many women didn't wear them. Short sleeves were acceptable, bright colors out of place.

Jean finally settled on a demure cream-colored blouse and a navy skirt. She added a sweater when Darroch mentioned that the old stone building was cold even in the hottest weather. The sweater made the outfit seem too casual so she put it away and took out her blazer, which she hadn't worn since the flight from Milwaukee.

Dubious, she surveyed herself in the mirror. I look like a teacher in a girls' school, she thought. But it certainly is proper.

Sunday morning she was ready half an hour before Darroch was due to pick her up. She had tried on the sweater and blazer twice but still could not decide between them. Finally she had an inspiration. She put the blouse back and pulled on a cotton crewneck sweater. With the blazer, it had the right look of casual formality.

She was so nervous on her way to kirk that her hands grew wet with sweat and she was glad she'd put a handkerchief in her pocket.

There was a visor mirror on her side of the Bentley. She pulled it down for the third time as they parked. Again she checked her hair, neatly tied at the back of her neck with a scarf, and her make-up, hoping her lipstick wasn't too bright. She thought that now she looked like the headmistress of a girls' school.

"You're fine." Darroch had noticed, amused, that she'd kept checking her reflection. "*Misneach*! That means courage." When she put her hand on the door handle he said, "No, wait." He got out and came around and opened the door for her. He gave her his hand as she got out.

She looked up at him, eyebrows raised. He smiled and tucked her hand in his arm. "We must do things the proper way here," he said.

The proper way was the Laird's way. They moved slowly towards the kirk door and Jean was reminded of seeing on television the Queen going walkabout, graciously nodding to everyone. Darroch was doing just that, greeting people by name, saying, "*Dè do chor?*" and "*Ciamar a tha?*" How are you keeping? How are you?

After a bit Jean got into the swing of it. "*Madainn mhath*," she murmured left and right. When she met Ian the Post and his Catrìona, she grinned and said, "'*Se là brèagha a th' ann*," to Ian. It's a beautiful day.

He grinned back, remembering her first attempt to speak the Gaelic to him. "Oh, aye, *a Shìne*. '*Se gu dearbh*! A very fine day indeed!" And he winked. Darroch raised his eyebrows. Ian blushed.

They went into the kirk and Darroch started to usher her into his customary back pew but abruptly changed his mind and walked forward with her on his arm. "This is the Mac an Rìgh pew," he said quietly, pausing halfway down the aisle. "It's usually empty but it won't be today." He stood, politely waiting for her to slip in. Parishioners stopped, nearly running into each other in their astonishment, and waited until Darroch had seated himself beside her. All around them was the sibilant hiss of indrawn breaths and fierce Gaelic whispers.

Jean was conscious of being stared at, both openly and covertly. "Is this how it feels, being an actor?" she whispered to him.

"Yes, but not all audiences are as friendly as this one," he said solemnly. She gave him a sidewise look but only a slight quirk of his lips betrayed his amusement.

The kirk was extremely plain and unadorned by candles, embroidered cloths or pew cushions. The only illumination came from a row of lights in clear glass shades suspended from the ceiling down the center aisle. There was no sign of an organ.

A heavy chill emanated from the stone walls and Jean was glad she'd worn her blazer. The wooden pew was very hard and she tried not to wiggle but she could feel her bottom getting sore and her back stiffening.

The Minister sat on a wooden chair on a small raised dais behind the pulpit. He wore the plainest black suit Jean had ever seen, with a white shirt and a straight, narrow black tie. His face was stern. Jean shivered, looking at him. She had seen him smile once or twice since she had known him but there was not the least memory of a smile in the lineaments of that grim face.

The service was entirely in the Gaelic. At one point she heard Darroch's name called and felt him move in surprise. Then he stood. She realized that the small leather-bound volume he had taken from his pocket earlier was a Bible. He opened it, slowly, deliberately, making sure he had his audience's full attention. Then he began to read.

His rich deep voice filled the kirk, reverberating around the old walls. He paused now and then for effect, his eyes scanning the congregation and coming to rest on the Minister. He and the Minister stared at each other in perfect communion as he finished reading the verses. Then he sat down and the kirk was absolutely still.

Darroch whispered in Jean's ear, "Psalm 52. The old fox." It was one of the Minister's favorite tricks, singling out for a relevant Scripture reading the person who was the focal point of the day's sermon. The congregation understood immediately: it was the scandal of the Laird's relationship with Mrs. Jean that was the issue. They slipped forward to the edges of their seats, ears quivering.

Jean, who had no idea what the Psalm said, was baffled.

The Minister was in the pulpit now, his fierce gray eyes under their heavy eyebrows sweeping over his flock. When he opened his mouth and the sonorous wave of the Gaelic poured over them they quailed visibly. Jean felt Darroch's shoulders shake as the sermon progressed and she looked at him in alarm. Was he upset? Distressed? Then she saw that he was valiantly trying to keep his mouth from turning up into a grin. He was laughing, she thought, astonished. What on earth was the Minister saying?

At last the sermon was over and several of the men were wiping their foreheads with large white handkerchiefs that Jean recognized as the Co-Op's last week's special, half-a-dozen for eleven shillings.

Reproachful glares were being flung at the small group of women responsible for spreading the scandal. In a pew directly under the Minister's glare, a woman slipped down in her seat, shoulders hunched, trying to make herself inconspicuous. The people sitting on either side had moved away ostentatiously, leaving a small but definite space around her.

Darroch poked Jean and she jumped. "Bridget MacDonough," he hissed in her ear, nodding in the direction of the shunned woman. Jean's mouth opened in a silent 'o' of understanding.

The singing came next. There were no hymnals. Instead, Angus Morrison, the precentor, stepped up to the dais and began to 'line-out' each psalm. The congregation repeated each line after him. Standing by Darroch, Jean heard the singing rise to the rafters and imagined the panes in the windows trembling in time.

Then it was over. Another passage from the Bible and the Minister closed the book and stepped from the pulpit. He walked down the aisle, looking neither left nor right. Stepping outside, he took up a position by the door.

The congregation stirred with relief and began to get up. Darroch, unused to being in the Mac an Rìgh pew, realized suddenly that they were waiting for himself and Jean to leave. But he'd had enough of the laird business for the morning. He shook his head slightly and nodded to the pews behind him, indicating that they were to leave first. The congregation relaxed and the pews emptied in turn. People flowed out, each man pausing to shake hands with the Minister and each woman pausing to nod and speak to him.

"If we'd gone out first," Darroch said in Jean's ear, "He'd have made us stand by him and greet every last soul here. This way we can blend into the crowd."

Jean doubted that Darroch would ever blend into any crowd, but she was relieved to have been spared the ordeal of greeting the Minister's flock with him. She was casting quick furtive looks at how the women were dressed, just in case this were to become a regular engagement on her social calendar. There were as many bare heads as hats, she saw with relief, and no short sleeves and no bright colors. Every woman wore stockings and heels and quite a few wore gloves. She made a mental note to buy a pair at the Co-Op. She'd seen plain cotton gloves there last week.

At last it was their turn to greet the Minister. He unbent so far as to give them a frosty smile.

Darroch said, "A fine sermon, *a Mhinistear*. I will be translating it for Jean on the way home."

The Minister said, "I hope you find spiritual solace in it, Mrs. Abbott. It was a pleasure to have you in the Mac an Rìgh pew today and . . . " a stern look at Darroch . . . "yourself as well, *a Dharroch*."

Darroch's expression so clearly said, don't push your luck, Minister, that Jean had to swallow a chuckle.

When Barabal, trailed by her family, came up to them Darroch looked surprised. "And what are you doing down here on a Sunday?" he said. "Minister Tormod will be wondering where you are."

"A wee bird told me that Minister Donald's kirk was the place to be today. I have always enjoyed a display of fireworks," Barabal said, smiling slyly.

"You got them today," Darroch said. "I am always surprised, after one of his special sermons, that the roof beams are not smoking. It is as well we got rid of that roof of thatch years ago."

"Aye, it was replaced with shingles shortly after he was called to the kirk. The elders were wise men. And thrifty. They did not care to spend extra money on fire insurance." The two looked at each other with broad grins.

Jean wondered who'd tipped Barabal off and realized it must have been Catrìona.

The small group gathered around them was suddenly silent. Bridget MacDonough was walking by. Cool stares followed her.

On impulse, Jean called, "*Madainn mhath*, Mrs. MacDonough. '*Se là brèagha a th' ann.*"

Bridget started visibly and looked at Jean. Finally she gulped, "*Madainn mhath*, Mrs. . . . er . . . Abbott. '*Se. Tha i blàth.*"

Jean smiled. Bridget glanced at the other members of the group and received reserved nods from several. Relieved, she scurried by, avoiding meeting Darroch's eye. He watched her grimly, his stare penetrating her shoulder blades. Her husband, looking acutely uncomfortable, glanced at Darroch, then at Jean. He started to walk by, then stopped. He squared his shoulders, lifted his chin and walked up to them.

"A word with you, *a Dharroch*," he said bravely. The others in the group turned aside as though to give him some privacy but it was obvious all ears were swiveled back to listen. He said, "I have spoken to my wife." This in itself was quite an acknowledgment, as Bridget was widely known as the ruler of her household, feared by spouse and children. "There will be no more letters."

Darroch said kindly, "Have you met Mrs. Abbott, *a Dhùghall, mo charaid*?"

Jean held out her hand. He took it and looked at her for a long moment. "I am very pleased to meet you," he said. "I apologize to you on behalf of my family. You have been grievously wronged and believe me, had I known, it would not have happened." He said, "It is in my mind to have Bridget apologize to you in person."

Jean smiled. "That's not necessary." She was feeling absurdly happy and she would have been uncomfortable having Bridget humiliated any further. "Everyone makes mistakes," she said.

"That is most generous of you," he said, and hurried away to his car where his wife stood waiting meekly. Only Jean had spoken to her after kirk. She was relieved that worse had not happened.

Jean peeled off the blazer before she got back in the Bentley. "That was almost fun," she said. "But I feel like a kid just let out of school. I wish I did have a hat so I could chuck it up in the air."

"The Mary Tyler Moore thing again, *nach*?" he said.

"*Tha*. Now I want to know . . . what did the Minister say and what is Psalm 52?"

"First things first. As you are all dressed up . . . " He glanced slyly at the jacket crumpled on her lap. "What about lunch out?" He pulled into the road.

She said, surprised, "Is there a restaurant open on Sunday here?"

"Of course, what do you think tourists do? It is the MacDougals' place, up near Airgead. They are Catholic. It's a grand arrangement. They feed the visitors on Sunday and Presbyterian consciences and the tourist office alike rest easy."

"Sounds wonderful. Now what about that Psalm?"

He considered. Finally he pulled the Bentley off the road into a scenic overlook. They sat for a moment, enjoying the wild sea dashing itself on the rocks below. Then he pulled the Bible out of his pocket again. "Read it aloud for me in the Gaelic," he said, opening the book, "and I will translate. You understand, this may not be a perfect King James version. I am used to it in our language."

She read, trying very hard to pronounce each word properly. He translated:

Why does thou so love mischief, O mighty man?
Thy tongue deviseth mischief, like a sharp razor, working deceitfully.
Thou lovest evil more than good and lying rather than speaking the truth.

She paused and looked at him. "My goodness, that's a bit harsh, isn't it?"

"It gets better. Go on." She continued and he translated:

Thou lovest all devouring words, oh thou of the deceitful tongue.
God shall destroy thee forever, he shall take thee away,
And pluck thee out of thy dwelling place,
And root thee out of the land of the living.
The righteous also shall see and fear and shall laugh at thee, saying:
Lo, this is the man that made not God his strength; but trusted in the abundance of his riches, and strengthened himself in his wickedness.

Jean sat silently for a moment. Then she said, "And what about the sermon?"

"I should have asked the Minister for a copy, it was quite *miorbhuileach*. It began with the Eighth Commandment: thou shalt not bear false witness. It moved smartly along to the evils of gossip and references to women's tongues being forked like the tongues of adders." Jean looked at him indignantly and he shrugged. "Remember, I didn't write this, *mo ghràdh*. Now where was I . . . I don't know where the adders' tongues come from but I think the part about a foolish woman being clamorous and simple is from Proverbs. Rather a neat twist because the bit in your letter about committing adultery and destroying your soul is from Proverbs too. The Minister doesn't miss a trick."

He stretched out his long legs. "Umm . . . let me see. Another bit from Proverbs, that deceit is in the heart of them that imagine evil. Something about the righteous being delivered out of trouble. And a hypocrite destroying his neighbor with his mouth but just people being saved through knowledge. Oh, and this was nice:

They that are of a froward heart are an abomination to the Lord.

"Since Bridget has the frowardest heart of anyone on the Island that was particularly apt. I think that's about it. But you really need to read it in the original. It loses some of its force in translation."

Jean was still indignant. "Now I'm mad at Bridget all over again," she said. "For being so foolish as to give him a chance to say such things about all of us women."

He looked at her, considering. "Oh, I don't know. It wasn't so bad. He finished with another bit from Proverbs:

Who can find a virtuous woman? for her price is far above rubies.
The heart of her husband doth safely trust in her . . .
She will do him good and not evil all the days of her life.

"Oh." Jean did not know what to say.

"Never think the Minister doesn't like and appreciate women, *mo Shine.* He knows our women are the backbone of our Island." He pulled her close. "Personally, my favorite part of the Bible about women is the Song of Solomon:

Behold, thou are fair, my love; behold thou art fair; thou hast doves'
eyes . . . Thou hast ravished my heart with thine eyes.

She smiled at him, bewitched. He smiled back. "Let's go get that lunch," he said.

Thirty-eight

I heard a bird sing
In the dark of December.
A magical thing and sweet to remember
We are nearer to Spring
Then we were in September.

Oliver Herford

*A*fter the scandal life settled back down. As November moved on the days shortened and became dark and rainy. Winds growled and gurgled around the cottage and poked in through every crack and chink. Nights were damply cold.

Jean built huge fires in her fireplace and thought with longing of central heating and her Milwaukee closet full of long underwear, wool socks and down jackets.

She went to the Co-Op and scavenged for warm things. When she found a heavy cotton flannel nightgown she took it to a clerk. "Do you have this in a smaller size?"

The clerk shook her head. "Sorry, Mrs. Jean, that is the only one left. We were nearly sold out by the first of November."

Jean sighed. "I'll take this one, then."

The clerk said, "But that is a size extra-extra-large. It will never be fitting you."

"I'll wrap it around me twice, then it'll be twice as warm."

Looking at the calendar one Friday, Jean realized that the upcoming Thursday was Thanksgiving in America. She invited Darroch, Màiri and Jamie for dinner and excused herself from Playschool so that she could cook all day. She'd gotten a turkey from Murray the Meat, who'd been puzzled by the request.

"We have turkeys at Hogmanay, Mrs. Jean; that is when most people are wanting them. I have some lovely chickens now and I could get you a fat goose, although it is a wee bit early for them too." But Jean persisted and Murray agreed to order a turkey for her from Inverness. Murdoch the Chopper dropped it off on Wednesday.

"Special delivery, Mrs. Jean, a turkey. The poulterer in Inverness did not know what to make of such a request but he got the turkey fresh from a local farmer."

She was lost in a flood of memories as she cooked. They'd always had a good time on Thanksgiving in Milwaukee and a full table: herself, Russ, Rod, Sally, Russ's family, her parents, friends. The women had cooked while Russ entertained the men in the family room with football games on television.

Russ had been in charge of making drinks and everyone except the kids had been a little drunk by the time dinner was served. There had been laughter and friendship and love.

Working alone in her kitchen Thanksgiving morning, she thought with longing of the women in her Milwaukee life: her mother, Sally, her mother-in-law, Russ's sister. What were Sally and Russ doing for Thanksgiving dinner, she wondered.

Oh, Russ, why did you have to spoil it for everyone? She could not regret what her present life had become but the past was sometimes hard to let go. She dissolved in tears several times. I've cried more in the last six months than I have in years, she thought.

She was exhausted by the time she served dinner, but the meal was wonderful.

Jamie said, pushing back from the table, "A fine party, Jean. Remind me what it is we are celebrating?"

She told them about Thanksgiving. They understood right away. "If we are ever free of the rule of the *Sasannach*," said Màiri, "we could celebrate a Thanksgiving ourselves."

Jean wanted to talk about Christmas. "I would be pleased if you came to me for dinner," she said. "But of course, I realize you may have other commitments. I mean, you may be used to going to friends to celebrate Christmas."

The three exchanged glances. "We don't make a fuss about Christmas in Scotland," Darroch said. "It is an ordinary day. It is the English who have the big dinners and the church services."

Jean's mouth fell open. "Not make a fuss? Don't you have a Christmas tree? Exchange presents?"

"No. Such things were regarded as Papist . . . Catholic, that is . . . and pagan and the Kirk forbade them, after the Covenanters." He said gently, "Christmas isn't regarded even as a holiday in parts of Scotland. In some places it used to be illegal to celebrate it."

She was shocked and disappointed. For the first time Eilean Dubh had failed to meet her expectations. "I will miss having a Christmas tree," she mourned. "And lights. And decorations."

Jamie said, "I will get you a tree, *mo charaid*. There are plenty growing here on the Island. What kind would you like? But I do not think we can find decorations."

"Never mind," she said, "I'll string popcorn and cranberries and make my own." As the others looked dubious she realized, "I'll bet there's no cranberries. And no popcorn, either." She felt like crying.

Darroch said, "I will look in Inverness for decorations for your tree."

"Okay." To hide her emotion she said gruffly, "Well, what do you do for fun in the dark of December?"

"Ah," said Jamie. "That'll be Hogmanay."

"Aye," said Màiri. "We have a grand time on Hogmanay and take two days to recover from it."

"What is . . . Hogmanay?"

"It's the first day of the year, what you'd call New Year's Day. On the eve of Hogmanay there'll be a fine *cèilidh* with music and dancing and lots of food. Everyone brings food to the party in the Hall."

"And whisky," said Jamie. "The whisky flows free, on Hogmanay."

Darroch said, "It's a grand party, Jean. You'll love it."

She was only partly convinced and invited them all to Christmas dinner anyway. "I'll have to beg another turkey from the guy in Inverness, I suppose."

The day before Christmas Darroch appeared at her door with a large basket. "I had it sent up from Fortnum and Mason's in London. Some things for your dinner."

In the basket were Christmas pudding, mincemeat, a specially blended tea, biscuits shaped like Santa Claus. "Father Christmas," Darroch corrected. "And these are Christmas crackers." He handed her a long tube covered with fancy crepe paper. "Take one end and pull."

She did and there was a bang and a smoky explosion. Several items fell out of the cracker: pieces of toffee, a plastic whistle and a paper which Darroch unfolded into a pirate's hat. He put it on her head. "Perhaps not all the English ideas are bad," he said, looking at her delighted expression.

After Christmas dinner the four sat around her tree. Darroch had found a string of lights decorating an Inverness shopkeeper's window and had talked him into selling them. Ornaments had been a problem until he'd thought to go into a toy store. Now her tree was adorned with Beanie Babies, model soldiers and the cups from a child's tea set, tied on with ribbons.

Jean had mailed presents to Milwaukee but had not been able to resist buying gifts for her Island friends, too. She presented Màiri with a beautiful edition of Gaelic poems by Sorley MacLean, purchased in Inverness.

For Jamie she had a cassette of American Civil War songs and the accompanying book of sheet music, ordered from Mad City Music in Madison. He examined both with delight and was immediately lost in the book.

"That's the last we'll hear from him for a while," said Màiri.

Darroch's presents she saved until the other two were gone. There was a pair of leather gloves. Pleased, he tried them on. "Just what I need, I ruined my good ones in the blizzard."

She had also knitted a long scarf for him using wool from Jamie's prized flock of Jacob's Sheep, with their distinctive coloring. The wool had been spun into thread by the women of the Knitters' Cooperative. He held it in his hands and looked at every inch.

He had a present for her, too, but it had not come from Inverness. It was a gold locket on a chain. "My mother's. My father got it for her in Edinburgh, for their tenth wedding anniversary."

She was so touched she got weepy again. He gathered her in his arms and said, "You're becoming a right little watering-pot, *mo chridhe*."

She smiled up at him. "Something in the Island air, maybe?"

PART V

Hogmanay

Thirty-nine

A guid New Year to ane an' a,
And mony may ye see.

Traditional Hogmanay toast

*I*f Christmas on the Island had been quiet, as Darroch had predicted, Hogmanay, the New Year's celebration, was not. Jean could sense the excitement building. The Co-Op bustled as the *Eilean Dubhannaich* swarmed in all week, selecting new blouses, sweaters, ties. It was the custom, she learned, to wear a new garment to the Hogmanay Eve *cèilidh*, just as it was customary to begin new projects, pay all bills and clean house thoroughly on Hogmanay day.

She had no need of new clothes since hers were far grander than people there owned. But not wanting to defy custom, she went to the Co-Op. Perhaps a new handkerchief, she thought. But that wasn't something to wear so she bought a flowered scarf to knot around the neck of her blouse, and added herself to the long checkout lines and the chattering mass of shoppers.

"Your first Hogmanay, is it, Mrs. Jean?" said Tòmas Mac-a-Phi. "You'll enjoy it, it's grand fun." Everyone in line nodded in agreement.

It was grand fun. In the Hall, which was decorated with holly, rowan berries and evergreens, she danced every dance, sang every sing-a-long and she and the other three played two new tunes in their performance turn. At midnight the band stopped playing and everyone gathered in a circle around the piper to sing *Auld Lang Syne*.

To her surprise the *cèilidh* broke up quickly after that. She'd expected, as in Milwaukee, that the party would go on for hours, but the floor cleared and the Islanders rushed to shrug into coats.

"Time for first-footing," said Darroch. At her baffled look he explained, "We visit friends' houses to wish them a happy New Year."

The most desired, the luckiest first Hogmanay visitor to step over a threshold, she learned from Jamie, was a dark-haired man carrying symbols of prosperity in his pockets.

And the Laird, jet-black-haired Darroch, was the most prized first-footer of all, the one who brought the most luck. He said, "Everyone wanted my father to visit, he used to wear himself out trying to please them. He'd have to go to bed for two days afterward, especially if the weather was damp and his asthma flared up."

Darroch, relentless in his goal of de-mystifying the Laird, had put a stop to all that. He confined his first-footing to the Seniors' Residence, the hospital wards (if anyone was unlucky enough to have to spend Hogmanay in hospital) and the cottages where there were new babies. And of course, the homes of his closest friends.

Jean understood why he limited his visits after the first stop. She, Darroch, Jamie and Màiri climbed into the Bentley and began to make the rounds, stopping first at the home of Mr. and Mrs. Cailean the Crab and their three-month-old twins.

Darroch dispensed the ceremonial gift of a piece of peat, a potato and a coin, tied in a handkerchief. Màiri explained to Jean that they symbolized a wish for warmth, plenty and prosperity in the New Year.

Cailean produced a 15-year-old whisky, poured a dram and offered it with a flourish to Darroch. "To your very good health, *a Mhic an Rìgh*," he said, using the formal style of address to the Laird. "*Slàinte mhath.*"

"*Slàinte mhòr*," said Darroch, raising his glass. Cailean and his wife poured drams all around and they toasted the New Year.

Jean was admiring the twins. They were identical girls with beautiful pale Island skin, bright blue eyes and delightful smiles.

When she commented on their beauty Cailean said, "Aye, they're bonny Hogmanay babies." He explained, "We think they were conceived on Hogmanay eve. Babies started that night always turn out to be especially bonny." He smiled at his wife who was blushing a becoming pink.

The first-footing ritual was the same at the next cottage. Remembering that whisky and beer had flowed freely at the *cèilidh*, Jean was concerned. "If everyone has a drink at everyone else's house . . . " she began when they returned to the car.

". . . why aren't the ditches full of crashed cars," Darroch finished. "Because the speed limit on the Island tonight is fifteen miles per hour, and anyone who has a crash loses the right to drive for a whole year. No exceptions."

"Not even you?" she teased.

"Especially not me," he said grimly as the Bentley crawled along. "If I can't set a proper example I deserve the punishment." He had made a point, over the years, of not finishing the dram he was offered at each stop as he had no intention of getting drunk.

The *Eilean Dubhannaich* knew he'd take only a sip at each house and the desire not to waste their most prized whiskies, saved for Hogmanay, warred with their notions of hospitality. Yes, the Laird was always abstemious but what if a household's whisky was so good he was seized with a sudden desire for a proper dram? There would no humiliation as great as not supplying a full measure. So the Laird's dram was always a full one, despite his efforts.

At the third house Darroch took a smaller taste, then passed his glass to Jean, next to him. Getting the idea, she sipped and gave it to Màiri, who in her turn handed it to Jamie. By the time they reached Barabal's cottage Jean felt her head beginning to swim and she wet her lips only. Jamie, last in line, shook his head slightly at Darroch, and at the next house Darroch took a sip and then handed it back to his host. "A fine whisky, Murdoch," he said. "You'll share it with me?" The four were thus able to preserve a measure of sobriety.

After the Rose and a proper dram of Gordon's finest, their last stop was the Seniors' Residence where nearly everyone had stayed up to greet the New Year with the Laird's party. A resident pounded out the old songs on a piano for everyone to sing.

A tiny, very elderly woman in an invalid's chair beckoned imperiously to Jean after the singing stopped. In careful English she said, "You'll be the *bana-Ameireaganach*."

"*Tha*." said Jean. "From Milwaukee. Near Chicago." She always introduced herself that way since she'd found everyone knew where Chicago was.

"*Ameireaganach agus Eilean Dubhannach*," the woman said. American and Islander.

Flattered to be accepted, Jean began, "It's kind of you to say so . . . " but the other shook her head impatiently. "*Chan'eil. Tha thu Eilean Dubhannach.*"

"What do you mean?"

"You're a MacChriathar. I knew you at once."

Flummoxed, Jean sat down by her. "How?"

"Lass, I'm a MacChriathar. Cairistìona MacChriathar Morrison is my name. Do you think I'd not know my own kin?" As Jean stared at her uncomprehendingly, she added, "Your hair. Your eyes. Only our people have hair the color of whisky and eyes like the tidal pool. And your skin is as pale as the old white rose that grows only on MacChriathar lands. It's called the Riddle Rose because *criathar* in the Gaelic means 'the riddler.' We are descended from a great *fiosaiche*, a soothsayer and prophet."

She leaned forward and looked steadily at Jean. "Look at me, child. Do you not see the resemblance?"

Jean stared. Cairistìona's hair was pure white, her skin had the translucence of extreme old age but her eyes . . . Jean saw her own eyes gazing back at her. A wave of dizziness swept over her.

Cairistìona Morrison raised her voice to a surprisingly strong shout. "*A Dharroch mhór!*"

Startled, Darroch and everyone else turned to look. He saw Jean, alarmingly pale, her hands clutching the arms of her chair. He rushed to kneel by her. "What's wrong, *mo chridhe?*"

Cairistìona smiled with satisfaction, hearing the endearment slip out. So that was the way of it. So a MacChriathar had caught the Laird, had she. The Riddler had predicted it centuries ago, that his house would one day unite with the Mac an Rìghs, though they were deadly enemies. "*Tapadh leat gu dearbh, a Dharroch,* for bringing me my kinswoman."

Darroch looked at her, baffled. "What are you saying, *a Chairistìona?*"

"I am saying your *leadaidh* is a MacChriathar, and my kinswoman. I am surprised you are not knowing that," she said.

Jamie was there, standing by them. She said, "You know this too, do you not, *a Sheumais.*"

"I do now and feel a fool for not recognizing it sooner," he said. "But in all fairness, *a bhean uasail,* there's not many of you MacChriathars left to make the comparison. But I knew she was an *Eilean Dubhannach,* no doubt about it."

Cairistìona said, "And she will be descended from Ùisdean *Mór* MacChriathar, he who went to *Ameireaga,* and my own many times great-grandfather, so we are cousins."

Jean said in shock, "But Ùisdean left, he had no descendants here . . . "

"Except his child by Mòrag Mac an Rìgh. That child was your many times great-grandfather, *a Dharroch*."

"Mòrag was a Mac an Rìgh . . . and she had a child?"

"Aye. Her father forced Ùisdean from the Island, then discovered she was with child. Mòrag was married to her cousin and the child raised as a Mac an Rìgh. Only a few of our clan knew his true father and always remembered that the child, the boy who became chief of the Mac an Rìghs, was half MacChriathar." She smiled. "We've never forgotten."

Darroch and Jean looked at each other. He said, "Ùisdean didn't translate the name, he just dropped the Mac and anglicized the pronunciation to Greer. A proper riddler, indeed. So we're related, then, *mo fhlùr*. My cousin." He raised her hand to his lips. Jean wept.

"The knowledge will be too much for her," observed Cairistìona. "She was not knowing who she is, then?"

"No. Mòrag's father wrote Ùisdean that she was dead and never a word about the child. Ùisdean had no reason to return to Eilean Dubh; he started a new life in America."

"Such wickedness." Cairistìona shook her head. "To break their hearts and deprive a child of his father. It is well you have returned, *mo nighean*."

Jean took the handkerchief Darroch handed her and wiped her eyes. "I'll bring Ùisdean's letters for you to read . . . Cousin Cairistìona. I only wish Mòrag's letters to him had survived."

"Aye. Come next week and visit me. I will tell you all about your family and I will have a surprise for you." She smiled to herself, thinking of the letter from Mòrag in her possession. "There are only a half-dozen or so of our people left now. Unless . . . " She brightened. "Have you children?"

"Yes, two. And Ùisdean had five children in America . . . you've got lots more cousins."

"Ah." The old lady smiled in pleasure, then leaned back in her chair in the sudden exhaustion of the very elderly. "We'll have a good long chat, then. *Oidhche mhath*." She closed her eyes.

Jean bent forward and kissed her cousin's cheek. "*Oidhche mhath, a Chairistìona. Dean deagh chadal*."

Her eyes flickered open, briefly. She murmured, "*Agus tha Gaidhlig aice. Glè mhath!*" You have the Gaelic. Very good!

On the way home Jean and Darroch were thoughtful in the front seat while Jamie and Màiri cuddled enthusiastically in the back. Jean was frankly envious, listening to Jamie whispering seductively and Màiri cooing in response. "Must be nice," she mumbled.

Darroch threw her a smile. "Aye," he said, then added softly, "Cousin."

Cousin. It warmed her down to her toes. She was part of this Island by blood, she belonged here. She had felt it, now she knew.

When they reached *Taigh Rois*, Darroch first-footed the cottage, then threw a triumphant glance at Jamie and his corn-silk yellow hair. "This is one evening where blonds don't have more fun," he said and seized Màiri and gave her an enthusiastic kiss on the mouth.

"No?" said Jamie, pulling Jean into his arms and kissing her with equal enthusiasm. Her senses reeled. A kiss from Bonnie Prince Jamie would turn any woman's head. She giggled, as giddy as a schoolgirl.

When Jamie's arms dropped from her shoulders, she looked at Màiri and impulsively stepped forward and hugged her. She could feel the stiffening, the slight resistance. "Oops," she said. "Too American."

"Nonsense," said Màiri and hugged her back.

Jamie and Darroch looked at each other dubiously. "Too American for me," Jamie said and extended his hand. "Best Hogmanay wishes, *mo chariad*."

Darroch shook it heartily. "As our American friend says, Happy New Year, *a Sheumais*."

They were all a little drunk, Jean thought, but not really from the whisky. It was the friendship, the music, the love.

Darroch led her out and over her shoulder she saw Jamie take his wife into his arms and kiss her, saw Màiri cling to him and kiss him in return.

At Darroch's cottage they got out of the car and stood for a moment. The night was chilly and velvet black, lightened only by stars and a huge full moon directly overhead. Jean glanced back at Jamie and Màiri's cottage. In the room she recognized as their bedroom the light went out.

When a cloud covered the moon they were plunged into darkness unbroken by streetlights or house lights, a darkness as absolute as that of a cave.

She realized suddenly that she was standing at Eilean Dubh's magnetic pole. With her identity confirmed as an *Eilean Dubhannach* it was clear to her that the center of the Island was where the Laird was. And Darroch was the Laird. He knew it and the *Eilean Dubhannaich* knew it. The soft respectful note in their voices when they spoke to him, the affectionate smiles that followed him, confirmed it. There was no escape for him and he knew that, rejoiced in it in his heart even as he rebelled against it.

He was their chief and like the old Scottish clans they would follow where he led with unswerving loyalty. They loved him and they loved their Island with a deep passion. She understood now why Màiri could not leave, why Darroch returned from his London exile with such profound happiness. She understood why Jamie and Sheilah and Lady Margaret, incomers all, had become so attached to Eilean Dubh. Within her she felt Ùisdean's spirit, joyful at his return home.

Reverence and love overwhelmed her. She put her arms around Darroch's neck, drew the dark head down and kissed him in absolute surrender. She was his, would always be his. There was no escape for her, either. And she too rejoiced in the knowledge.

She whispered, "Leave the car here, lovie. Let's walk under the stars."

They walked hand in hand through the solemn darkness to her cottage and when she would, unheedingly, have gone in first he stopped her and made his entrance. "Peace to this house and all who dwell in it," he said, then held out his hand to lead her inside.

"I'll get your dram for you, my lord," she said but he answered, "That's not what I want," and pulled her into his arms. They kissed until she wriggled free. "Make a fire, let's sit together."

Seated on the sofa, she watched him kneel at the fireplace. Then he turned, rested his elbows on her knees and asked, "Did you enjoy your first Hogmanay?"

"I sure did," she said, stroking his hair.

"It gets better," he said and rose up on his knees to lean towards her. She opened her legs and took him close. Their mouths met. When he seized her tongue and suckled it she felt as though she was being turned inside out.

She said, "Darroch . . . I was told that on Hogmanay it's the custom to begin things that you want to be lucky with all year. Is that right?"

"Aye."

"What I want to begin . . . I want . . . I want to make love with you. I want you to make me yours tonight."

He drew back and looked at her. "Are you sure, *mo chridhe?*"

"I've had lots of time to think about it, haven't I?" she whispered. "And nothing matters but you and me."

"Aye." Tempted beyond restraint, he let caution go. She was right, nothing else mattered. They were fated to be together; she was meant to be his and he to be hers. Passion flared between them, sweet and hot.

He slipped his hands under her skirt. "We'll have these off, for a start," he said, pulling on the waistband of her tights. She lifted her hips as he pulled the tights down to her feet and stripped them from her along with her shoes.

His hands went to her waist again, finding buttons and zipper, and again she lifted her hips as he pulled off her skirt. He ran his hands up and down her bare thighs, then rubbed his face against them.

A delicious need filled her and she thought, all over the Island people are doing this, in bed, on the sofa, on the floor in front of the fire. Making love. Maybe making Hogmanay babies. I'd like to make a baby tonight, she thought recklessly, and the idea of Darroch's child in her stirred something deep in her soul.

He unbuttoned her blouse, untied the flowered scarf, slipping it all off until she was wearing only bra and panties. He ran his hands over her simple cotton underwear. "Such a plain wrapping for such a beautiful package. You should wear satin and lace."

Remembering the puce panties she said, "I'll run right down to the Co-Op tomorrow and stock up on sexy lingerie." He chuckled.

"My turn now," she said and pushed up his sweater. "Come on, off with it," she commanded. He pulled it off and she stroked his bare chest, tangling her fingers in the crisp hairs. His body was wonderful, she thought, lean and muscular. She caressed him where he rose against the fabric of the kilt. "You are so big," she whispered. "You'll have to go slowly, let me open to take all of you."

"I'll open you with kisses," he promised and she shivered in anticipation. She was as wet between her legs as the burn that flowed between her cottage and his. Only the burn water was icy cold and she was hot, her thighs burning with moisture.

He opened her bra and kissed a trail from her throat down her body, moving between her breasts, rubbing them with cheeks rough with evening whiskers, to her belly and lower. He slipped her panties down and blew across the soft curls until she shuddered with anticipation.

Jean trembled and whispered, "I want you," and he murmured in the Gaelic. She did not understand the words but the meaning was clear. Love and passion and surrender filled her senses. "Please," she whispered and his hand went to the top buckle of his kilt.

The telephone rang, startling them so much they nearly fell off the sofa. Darroch cursed in the Gaelic. Jean swore in English.

"*A Dhia*," he said. "There must have been an accident."

She cried, "Something's happened to my family!" untangled herself and struggled to her feet. The panties threatened to slide down and trip her and she tugged them up impatiently.

She stumbled through the darkness beyond the firelight trying to remember where she'd left the phone. She followed the insistent 'brrp-brrp' until she located it on the kitchen table. She snatched it up, fumbling for the button that turned it on. "Hello?" she gasped.

"Jean!" said a hearty voice. "Happy New Year!"

"Russ?" she said in disbelief.

Darroch, on the sofa, cursed softly and fluently.

"Russ, what's wrong? What's happened?" Now she really was panic-stricken.

"Nothing's wrong, Jean. I just wanted to wish you a Happy New Year."

She fumbled behind her for a chair, her heart thudding. "Russ, do you have any idea what time it is?"

"Umm . . . well, six hours difference . . . it's nine o'clock here so it should be . . . three o'clock in the afternoon. Right?"

"Russ, it's three in the morning. We're ahead of you, not behind."

"Oh. Hey, I'm sorry. Did I wake you? You don't sound sleepy."

"No. We've . . . uh . . . just gotten back from a party. Russ, you frightened me, I thought something terrible had happened."

"No, everything's fine." His voice sharpened with suspicion. "Who's 'we'?"

"What?"

"You said, 'we've just gotten back'. Who's with you? Is it a man?"

She was silent. "It is a man," he said. "Who is he?" When she still did not answer he said, "What's going on? What are you doing?"

"It's really none of your business, Russ," she said stiffly.

"I see. Found yourself a boyfriend. Didn't take long, did it? What are you up to with him at three in the morning?"

"It's none of your business," she repeated. "If everything's all right there, I'll ring off . . . I mean, hang up. Happy New Year, Russ."

He said, "Good night, Jean. Don't do anything I wouldn't do."

"That leaves me a lot of leeway, doesn't it," she snapped and clicked off the phone.

She made her way back to the sofa. "What did he want?" Darroch demanded, trying unsuccessfully to keep the jealousy from his voice.

"He said he wanted to wish me a Happy New Year. He said he got the time difference mixed up. I don't think I believe that, though. I think he just wanted to know what I was doing on New Year's Eve."

"Forget him," said Darroch fiercely. Mad with passion and jealousy he pulled her beneath him on the sofa, desperate to claim her and furious at his rival's intrusion.

"Darling, please," she gasped. It took all her control to deny him, she was as eager as he was. "Not like this, please, lovie."

He stopped, hovering above her. "*A Dhia*," he said and bent down to rest his head on her belly. He mumbled, "I'm sorry. I would have taken you . . . to erase him from your mind."

"We've got the rest of the night. No need to rush," she crooned tenderly.

She rubbed his back until he began to relax. She was right again; there was no reason to rush. She would be his soon. Her soon-to-be-ex-husband was just a distant voice on the telephone, an echo from the past.

He lifted his head and smiled at her. "Where were we?"

She said, "It was just getting really interesting when we were interrupted."

"Damn, I've forgotten where I left off," he teased, then moved his hand down her belly. "It was right about here," he said and replaced his hand with his mouth.

"My God," she said. Every ounce of feeling in her body was concentrated on the movements of his mouth on her skin. She was wet again, as deep and wet as the ocean.

He looked up and grinned. "Tell me if you don't like it."

"Oh, I like it fine . . . " she began, not caring if she sounded like a gusher, when the telephone rang again.

Darroch growled with fury. "I'll answer it. If it's him . . . "

"No, no, let me. It might be someone from the Island this time." Again she stumbled across the floor, found the phone and turned it on.

"Hi, Mom," said a bright voice in her ear.

"Sally!" she gasped.

Darroch slumped in despair on the sofa. He put his elbows on his knees and rested his head in his hands. The husband he could compete with but not the daughter.

Jean sat down on the chair. She was suddenly aware that she was almost naked and it made her acutely embarrassed. "How are you, sweetie?" she said.

"I'm fine. And Mom, I know what time it is there, I'm not confused like Daddy. I wouldn't have called this late but he said it was okay, you were still up."

I bet he did, thought Jean grimly.

"So I decided to call because I have something so exciting to tell you, I just couldn't wait."

"What is it, Sal?"

"Daddy's just given me the most wonderful present. He's buying me a ticket to come and visit you on your Island. Isn't that great?"

Her joy at the idea of seeing her daughter again was tempered by resentment as she suddenly realized why Russ was sending Sally. So he can find out what's 'going on', she thought. She said, "That's great, I've missed you so much. When are you coming?"

"That's the best part. Today's Friday. I can leave Tuesday. I just need to get my passport out of the safe deposit box and book the ticket. Is Tuesday okay?"

"Oh, yes. But Sally, what about school? Isn't the new semester about to begin?"

"It's independent study month all through January. I'll have to write a paper. Maybe I can find something to study on your Island. What do you think?"

"I'm sure you can. We'll help."

On the sofa Darroch listened to Jean's soft voice murmuring. It was cold in the cottage. He found his undershirt and pulled it on, then his turtleneck. He located her blouse and a blanket and went to her.

He held out the blouse and helped her into it, first one arm, then the other, while she transferred the phone from shoulder to shoulder. He tucked the blanket around her.

"Thank you, lovie," she whispered. He nodded and walked back to the sofa.

"Who are you talking to? Do you have company, Mom?" asked Sally.

"Just a friend, darling. Now tell me again when you'll arrive . . ."

Just a friend. Darroch was wounded to his soul. Is that all I am? he thought. He knew he was being irrational. She could not tell Sally about him in these circumstances, but he had a searing desire to snatch the phone and shout to Milwaukee that Jean was his and they were lovers. Or they would have been if the damned phone had not rung. Twice.

"I'd better hang up, Mom, don't want to waste Daddy's money. I'll phone you as soon as we book the ticket."

"Wonderful." Mother and daughter cooed their goodbyes and hung up.

She came back to the sofa to sit by him. He put an arm around her, realizing that the evening's hot passion was over. "I gather we're going to have company," he said.

"Yes. I can't wait for you two to meet. You'll love Sally, she's a terrific kid. And she'll like you too."

Of course. She'll be thrilled to meet her mother's lover, he thought wryly. They sat together in front of the dying fire. Jean yawned.

"I should go home, *mo chridhe*," he said.

"Darroch, I'm sorry about . . . the interruption. I really wanted to . . . you know."

"I know. There'll be other times, don't worry. What we did was fun, though, wasn't it?"

Her body tingled at the memory. "Fun is not the word for it."

When he left Jean stood by the kitchen window and watched the tall figure stride down the road to his cottage. Darling Darroch loves me, she thought, and my sweet Sally is coming to visit. And I've found my Island family. A good start to the New Year.

PART VI

Mòrag and Ùisdean

Eilean Dubh

words: Audrey McClellan and Sherry Ladig
music: Sherry Ladig

1. A — maiden fair as the island sky, be—neath the oak tree softly sleeping, I'll
2. O — maiden fair as the island sky, with — sorrow now we must be — parting. I'll
3. O — maiden fair as the island sky, It — is I would forget you ne—ver. Deep

1. wake her with a — tender kiss, our   hearts will rise, and rise for — ev — er. Oh,
2. leave you with a — tender kiss, our   hearts will break, and break for — ev — er. Oh,
3. ocean parts us, the song remains, our   hearts will sing, and sing for — ev — er. Oh,

1. Eileen Dubh, where my heart does dwell, here — I will stay with my love for — ev — er. Oh,
2. Eileen Dubh, where my heart does dwell, I will leave my heart with you for — ev — er. Oh,
3. Eileen Dubh, where my heart does dwell, I will sing the song of you for — ev — er. Oh,

1. Eileen Dubh, where my heart does dwell, here — I will stay with my love for — ev — er.
2. Eileen Dubh, where my heart does dwell, I will leave my heart with you for — ev — er.
3. Eileen Dubh, where my heart does dwell, I will sing the song of you for — ev — er.

Forty

*The Sons of the King shall rule the Island for many years
but the Daughter of the King shall be conquered by
the Riddler's Son . . . blue eyes will yield to green . . .*

From the predictions of Tormod Alasdair MacChriathar,
"Tormod the Riddler," translated by Isabel Ross

Cairistìona MacChriathar, balanced on two canes and standing fiercely upright, was waiting for Jean and Darroch when they came to the Seniors' Residence two days after Hogmanay. She served them tea, then said, "Have you brought Ùisdean's letters?"

"Photocopies," said Jean, handing them over. "The originals are in my safe deposit box back in Milwaukee. I'm afraid they're not easy to read," she added, watching Cairistìona peer at the first letter.

"At my age nothing is easy to read," she replied and gave the letters to Darroch. "Read them to me, *a Dharroch mhór.*"

Darroch read them aloud. He did not censor them, giving the author's passion for his beloved Mòrag full rein in his beautiful voice. The old lady kept a stern impassive look on her face. It was not until the last letter that she broke down.

"We are sorry to upset you," Darroch began but the old lady shook her head.

"It was a long time ago," she said but Jean realized that here on the Island the past was always with them; the events of two hundred years ago were as real as today.

Cairistìona turned to Jean. "Thank you for sharing his letters."

"I wish we had Mòrag's letters to him," said Jean. "I wonder what became of them. He certainly would have kept them."

The old lady smiled. "I have a surprise for you. Mòrag's last letter to him." As Jean and Darroch stared at her she added, "It was never sent. It has been passed down in our family from each eldest daughter to her eldest daughter. It's there on my table. Bring it to me, please, *a Dharroch*."

He brought a packet wrapped in yellowed silk to her. She opened it and took out a letter as old as Ùisdean's.

"Before you read it I will tell you the story of these two, as the women in my family pieced it together and have told it to each generation of MacChriathar women." She smiled at Darroch. "Never to the men. Only women can be trusted with secrets."

Even the chief's daughter had work to do and in the spring it was the young girls' duty to take the sheep to summer pastures in the hills.

Each girl had her special spot for her sheep and Mòrag's was by a loch in the hills above Ros Mór. When Mòrag and her dogs and flock arrived one morning, she was startled to see a young man kneeling by the loch, hands cupped for a drink of water.

She knew immediately he was not a Mac an Rìgh; she knew every man of her clan. She whistled the dogs to her and challenged him. "You are on my lands. Who are you and what do you want?"

He smiled. "Water belongs to everyone. Would you begrudge me a drink?"

She glared, realizing who he was. That shining red-brown hair was as telling as a banner would have been. "Have the MacChriathars no water of their own, that they must poach from the Mac an Rìghs? You steal water as easily as you steal sheep."

He sat back on his heels, still smiling. "Harsh words on such a beautiful morning, from such a beautiful mouth. Has no one taught you that women should be soft and gentle and kind to strangers?"

With the dogs at her heels for protection she edged nearer. The young man was handsome and his smile charming, but she would not be sweet-talked into allowing him to encroach on Mac an Rìgh territory. "You are my enemy; you are not welcome here. Drink your fill and leave. Hospitality demands no more than that."

He stood. Instead of turning to leave he walked up the grassy bank from the lake and sat down again, quite at his ease.

"I told you to leave," growled Mòrag and the dogs, catching the sound in her voice, growled in their turn.

"Come now, lass. I am tired and must rest before I climb that hill back to MacChriathar lands. Would you deny me that? Searching for lost sheep is hard work."

"Reiving, more likely," she said. "Everyone knows that the MacChriathars are notorious sheep-stealers."

He frowned. "Among my people it is known that Mac an Rìghs own but one sheep each and the rest of their flocks are . . . borrowed . . . from their neighbors."

"You dare to accuse my clan of stealing sheep?"

He lay back on the grass. "Aye, I dare, but right now I am too tired to argue and the sun's warmth is making me drowsy. Let me have a little nap and then you can abuse me to your heart's content." He closed his eyes.

Flummoxed, Mòrag drew nearer. She could set the dogs on him, and probably should, but his casualness was disarming. He was, after all, doing no harm, even though he annoyed her by his presence. She sat down on the grass a safe distance away and studied him as he stretched out.

His hair changed colors in the sunlight, now sandy, now red, like the color of the *uisge beatha* distilled by her father's *grùdair*. His full mouth still wore a teasing smile even as he feigned sleep.

"What is your name?" she demanded.

He opened one eye. "Ùisdean MacChriathar, at your service, my lady. I have the honor to be the second son of our chief, Alasdair MacChriathar."

"Only a second son," she scoffed. "I am the daughter and only child of our chief."

He rolled over on his side and looked at her. "Does the chief's daughter rejoice in a name? Or is she simply called 'your ladyship' by all the humbler folk, who no doubt are never allowed to raise their eyes above her shoetops?"

She had not meant to sound so haughty. "My name is Mòrag," she mumbled.

"Mòrag," he said and repeated it several times with varying inflections. "A beautiful name . . . but not as beautiful as its possessor."

Few of the young men in her clan dared flirt so openly with her and she didn't know how to deal with it except by haughtiness. She put her chin in the air and looked away from his grin.

What a beauty, he thought, eyeing the black hair tumbling down her back and the luscious curves of her young figure. And so full of herself that he longed to take her down a peg or two. "Tell me," he teased, "why so great a daughter of so great a chief is tending sheep like a peasant girl?"

Mòrag sniffed and stuck her nose higher. "Among my people everyone has their duties. There are no lie-abouts and wastrels."

He groaned. "I am wounded to the heart. My lady thinks me a lazy-bones, a thief of sheep and water and, no doubt, every other kind of scoundrel."

"I am not your lady," she snarled.

No, he thought, not mine but wouldn't I enjoy it if you were. That idea surprised him. At sixteen he had done his share of flirting, was notorious among the MacChriathar women for his charm, but he'd not had a woman yet because he'd not found one to whom he could commit his life. He'd looked and fantasized, but in their close-knit community the chief's son could not bed a woman without some promise being expected from him. And he was not ready for marriage, not yet, and when he was, his bride would be chosen by his father.

He was staring at her with such intensity that she felt herself blush. No man had ever looked at her that way. The blush made her pale skin glow and the wind ruffled her black hair like a lover's hand.

"*A Dhia*, you are lovely," he said softly. A warmth was rising in his groin, more intense than he'd ever felt before. "The men in your clan must be mad for you."

She was used to having her person coveted, but it was only from men's ambition, or so she believed. To be desired for her beauty alone was a new thought. She was her father's only child and the next in line after her as heir were twin cousins so deficient they could not feed themselves or control their bodily functions. Imperfect men could not lead the Mac an Rìgh clan. It had been agreed for years that Mòrag's husband would be the next chief.

"My second cousin wants me," she said, "but I think it's only because he knows that if he marries me he will be our chief."

"Will your father let him have you?"

"I don't know . . . I am afraid he will." The memory of her cousin's lustful leer was suddenly fresh in her mind. Perhaps he wanted more than the chieftaincy. She shuddered. She did not like her cousin.

"You should choose your own mate," he said. "Life is hard enough without one you love at your side."

"I am the chief's daughter. The choice is not mine to make."

He sighed. "Aye, for me as well. My father will choose my wife."

They looked at each other in sudden sympathy. He said, "We have much in common."

Suddenly wary, she snapped, "Perhaps. But you are still my enemy."

He said, "I have often thought that a shame. Why should our clans be at war? The Island is big enough for us all, with game and water and pastures in plenty."

That was a new idea to Mòrag, who'd grown up on stories of the evil MacChriathars. She should fear him, but she did not. He didn't have horns or a tail and he seemed quite harmless.

Ùisdean said softly, "Perhaps we could begin to heal the feud by being friends." As she hesitated he added, "A lad and a lass, friends, on a beautiful summer day."

She smiled. *A Dhia*, he thought, her smile is more beautiful than the day itself. He stood up reluctantly. "I must go. Could we meet again, Mòrag? And talk . . . as friends?"

She was silent, then said, "I come here often, to check on my flock. Every third day."

"I will be here whenever I can."

"Until our next meeting, then. Goodbye." He walked up the hill and was soon lost to sight.

Two days later she was back at the loch. She had taken a larger lunch than usual, sneaking an extra piece of cheese and a loaf of bread into her basket when the cook wasn't looking. After all, he was on her land. Would not the law of hospitality dictate that she offer him something to eat?

But he was not there. Disappointed, she sank down under the tree and closed her eyes in the sunshine. She awoke to the sound of a warm voice singing, improvising:

A maiden fair as the Island sky,
Beneath the oak tree softly sleeping.
I'll wake her with a tender kiss.
Our hearts will rise and rise forever.

She opened her eyes to meet his.

He grinned. "Ah, she is not dead, she only sleeps."

"That voice of yours would wake the dead," she said tartly. "But I like the song. Is there more?"

"Hmmm . . . " said Ùisdean. He was well known in his clan for his ability to make up songs for any occasion. He sang:

Oh Eilean Dubh, where my heart does dwell,
Here I'll stay with my love forever.

Mòrag could play that game too. She began a new verse:

Oh maiden fair as the Island sky
With sorrow now we must be parting.
I'll leave you with a tender kiss . . .

She paused, stymied. Ùisdean added:

Our hearts will break, and break forever.

"A lovely tune, but such sad words. How does it end?" challenged Mòrag. Ùisdean thought for several long moments, than sang:

O maiden fair as the Island sky
O I will forget you never.
Deep ocean parts us, the song remains.
Our hearts will sing, and sing forever.

Mòrag clapped her hands, delighted, and joined him on the last lines.

O Eilean Dubh, where my heart does dwell
I'll sing the song of you forever.

They looked at each other. "Your voice is as sweet as a breeze over the heather," he said softly.

Flustered, she looked down and spotted her basket. "I have brought food. Will you join me?"

"A MacChriathar and a Mac an Rìgh, taking bread together. My lady honors me."

"I am not your lady. Why must I keep telling you that?" she snapped, pleased.

After that day they met often to talk, laugh and make music, and said goodbye reluctantly when it came time for Mòrag to drive her sheep back to winter pasture. All through the winter she dreamed of red-brown hair and green eyes and found herself trembling with eagerness when it was time to take the sheep to the loch.

Would he be there?

He was. He went to her and took both her hands in his. "I have come every day, waiting for you. I claim a kiss for my fidelity."

Memories of her dreams flooded Mòrag's mind and made her tilt her head willingly up to his. He bent to her mouth. When the kiss ended, she pulled away, breathless and shivering.

"Have you never kissed a man before, *m'eudail?*"

"No." Her cheeks blossomed with pink. Her mind picked out the key point in what he had said: last year he had been a boy, but this year he was a man and kissing him could be very, very dangerous. She swallowed hard.

They talked as easily as they had last year, sang and laughed together but both sensed something different between them. Over the winter Ùisdean had shared kisses with several young women in his clan, each eager to become his bride. His father had watched in amusement. He had already selected a wife for his son, but saw no harm in letting him have a bit of fun before marriage.

It had awakened Ùisdean. The older boys' tales of their conquests had aroused his interest and a newly married man's boasting of his pleasures with his wife had awakened his passion. Mòrag's mouth was sweet and her innocence arousing, but it also stirred a deep protectiveness.

Throughout the summer love and lust grew. Their kisses grew deeper and their dreams more passionate. One day she let him pull down the neck of her blouse and feast on her breasts. "I love you, *mo Mhòrag*," he said. "I love you, Ùisdean," she replied.

They began that day to talk of marriage. Of being together forever.

A week before the end of the summer pasturing, Mòrag's father summoned her. "I have selected your husband and our next chief," he announced without preamble, and motioned to a man standing in the shadows. "Give your hands to your cousin, who will wed you at our winter feast."

Her cousin strode forward and kissed her. "I dream of the day when I have you in my bed," he whispered in her ear and she shivered with terror. Ùisdean's mouth was tender; this man's was hot with lust.

Ùisdean found her in tears the next time they met. Sobbing, she recounted the story of her betrothal. Fierce anger raked him. "You are mine. You belong to me." He pulled her into his arms and kissed her furiously.

She gasped, "Handfast yourself to me, so that I may refuse to marry my cousin."

"We should have witnesses . . . "

"God is our witness." When he swore to pledge himself to her for a year and a day, she smiled in triumph. "Now take me. I give you my body as well as my heart."

He moved back in shock. "It would not be honorable to take your virginity . . . "

She reached for the heavy leather belt that held his plaid pleated around him. When it loosened in her hands she pulled it away from his body so that he wore only his hip-length shirt of saffron linen. She spread out the plaid around them.

"We are handfast and my virginity is yours. I give it to you freely."

Lust and duty warred in him. "I don't want it to be this way," he cried.

"And what would you prefer, *mo chridhe?*" she teased. "Silks and satins and a feather bed? Walls hung with tapestries?"

"All those things and more. No finery is too good for you, *mo Mhòrag*."

"What does it matter, if we are together?" She pulled the belt from her skirt and tossed both away. Her shift was of a finer, creamier fabric that barely reached her knees.

"You are determined, then," he said and she replied, "It's the only way." Her hands reached out to lift his shirt, then hers so that their lower bodies touched. "Let us join as lovers, as we've both wanted for so long."

They'd shared kisses and intimate caresses, but he'd never felt the warm length of her nakedness from her belly to her strong smooth legs. Always he'd restrained himself from liberties that a betrothed lover or a husband might rightly enjoy.

Still he hesitated. She whispered, "Perhaps my cousin will not want me if I am no longer a virgin. Perhaps my father will let me marry you if you get me with child."

She moved into his arms with all the sensual grace of the seductive fairies of Island legend, slipping her hands down to his hips, then lower. "So this is how you are made," she whispered. "Are all men so hard and so strong?"

"Are all women so wet and warm as you?" he murmured, slipping his hand between her legs. With his other hand he pushed up her shift and his mouth captured her breast.

"Come into me, make me yours," she begged and he moved on top of her.

"It hurts, for women, the first time. Forgive me if I cause you pain."

She answered by thrusting her hips upward until he found and entered her. She was small and tight and it terrified him to force his hard length into her. When he met the barrier of her maidenhead he forced himself to stop when she moaned in agony. She had not expected such pain, but it would not deter her.

"Take me," she commanded and he dove deep. She screamed and the sound echoed through him as he thrust again and again, lost in an ecstasy he'd never imagined in his most erotic dreams. The pure male joy of possession filled him and he gathered her to him, pressing her hips against his with strong hands. His, at last. His woman, bound to him for all time by the entry that she'd demanded so fiercely and given so freely.

She wrapped her legs around his hips, imprisoning him inside. He moved in her again and this time she screamed with the pleasure of surrender.

They made love every time they met at the loch. Their passion grew and was so intense that there were times when they did not even disrobe, falling to the ground in each other's arms. There were other times when he spread out his plaid and they took off their clothes and spent long leisurely minutes bringing each other pleasure.

One of Mòrag's friends was a young woman with a very great curiosity. She thought the chief's daughter was spending a great deal of time up at the loch and she wondered why. She followed Mòrag one day and just as she was about to run down to the water and surprise her friend she heard voices. She saw them, lying on Ùisdean's plaid, legs entwined. She watched, eyes wide, as the young man moved on top of Mòrag. She heard the cries of the lovers ring out in the grass-scented air.

It was shocking, it was *miorbhuileach*. She could not keep it to herself, she had to tell her closest friend. "Our Mòrag has a lover, a wonderfully handsome young man with hair like the sunrise. They meet at the loch, they lie naked together. I heard him say that he loved her."

The young woman in whom she had confided felt it was her duty to tell Mòrag's mother, who could not keep such a story from her husband the chief. The storm that broke over the household was made more terrible by the Mac an Rìgh's shouts of fury that soon changed into cold hard anger. Mòrag was summoned to her parents' presence.

"You foolish girl, you have given away your honor like some worthless slut. Who has defiled you?"

Mòrag stared at him defiantly. "I have done nothing wrong. I love him."

The Mac an Rìgh roared, "Who is your lover?"

Mòrag lifted her head bravely. "He is the second son of the MacChriathar chief."

Her mother drew her breath in sharply and her father's face twisted in fury. "You have given yourself to our enemy. No doubt he laughed with his father over how he has cheated your bridegroom."

"No! He wants to marry me."

"Marry you? A MacChriathar marry my heir? Are you mad or merely stupid to think that such a thing could happen?"

"Why not? We are in love." Her mother looked at her in appalled pity.

"Use the small amount of brains you have, girl," said her father cruelly. "How do you think our clansmen would react, if I give my daughter . . . and my chieftaincy . . . to a MacChriathar?"

"Why . . . " Mòrag stopped. She had thought only of the two of them.

"What do you think your cousin would do if he were cheated of his bride? He is a ferocious swordsman. Do you think your lover could best him in a fight?"

She was pale with fright. "You could stop it . . . "

"I would be lucky if I could stop an attack on the whole cursed band of MacChriathars if word of this outrage gets out. Fire and sword and slaughter, the old and the children, no one spared. Is that what you want for your people and his? By God, it's small wonder women are never allowed to rule, when they let their lust overcome their duty to their clan."

"We are handfast. We want to unite our clans with our love."

"You wanted to gratify your lust." The words were final and harsh. Mòrag dropped her head into her hands. She loved Uisdean deeply but she could not deny she had wanted his body.

"And suppose . . . " her father lowered his voice to a whisper more threatening than shouts. "Suppose he survives to wed you in peace and become our chief. Do you think he will ever be accepted? Will he not always fear the knife in his back some dark night? The arrow gone astray when he hunts? The sword turned against him in battle?" He shook his head. "What will happen to your love then, girl, if your husband can never feel safe amongst your people? You'd sign his death warrant with the marriage vows."

Weeping, Mòrag heard the truth in what he was saying. "We will go away together, we will live in the hills where no one will find us."

He shook his head in dismissal. "Your cousin would not permit it. He would hunt you down, kill your lover and take you. Even dishonored, you are still the heir to the chief. And he wants to be chief."

He looked at her without a hint of pity. Then he turned to her mother. "Who else knows of this?"

"Ealasaid, who brought me the story. And the girl who told her. I don't know which one it is."

"Foolish brats. No doubt they've spread the story far and wide."

"No. I swore Ealasaid to silence and she promised her friend had not talked."

"They must be dealt with. And that bastard who is her lover."

"You can't kill Ùisdean! I love him." Mòrag glared at her father.

"I don't mean to kill him." A trip to the Colonies would seal his mouth forever, and the two girls could go along as well, unless he decided they could keep silent.

Mòrag took a deep breath and played her final card. "What if I am with child?"

"And are you?" Her father's voice was as cold as death.

"I don't know . . . I may be. I have been sick, mornings . . . and I am late."

Her mother broke down in hopeless tears. "We are ruined. They will kill each other over the succession."

"Stop wailing, woman," snarled the Mac an Rìgh. "Is there a way to get rid of it?"

"No way that is safe. She might die."

The Mac an Rìgh muttered under his breath that it might be the best solution but he could not condemn the daughter he loved to death. "You must wed your cousin at once."

"Husband, he will want to know why the wedding has been hurried up. He will suspect and Mòrag's life and the baby's will never be safe."

The Mac an Rìgh turned to his daughter. "A task for you, girl. You must seduce your cousin and make him think he has put his brat in your belly."

Mòrag collapsed in tears in her mother's arms. "I hate him . . . " Her mother whispered in her ear, "But you will love your child. Do it for the child."

Her father smiled grimly. Life was uncertain, especially for children. Disease, accidents, real or arranged, and a small inconvenient person could be removed easily. The brat might not live to see its first birthday and by then Mòrag would be safely married, perhaps even with her womb filled with a true heir for the Mac an Rìghs.

"Lock her in her room. Let her think about it."

As her mother led their daughter away, the Mac an Rìgh turned to his own thoughts. Two more tasks and the clan would be safe. The first was the two girls who knew of Mòrag's disgrace. An interview with their terrifying chief had them on their knees weeping and promising on the lives of their mothers they'd never tell. To make sure of their silence he wed them both, at once, to two shepherds who spent their lives year around in the dark lonely hills far from their village.

The second task was to rid the Island of the MacChriathar's second son. The men assigned to Ùisdean's kidnapping knew only that the MacChriathar had offended the Mac an Rìgh and stealing the chief's son would be his revenge. Exile was a sweeter revenge than death.

Ùisdean fought like a devil when they sprang on him by the loch where he'd gone to meet Mòrag. They bound him hand and foot and delivered him to a fishing boat leaving Eilean Dubh waters for the mouth of the Clyde by Glasgow. Drugged into unconsciousness, he was put aboard an immigrant ship leaving for America. When he awoke he found himself in the steerage, seasick and alone despite the company of fifty others: men, women and children leaving the poverty of their homeland and the treachery of their landlords.

He was dumped unceremoniously on the docks at Baltimore.

Mòrag, unaware of her lover's fate, knew she was pregnant. Irrational love grew for the child in her womb, Ùisdean's child, and the only part of him she would ever have. She would protect the child and if it were a boy, he would rule her clan.

With her mother's help she contrived to be alone with her cousin and made it seem she was falling prey to his advances. On the third such occasion she let him pull her down beside him in the grass, suffered his fumblings beneath her skirt, let him move on top of her. Remembering her lost lover made her burst into tears and a natural revulsion made her try to fight him off. He took her hard as she struggled and screamed and he never noticed her lost virginity. All he knew was he'd solidified his claim to the chieftaincy by possessing the chief's daughter.

It was the Mac an Rìgh himself who discovered them, or pretended to do so, for he'd kept a shrewd eye on them all evening. He roared with rage at what he called his daughter's lost honor and demanded that her cousin wed her at once.

The priest was summoned and they were married in the chief's chapel. The cousin, wild with triumph and lust, enjoyed her twice more that night while she wept in despair.

It was the custom for a woman to seclude herself in the last weeks of her pregnancy. Mòrag was very close to term when she retired with her mother and two trusted women, the shepherds' wives. By now both women were sick of exile and would have done anything to be allowed to live once more in their village. It was no hardship to them to swear silence about the date of the child's birth.

Fate was kind to Mòrag and her child, as it was not to her clan. A deadly disease swept over the village and no one thought it strange when she insisted on remaining in seclusion with the child until the epidemic was over. It was several months before they returned to their people and no one realized the baby was a month older than claimed.

Cairistìona finished her story and there was dead silence in the room. She said, "Mòrag's father died suddenly, a year after the birth, taking his secret with him. Her husband was too busy consolidating his power as chief to question his son's parentage. They had five more children, but Ùisdean's son survived to be the next chief. Your ancestor, Darroch."

She leaned forward. "Here's Mòrag's last letter to Ùisdean. We don't know why it was never sent. We think perhaps her mother intercepted it."

"Will you read it to us, *a Chairistìona*?" said Darroch.

She unfolded the letter carefully and began to read, Darroch translating for Jean:

> *My adored Ùisdean,*
>
> *Sailors have brought me the letters that you have written from your new country, and a sailor took the two I was able to write to you. I hope you received them, and the words of my undying love for you.*
>
> *I thought at first you would come to claim me and be damned to our fathers and our clans. When you did not come I thought they had killed you. My heart swelled with happiness to read your first letter, telling me you were safe in that town of Baltimore so far away. My happiness increased to hear in your following letters how well you are faring in the New World, and I rejoiced to hear you are making yourself a part of that World, so strange in custom and sights.*
>
> *My heart broke when you wrote that I should wait for you, and it breaks anew every time I read your letters. Gladly would I have waited and gladly gone with you, had God granted that boon to me.*
>
> *But I am with child, beloved, and it is yours. I cannot tell you how*

sweet it is to have your child in me, to have some part of you still here with me. I talk to our baby and I hear it answer in your voice.

I will never join you, m'aingeal, they will not let me go. I have married my cousin and I have convinced him our child is his. I pretended to let him seduce me and he took me with cruelty. He is not unkind to me now, he is happy to think he has planted a child in me so quickly. I think he may even be beginning to love me. I wish that I could love him but my heart is yours forever.

But I know my duty to my clan and to our child. Perhaps God will grant me this, as he would not give me you: that our baby be delivered safely and live a long life.

God willing, then, my Ùisdean, know this, that your child will be the ruler of the Mac an Rìghs. We have united our clans although they do not know it.

And they have exiled you but you remain on our Island forever!

Ever yours and trusting we shall meet in Heaven,

Mòrag, daughter of the chief, wife of the chief to be, mother of the one who will be chief of Clan Mac an Rìgh

Jean wept. She buried her face against Darroch's shoulder and his arms went around her. His eyes met Cairistìona's. Yes, he said silently, *this is how it is. A MacChriathar and a Mac an Rìgh, united at last. Forever, this time.*

"Take the letter, *mo Shine*, and keep it with his," said Cairistìona. "It no longer needs to be secret. Ùisdean has come home at last."

"I have something else for you," she said, and began to sing in the clear, quivery voice of old age a beautiful melody, the words in the Gaelic:

A maiden fair as the Island sky . . .

Jean gasped, and trembled as Cairistìona sang, and when the older woman had finished Jean took up the tune and sang it, the same tune with English words:

Down by the banks of the Ohio lies Sarah softly sleeping-o.
Then comes good Thomas, her own true love
To wake her with his kisses-o.
O you shall sing, my own true love and I shall fiddle a tune so low.
O you shall sing and I shall play and we'll while away the evening-o.

Tears rolled down her cheeks as she sang. It was her father's song. He'd taught it to her when she was very young, sung her to sleep with it often, and after he'd died she'd put it out of her mind, unable to bear hearing it. She'd not sung it in years.

Darroch, comparing the English words to the Gaelic Cairistiona had sung, hearing the same themes of love and music and parting, realized it was the same song, transformed in the New World into an Appalachian ballad. The words and music resonated in the deepest part of his consciousness. *It's a haunted tune,* he thought in wonder, *something very rare. You can hear the souls of its creators in it.*

"How can it be, that you both know this song?" he asked.

"It's from the part of North Carolina where Ùisdean settled, where our family began," said Jean. "So old no one knew where it came from, but always linked to him."

"It is Ùisdean and Mòrag's song. They made it together one day, up by their loch. Another secret she passed on to the women in our clan," said Cairistìona.

Two elderly women poked their heads into the room, faces alight with curiosity. "That is your song, *a Chairistìona,* we've heard you sing it many times," said one. "How is the American lassie singing it, and the words in the English?" said the other.

"Because it is a MacChriathar song, and she is a MacChriathar," said Cairistìona proudly. "And she has brought the song home from America, and herself with it."

Sarah & Thomas

(Appalachian version of Eilean Dubh)

Down by the banks of the Ohio lies Sarah softly sleeping-o.
Then comes good Thomas, her own true love,
To wake her with his kisses-o.
Oh you shall sing, my own true love, and I shall fiddle a tune so low,
Oh you shall sing and I shall play, and we'll while away the evening-o.

Oh, Sarah, why do you weep and sigh? It's because you're leaving O-hi-o,
Across the ocean deep and wide, and never again see my Thomas-o.
Would you forget me, Thomas dear, would you forget your Sarah so,
I never could forget my dear, even if we part in deep sorrow.

So I will fiddle and you shall sing, even as our hearts are breaking-o,
And when I'm gone and far away, our hearts will still remember-o.
And when I fiddle and when you sing in notes so mournful and so low,
We will remember our true love, down by the banks of the O-hi-o.

lyrics by Sherry Ladig

PART VII

Sally

Forty-one

Scene 6. Little girl on the roof, inches from the edge.
    Magician approaches cautiously.
Girl: You're the magician from the theatre. Can you do . . .
    real magic?
Magician: Can I do real magic? What is real magic?
Girl: Can you make things . . . disappear? Bad things?
Magician: Well, I can make things . . . good things . . .
    appear. (Pulls rabbit from pocket.) His name is Harry.
    He's named after my friend, a real magician . . . Harry
    Houdini. Would you like to pet him?
Girl stretches her hand towards the rabbit and moves away
    from the edge.

The Magician, episode 12: "Rings of Fire"

*I*nverness's train station is largely outdoors. Trains arrive on uncovered tracks and those waiting to meet them are subjected to all the vagaries of the weather. Today it was windy, cold and drizzly, with a particularly Scottish January dankness. It was four in the afternoon and the gray air was filled with a thick watery mist.

Shivering, Darroch jammed his hands into his pockets and paced on the platform to keep warm as the London train slid into the station. The seven passenger cars were all full and he feared he'd miss Sally in the confusion. As passengers trickled out he looked around, baffled, until a young woman emerged from the last car. She hoisted off a bag, then went back for more.

Aha, thought Darroch. Unmistakable. The girl was very slender and very tall, with wide shoulders and a slim waist, and her hair was golden red-brown, the color of Lagavulin whisky. She was the image of her mother, only taller and lankier. He strode up to her, impatiently pushing his wind-ruffled hair out of his eyes.

"Sally?" The girl stared at him with eyes as green as the tidal pool off Airgead Point. He plucked the backpack from her hands. "Yes, of course, you're Sally. I've never seen anyone who looked more like Sally than you do. Except your mother and you look just like her."

"Umm . . . you're not a lunatic, are you?" She couldn't help responding with a smile. He had an immensely likable face given character by an elegant nose and sapphire eyes dancing with amusement and admiration. He looked familiar but she could not imagine why.

"No, I'm only a friend of your mother's, sent to collect you. My name is Darroch." He was quite dazzled. He wanted very much to kiss her cheek, she reminded him so of Jean. Instead he offered his hand.

She looked him up and down before reluctantly taking it. The friendliness was gone as soon as she realized who he was. Only a friend, indeed. She had sensed much more than that from her mother's letters. "Where's my mother?" she demanded.

"Home, sick with flu. She's been . . . what was her expression? 'Throwing up,' she called it. Very picturesque phrase. I assume you know what that means?" She nodded. "She's feeling much better and wanted to come meet you. I had to dissuade her by mentioning the vicious little updraft we get over Eilean Dubh as the chopper comes in. That dampened her enthusiasm and she agreed I could be your escort. Now, if it pleases you, I have a taxi waiting. Ready?"

"Okay." He picked up her suitcase but after a brief, silent and determined struggle she retained custody of her backpack. Glowering, she slung it over her shoulder. She was determined not to be treated like a weak female.

On the ride to the helicopter he said, "I hope you had something to eat on the train so you're not famished?"

"I had a sort-of-a-chicken sandwich and some it-must-be-tea-it's-too-strong-to-be-coffee from the BritRail buffet. That and jet lag have squashed my appetite."

"The chopper ride's just an hour and you'll have supper when we get home. I'm sure your mother is cooking even now if she feels at all well."

She said hungrily, "I hope it's chicken. Mom does great chicken. Or fish. I'll bet you get terrific fish here. Maybe I could force down a few morsels after all."

The rain had thickened to a steady fall by the time they reached the helicopter pad and the flight was bumpy. Darroch, his stomach iron as usual, thought of Jean and her bout with flu and was glad he'd persuaded her not to come. She had no business out in this weather; he would have ordered her to stay home if necessary. Amused, he wondered if she would have obeyed him.

Sally matched him for custody of the stomach. Calmly she peered out of the tilting windows as the chopper rocked in the wind. "Off to see the Wizard," she said.

Dusk was succeeded by a heavy velvet darkness. Lights defined the shape of Oban as they flew over. Above the harbor the pseudo-Grecian shape of McCaig's Folly glowed like a beacon.

Darroch shouted over the helicopter noise, "Our Island will be coming up soon. That's Islay below, and Jura just beyond, like a football at the tip of a boot."

Sally watched and absorbed the Islands by twilight, conscious that the thick sea lay just below. They landed on Eilean Dubh in a cloud of rain that lashed them as they got out and stood, shivering, waiting for her bags.

A figure ran out of the waiting room, straight at Sally. "Sally! Sally, darling!"

"Mom!" Sally caught the figure around the waist and they hugged.

Darroch made a small exasperated sound. "Sally, take your mother into the waiting room, please. At once. No, leave the suitcases. I'll take them and bring the car around. Stay inside till I come back."

She obeyed automatically, taking her mother's arm and urging her into the office. Inside, she said, "He's sort of bossy, isn't he."

Jean laughed. "He's the least bossy man I've ever met. He's just fussed because I came out in the rain after being sick."

Darroch appeared at the door. "Hellish weather, Jean. What are you doing out in it? And how did you get here?" He frowned at her.

"Don't scold, lovie. I couldn't wait to see Sally. I got a ride with Ian the Post."

"What, standing in the rain waiting?" He said something in the Gaelic.

"You forget I know Ian's schedule to the minute. I hardly had to wait at all." She smiled at him. He said something else and Jean giggled. Sally stared first at one, then the other. Her mother seemed different and Sally wasn't sure she liked it.

They went out, Darroch gripping the door with a firm hand. "Wait, Sally. I'll be right back," he said.

Sally snorted. I don't need an escort, she thought, I'm not some feeble girlie. She grabbed the backpack and opened the door. She staggered as a howling gust of wind pulled the door from her hand and slammed it against the wall.

Darroch, settling Jean in the back seat, did not notice. "I'm all right," Jean protested as he wrapped a travel rug around her. Damp and tired, she snuggled into the rug's warmth and smiled at him.

Darroch turned to go back for Sally and was at first taken aback, then amused, by the sight of the slender, soaking wet figure tacking relentlessly toward what she could just identify as the interior lights of a car. Once out of the waiting room and into the storm she had no intention of turning back, regardless of whose car it was. She would get into it as quickly as she could, hoping it wasn't the local mad killer driving.

Darroch peeled off his coat and wrapped it around her before opening the passenger door. She allowed herself to be belted into the seat. It was too dark to assess her surroundings but she had a brief intimation of luxury. A smell of leather tickled her nostrils. What sort of car was this?

Jet lag and the seductively warm coat with its faint odor of peat smoke combined to make Sally drowsy. Darroch thought of providing a travel commentary but a glance at her nodding head kept him quiet.

When they arrived at Jean's cottage both women were asleep. "Sally," he said gently. Then, "Sally," a little louder.

From the back a sleepy voice said, "What do you want with my Sally?"

"We're home, Jean."

"Oh, *miorbhuileach*. I suppose she's asleep?"

"Yes."

"Jet lag. If I can get unwrapped from this rug I'll go inside and build up the fire while you bring her in."

"Steady on, who's been sick? Go warm your famous soup, I know that's what you've been up to this afternoon. I'll see to Sally and the fire." Jean, feeling a little peely-wally from the flu's aftereffects, was glad to go into her kitchen to finish supper.

Once out into the rain Sally roused quickly. "Are we here?"

"Yes, go in, hurry."

Inside Sally headed for the kitchen's bright glow but stopped awkwardly. "Here's your coat. Thank you."

"My pleasure. Come sit on the sofa. No, don't go into the kitchen. You'll be warmest by the fire; you're wet." His arm behind her, Darroch herded her to the sofa and draped a blanket over her before he knelt to make the fire.

Why did she keep doing whatever he told her to do? She thought, you've wrapped my mother around your little finger, honey pie, and you'd like to do the same thing with me. We'll see who pulls the strings. Metaphors thoroughly mixed, she stared at his broad shoulders. She herself had quite a little reputation in her circle as a charmer. It takes one to know one, she thought.

Darroch had a fire going brightly by the time Jean announced that the soup was hot. She took Sally into the bedroom, relieved her of her wet skirt and blouse and inserted her into a warm robe.

When they came back to the kitchen Darroch said, "I'll be off, then, *mo Shìne*."

"You certainly won't," said Jean indignantly. "You'll stay and have your supper."

"You should have time alone with your daughter," he protested.

"We'll have plenty of time. Sit down, both of you."

The fish chowder was so good that no one said much for the next few minutes as they ate. "Mom, this is terrific soup," said Sally, emerging from her first bowlful.

"All fresh ingredients, that's why. Cailean the Crab dropped a packet by for me today, wasn't that kind? He'd heard I had the flu and he said fish chowder was just the thing to build my strength up again. And it was funny, I was afraid the smell of raw fish would bring the nausea back but I got so absorbed in cooking I forgot to feel sick."

After the edge was off their hunger they relaxed and began to talk. Darroch took little part in the conversation and sat back, listening to the two catching up. The firelight danced off both whisky-colored heads as they bobbed back and forth. He could see both were kept awake only by the excitement of their reunion.

After the second bowl they were replete. "All done?" he asked and at affirmative nods he began to clear the table.

"Leave them, Darroch," began Jean but he shook his head at her. "I don't mind," he said as his hands busily washed dishes. The clean-up didn't take long. He said, "And now I really am going to go. Good night, Sally. I am very pleased to meet you at last."

Sally muttered an ungracious good night, remembering how she felt about this interloper in her mother's life.

Jean said, "I'll walk you to the gate." Since the rain had stopped he agreed.

After a few minutes Sally could not resist peering through the lace curtains. She saw one figure, her mother wrapped in the tall Scottish stranger's arms. Then the figures parted and they looked at each other, talking, and she thought, probably laughing as well. Then Darroch bent and kissed Jean. Sally saw her mother's figure reaching up to him and the silhouettes merged again. Annoyed, she twitched the curtains closed.

When Jean came in, her expression dreamy, Sally said, "So . . . where is he going?"

"Down the road to his cottage, just below mine. Look at the headlights on the road, it's his Bentley. Now he's pulling into his lane and he's home." Jean looked wistfully out the window.

"Bentley? Is that the car he drives? Mom, a Bentley, really?"

"Yes, dear."

"But Mom, they're fantastically expensive."

Jean wrinkled her brow. "This is an older one, Sally. It's about fifteen years old."

"Mom, they're even more valuable when they're older. Is it in good shape?"

"Oh, yes." Jean nodded. "He says the only reason he keeps it is because he has a mechanic here who loves it and does all the tune-up work. Otherwise he might get a Land Rover. More practical. I love the Bentley, myself. Makes me feel like the Queen. Only she has a Rolls, of course, but a Rolls is like a big brother of the Bentley."

"I don't see how a farmer could afford a fancy car."

"Oh, he has another job. Everyone here has one, especially if they're crofters. You can't make enough to live on, crofting; you need a second job to make ends meet. Darroch's a television actor. In fact, Sal, he's the . . . " She remembered she'd never written Sally she'd met the Magician and was about to tell her when the girl interrupted.

"But Mom, his clothes aren't anything like fancy. That's a good overcoat he has but it's obviously old. How could he buy such an expensive car?"

"Well, he says it was his big splurge after he got his television series that turned out to be so successful. But there'd be no reason to buy fancy clothes for the Island, no one else has them. Most of my clothes are too new and cost too much. I've been wearing them at home to break them in so people wouldn't think I was showing off."

Sally digested this, then started on another tack. "So he lives down the hill."

"Yes, and our friends Mairi and Jamie live just below him. Sally, I'm worn out, I have to lie down. You must be tired too. Get ready and climb in bed. I'll smoor the fire."

Sally's questions were by no means answered but she was beginning to yawn uncontrollably. She dug her toothbrush and nightgown out of her bag and washed up. Jean called, "There's just the one bed, but it's big. I hope you don't mind sharing."

"No problem." Sally got into bed and collapsed into sleep. She did not hear her mother come in, or see her pause and look down at her little girl, or feel her kiss upon the cheek. Jean got into bed and she was asleep almost as fast.

Forty-two

The curtains open on a figure standing in the middle of a stage, back to the audience. He turns. He's dressed as an Edwardian dandy, in a burgundy frock coat, slim black trousers and a white shirt with lace at the neck and cuffs. He sweeps his top hat off as he bows. He pulls a wand from his pocket, taps the hat, and a cloud of smoke fills the stage behind him.
Magician: Good evening, my friends. And welcome . . . to a world of magic!

The Magician, episode one: "The Tragedy in Lambeth Marsh"

*T*he morning dawned sunny and clear, a bright blue sky glowing through the cottage windows. Jean jumped out of bed, invigorated, the last traces of flu gone, and bent to look at her sleeping daughter. Then she went into the kitchen to start breakfast.

Sally appeared just as Jean was about to call her. "I hope you've not become a vegetarian because I've fixed bacon and eggs. I've gotten used to fixing that for Darroch. I didn't think that you might prefer something else."

Sally's joy in the food was dimmed by the knowledge that her mother routinely had breakfast with that man. *So they are sleeping together,* she thought angrily. *Last night was just a sham.* She ate her eggs, simmering.

Jean knew she was angry but she didn't know why. She decided to wait till Sally said what was bugging her. She knew her girl couldn't keep things bottled up forever.

Sure enough, Sally began her attack with the second cup of tea. "You know, Mom, I can get a hotel room. I don't want to cramp your style."

Aha, thought Jean, now we're coming to it. "I don't know what you mean. Of course you'll stay with me."

"What about him? Doesn't he mind not staying the night with you?"

"Darroch lives in his own cottage," Jean said patiently. "We're not sleeping together, Sally. We love each other but we're not lovers."

"Mom, you don't expect me to believe that."

"I most certainly do. When have I ever lied to you?" Jean looked at her indignantly.

"Never," said Sally. It was true. Her mother was the most honest person she knew. She couldn't even bring herself to lie on the telephone about whether or not someone was home. The answering machine had been a great relief to Jean's conscience and the rest of the family's convenience.

Sally said crossly, "I don't know why you aren't sleeping together. Everyone does."

Jean laughed. "We don't, because I'm married."

"Well, that certainly hasn't slowed Daddy down," Sally blurted. "He sleeps with whoever he wants to."

Dismayed, Jean said, "Whomever. How on earth did you find that out?"

"Because I saw them. Well, not in bed, of course," as her mother's jaw dropped in shock. "It was finals week last semester. I was going to study at school but I'd left my history notes at the house. So I got up early and drove home, intending to grab my stuff and go back to school. I walked into the kitchen because I smelled coffee, so I knew Daddy was up." She smiled bitterly. "They were sitting at the breakfast table together. In their robes. So it was pretty obvious."

"Who were?" said Jean faintly.

"Daddy and Mrs. White from next door, of course. Who else would it be?"

"Oh, my," said Jean. She leaned her head on her hands.

Sally stared at her. "That's not who you expected, was it. Who else has he got?"

Still in shock, Jean murmured, "Mary Lu. From work." Then she wished she hadn't said anything.

"Really." Sally stretched the word out in prolonged syllables. "That fubsy-faced blonde with the electric blue eyeshadow? Who sends those mushy cards to 'the family' at Christmas? That witch! That hypocrite! Mom, how long has this been going on?"

"Sally, I didn't want you to know all this and I'm sorry you found out. I'm not going to say any more. It's between your father and me."

"Mom!" Sally's voice rose alarmingly. "Do you know what awful things I've been thinking about you since you left? I've felt so betrayed that you could just walk off and leave us. I've been feeling sorry for Daddy, that weasel. When did you find out?"

"He told me about Mary Lu several months before I came here. I didn't know what to do. I finally decided I had to get away from him and home to figure out what to do with the rest of my life." She looked at her daughter. "And now I've done just that."

"You should have told us why you left. Rod and I thought you were having a middle-aged crisis or breakdown or something."

Jean did not mention that Russ could have done some explaining too. Instead she repeated mildly, "It was private, between your father and me."

Sally started to protest again but Jean said, "Sally, please understand. I was humiliated. I didn't want anyone . . . especially you kids . . . to know that he preferred someone else to me. It was awful. I felt like a nothing, a nobody. But now I've got myself together and I've made my decision." She looked her daughter straight in the eye. "I'm divorcing your father."

Sally burst into tears. "Oh, Mom, no. Can't you take him back? Can't you make him stop?"

Jean put her hand over her daughter's. "He doesn't want to stop, Sally. He told me so. He says he's addicted to infidelity. I don't know if that's true or just an excuse. But I don't want him back, I want Darroch. I love him and he loves me."

"But where are you going to live? Aren't you coming home?"

"Home is here," Jean said gently. Sally's response was to put her head down on the table and sob.

"Sally, please. You're almost grown-up, you and Rod don't need me any more. It's obvious Russ doesn't need me either. I don't want to be his second-best." She stroked Sally's hair. "I love this Island and I have friends and useful work to do here. I have gotten my music back. And I have Darroch. Wait till you get to know him better. You'll really like him."

A muffled snort of protest came from Sally. "Even if you don't like him you'll see that he and I are perfect for each other. We belong together."

Sally lifted her head, eyes streaming. "Then why aren't you sleeping with him?"

"I'm still married. And even if we could get over that hurdle in our own minds the Island would not approve. Adultery is frowned on here." She remembered Hogmanay night with embarrassment. Saved by the phone, she thought.

Sally shook her head. "I can't believe this is happening. I always thought you and Daddy had the perfect marriage. I used to feel so sorry for my friends whose parents were divorced and here the same thing was going on right under my roof." She sniffled loudly.

Jean handed her a tissue. "Maybe not. I know he was faithful the first years of our marriage. I think it started with the woman he got to replace me as office manager. She was lonely and she really liked your dad. If she threw herself at him it might have been too much to resist. I don't know the details and I don't care. I've put it all out of my mind and I'm trying to remember only the good times we had together as a family. There were lots of them, Sally, you know that. But things change. People change."

Sally wiped her eyes. "I'm so glad this didn't all blow up when I was young. It would have been really hard then. At least now I have my own interests and can see myself as separate from the family."

"This may sound disloyal and unmotherly, but I feel exactly the same way. I'm separate from my family. I love you and Rod but I'm my own person. I'm enjoying being independent." She paused. "Of course, it's not as if I'd gone off to live in a log cabin in northern Wisconsin. But I live alone and I make my own decisions. I've never done that before, except for a few months in college. You'll be off on your own pretty soon. And you know that your father and I will always love you, whatever happens. But he and I can't live together any more."

Jean looked at Sally. "Since you've come here to see what's going on I want you to meet my friends and see what my new life is like. And I want you to get to know Darroch. Please give him a chance."

"Is he good to you, Mom?"

"He is wonderful to me. He's honest and sweet. He is a man of absolute integrity. And Sally, wait until you hear us sing together."

Sally shook her head again. "I don't know what to think anymore. Show me your Island, Mom. I'll try to understand."

Jean smiled. "Let's do the dishes and then walk into town. You can meet people and I can show off my beautiful daughter."

Sally said shyly, "When will we see him again? Darroch, I mean."

"We'll fix dinner and invite him, shall we? We'll do the shops and get something wonderful to cook." She stood and began to clear the table.

Sally rose to help. "Well, I think he's sexy and I'd want to sleep with him if I were you," she said suddenly.

Jean laughed, embarrassed, and decided on complete frankness. "Oh, I do, dear, I do. It's all been a tremendous hassle, you can't imagine."

"Well, I can, Mom. You know, I've had feelings like that about guys."

Jean looked at her in shock. "You have? Sally, you're much too young. You haven't. . .. you haven't . . . "

Sally laughed. "Well, you're the one to question me, aren't you. I know perfectly well that you had to get married and give up your education because you were pregnant with Rod. That experience would be enough to keep me a virgin forever." She dried dishes vigorously.

Jean did not know what to say. She had always soft-pedaled her wedding anniversary, hoping that the kids wouldn't figure out that she was pregnant when she got married. And she realized that Sally hadn't answered her question.

"You know," said Sally, "Darroch looks sort of familiar. Did you say he's an actor? Maybe I've seen him on television."

"You certainly have, for hours and hours. Remember how you and I used to curl up together to watch television when you got home from school? Remember why we switched dinner from six to six-thirty and how mad Daddy got because it wasn't ready when he got home?" She grinned. "Remember the rabbit?"

Sally looked puzzled. Then Jean saw the recognition growing in her face.

"Oh, my God, I am so dumb. And I never even recognized him!" Still holding the dishcloth, Sally sat down at the table. "Oh, Mom. However did you manage to meet the Magician?"

"Just a lucky quirk of fate. If you're wondering why I didn't tell you who he was, he thinks people should know him as himself, not as a television character. I don't even think of him in that context any more. Except . . . " She looked dreamily into the distance. "Sometimes there's a certain something about him that brings the Magician to mind. Facial expressions . . . the way he moves . . . "

"I was madly in love with him when I was ten years old, Mom."

"So was I, when you were ten years old. But that was the Magician. Now I love the real man. He's even better."

"Mom," said Sally desperately, "please don't let me gush over him, you know what I mean. I've always wanted to meet him and now I'll either be afraid to talk to him or I'll babble. Help me out till I get used to him, okay?"

"Just think of him as the boy next door," said Jean. "Because that's what he is."

Forty-three

Season trout with herbs and roll in ground almonds.
Finish with a dusting of rock salt.
Sheila Morrison's recipe for fried trout

The walk down the hill to Ros Mór was strenuous, Sally thought, and looked admiringly at her mother striding along. Jean said, "Wait till we come back, all uphill. That's when I slow down. I walk it every day and it's been great for my waistline and hips. Usually get a ride from Ian the Post if it's raining, though."

"What's an ee-an the post?"

"The mailman." Jean explained the Island's system of nicknames.

They entered the bakery and began the pattern that continued all morning. Beathag the Bread said, "*Madainn mhath*, Mrs. Jean, and this must be your daughter."

"*Thà gu dearbh, a Bheathag*," said Jean and performed introductions. At the fishmonger's next door, the greeting from Cailean the Crab was the same, except he said, "your lovely daughter." On the Island he was considered a gusher.

At each stop Sally was welcomed, asked if she was enjoying her holiday and told she looked exactly like her mother. They squeezed in shopping between pleasantries and when they were done Jean said, "Come on, I'll take you to lunch."

It was a light day at the Rose, most of the guests, armed with box lunches, having gone out on Murdoch the Taxi's bird-watching tour. Sheilah was delighted to meet Sally. "You can have whatever you want for lunch. I've tons of things. Cold game pie? Venison stew? Trout fresh from the burn?"

Sally's eyes were glassy with pleasure. "The trout, please."

"Yes, trout by all means. Sheilah, can you join us?"

"Yes. Eat in the kitchen or the dining room?"

"The kitchen, please, Mom, can we?" said Sally, like a little girl. "I'd love to see a hotel kitchen. Did I tell you I worked part time in a Thai restaurant last fall? It was fascinating. I'm thinking of becoming a chef."

Sheilah rolled her eyes. "A look at a hotel kitchen is more likely to dissuade you than anything else, but come on."

They spent a pleasant two hours in Sheilah's kitchen. She found herself explaining all about her work and demonstrating her special method of cooking trout.

"It's wonderful," said Sally, eating with gusto. "Tell me about chef's school."

Jean watched her daughter as she listened avidly to Sheilah's description of the culinary institute she'd attended. She had no idea Sally was interested in being a chef. It must have happened since Jean had left Milwaukee.

Sally had just drawn Sheilah out at length on the making of cream sauces when Sheilah noticed that Jean's eyes were glazing over. "We're boring your mother, Sally. Why don't you come back another day and we'll chat."

"Do you think . . . " Sally hesitated. "Would you mind if I came and watched some day while you're cooking a meal? I promise I'd keep out from underfoot. It's just that you're the only real chef I've met and it's only because you're a friend of Mom's that I have the nerve to ask you."

"Of course," said Sheilah. "Do you want to chop veg, like your mum?"

"Oh, I'd love to help."

Sheilah said, "It must run in the family, Jean."

Surprised, Jean said, "Do you think so?" And then she remembered the pleasure she took in working with Sheilah, the concentration, the controlled frenzy of meal preparation. Another similarity with herself she hadn't recognized in Sally.

She glanced at her watch. "Ridiculous as this sounds, we have to leave the scene of this lovely lunch and scurry home to fix dinner. Eating and cooking, that's what we spend most of our lives doing."

"Yes. Tedious, isn't it?" said Sheilah.

"What else is there?" said Sally dreamily. Jean and Sheilah looked at each other. "Thank heavens I'm not that much of a fanatic," said Sheilah.

"Well, you're married," said Sally. "You have other things to think about. I have to sublimate, you know."

Jean was too shocked to comment.

Later, when Jean was preparing salmon and Sally was telling her mother about a potato recipe she'd invented, preparing the recipe as she talked about it, there was a knock on the door.

"I'll go," said Jean firmly, forestalling her daughter's impetuous movement. "Me. Just me, okay?"

Her daughter, bemused by the elderly British measuring cup she held in her hand . . . a pint was 20 ounces, not 16, Jean had told her . . . said, "Huh? Oh, I get it. I should be staring out the window, I suppose."

"Yes, please," said Jean, halfway to the door. Sally moved around the table and ostentatiously turned her back.

Jean opened the door to Darroch, who held a bottle of wine out in front of him. He looked anxiously at Jean. "Is everything all right?" he whispered.

"Everything's fine," said Jean, and drew him down for a kiss. She intended to make her point about complete frankness with Sally.

Darroch, bewitched by her mouth, at last tore himself away. "Umm . . . Jean . . . perhaps this is not the time . . . " She saw, amused, that he was slightly red-faced.

"This is the perfect time," she said and kissed him again. His arms went around her, the bottle of wine held carefully to one side. When he lifted his head he saw Sally at the kitchen table. She was sitting with shoulders rigid from the attempt to keep from either turning around or eavesdropping.

"*Feasgar math*, Sally," he said. She took that as a cue it was safe to look. She turned and sized him up frankly, staring at him without reserve.

He became uncomfortable after a few moments. "Umm . . . is something wrong with me?"

"No," said Sally. "I'm waiting for you to pull a rabbit out of your pocket."

"I see the kitten's out of the strudel, as you say in Milwaukee," he said to Sally's bafflement and Jean's amusement. "Well, sorry, they repossessed the rabbit when *The Magician* ended. I never liked that rabbit anyway. He always bit my finger when I reached in my pocket."

"That explains the looks of agony." Sally's smile lit up her face.

"Right. It was too dear to re-shoot so the agony stayed in."

"Well, I just want to tell you I enjoyed *The Magician* tremendously and I'm thrilled to meet you. But I want to get to know you as Mom's Darroch."

Tickled, he said, "I suppose that will become my Island nickname. Jean's Darroch."

"Nonsense," said Jean, "you don't need a nickname. There's only one of you."

He said softly to her, "Do you know they're calling you Darroch's Jean? To distinguish you from Jean the Frills who runs the lingerie shop up in Airgead."

"Just so it's not Jean the Yank," she said. "I haven't come three thousand miles to be called a Yankee. My rebel ancestors would turn over in their graves."

Darroch looked puzzled and Sally said, "Better start the salmon, Mom. Aren't you guys hungry?"

That night Darroch was reluctant to go home and Jean was reluctant for him to leave. Sally went to bed, admonishing him "not to keep Mom up late, she's got school the next morning."

"Yes, ma'am," he said solemnly.

On the sofa, they chatted and cuddled until the subject of music came up. Jean said, "Oh, you must have heard it. It's a traditional American song."

"Sing it. Perhaps I know the tune."

Quietly, so as not to wake Sally, she began.

Down in the valley, valley so low,
Hang your head over, hear the wind blow.

He rose and brought over the guitar. "Play it for me."

"*Down in the valley . . .*" Jean's voice soared and Darroch joined her in harmony.

Sally, drowsing, was brought awake by her mother's voice. Suddenly she was home in bed and eight years old, listening in terror to her brother wheeze and gasp in an asthma attack. She was huddling under the covers, frozen until she heard Jean sing. That meant the attack was subsiding and Rod could breathe again. It meant Jean was rubbing Rod's back and singing to help him relax. Sally could relax then, too.

She got up, put on a robe and walked to the bedroom door. Yes, Darroch was still here, she could hear him harmonizing. So that was how they sounded together. It was very pleasant. She crept out and hovered, listening.

If you don't love me, love whom you please.
Put your arms round me, give my heart ease.

"That's lovely, *mo chridhe*. Sing something else." Sally could hear the affection in his voice.

"I don't want to disturb Sally . . . " Jean began.

"You're not disturbing me," Sally said and they both jumped. "Sing 'Suo-gan,' please, Mommy."

"'Suo-gan?'" said Darroch in amazement. "How do you know a Welsh lullaby?"

Jean laughed. "Well, why not? I have a Welsh friend who used to live in Milwaukee, Laurel, from Betys-y-Coed. She played the harp and a guy named Dan played penny whistle with us. We were a trio until she moved to California to become an astrologer and Dan was downsized and went to Door County to run a resort. Laurel taught me Welsh songs. And I suppose your accountant taught you 'Suo-gan?'"

"Well, why not?" he echoed and laughed back at her. "Go ahead, sing it for the lassie, then."

"Don't know if I can remember all the Welsh words . . . hope you can."

"Da iawn, certainly I can." He sang:

Huna blentyn ar fy mynwes
Clyd a chynnes ydyw han.
Brechiau mam syn dyn am danat
Cairad mam sy dan fy mron.

He had not been joking; he did know all the words. Listening, lost in memory, Sally felt her eyes spill over with tears. She wiped them away and moved forward to perch on the sofa arm by her mother. She noticed the guitar. "Oh, Mom! How beautiful! Where did you get it?"

"It's Darroch's."

Sally looked at him. "Do you play?"

"No, just buy." He grinned.

"It's getting late, I suppose we should all go to bed," began Jean, then felt herself growing warm with embarrassment. "I mean home, or whatever."

"Oh, don't fuss, Mom. This is fun. Go on, sing something else."

"Well, join in, Sal." They sang "My Darling Clementine" and "Casey Jones" and "The Wreck of the Old Ninety-Seven." Sally's voice was sweet and clear, Darroch observed, not polished but promising. He wondered if they could get her on stage to sing with them.

"Now sing something with Darroch, Mom. In his language, what's it called?"

They sang *"Fear a' Bhata"* and Sally said, "You're right, Mom. You're perfect, the two of you. In singing, I mean." They fit together like a patch-work quilt, she thought. Kind of a crazy thing, but it worked.

Forty-four

Seek truth in travel, and enlightenment at home.
Eilean Dubh proverb

*S*ally's visit passed all too quickly. When it was over Jean realized she couldn't bear to put her daughter on the train in Inverness and send her off alone. Darroch suggested that the three of them go down and spend several nights in his flat and he'd show them London. They eagerly accepted.

Jean's eyes widened when they walked into his apartment. It was spacious and open, one large room, the river side all windows with sliding doors opening onto a balcony that ran the length of the flat. The two bedrooms upstairs were reached by an open wooden staircase.

They spent their evenings on the balcony watching the Thames flow by, after exhausting themselves touring the city. Sally got a guidebook and compiled a list of sights she wanted to see: the Tower, St. Paul's, the Victoria and Albert Museum. Darroch added the Museum of London. And Jean wanted to see MOMI, the Museum of the Moving Image, dedicated to film and television, because Darroch had once mentioned that there was a picture or two of *The Magician* in the collection.

Jean and Sally were taken aback to round a corner in MOMI and discover, not just a picture, but the original set of *The Magician*, with life-size cutout figures of Darroch, his blonde assistant and several of the villains from the program. They stared.

"My goodness!" said Jean. "You're a hero."

"Not me, the Magician," he said uncomfortably. "They make a bit of a fuss here."

Sally got out her camera and started snapping. "Go stand by your figure, Darroch," she ordered. "Mom, you stand on the other side."

A museum guard was brought quickly by the flashes. "No picture taking here, Miss; the flash is bad for the exhibits." Then, seeing Darroch standing next to his image, he said, "Why, it's the Magician himself. How do you do, Mr. Mac an Rìgh. You might remember me, I was here when the exhibit opened. Are you ladies fans of the program?"

"From America," said Sally.

"Is that right? Well, perhaps one picture won't do too much harm. Give me your camera. I'll take the snap and then the two of you can be in it with Mr. Mac an Rìgh."

Several visitors wandering by recognized Darroch and asked for autographs. One woman was from Australia and said the program was still being shown there.

Jean watched with pride as he talked and laughed with his fans. "You've caught yourself a somebody, Mom," Sally said. Jean said, "It doesn't take a television show to make him a somebody."

After they had extracted themselves from MOMI, Darroch proposed a Chinese restaurant he liked but Sally said, "Where do the television people eat? Let's go there."

He groaned inwardly, foreseeing an evening of noise and mindless chatter. He loved his theatrical friends but it took him time to adjust to them after the tranquillity of Eilean Dubh. But Sally was adamant. "Let's go someplace exciting I can tell my friends about when I get home."

So they went to Cosetta's, a little Italian restaurant near the theatre district, and as Darroch had expected it was full of people he knew. So many people dropped by their table to say hello they scarcely had time to eat. So this was theatre life, thought Jean.

"Beautiful ladies from America!" said one charming man, introduced as Max. "Have you been holding them prisoner on that tiny island of yours, Darroch, dear boy?"

"Oh yes," burbled Sally. "Chained hand and foot."

"Delicious," murmured Max. "I must pay a visit, if that's what goes on there."

Later, on the balcony overlooking the Thames, Sally excused herself to go to bed.

"Isn't she sweet," said Jean. "Giving us a little privacy." They took advantage of it, wrapping themselves around each other and necking enthusiastically.

"It's a good thing we've a chaperone," murmured Darroch, thinking of the king-sized bed in his room.

Jean cried and Sally cried at Gatwick. Later, on the train back to Inverness, Jean was unusually silent. "What are you thinking, *mo chridhe*?"

"I'm thinking I should go back to Milwaukee," she answered.

Darroch's heart lurched and contracted into a knot in his breast. "I see," he said dully.

"It's the only way, I'm afraid."

He detached his arm from her shoulders and moved away. "When do you want to go?" It was exquisite, the pain he felt. So he was going to lose her after all.

"I don't want to go, period, but I think it's the only way I'm going to get Russ to move on the divorce. I have to see him to convince him I'm not coming back. We can work out terms and I can finally be free. Then we can be together. Lovie, can we spend our honeymoon in London? I love your flat and there's lots more we didn't get to see in the city."

He put both arms around her and squeezed her so hard she yelped. Heads in the seats two rows in front of them turned. "You can have your honeymoon anywhere you like as long as it has a big warm bed."

She leaned against him. "No reason to go any farther than my cottage, if that's all you want," she said.

She meant it about going to Milwaukee. She tried talking to Russ on the phone, hoping that Sally's report about herself and Darroch would make him understand she was not coming back to him. But he was evasive and refused to discuss the divorce.

So she bought her ticket for a flight out of Glasgow, doing it impulsively one morning without telling Darroch. It turned out the day she'd chosen to leave was the same day as the semi-annual Co-Operatives Association meeting in Airgead, with visitors coming from all over the Highlands.

Darroch ran his hand distractedly through his hair when he heard what she had done. "If you'd consulted me first . . . I'd like to take you to Glasgow. I don't want you traveling alone . . . "

"But you can't miss the meeting. Never mind," she said firmly. "I'll do just fine. I'm taking suitcases that are mostly empty, anyway, so I can bring stuff back. My luggage will be easy to carry."

He fretted up to the day of her departure, issuing orders all the way to the helicopter. "Now mind yourself, Jean, have a care, especially when you get to Glasgow."

"I know, I know. Have the conductor tell you where to get off the train. Watch your purse. Lock the door when you go to the bathroom. And don't speak to strange men." She laughed at him. "If . . . and this is a big if . . . I meet any stranger than I've met on Eilean Dubh."

He put his hands on her shoulders and kissed her with a searching intensity that weakened her knees. "Darroch, what about Murdoch? He'll see us," she whispered.

"To hell with Murdoch," he said. "Jean, you'll come back?"

"If you kiss me like that again I might never leave."

Behind them they heard Murdoch clearing his throat. Darroch sighed. "Safe flight, *mo chridhe*. Call me when you get to Milwaukee."

"Yes. I love you." She walked to the helicopter. She said to Murdoch, "You didn't see anything, right?"

"You'll be mistaking me for my cousin Murdoch the Taxi," he said with dignity. "He's the gossip. I keep my mouth shut. As if I would be spying on the Laird and his lady and talking about what is none of my affair." He winked.

That bloody laird business, she could hear Darroch saying. She returned Murdoch's wink and settled back to enjoy the flight.

PART VIII

Jean and Russ

Forty-five

So far away, so deep the sea that parts us!
But we will be together one day, trust in me . . .

Ùisdean's fourth letter to Mòrag,
translated by Lady Margaret Morrison

*M*ilwaukee hadn't changed a bit, she thought, as the plane glided over the skyline of old Gothic buildings and smart new glass ones. There was the enormous pillared front of the Museum of Milwaukee, standing like the Parthenon on its hill. There was the old Pabst Brewery building, its chimney piercing the sky. And the river was a green-brown ribbon twined through the streets. Jean loved that river. She'd hoped someday she and Russ would buy a retirement apartment downtown on its banks so she could fall asleep to the sounds of water lapping against walls and pilings.

Russ looked much the same when he met her: tall, handsome, smartly dressed. He kissed her mouth before she could turn her head and present him with her cheek. She was not surprised to feel nothing from the kiss but embarrassment.

The house surprised her as Russ had not. It was so big, so imposing, so . . . decorated. She felt as though she was in a hotel, half expecting her voice to echo off the high ceilings. It was immaculate. Russ must have had the house-cleaner working for days.

She marched upstairs to a guest room, carrying her overnight bag. Russ followed with her suitcases. "These are pretty light, they feel almost empty."

"I didn't bring much. I'm going to pack them with things to take back."

That wasn't the response he wanted. He'd hoped she was home to stay. "What sort of house do you live in on that Island? Sally said it was a little place. Sounded like it's barely big enough for one, let alone two."

"It's big enough for me, and there's just one of me," Jean answered.

He wandered around the room, getting in the way of her unpacking, to her annoyance. It was with some reluctance she pulled her nightgown out and put it on her pillow.

He eyed it. He said suddenly, "Jean, come back to our room and sleep with me tonight. I've missed so much having you by me. We can just lie together and talk, nothing else, if that's what you want."

"I don't think so," Jean answered coolly. She felt as though she was in Darroch's fabled French farce. Great, she thought, asked to cheat on my lover with my husband.

"We're still married, Gina, don't forget that. Why won't you sleep with me?"

"Why? Well, to begin with, I don't want to." He winced. She was glad, then faintly ashamed of her cruelty.

"And in the second place I'd be worried about catching some awful disease. I know you've been sleeping around. Really, Russ, anyone would think you've never heard of AIDS."

"What!" He was outraged. "What are you talking about? I'm always careful."

Jean noted with interest that he did not deny the sleeping around charge. "Careful? Oh, yes, I remember how careful you are. Rod is the living proof."

He tried a different tack. "I have not slept with anyone who might have caught something. That's insulting, Jean. You know I'd never go to a prostitute."

She said wearily, "That's stupid, Russ. Anybody can get a sexual disease if they sleep around. It only takes one person to infect a lot of others. Anyway, no thanks."

He stalked to the door. He was halfway out when he turned around. "For your information I have had an AIDS test. And all the other tests. They were all negative."

After unpacking she headed down to the kitchen, wondering what to do about dinner. It was exceedingly awkward. She did not know whether to behave as a guest or as the woman of the house. Still, she expected dinner preparations would be up to her as if she'd never left. She hoped Russ had at least gotten in some groceries.

A delicious odor greeted her as she entered the dining room. The table was laid with her best china and her mother's sterling. She thought, Sally! Sally's home!

She pushed open the kitchen door and saw Russ at the stove, stirring something in a large pot. She stared, astonished.

"Ready for dinner?" he said.

"Russ . . . are you actually cooking?"

"A specialty of mine. *Boeuf bourguignon,*" he said proudly. "Something to drink?" He handed her one of her best glasses, filled with red wine.

She sat at the table watching him fuss over the stove, trying to take it all in. "When did you learn to cook? Did Sally teach you?"

"You needn't be so surprised, Jean. I am capable of looking after myself. I took a couple of cooking courses through community ed." He was very casual about it.

In fact, food had been the biggest ordeal after Jean's defection. Russ had the housecleaner in twice a week to keep things tidy and he discovered their local dry cleaner would do laundry, so he had an ample supply of clean shirts and socks, as long as he remembered to take his clothes in.

But meals utterly defeated him. Breakfast was easy, since the toaster and the electric coffee pot held no terrors for him. Lunch he ate out. It took time he was unprepared to lose from work and he missed Jean's tasty, healthy, low-fat sandwiches on homemade bread, accompanied by pickles, vegetables and fruits and a thermos of skim milk, all easy to eat at his desk so he could work straight through.

He had made fun of her obsession with feeding him foods that were good for him, but now he missed them every day after lunch when he returned to the office with his waistband uncomfortably tight, a bout with indigestion more than likely. And the cocktail or glass of wine he couldn't resist with a restaurant meal made him sluggish and sleepy, so he began drinking more coffee in the afternoons, with heartburn the result.

Dinner was the real problem. He worked hard and often returned home too exhausted to think about food preparation. For the first few weeks he alternated between fast foods and Chinese and Mexican take-out or called for pizza delivery.

It was fun, at first. He felt like a teenager gobbling all his favorite foods with his feet up in front of the television, no one to nag him about eating his vegetables. But he grew quickly tired of double cheeseburgers, Moo Goo Gai Pan and greasy pepperoni. His indigestion reached epidemic proportions.

Worse, his shirts were beginning to strain at the buttonholes and his pants were harder to get into. When he put on a pair of favorite jeans one Saturday and buttoned them up he felt like a sausage stuffed into a casing. He looked at himself in the mirror with horror.

Go to the health club and work it off, he thought. More exercise, that's what he needed. But he didn't have time. Even with a housecleaner, drycleaner and laundry, there weren't enough hours in the day to do the work needed to run the house. The grocery store was necessary one night. Then he realized he'd forgotten toothpaste and that meant a drugstore stop the next evening.

The furnace refused to start one cold morning, so he had to take an afternoon off and wait for a repair person who never showed up and never called. The lawn was suddenly ankle deep in leaves and raking took all one Saturday. Then the gutters overflowed in a torrential rain, puddles appeared in the basement corners and he realized he'd forgotten to call his handyman and schedule the quarterly gutter cleaning. And then there were bills to pay and the checkbook to balance.

It went on and on. He understood now why single people lived in apartments. A large house was too much for one person and Jean had always taken care of the details.

Sally came home on weekends and tried her best to help. She fixed him huge meals "so you can have leftovers for a couple of days, Dad." She put containers of food in the freezer, carefully labeled with preparation directions. But when her midterm exams started, she had to beg off. She needed to stay at school and study.

Russ felt himself slipping into a state of hopeless lethargy. It began to be easier to come home to a couple of drinks, packages of snacks and falling asleep in front of the television. He wondered what was becoming of him.

Mary Lu, his mistress from the office, would have been glad to help, he knew. She would fix his meals and welcome him in her bed. But with an insight born of self-preservation, he did not tell her Jean was gone. She would have moved in on him, eager to fill Jean's place, pressing him for a commitment he was entirely unwilling to give. He began to understand, dimly, that he wanted her in her own little box, free of domestic entanglements, there just for fun and games.

What he wanted was Jean. Jean and his cozy well-run house, well-organized life, meals on the table at regular intervals, and a warm, loving presence in his bed. He missed making love with her desperately and he had no desire at all for sex with Mary Lu.

Waking up one Saturday morning with a hangover and a splitting headache, Russ reached his lowest point. He could not remember much of the night before except that it had involved a pitcher of martinis, a take-out pizza so undercooked he couldn't eat it, and an endless stream of Schwarzenegger films on the VCR. Or had it been Bruce Willis? He couldn't remember.

Lying alone in bed he faced his problems squarely and made a decision. He would apply the organizational skills that had made him a successful businessman and he would get his life together.

With nausea rolling over him and his stomach burning and cramping, he decided food was the key. The answer to that was simple: he'd learn to cook. Other men cooked and many even enjoyed it, so why shouldn't he? He would take a course at the local community ed center. Jean had taken classes and acquired tasty recipes.

He signed up. Unfortunately, the classes were all very specialized. Thai appetizers. Mexican pizza (he shuddered at the idea). Italian desserts. Peasant French.

He chose the latter. Perhaps he could sneak in a few questions about how to boil an egg and how to make a decent spaghetti sauce. Peasant cooking sounded pretty basic.

Things looked good at first. The instructor was from Marseille and so chic, so sophisticated, so French that he was captivated and missed the first half hour of instruction wondering if she was married and if she'd be receptive to a cappucino after class.

When he came to, she was talking about bouillabaisse and how to judge the freshness of eels by the brightness of their eyes. When they arrived at the hands-on part of class, he looked at his fellow students who were happily deveining shrimp and filleting fish and knew he was in over his head. Way over his head.

The instructor, whose name was Antoinette, eyed him out of the corners of her bright black eyes and wondered what the hell she was going to do with him for the next seven weeks. She doubted he'd ever stepped foot in a kitchen, let alone having the skills needed for a class in French cooking.

The next week, after a disastrous workout involving scorched milk and curdled cream sauce, she asked him to stay after class. By now he recognized this would have nothing to do with seduction in any way, shape or form. She took cooking seriously and she was obviously going to throw him out of class.

"Tell me why you are in this class, *M'sieu'* Abbott," she began. "I do not think it is to learn about truffles and *grenouilles*."

"Well, I . . . " he began, "I didn't know it was so advanced, I thought peasant cooking would be simple . . . "

Her nostrils flared. *Ces Américains*! "There is nothing simple about any aspect of *la cuisine Française, M'sieu'* Abbot. Especially when the boiling of water is to one *un très grand mystère*."

"Boiling . . . Oh. You mean me."

"It is quite obvious that you are not an experienced cook and that is for whom this class is . . . for. Did you not read the description in the brochure?"

He had, but had ignored it. "Umm . . . "

"*Je regrette*, I must tell you that you may not continue with us. Your money will be refunded, of course. Except for the two classes you have attended," she added thriftily.

Russ's expression was so unhappy that she felt sorry for him and a little guilty. "Perhaps you can find a class more suitable."

"No, I can't. There are no classes for beginners." He blurted, "My wife's left me, I can't cook, I'm sick to death of Big Macs and sausage pizza, and I'd rather starve than eat another order of chicken fried rice."

She was shocked. *Mon Dieu, quelle horreur*! To have to eat such stuff! "You can't cook at all?"

"No, you were right. I can barely boil water."

Beneath her tough practical exterior Antoinette was very softhearted. "Your wife has left you for good?"

Miserably he said, "I don't know. She's gone off to Scotland and she hasn't said when . . . or if . . . she'll come back."

"*M'sieu'* Abbott . . . "

"Call me Russ."

She made a sudden decision. " . . . Russ . . . I will help you. If you would like to come to my house on Sunday, I will give you a . . . crash course, I think it is called . . . in the basics of *la cuisine*."

"You will? That would be wonderful!" He was so thrilled that he did not even think of the possibilities for seduction involved.

She did, and added, "My husband will be home. He is a chef. We own a restaurant, *La Belle Française*. Perhaps you have heard of it."

"I sure have. My wife and I ate there for our anniversary last year. Best food I've ever tasted."

"*Alors.* I cannot promise to make you a chef, but in one day we can give you a start. But you must work. Go to a bookstore and buy a good cookbook, a simple one. Read it carefully before Sunday."

"One that starts by telling you how to boil water?" He grinned.

He bought two cookbooks and immersed himself in them. Sunday Antoinette worked him hard and her husband Henri watched, at first skeptically, then with interest and finally with enthusiasm. The American was smart and learned fast. "We will make a cook of you yet, *mon ami*," he said, tasting Russ's mashed potatoes.

The two of them battered him with advice. "Never start a recipe without checking that you have all it calls for," Antoinette ordered. "Measure with precision," Henri ordered. "When you are experienced you can season with a pinch of this and a *soupçon* of that. Beginners must always measure."

"Cooking temperature is *très important.*" "Use only the freshest ingredients." "Simple foods can be the most perfect. Learn to cook simply." He drove home with their admonitions ringing in his head.

He came home after that fired with enthusiasm, arms full of grocery bags of meticulously chosen meat and produce. He started slowly, with hamburgers, then pork chops, then a slice of ham simmered in sherry. Thursday night, exhausted from work, he decided to cook something simple and quick: scrambled eggs.

It was a disaster. He got distracted, forgot to turn the fire down and in seconds they congealed into a frizzled mass. He was so discouraged he reached for the phone to order a take-out pizza. No, he thought. He dined instead on cinnamon toast and tea.

Antoinette called that evening and was all sympathy. Eggs, she said, were a very complex food and she discoursed on the coagulation of protein in high heat until he felt much better.

The three of them became good friends. Antoinette continued his cooking lessons, confiding to her husband, "He will never be a great cook. Like all Americans he is too impatient, too rushed to understand the art of cooking. But he will not starve now, I think." She smiled in satisfaction.

Antoinette had been right. He would never be a great cook but he could develop a repertoire of a few dependable specialties. It certainly beat chicken fried rice, he thought in satisfaction, bending over his *boeuf bourguignon* and inhaling the rich odor. And it was going to impress the hell out of Jean. He'd take her to *La Belle Française* on Saturday and introduce her to Toinette and Henri. That would impress her, too.

For now he was content to serve her dinner, adding French bread and salad and putting his main dish on the table with a modest flourish. He refilled her wine glass and held her chair for her.

He watched her eat, and wondered if the quickest way to a woman's heart was through her stomach. He sure intended to find out.

Later, Jean lay in bed, musing on the irony of being in her own home in the guest bedroom, thinking about a man three thousand miles away while listening to the familiar sounds of her husband getting ready for bed in their bedroom.

The sound of a drawer opening on the other side of the wall told her he was getting his pajamas out of his half of the double dresser. His use of pajamas had always struck her as stuffy. She remembered with pleasure that Darroch didn't own pajamas.

Russ's footsteps were retreating now across the bedroom and she knew he was heading into the bathroom to brush his teeth. She saw him clearly in her mind, leaning close to the mirror, carefully examining himself, turning his head this way and that.

She had never known what he was looking for. Wrinkles? Did men worry about those? It could not have been a receding hairline that bothered him. His blond hair in its expensive cut was still thick.

Now, she thought, he'd be putting toothpaste on his brush, a neatly centered column an inch long. The tube he'd drop on the counter without concern and often the top would pop off and the paste would ooze out, leaving a little glob for her to encounter. After a while she'd bought her own tube and stored it at her end of the counter, its top carefully screwed on. Then she only had to worry about the globs at sink-cleaning time.

The toilet flushed, water ran and Russ's footsteps came back into the bedroom. She heard the bed creak as he sat down and imagined him stretching out on their bed, with a wall and three thousand miles between them.

She tossed restlessly and tried to soothe herself with thoughts of Eilean Dubh, which turned at once into thoughts of Darroch. I wonder what he's doing? Is he missing me? She thought of their kiss at the helicopter pad. Good night, darling Darroch, she thought. I hope I dream of you.

The moon was full and it sent a bright shaft through the window, lighting her collection of glass animals on the table. She flashed back to a wide whitewashed stone windowsill with a bunch of wild flowers stuck in a jar, and on the table a smaller bouquet in a tiny glass vase Darroch had bought for her in an Inverness antique shop. The color was a deep red-violet that fluoresced to rich ruby in sunlight.

The number of objects illuminated by the moon began to irritate her. Why was there so much in this house? Why so many things, so many windows, doors, halls? Why had they had bought such a large house? They had never needed more than three bedrooms but the house had five. They'd wanted guest bedrooms, but she could count on the fingers of one hand the number of times they'd had overnight guests.

Well, she didn't have to think about this house anymore, didn't have to clean it, decorate it, landscape it or entertain clients in it. She was going to walk away from it. I've served my time, she thought. The judge is going to commute my sentence. It occurred to her that this type of thinking was childish and insensitive. Good, she thought.

Jean had a vision of the stark simplicity of her cottage and was soothed immediately.

How pleasant to live without all this stuff, she thought, and fell asleep.

Forty-six

If ye be for Miss Jean, take this frae a frien',
A hint o' a rival or twa, man:
The Laird of Blackbyre wad gang through the fire,
If that wad entice her awa', man.

Robert Burns

Sally had been alarmed by Russ's constant references to "when your mother comes home." As gently as possible she tried to warn him there was another man in Jean's life.

Russ refused to listen. He was confident he could win Jean back if he could just get her home to Milwaukee. Now she was there he turned on the charm. He encouraged her to talk about the Island and countered each story with news about their friends. He got her sentimental about Sally and Rod and nostalgic about the old days. One night he hauled out the slide projector and showed pictures of their camping trips when the children were young. Jean was in tears by the end of the evening.

He wormed out of her what she missed about Milwaukee and took her to all their special restaurants. La Cucuracha, for fajitas. The Saigon, for lemon grass soup. Sakura, for tempura. And the first restaurant where they'd ever had dinner together, Vescio's, near their high school.

He'd made a round of phone calls collecting gossip about their friends and regaled Jean with it throughout a dinner of their favorite lasagna: who was married, who was divorced, whose children were accepted at Harvard and whose had run away to homestead in Alaska. He was as amusing and charming as only Russ could be.

It was paying off, he thought optimistically. She looked at him now with affection and the formality was disappearing from her manner. She laughed

at his jokes and listened admiringly to his stories about the business. All he
had to do now was get her into bed and he'd home free.

For the *coup de grâce*, as Antoinette would say, he took her to *La Belle
Française*. "A special table, please, Henri. Romantic. Your best wine. You
order for us."

A new mistress, thought Henri, but Antoinette knew better. "My wife is
back, Toinette. I want to keep her." She was all sympathy. Courses arrived,
each one more delectable than the preceding. The dessert, profiteroles
smothered in a chocolate sauce of Henri's devising, was positively voluptuous.

Jean was thrilled to be introduced to the chef and his charming wife and
to learn at last who had taught Russ to cook. He always lands on his feet,
she thought, and remembered how that had first attracted her to him. So
self-assured, so together.

No wonder he went after other women, she thought on the way home. I
wasn't enough of a challenge for him.

Now she was a challenge. Upstairs, outside their bedroom door, he put
his hands on her shoulders and drew her close. She could feel desire rising
from him in waves.

He kissed her with practiced tenderness. "I haven't slept with anyone
since you left, Jean. I discovered you were the only one I wanted." That was
almost true. He'd extricated himself from his mistress's clutches by feigning
a sudden overwhelming guilt over deceiving his wife. The only satisfying
sexual encounter he'd had since Jean's departure had been with Ruth next
door, and she'd been horrified afterwards by her first and only lapse into
adultery. He'd not been able to persuade her back into his bed.

"Please, Russ . . . " She put her hands against his chest.

"I want you, Jean. Remember how good it was? Come to bed with me,
let me love you . . . " One hand moved down her back to her hips, pressing
her against him, making his arousal perfectly clear.

It had been good, sometimes very good. God help her, she was tempted.
She wrenched herself away, ran to the guest bedroom and shut the door.

In bed, she tossed, turned, yearned and burned with desire. She wanted,
she wanted . . .

Her mind suddenly became perfectly clear. Darroch. She wanted
Darroch.

She turned her head and looked at the clock. Two A.M. Eight A.M. on Eilean Dubh. Perfect.

She switched on the light, jumped out of bed and ran to her purse. She rummaged for her notebook with the international calling instructions. She climbed back in bed, picked up the phone and dialed.

Brrup, brrup, the funny British Telecom ring. Please be there, she thought.

"*Tri-coig-tri-coig,*" said the familiar voice, as sweet and sexy as any chocolate sauce.

"Hello, lovie. *Ciamar a tha?*" she said.

"Jean." There was such pleasure in his voice she felt warm all over. He said, "*Tha mi gu math, mo chridhe. Agus thu?*"

"Oh, I'm *glé mhath*, lovie, but I miss you so much."

"Aye, me as well. It's late there, Jean, why aren't you asleep?"

"I'm in bed but I can't sleep, thinking about you. Wishing you were here by me."

"Ah." His sigh came through the telephone lines, making them quiver. He was picturing her in a huge American bed, perhaps with satin sheets. In a silk nightgown. Or nothing at all. He had to bite down hard on his lower lip before he could talk again.

She whispered, "Tell me about the Island."

He did, distracting himself from the vision of her in bed by talking about everyday life. Màiri, and her latest rage against the Tory government's education policies. Jamie, and how he had shocked everyone at the *cèilidh* Friday by throwing jazz riffs into his version of *Eilean a' Cheo*. The Minister, and his fire-breathing sermon denouncing teenagers for laughing on Sunday afternoon down by the pier.

She laughed and sighed and tried to visualize him as his wonderful voice purred in her ear. She could almost feel the silky fall of black hair brushing her cheek as his lips sought hers. She flexed her fingers, imagining the strength and hardness of the muscles in his shoulders when she massaged his back.

She was silent so long, lost in fantasy, that he said, "*A Shìne?* Are you still there, *mo chridhe?*"

"Oh, yes. I was imagining you in my arms."

"Ah, Jean. When are you coming home?"

Home. Yes, it was home. "Soon, lovie. As soon as I get things sorted here."

She tended to business, organizing her possessions to take back to the Island. She sat in the sunroom with her sewing box, deciding which spools of thread should go. The Co-Op had every shade of black and white thread imaginable but their stock of colors was limited. She selected scissors, needles, tape measures. She found herself stroking a skein of embroidery silk, thinking that the color matched Darroch's eyes. Don't be soppy, she admonished herself but she couldn't help it.

She watched the dust motes dance in the sunbeams shining through the windows. With no trouble at all she could conjure up her Island kitchen.

There was Darroch, lean body draped over a chair, elbows on the table, long fingers of one hand emphatically gesturing in support of some point he was making. Across the table sat Màiri, eyes snapping, red-gold curls rioting about her shoulders, arms folded over her breast while she waited, trembling with impatience, to reply.

Jamie was making the tea, smiling to himself, thinking about a new tune. Just another day on Eilean Dubh, and she missed it beyond words.

Have her hair done, one last cut from Marlyce, who'd done her hair for fifteen years with skill and imagination. She would miss Marlyce.

Frustrated, she'd asked Màiri, "Is there a hairdresser on the Island?"

"Well, there's frizzy Fiona in Airgead."

"Frizzy . . . Fiona?"

"That's what Eilidh and I call her. It's not for general publication."

"How is she with haircuts?"

"I wouldn't know. I went to her only once. She wanted to give me a . . . what do you call it . . . a perm."

"A perm?" She stared at the mass of ringlets. "But your hair is naturally curly."

"Yes. She wanted to cut it all off and give me a perm, she gives everyone that Margaret Thatcher look. I said no thanks, and left. Eilidh and I learned to do each other's hair and have done so ever since." She looked at Jean. "Why do you need a hairdresser?"

Jean pulled at the hair around her face. "It's falling in my eyes."

Màiri said, "I could trim your fringe for you if you like."

Jean hesitated, then thought, why not. "Okay. Snip away."

When Màiri finished Jean looked in the mirror. "That's great, Màiri, you're very good."

"Just one of those things you learn to do in self-defense. Eilidh always does mine when she comes home. She's a dab hand with haircuts. She'll do yours too, if you like."

Jean's hair had grown. It reached below her shoulders now, falling in waves with a hint of curl at the ends. She wore it tied back with a ribbon. Darroch loved to untie the ribbon, lift her hair, let it fall through his fingers.

She had to be very firm with Marlyce who wanted to cut it short and give it the sophisticated styling at which she excelled. "I've been asked to leave it long," she said. Not wanting to say who had asked, because Marlyce knew she was married, she added casually, "You know men like long hair."

Marlyce liked her in short hair but a man's request couldn't be argued with. So she grumbled while she shaped, layered and fluffed, but left it long and beautifully styled. Jean looked at herself with pleasure.

"I'll miss you, Marlyce," she thought, sighing.

Remembering the Co-Op's puce panties she went through her dresser and selected her best lingerie. Then she went to the mall and bought more, sexy satin and lace. She ordered a white nightgown from her dressmaker.

"For a wedding night," she told the dressmaker, who smiled. "We'll make it special, then," she said.

Sally helped Jean go through her clothes. She selected warm sturdy things for the Island and bagged up what Sally didn't want for Goodwill. She packed treasured photos and memorabilia in boxes and they lugged them up to the attic, both in tears the whole time. So many memories, thought Jean.

She plowed doggedly ahead and after two weeks had everything well organized. But she made little progress with Russ. He twisted and turned and hemmed and hawed. Finally she saw her lawyer. He was adamant: her husband's co-operation was essential if they were to achieve a prompt settlement.

So she turned her attention to Russ. He was not the only one who could get what he wanted with charm and good cooking. She fixed his favorite dinner, fried chicken, and served a delicious Chardonnay. She made a lemon meringue pie for dessert.

Afterwards they went to the living room sofa in front of the fire and she brought in a silver tray with two glasses and a bottle of twenty-five-year-old Glenmorangie. She'd flinched at the price at the liquor store but bought it anyway.

By the second dram they drifted into a conversation about their marriage and the subject of sex came up.

"I don't know why you had to go outside our marriage to find sex. We did pretty well together," she said.

"Yes. Though you were always rather restrained. A man likes a bit of the tiger."

"Nonsense. Not in a wife. It would get tedious."

"Perhaps you're right. Safe cozy sex at home, tigers on the outside." Whisky had loosened his tongue.

"Are you saying you wrecked our marriage because you wanted variety?"

"Not variety so much as . . . adventure. The thrill of the chase, of wooing a new woman, getting her into bed. My trouble is I'm a romantic, Jean."

She snorted. "Your trouble is you think you're Casanova."

"Exactly. He was a romantic, too. I can't help myself," he said with a trace of smugness. He lifted his glass and sipped. "This is good, by the way."

"It's a single malt whisky."

"So you're learning about whisky in Scotland? What else are you learning?"

"Oh, an obscure language and lots of folk music."

"You're back doing that Judy Baez thing?"

"Yes. I sing at *cèilidhean* . . . musical evenings . . . with Darroch and our friends Jamie and Màiri. I also volunteer at a playschool, doing computer stuff."

He was intrigued, as he always was when computers were involved. "Tell me about the computer stuff."

So she talked about the Playschool and the hopes and ambitions they all had for it.

"Hmm," he said. "Why do they want to keep their language? What good is it?"

She talked about that. At the end he shook his head. "I can't say I follow all that but it sounds very earnest. Who knows, it might come in handy as a secret code one day, like that Indian language was for the U.S. during World War II. Does the school need anything for its computer setup?"

"A scanner would be nice. And I need a PC for my cottage. Can you send me one? I've been using Darroch's but I'd like one at home so I can use it at all hours. You know what a night owl I am."

"Okay. You can try out some new software for me." He added casually, "Who's Darroch? Is he the boyfriend? Doesn't he keep you too busy at night for you to play with the computer?"

"Don't be vulgar, Russ. We're not sleeping together."

"What?" He was astonished. "Why not?"

"Because I'm married."

"My prim little Jean," he said and grinned when she frowned. "I've given you every reason to be unfaithful. Get your own back, have some fun."

Jean said defensively, "It's not that simple. The Island is like a small town. People would be shocked if we have an affair because they know I'm married. Darroch is . . . well, an important person there. There'd be talk. Denunciations from the pulpit."

"Good God," he said, appalled. "What have you gotten yourself into?"

"I know it sounds weird but I love the place. The people are wonderful, the music is incredible. And I really love Darroch."

"Hummph. What's he like, this guy you really love?" Important person, she'd said. "So is he the mayor or what?"

She wasn't going to try to explain that bloody laird business to Russ. "He's a crofter. That is, he has a small farm."

"You're in love with a farmer, Jean?" he said incredulously. "All sweaty and muscular, manure on his boots? Better try him out, make sure he takes them off before he gets into bed."

She chuckled at his mental picture of her elegant Darroch. "So you wouldn't object to adultery on my part?"

"Would it make any difference if I did?" Time to make his move, he thought, and leaned forward and kissed her hard on the mouth, his hand firmly grasping her chin.

Used to Darroch's more sophisticated approach she drew back, then reconsidered. The whisky was affecting her too; her normal caution in dealing with Russ had vanished. He'd played games with her all these years, now it was her turn. She'd show him. She wasn't sure what she'd show him but she knew it had something to do with sex.

"Shh, be still," she said. She rubbed her thumb slowly across his lips, kissed him on the corners of his mouth, then bit his lower lip.

He opened his eyes wide in surprise. "Something else you've learned, eh, Jean? Lessons from your Scottish lover?"

"Um-hmm." She flicked her tongue across his mouth and heard him growl in his throat. She realized suddenly that he was unbuttoning her blouse. Her little experiment was getting out of hand. "What do you think you're doing?"

"Just what I want. And what you want, too." He slid her blouse off her shoulders, unhooked her bra and slipped his hand inside, all in one practiced motion. "You have the most beautiful breasts of anyone I've ever slept with, Jean, have I ever told you that?" he purred.

"You used to laugh at my breasts, remember?" she said, trying not to enjoy his fondling hand and feeling an unwanted warmth in the lower half of her body. "When I was so flat, before I got pregnant?"

"Ummm. Little rosebuds, back in high school. I could hardly sit still in English class for thinking about your breasts. Remember when you first let me touch them? And that night we first made love, on the hill overlooking the lake. I was nervous, I didn't want to hurt you. You were my first virgin." He considered. "Come to think of it, you were my only virgin, ever."

"What about Amy Jones? You slept with her, didn't you? You went steady with her the year before me."

"Of course I slept with her, but she was no virgin, believe me." Jean looked shocked and said, "And her father was a minister."

"Didn't slow her down at all." He kissed her with unexpected tenderness and she gave up the fight for self-control and succumbed, suddenly and completely. It's just Russ, she thought, like in the old days, when he could always get what he wanted from her by being sweet. She let him lay her down on the sofa, the leather cool against her bare back. Memories teased her mind. Desire rose, thick as an Eilean Dubh mist. Time slowed.

When he eased off her skirt she tried to summon restraint but felt nothing but an intense need for sex that was spiraling out of control. It had been too long; the frustrating cuddles with Darroch had built up too much suppressed desire. One last time with Russ, one final memory. What could be the harm in that?

He kissed her again and her mouth opened to him.

"Why, Jean. Not so prim any more, are you." He pulled off her remaining clothes and his own and his hands moved over her, reacquainting themselves with her body. She sighed, deep in her throat. Now, he thought, with the cool calculation of a skilled seducer, and thrust into her. She climaxed in a shattering burst of physical pleasure that was like nothing she'd ever experienced before.

Russ had felt it too, he tingled to his toes with awareness of her response. "That was terrific, Gina. Why have we never had sex like that before?"

Still shaken by the sensuality of the experience, she wondered about it herself until realization hit her: she'd held nothing back, she wasn't protecting herself. She wasn't afraid any more that he might reject her or laugh at her eagerness. "The best for the last time," she murmured.

"The last time, Jean? But it was so good. Will your new lover make you as happy? Tell me more about him." He'd just given her the time of her life; maybe the new boy would pale in comparison once she thought it over.

It was weird, lying naked in Russ's arms, talking about Darroch. "He's sweet, sensitive, funny. Gorgeous blue eyes. Sings beautifully. He's an actor."

"An actor," he said, astonished. "How in hell did you meet an actor on that Island?" Resentment surfaced in Russ. He's probably a wimp, he thought. A tree-hugger. Celery-munching veggie-head. Then he had another thought: weren't most actors homosexuals? My God, he thought, no wonder they haven't slept together. His passionate, sexy . . . and dumb . . . Jean had gotten herself involved with a guy who doesn't even like fucking women. He said urgently, "Jean, don't commit yourself until you go to bed with him."

"We can't, Russ."

He scowled. "You always preferred that artsy kind of guy, anyway. I can see that a boring old computer nut and husband of twenty years is no competition. I just happened to come along and get you pregnant."

She said, "I did love you, Russ. And we had lots of good times. We've shared twenty years and raised two children. I hope we'll always be loving friends."

He said urgently, "I want you back, Jean, I miss you. I hate coming home at night and being alone in this house, solitary meals, television, all the refuges of the lonely."

He sighed when she shook her head sadly. He wouldn't beg, he had too much pride. Might as well come out of this with his dignity intact, if nothing else. "But we can't go back to the way it used to be, can we. We'll talk to the lawyers tomorrow and work something out. Just don't ruin the business, okay? We'll set up something that's fair. I always meant to treat you right, Jean, you know that."

"Yes, I know." She sat up and gathered her clothes and slipped into her blouse. He reached over to grip the fabric. "Let me button that, Jean. I like dressing women after sex. Ummm . . . I suppose you wouldn't consider another round, for old times' sake?" His fingers dallied between her breasts.

"No. Please, Russ, I can't. I feel guilty enough about this time." Guilt was seeping into her mind like the first wisp of smoke from a newly-lit peat fire.

"Why should you feel guilty about sex with me? You're my wife and I have every right to have you."

"I'm not an ice cream cone, nobody has the right to 'have me'. And Darroch won't like it." That was the understatement of the year, she thought uneasily.

"Why tell him?"

"We don't have secrets like that from each other. And he'd know, anyway."

"I envy you, Jean, beginning a new love affair. It is quite, quite delicious. Intrigue and passion and secrecy and betrayal."

"All those things that make life worth living."

Her sarcasm was lost on him as he was overtaken by a sudden bonding of jealousy with lust. He'd show her how a real man made love, give her something to think about while she waited for her wimpy pretty boy to get it together. He tightened his arms around her, kissed her, his tongue exploring her mouth without restraint. He pushed her back on the sofa and took her before she could react. She arched up to him as he came deeply inside, moaning her name.

He lay, spent, against her breasts. She stroked his hair. Definitely the last time, she thought.

He knew it was the end for them, too. Even sex hadn't worked. It had always worked before; taking her to bed had always ended arguments because she enjoyed making love so much, especially if he turned on the tenderness. He was out of weapons. For a moment he was close to tears. "I'm sorry. You said no. But I couldn't resist."

"I know. Me too. I'd forgotten how wonderful it feels to have you inside me. It's been months since I've made love."

"How do you manage, you and what's-his-name? I'd think you'd be nuts by now."

"Quite, quite nuts," she said, thinking of Darroch's mouth and hands intense upon her and their mutual frustration. "Please divorce me to save my sanity. And his."

"And you're going to wait until you're married for sex? That's not healthy, Jean, not at all." Especially with that actor guy, he thought.

"No, just till I'm divorced. It's adultery the Island objects to; the population's too small for messing around. It's okay for engaged couples to be lovers, it doesn't hurt anybody or start any clan wars. I've had enough, Russ. I'm going to bed. Good night."

He whispered seductively, "Sleep with me, Jean. Just once more, in our bed."

She fled to the guest bedroom.

Lying in bed she realized that for the first time in her life she had used sex as a weapon to get something she wanted. Russ had done it, too. He had wined her and dined her—courted her, she understood now—and seducing her was his final effort to win her back. She'd showed him that wouldn't work. He had lost and she had won.

She shuddered as waves of guilt overwhelmed her. She'd had to do it, she'd wanted to do it, but how was she ever going to explain it to Darroch?

PART IX

Homecoming

Forty-seven

Away, away, over the sunset sea,
Home to the beloved Island.

"The Emigrant's Lament," traditional Eilean Dubh folk song

*R*uss kept his word. They saw their lawyers two days later and worked out an agreement. When they left the lawyers' office, Jean felt a heady sense of freedom. Guilt had kept her awake the last two nights and she hadn't even the option of calling Darroch, who was in Inverness.

It was just as well, she thought, for she probably would have blurted out her transgression over the phone and that would have been unbearably hurtful to him. She had to tell him but she needed to choose time and place carefully. She tried not to think about his reaction.

But it had been worth it, hadn't it? Russ had let her go. "Come on," she said, "I'll buy you lunch to celebrate."

He looked at her angrily. "Celebrate? You think we've something to celebrate? The end of twenty years of marriage?"

She stammered, "I'm sorry . . . I didn't mean it that way. It's just . . . we can be friends again." She squeezed his arm. "Let's go home. I'll fix you fried chicken for dinner."

Suddenly he smiled. "May I have your recipe, Jean?"

The morning of her departure Russ came into her bedroom. "We need to talk."

"I'm packing these last bits. Could it wait?"

"No." He took her hands and pulled her down to sit on the bed beside him. "There's something I've been thinking about. Are you still taking the Pill?"

"No, I ran out."

"Ah. We didn't have any protection, did we, three nights ago."

She looked at him, aghast. "My God, I never thought about that."

"Jean, I want you to know I'll take you back if you're pregnant," he said solemnly.

"Pre . . . preg . . . " Jean could not get the word out.

"We'll get together and start all over. This time we'll make it work, for the baby."

She pulled free and jumped up. "No. It can't happen again, I can't be trapped again."

Russ stood and tried to put an arm around her. "Trapped? You felt trapped into our marriage?"

She pushed him away. "What does that matter? I can't be pregnant now! There must be some way . . . " But she realized it was hopeless. Three days afterward and five hours from her flight there was no option. She burst into tears.

"Promise you'll tell me if you're pregnant," he insisted. "I'll come and get you."

"How do I know what I'll do? Leave me alone." She seized his shoulders and pushed him out the door. She shut it violently behind him, threw herself on the bed and had hysterics. Then she got up and finished packing.

Tears flowed at the airport. Russ whispered, "If you're pregnant, let me know right away." She said only, "Take care of yourself, Russ."

Sally hugged Jean. "Oh, Mom, I'm going to miss you so much." Jean said, "Come visit me, sweetie."

When she got on the plane her eyes were red and swollen. Her seatmate looked at her uneasily and edged away. Jean didn't notice. Somewhere over the Atlantic she quit trying to remember the date of her last period and made her decision: she wasn't going to worry about being pregnant. She was going home. When she climbed into the helicopter at Inverness she was almost too excited to greet Murdoch.

On the Island she tumbled out of the chopper and stood for a few moments on the tarmac getting her land legs back. Murdoch had shut down the engine and the rotor blades were turning slowly. The wind they created brought the sharp cold smell of Eilean Dubh to her nose, pine and sea and some early blooming wildflower. Peat smoke from the waiting room fireplace was sucked in by the blades and flung back into her face, rich, intense.

Beyond the blades' swath she saw a tall dark-haired figure in a shabby black coat. She took off and ran at full speed, ducking below the lazily-revolving blades, and flung herself at him.

"Ooof!" he gasped and wrapped his arms around her. "I take it you're glad to be back."

She didn't try to talk. She plunged her hands into his hair and tugged him down for a kiss.

When he lifted his head he murmured, "I think Murdoch's watching, *mo chridhe*."

"To hell with Murdoch," she said. "Anyway, he and I have an understanding. He doesn't gossip about the Laird's business and I don't confuse him with his cousin Murdoch the Taxi."

Darroch stared at her, puzzled. Murdoch, leaving the helicopter, carefully averted his eyes. "*Feasgar math, a Dharroch,*" he said. "Cheerio, Mrs. Jean."

"Bye-bye, Murdoch, *agus mòran taing.* Wonderful flight, *miorbhuileach.*"

Murdoch nodded and walked off. He was remembering the mist that had swept without warning over the chopper as they'd left Inverness, the sudden turbulence as they neared the Minch and the stomach-churning updraft that had struck as he was landing on Eilean Dubh. And she thought it was a wonderful flight! Now that was a woman who was either *as a ciall* . . . crazy . . . or very glad to be back on the Island.

Deirdre MacQuirter, the helicopter firm's secretary, peered out the window as she always did when the chopper was landing. She observed Jean's headlong rush into Darroch's arms and the passionate kiss. Unlike Murdoch she was not reluctant to gossip and the telephone wire hummed with the news. "The American woman's back . . . you know, Mrs. Jean, who weeded the cemetery . . . and the Laird was so glad to see her. *A Dhia,* you should have seen them kissing!" Her sigh echoed down the wire.

Riding along, Jean turned her head from left to right, looking for signs of spring though it was only late February. Here was a hint of leaves coming, there a patch of grass contemplating turning green and in the fields were heavily pregnant ewes, moving ponderously.

"It's all so beautiful," she sighed. "I was afraid I'd miss my first spring on Eilean Dubh. Darroch, can we go up Cemetery Hill?"

"Of course." He turned into the road and they parked, then started up the hill.

To their dismay they were not alone. Parked quite illegally upon the brow of the hill, out of sight of the road and perilously close to a charming stand of early wildflowers, was Murdoch the Taxi's minibus. On top of the hill stood the man himself in the center of a semicircle of tourists, waving his arms and expounding vigorously.

Alarmed, they saw him beckoning his little flock to follow as he headed back to the bus, still talking. They turned to retreat but it was too late. He'd seen them.

"*Feasgar math*," he called to Darroch and switched to English to greet Jean. "Hello, Mrs. Jean. Welcome back to the Island."

Jean said, "*Tapadh leat, a Mhurdoch. Tha mi toilichte a bhith an seo.*" I am happy to be here.

"Oh, Mrs. Jean, I am forgetting you have learnt our language," he cried and switched to a voluble stream of the Gaelic.

Jean was quite lost. Darroch whispered in her ear, "Just smile and keep walking."

They nodded and swept hastily by. Darroch said something stern to Murdoch, gesturing at the minibus and the wildflowers.

"*Tha mi duilich*," was all Jean understood of Murdoch's reply but she gathered he was explaining. Elderly ladies in his party who couldn't walk up the hill, perhaps.

After they had passed they heard Murdoch saying proudly to his tourists, "That's the American lady who's come to live on our Island. She's going to marry our Laird."

Dumbfounded, Jean and Darroch slowed and looked at each other. "I might just as well have made love to you in the middle of the square. There are no secrets on Eilean Dubh," he said ruefully.

The tourists were glancing surreptitiously over their shoulders. "Is that the Laird with her?" said one woman reverently.

"Och, aye. He's a famous actor. You'll have seen him on the *teilebhisean*."

All of the tourists' heads swiveled around and they stared avidly at Darroch who turned quite red. He cursed with feeling, took a firm grasp on Jean's arm and hurried her up to their bench.

The tourists disappeared around the bend and Jean and Darroch sank down on the bench. She began to laugh and he joined her after a reluctant moment. "I love being home! What a blissful place this is," she cried.

She looked at him. He had not changed; he was as she remembered: blue eyes shining with life and intelligence, black hair rumpled by an impatient hand, shabby coat unbuttoned despite the crisp wind polishing his high cheekbones and elegant nose to pink.

Darroch, after a glance back to make sure they were finally alone, pulled her into his arms. "You came back, Jean."

Astonished, she said, "Did you think I wouldn't? How could you doubt me?"

"It's myself I doubted, that you could want me enough to escape the lure of America. All that cable television and those microwave ovens."

"I missed the peat smoke. It felt weird being able to breathe without gasping."

"I've been mad with jealousy thinking of you there with him," he said into her ear.

"I slept in the guest bedroom," she said but something in her voice left him uneasy. "Jean," he began but she interrupted. "Don't talk, kiss me. I'm hungry for you."

He complied but could not stop himself from saying, "Did he kiss you? Did he try to touch you?" He slipped his hands under her jacket and pulled her closer.

"Please, Darroch," she said, her voice trembling.

"I would like to kill him," he said fiercely. "What happened?"

"Why are you so sure something happened?" She was positive this was not the moment for confession.

"Because Adrienne tried it on with me our last night together." He sighed. "We made love and she thought she'd gotten me back. The next morning I left her for good."

His hands under her jacket were becoming more adventurous. "Lovie, please. What if Murdoch comes back with more tourists? Or Liz with her Girl Guides? Or the Cemetery Beautification Committee?"

"Frankly, my dear, I don't give a damn." He nuzzled her neck, then said, "The Cemetery what?"

"Darroch . . . should we be doing this here?"

"Why not? Màiri and I used to, all the time."

She was quiet for a moment. Then she said, "In broad daylight?"

"If we couldn't wait till dark, which was most of the time. I can show you the exact spot where we first made love, the first time for both of us. I believe the grass is still scorched. I've thought of putting up a plaque."

"You really loved Màiri, didn't you?"

"She was my first love. I thought I'd never love like that again, until I met you."

"Russ was mine, too. It was hard saying goodbye but I realize now there'd been something lacking in our marriage for a long time. Communication, respect, honesty. We have all that, Darroch."

"And sex. Don't forget sex. Jean, I need very badly to make love to you. Do you fancy the grass?"

"A roll in the hay, is that what you're proposing?" She laughed at him. "I want to go to my cottage, Darroch. I'm quite starved for a delicious cuddle with you. And I want to know everything that's happened here since I left, all the gossip."

"Well, the big scandal . . . apart from you and me, of course . . . is that Iain MacShennach's been having an affair with Oighrig, wife to Angus the Shop in Airgead."

"Oh, I knew that two months ago."

"Never! I only just found out last week. How could you have known?"

"Barabal told us, Màiri and me, at the Playschool one day. Shocking, isn't it. What did the Minister say?"

"He reserved comment because the guilty parties belong to Minister Tormod's kirk, but his lips have been more pursed than ever all week and last Sunday's sermon was on sex and sin. It was a scorcher, I wish you could have heard it. You'd have gotten the point even though you don't have the Gaelic."

"I love this place, something's always going on. Think it'll take the heat off us?"

He said with resignation, "We're special. Open to view, like a stately home."

"Well, in the immortal words of Bonnie Raitt, let's give them something to talk about." She flung herself into his arms. Sex with Russ had eroded her restraint and kissing Darroch was arousing her to a fever.

He said hoarsely, "Have you fully considered the advantages of a roll in the hay?"

She rubbed herself against him like a cat. "Lovely, but that's not how it's going to be, the first time. I want something more . . . private. And prolonged."

"Champagne."

"Whisky," she said.

"My bed, under the skylight."

"Do we have to wait for a full moon?"

He chuckled. "If you're going to laugh at me we may as well go to the cottage. I can see you're not in a romantic mood."

"If I felt any more romantic I'd go up in flames." She ran her fingertips over his face. "You are the loveliest man." She looked at him closely. "Are you blushing? If you're not, you should be. You know, I absolutely adore you."

"Let's go, Jean. There are parts of you I cannot reach on this bench."

They got up. Jean smoothed out her clothes. They strolled hand in hand down to the car and drove home.

Forty-eight

For aught that I could ever read,
Could ever hear by tale or history,
The course of true love never did run smoothly.

William Shakespeare

*J*ean walked into her cottage like a queen returning to her palace. "Home at last! Light the peat fire flame, put the kettle on, pour the whisky! Let's celebrate."

Darroch said, "Sit you, Jean. I'm making this meal." He took a package from her refrigerator.

"I'll peel potatoes. I need something to do with my hands." Otherwise I'll not be able to keep them off you, she thought.

He smiled, reading her mind. "Later, *mo leannan*. Lobsters first."

"Lobster! *Miorbhuileach*!" Then she said cautiously, "We don't have to kill them, do we?"

"I took the easy way out, Sheilah cooked them. And Màiri sent a dish of potatoes with cream and cheese."

"Wonderful low fat Island cooking. I need to start walking again, I've gained weight on American food." She smoothed the skirt over her stomach self-consciously.

"Let me feel." He knelt beside her and rubbed her belly. "Deliciously rounded." He put his face against her and she felt the warmth of his mouth through the fabric. Desire flooded her and only the thought of pregnancy kept her from pulling him into the bedroom. "Lobster first," she said firmly.

He stood up. "Greedy wench." He put the potatoes into the oven, then took another dish from the fridge. "From Sheilah too, a prawn salad starter, and chocolate cake and a pint of cream for it. And this is from Jamie."

He took a bottle from the cupboard and set it in front of her with a flourish.

The label was old, faded and torn around the edges. When she looked more carefully she saw that the information on it was hand written. "What in the world . . . "

"A prize from his collection. A whisky distilled at the world's smallest distillery, at Broadford on Skye. Made by his uncle and quite, quite illegal. Twenty years old, aged in prewar sherry casks, only about a hundred bottles made. He insisted I take it for your return." And make love to the woman, Jamie'd said. No more waiting about, both of you nervous wrecks.

Jet lag and emotion caught up to Jean and she began to cry. "I can't bear it, everyone is so nice."

He took her in his arms. "They love you, Jean. And I love you too."

"I love you, darling Darroch. I love this Island and everyone on it. Even Minister Donald."

"Oh, I forgot. He was asking about you, wondering when you were coming back from Mel-wah-kay. He said to give you his sincerest *fàilte* when you got home."

Overcome, she said, "I think I'll go to kirk with you on Sunday."

"Steady on, let's not get his hopes up."

She wiped her eyes. "Do we open the whisky or shall we just sit and admire it?"

"Let's open it and take a dram to bed." He stared into her eyes with naked yearning.

Russ's voice whispered in her ear, "You could be pregnant." She said quickly, "Let's taste it and then eat lobster until we're stuffed."

Darroch sighed. He picked up the precious bottle and opened it while Jean fetched glasses. The whisky was as soft as velvet, as mellow as honey and as hot on the throat as chili peppers. It was also extremely strong. "*A Dhia beannaich mi*," said Darroch, when he could talk. "I wish I'd known Jamie's uncle. He should have been revered as a national treasure."

Jean gasped, "Let's go to Skye and scatter flowers on his grave on our honeymoon." She took another, careful sip. "Let's have supper and then sit in front of the fire with chocolate cake. That's almost as good as sex."

"What do you mean, almost. It is Sheilah's chocolate cake we're talking about."

After supper, lying across his lap, full and happy, Jean decided to leave her confession about Russ to another day. Why spoil a perfectly good evening, she was thinking, when Darroch read her mind.

"Tell me about it."

"What?" she said guiltily.

"You and Russ." Then, as she looked frantically at him, he said in surprise, "About the divorce. Is everything settled?" He stared at her. "What's wrong, Jean?"

"I have to tell you something," she blurted, shaken out of her composure.

"There's nothing wrong about the divorce, is there? Answer me, Jean."

Her heart began to pound so loudly it echoed in her ears. She sat up and gazed into the fire. "We've reached an agreement. The lawyers are drawing up the papers. The divorce will go through within the month."

"There's something else." He ran a hand distractedly through his hair. "Oh, God. You didn't, Jean. Please tell me you didn't go to bed with him."

"I can't lie to you. I intended to tell you but I didn't want to spoil our evening."

"To hell with the evening, what about our lives? What have you done?" He was clearly furious, he was trembling with it. She had never seen him so angry.

"Please let me tell you what happened."

He was barely able to talk, his throat was so choked with pain. "What do you think I am, a voyeur? Do you think I can stand to listen while you tell me how he kissed you and you kissed him and then . . . Was it in a king-sized bed, Jean?"

He was so close on the details she was floundering. "No bed. In front of the fire on the sofa. After a whisky. Glenmorangie, twenty-five years old," she added stupidly.

He stood up, face frozen, eyes icy, voice frigid. "I'm going home, Jean. Good night." He stalked to the door and yanked it open.

Things had blown up so quickly that her reaction time seemed glacial. "Darroch, please don't go . . . You forgot your coat," she said to an empty room. The cottage suddenly seemed as cold as the ruins of old Airgead Castle, and as lonely.

She hugged his coat to her, breathing in the familiar smell of peat smoke. My God, she thought, I've ruined it. She wanted to run after him but her legs refused to move.

The pain and fear were too deep, at first, for tears. It's all over, she thought, desolate. He'll never speak to me again. Màiri will never speak to me again. And Jamie . . .

No more love. No more music. She'd have to leave the Island.

This is not fair, she thought bitterly. Why am I always punished for what everyone else gets away with? Pregnant by my first boyfriend. Seduced by my soon-to-be ex-husband. Abandoned by my almost-lover.

She dragged herself into the bedroom, not caring that it was barely eight in the evening. She put on the flannel nightgown and got into bed planning on a good long cry.

She couldn't squeeze out a tear. Jet lag and despair caught up to her and she fell asleep as though falling into a deep pit.

Forty-nine

Mountains will wear away, rivers will run dry,
trees will tumble in the forest and turn to dust
but my love will endure, you will be in my heart till the end of time.
Ùisdean's fifth letter to Mòrag, translated by Darroch Mac an Rìgh

*J*ean woke exhausted from a night of horrible dreams in which Russ made love to her endlessly, then turned into someone with beautiful blue eyes who disappeared at the crucial moment. In the dreams she reached out to him, yearning and hopeless. When she woke she ached with frustration and the bed was large, lonely and cold.

She stayed in the cottage all day but Darroch did not phone, he did not come by. She had no energy. When she tried to fix something to eat she became exhausted and had to sit down. Finally, overcome by hunger, she heated canned soup. She took one mouthful, gagged and rushed to the sink to spit it out.

She drank endless cups of tea. For supper she had two oatcakes.

That night she went to bed at seven, worn out. The tears came finally and she sobbed for what seemed like hours. She slept, woke, cried, slept. All through the night it went on and she woke next morning feeling as though she'd been thrown off a cliff.

The phone brrped in the kitchen.

She sat up, stunned, then flung herself out of bed, tangled in the huge nightgown. She saved herself from falling by grabbing the bedstead, banging her leg painfully on it.

Nursing a wrenched arm and a bruised leg she hobbled to the phone. "Hello?"

"Jean? Sheilah here. Did I wake you? I've just heard via the Island grapevine that you're home. I've sorry to bother you but I'm desperate. Ian's Catrìona's mother sprained her ankle and Catrìona's got to stay with her little brothers. Any chance you could spare a few hours to help with the Co-Op meeting? Just lunch, but fairly elaborate because I'm trying new things. And I was short-handed before I lost Catrìona."

Disappointment enveloped her like a shroud. "Sure, Sheilah, I'd be glad to. I'll come about ten, okay?" She was amazed how calm she sounded.

"Thanks, Jean." Sheilah's gratitude was heartfelt.

It occurred to Jean as she hung up that she would see Darroch at the luncheon. Perhaps he would ignore her, snub her before the whole Island. She shuddered. No more than you deserve, she thought in an agony of self-reproach.

She bathed her eyes with ice-cold tap water until the redness disappeared. She forced herself to apply a little make-up, then realized mascara and eyeliner only accentuated her pallor and the haunted look in her eyes. Lipstick made it worse; she looked like a cartoon ghost.

She gave up. She tied her hair tightly back, dressed without knowing what she was putting on and trudged to the Hotel. Each step was an effort and she wondered how she'd be able to stand the day.

The kitchen work was so intense she was able to forget Darroch at first. Then she walked into the dining room with a salad tray and saw him coming in the door. She put the tray down and fled.

She rehearsed excuses to keep her in the kitchen while others served but nothing occurred to her that wouldn't involve painful explanations. She gritted her teeth, picked up another tray and marched into the dining room like Joan of Arc going to the stake.

She cast a despairing look toward his tall elegant figure. Just beyond him, Màiri waved and Jamie smiled at her. All, all gone, she thought, and hoped she wouldn't disgrace herself with tears. She waved back, smiling brightly, and realized Darroch had seen her. She turned away so that she would not see his expression. She was suddenly aware she'd eaten practically nothing over the last thirty-six hours. She felt dizzy.

All through the long dreadful luncheon Jean moved in and out of the kitchen, bringing food in, carrying dirty dishes out, always intently aware of Darroch's presence, as conscious of him as if he were touching her. When she had to pour his tea she trembled so much the tea splashed into the saucer.

Patiently he lifted the cup and wiped the saucer with his napkin, not looking at her.

He was so in tune with her that he could read the waves of emotion that enveloped her: despair, desire, fear . . . and love. She loved him, he knew it. What had gone wrong?

Jamie, across the table, read the emotional turmoil with deep alarm. He quirked his eyebrows inquiringly at Jean and she turned away, her eyes filling. Stunned, he frowned at Darroch who ignored him.

Finally the meal was over and the diners turned their chairs around to listen to the speakers and gear up for the usual hours of acrimonious discussion that, Darroch had told Jean, inevitably followed the proposals put forth by the Committee of Management. "They always accept them in the end," he'd said, "but they enjoy wrangling about them first." Jean had laughed and said her experience with meetings was the same.

The Co-Op members sat in a drowsy haze, brought on by a large lunch and the current speaker. Ewan MacCorkle was acknowledged by everyone to be the most boring man on the Island. Even though he was speaking on his extensive research regarding a subject of vital interest to every farmer in Britain . . . the role of animal feed in mad cow disease, and the idea of using natural foods for sheep and cattle instead of those processed from animal cadavers . . . his slow, methodical delivery and his monotone voice induced a torpor in everyone.

Darroch had already had an extensive discussion on the subject with Ewan, agreed with him and knew he would vote for his proposal. That was fortunate for he found himself unable to listen, entirely absorbed in his thoughts of Jean.

He'd had the worst day—and two nights—of his life since he had stalked out of Jean's cottage. The moment he got home he regretted his impulsive action. He didn't lose his temper very often but he was so in love with her and so frustrated that he was on the brink of coming apart. His customary self-control was fraying badly and he felt as though tiny knives were ripping his heart to pieces.

He spent the first night listening for the telephone's insistent burr, hoping she might call. When that didn't happen he lay in bed hoping for a knock on his door. Perhaps she wouldn't knock, perhaps she'd just slip inside the door . . . she knew it was never locked . . . and come to his bedroom. He roused out of a restless doze several times thinking he'd heard a quiet step on the spiral staircase.

Maybe she'd come upstairs and sit down on his bed. "I have to talk to you," she'd say and burst into tears. And he'd pull her into his arms and comfort her. Then he'd make love to her until they both wept with pleasure. He dreamed of Jean in his arms every time he managed to fall asleep.

Jamie had been right. Women keep the memory of past lovers in their heads, he'd said, and the only way to get rid of those memories was to replace old images with new ones. He should have made Jean his before she'd left for Milwaukee. If they'd been lovers she never would have given herself to another man, husband or not. She had too much integrity.

But this strange half-life of love and stifled desire they'd been leading had been as hard on her as on him. Perhaps that had made it difficult for her to make the final break with Russ.

After all, what had she done that was so wrong? She'd offered the comfort of her body one last time to that poor bastard who'd lost her. Hadn't he done the same thing when his marriage was ending? So hard to let go, he thought.

He realized suddenly that she was not his possession, she would never be his possession and she would not always act as he wanted her to. She would do what her mind and heart and conscience told her to do. This was not the same as Adrienne's infidelity, nor could he end this relationship by walking away. He was going to fight for Jean. He was going to understand what had gone wrong and make it right.

He could not, would not, give her up. It would destroy him to lose her.

He came to a decision: he would ask her why it had happened. He should have asked her two nights ago. How very simple, and what a prat he was not to have thought of it sooner.

Lost in his thoughts, he chuckled aloud at his foolishness and his dozing neighbors on either side looked up in surprise. Had they missed something? Had Ewan MacCorkle actually made a joke? They leaned forward to listen with awakened interest.

The luncheon's end meant Jean could escape into the kitchen to help with the washing-up. All the helpers were dead on their feet and no one noticed that she was quiet and tight-lipped. She didn't volunteer to restock the tea and coffee tables. Someone else can do that, she thought. I've had enough.

She thought that if she had to endure one more moment of looking at the proud dark head turned so pointedly away from her she'd go straight home and get her suitcases and leave. Walk right into the sea and start swimming to America. Lucky I haven't unpacked yet, she thought grimly.

The afternoon wore on and the lowered sound of voices from the dining room told them in the kitchen the meeting was winding down. Tired beyond imagination Jean latched the door of the dishwasher and turned it on. The other helpers had gone.

Sheilah said, "How about a wee dram of Gordon's finest?"

"I'd love it." Jean welcomed anything that would deaden the pain. She sat with Sheilah drinking whisky, both too exhausted to speak except in occasional sentences.

"I think the roast beef went over well, didn't you?" "They loved the lemon tarts but they're a hellish lot of work to make." "They ate tons of potatoes; there's all the profit gone."

They looked up as Darroch pushed open the door. Jamie had grabbed his sleeve urgently, just before Màiri'd marched him away for one of her countless errands. "What the hell are you playing at?" he'd hissed. "Jean's in the kitchen. Get in there." Darroch, furious, shook him off. "Where the hell do you think I'm headed?" he'd growled.

He said, "Lovely luncheon, Shee. Thanks for all your work." He looked across the room and nodded noncommittally. "Jean."

She trembled and her face flamed but she said nothing. Her love flared so intensely that she wanted to throw herself at his feet. Clutch at his ankles, weeping.

Sheilah looked from one to the other and realized immediately that something was very wrong. She was up from her chair and out the door in a flash, saying as she fled, "Ooops! Just remembered something I have to tell Gordon right away."

Jean sat at the table, her head bowed. Darroch said, "I'll take you home."

"I can walk."

"Nonsense, you're exhausted. Get your coat." It was the Laird's voice, low and firm, demanding obedience. Mutely she obeyed.

Sheilah encountered them in the lobby. Looking at Jean's tense face and Darroch's carefully controlled one, she said, "Are you all right, Jean?" She stared hard and accusingly at Darroch.

Despite his distress he had to smile. Jean's friends looked after her, even at his expense.

Jean said, "I'm fine," and meant it. At least he was speaking to her now. "Bye, Shee, let's do this again sometime." And she let him lead her out. She felt as though she was floating, dazed with emotion, fatigue, whisky and lack of food.

The silent ride to her cottage had never seemed longer but he passed the turnoff and continued to the road up *Cladh a' Chnuic*. She let him take her there without comment. He parked and they walked up. His grip on her arm was like a policeman's but she relished even that contact with him.

They sat on their bench.

"You look terrible, Jean."

"You look worse. Have you had any sleep at all?"

He shrugged. "A couple of hours last night. How about you?"

"Oh, I can sleep. I cry myself to sleep. Men don't know how to do that, do they."

He said accusingly, "You wouldn't look at me at that dreadful luncheon."

"Did you want me to burst into tears in front of half of the Island?"

He leaned forward until he was very close. "Can you forgive me, Jean?"

She was so astonished she nearly fell off the bench. She said, "Forgive you? Why am I forgiving you?"

"For walking out on you instead of talking it out. Jean . . . while you were gone to America I had the most awful dreams, like the morphine dreams after I had my appendix out. You'd keep disappearing down a hall." He smiled faintly. "And it seemed two nights ago the dreams had come true. I couldn't bear the thought of him making love to you. I thought I'd lost you.

"Today it dawned on me that although you'd slept with him you came back to me, so perhaps all wasn't over. But you wouldn't look at me today, wouldn't give me a sign."

A faint ray of hope dawned in Jean's heart. "Darroch, what happened had nothing to do with us. It was about Russ and me and twenty years of marriage."

He was quiet for a moment, then said, "If you want to talk, Jean, I'll listen."

She took a deep breath. "It was . . . sort of . . . a summing up of our relationship. I was reliving our past sex life, from the first time, on a hill overlooking Lake Michigan, like right here and you and Màiri. Isn't that funny? While he was . . . while we were . . . " Uncomfortable, she looked away.

"In my head I was remembering all those years of lovemaking. Necking in his car when we were teenagers. Being pregnant and so full of hormones I was crazy for sex. The years with the kids when we had to give up making love on the living room floor and go to our bedroom instead.

"Wondering why his interest lagged at times, resenting it, knowing something was wrong. Knowing he was gradually shutting me out of his life and wondering why.

"Sex and the kids were the best things we had together. Now the kids are grown up. And sex isn't enough. I won't lie to you; I don't regret making love with him one last time. It was a way of saying goodbye, a way he understood. Sex was always the language we communicated best in." She saw the pain in his face. "I am so sorry to have hurt you. But it was the right thing to do.

"And it liberated me. I'm yours entirely if you still want me. If you don't want me I'll understand." But my heart will shatter like glass if you don't want me, she thought.

"My darling girl, I have no choice in the matter. Even if I didn't love you to distraction there are too many people who want you to stay. Didn't you see the way Sheilah frowned at me? If you leave I'll probably be run off the Island."

She said, "I love you. I love you even more than when I went to Milwaukee. And I know what I want our relationship to be, Darroch. I want us to be partners, loving, trusting partners. Best friends. I want to sing and cook and dance with you. And talk. We must always talk things out, always.

"I want lots of sex . . . wonderful sex . . . I want to make love like I never have before. I want more passion than a romance novel. I want us to go to bed together and burn up like meteors." She flung her arms wide, then took a deep breath. "I want to have a baby with you. Maybe two. Maybe half a dozen."

He gawked at her, overwhelmed. "You are *miorbhuileach*. I adore you."

"Russ says we should be lovers."

"What?"

"Russ says . . . "

"Aye, I heard that," he said impatiently. "What the hell does it mean?"

"He suggested it." She watched the amazed expression grow on his face. "He says it will help us to get to know each other. We've settled the divorce. It's just a matter of waiting for the court. I'm almost not married."

"Almost not married. Well." He shook his head. "It's nice to have the almost not husband's *ceart math*, I suppose."

She grinned at him. "Let's go home and fry chicken."

Back at her cottage they fixed dinner. Then he got out the rosewood guitar and they made music until they were hoarse, then cuddled until both were frantic and disheveled and dazed with desire.

She was on his lap, clothes askew, and he was painfully aroused. He growled into her ear, "I want you. Let's go to bed."

"Umm . . . " You could be pregnant, said Russ's voice in her head. She blurted out the only excuse she could think of. "I'm having my period." Russ had studiously avoided her the entire week of her menses.

Darroch wanted to tell her that it didn't matter in the least to him. He and Morgan had indulged during her time of the month; she'd said it helped with the cramps. But he hesitated, afraid of shocking Jean with such uninhibited lust. "I don't care," he said at last.

A vision arose in Jean's mind of herself pregnant for nine months, not knowing the father of her baby, and presenting Darroch with a beautiful yellow-haired son, the image of Russ. She shuddered with horror. "Oh, no."

He muttered something unintelligible and said, "Then get off my lap, and mind how you go."

She took that to mean she should move with care. She levered herself up awkwardly and sat on the sofa.

Pain sliced through his groin and he gritted his teeth. "This has got to stop."

"I'm so sorry, lovie," she said and stumbled through an excuse. "Just a couple more weeks. Till the papers come. Till I sign them and send them back."

She hesitated, then blurted, "I'm not really having my period. I just want to wait."

He accepted her explanation without comment, slammed the door on his libido and pulled himself together. "I can handle it. We're adults, not sex-mad teenagers."

"You don't have to be a teenager to be mad for sex," she muttered but didn't try to change his mind when he announced, briefly, that he was going home.

Be steadfast and faithful, my Heart,
and speak only to the One Who Listens.

Ùisdean's fifth letter to Mòrag, translated by Darroch Mac an Rìgh

*J*ean could not share the pregnancy problem with Darroch; she'd thought she'd caused him enough pain. Again, like twenty years ago, she counted the days, waking up each morning to inspect her nightgown and sheets for signs her period had arrived. And each morning there was nothing, and each morning she wanted to scream and stamp her feet and break things.

I can't stand this, I'll have to tell him, she thought. I can't figure out what to do by myself. There were no acceptable solutions. She couldn't deprive Russ of his child; she couldn't ask Darroch to accept another man's baby. And she could not give Darroch up.

She was sleeping badly and eating little. Twice she began to cry while the four of them were rehearsing. To their anxious inquiries she said, brushing the tears away impatiently, "It's nothing, just these sad old tunes. Did no one on this Island ever make up a happy song?"

Màiri and Darroch looked at each other, puzzled. He said, "That is a good question. I know one or two but they're naughty. I wonder if Kenneth has any more?"

"Teach me a naughty one. It'll improve my Gaelic if I have to figure out the translation."

They all laughed but Màiri and Jamie glanced at each other, then at Jean. Jamie lured Darroch outside on the pretext of asking him about his truck. Darroch knew next to nothing about trucks but shrugged and prepared to follow. But first he put an arm around Jean and whispered in her ear, "We can go home now, if you like, *mo chridhe*."

She shook her head. "No, it's all right."

He kissed the corner of her mouth and gave her a look of longing as he left.

Màiri was deeply moved. "Why don't you put the poor man out of his misery," she said, "and yourself as well?" Half joking, she was startled to see tears spring again into Jean's eyes, enormous pools of green in a face suddenly pale and pinched.

"If only it were that simple," she murmured.

"Jean, if you have problems you can always talk to me," she said awkwardly. Intimacy did not come easily to Màiri.

Jean sighed. "There's nothing you can do, but thanks." The urge to confide was strong but she was too ashamed to talk about it. Màiri could not possibly understand what had happened between her and Russ and she could not bear to lose Màiri's respect.

Later, Màiri said to Jamie, "It's sex, isn't it. Why are they torturing themselves so?" Jamie shook his head. It was beyond his understanding.

Darroch knew there was something very wrong and it did not seem to him to be just frustration. The suspicion began to grow in his mind that she regretted what she had done in divorcing Russ.

It didn't make any sense. She'd flung herself at him when she returned from Milwaukee and she seemed deliriously happy to be back on the Island. What was wrong? Was she missing Sally? The good life in Milwaukee? Or . . . God forbid . . . Russ?

She even seemed reluctant to be in his arms at the end of an evening and he felt acutely the lack of their determinedly chaste cuddles.

He refused to believe she did not love him any more. But she was increasingly miserable about something and he had no idea what it was.

A call from his agent, wanting a conference in London, made his decision for him. He'd go away for a few days and let Jean work through whatever was in her mind without the distraction of his presence.

He felt he'd made the right decision, one that would take the pressure off Jean. Now all he had to do was tell her about it.

It was a bitter March afternoon with a stinging rain lashed by a wind off the ocean. At least the weather could cooperate, he thought grimly as he staggered up the hill toward her cottage. It was not a day to endear the Island to its inhabitants and it would certainly not encourage an incomer to stay.

He knocked, then opened the door and was struck by the blazing kitchen lights in a shimmering atmosphere of warmth. A fire snapped on the hearth. The cottage smelled deliciously of cooking.

Jean came to him and stripped him of his dripping coat, grumbling about his exposure to the dreadful weather. "Let me see if you're wet through," she instructed and patted him. He laughed, caught her around the waist and pulled her close.

She was pressed tightly against him and he could sense . . . almost taste . . . the yearning and yielding before she pulled away, looking hunted.

But she made light of it. "Did you come for kisses then, or for supper?"

"Depends. What's for supper?"

"Ashes and charcoal unless I stir that stew right now." She wriggled away.

A plump, steaming loaf of bread sat on the table. "Ah," he said, looking at it with pointed interest.

She cut a thick heel slice and buttered it. He sat down, took a bite and looked up at her as she waited for his opinion. He said, "Heavenly."

Such a rapport between them at that moment in her little cottage, with the rain pelting away outside. He put the bread down and wrapped his arms around her, pillowing his head against her belly. "Darling Jean, *mo chridhe.*"

She stroked his hair and he could tell she was crying, trying hard not to let him know. Take her to bed, he thought, love her, end all this. He stood up with determination and was stunned into immobility by the tortured look on her face.

"Jean, why won't you tell me what's wrong?" he whispered.

She said something.

"What?"

"I can't."

Utterly baffled he held her until she pulled away. "Come on, supper's ready."

They ate a silent meal. Afterwards he told her he was going away. He thought despairingly that she seemed almost relieved.

He left the next morning.

So Jean waited, flashing back to twenty years ago when she was unmarried, pregnant and nineteen, her future in doubt and her college education abruptly halted. The misery and shame of that period engulfed her.

She was unapproachable. At the Playschool Barabal tried, and Catrìona.

What is wrong? they whispered to Màiri, who shook her head. Jean canceled her Wednesday afternoon with Jamie and Gordon, didn't go to the Thursday evening *seisean*, didn't go to Airgead with Ian the Post on Friday.

She was keenly aware of her body, listening to it for signs of pregnancy. She sat alone, thinking of Mòrag and Ùisdean. How had Mòrag felt, carrying her lover's baby, knowing he would never see it? Oh, Mòrag, what shall I do? she thought and as though a voice had whispered in her ear she was suddenly reassured. She was in control of her life; she would work it out.

As if her body had been waiting for that, she woke in a pool of blood on the twenty-ninth day. Her period had come in the night like the tide rushing into Airgead Bay. Jean got up, dizzy with relief, murmuring grateful prayers under her breath. To whom the prayers were addressed she couldn't say but she remembered Darroch's expression, the One Who Listens.

That has got to be a female, she said to herself. Is it you who listens, Mòrag?

She was deliriously happy but her back ached as though she'd been kicked. She took a hot shower. Then she pulled out the box of tampons she'd almost thrown away in the mad thought that her period would certainly come if she didn't have any supplies.

She made a pot of tea and fixed cinnamon toast just as her mother had done for her when she'd been a young girl miserable with her period. She took the tray and a paperback romance to bed, luxuriating in her freedom to begin the rest of her life.

Ian the Post knocked at her door several mornings later. "This looks important. I did not think I should leave it in your box." He handed her a thick manila envelope.

It was from the lawyers. She put it on the table, staring at it while she waited for the kettle to boil. Nuts to tea, she thought, I need something stronger. She rummaged through her cupboard and found the small stovetop percolator and the coffee she'd brought from Milwaukee.

It was only when a cup of coffee sat steaming in front of her that she was able to summon up the nerve to open the envelope. Even now, she was thinking, something could go wrong.

Nothing had gone wrong. The papers said exactly what she'd worked out with Russ and the accompanying letter instructed her to sign the agreement and return it. She could expect her divorce to be granted soon, a matter of a week or two. She was free.

Strangely, she did not feel like rejoicing. She sat for a good half-hour, lost in memories and an overwhelming sadness. It was like a funeral.

Then she pulled the papers to her and signed them. She addressed an envelope, put the papers in and sealed it. She dressed to go into the village to the post office.

Eilean Dubh, this morning, was more beautiful than she had ever seen it. The air was crisply cold and a sharp wind brought tears to her eyes. Peat smoke tickled her nose. Cars passed and the occupants honked at her and waved. Somhairle Mac-a-Phi, Barabal's eldest, straining uphill on his bicycle, shouted a greeting.

Wildflowers were blooming along the road. She knelt and picked a yellow blossom with no idea of what it was and stuck it in her buttonhole.

She came to the rise in the road overlooking Ros Mór and the harbor. The Cal-Mac ferry, out in the sea, steamed majestically toward the docks in Airgead and fishing boats were sailing back home.

Dogs barked. A blackbird sang. On a nearby croft chickens cackled and a lone cow mooed vigorously.

It was an entirely normal morning and she was part of it. She stopped in the verge and felt her feet, inexplicably, rooting into the ground as if she were a tree. She was becoming one with the soil of Eilean Dubh.

She chuckled and strode confidently down into the village. Darroch would be home tomorrow and she would fix him a supper such as he had never eaten before.

Fifty-one

What is it men in women do require?
The lineaments of Gratified Desire.
What is it women in men do require?
The lineaments of Gratified Desire.

William Blake

*D*arroch came home desperate to see Jean, hoping she'd worked out her worries. He put on comfortable Island clothes and went into town for a bottle of wine, then parked at her cottage.

The weather had broken that morning and the winter sun disappearing over the horizon bathed the cold sky in an array of color. He called her outside to see the sunset.

She seemed more cheerful, he thought, even high-spirited. After supper she suggested a walk and they tramped down to *Taigh Rois* and chatted their way into an impromptu music *seisean*.

But he was determined not to put pressure on her. When they got back to her cottage he kissed her and turned to go. "I'll not come in, Jean. *Oidhche mhath.*"

"Okay . . . " The word was barely out of her mouth before he was striding to the car. She watched him in dismay. "Darroch!" She ran after him. "Wait!"

He stopped but didn't turn. "What's wrong?" she said. "Darroch, are you angry with me?"

He swung around and stared at her in surprise. "Why would I be angry, *mo chridhe?*"

She said, remembering Russ's day-long sulks that had erupted without explanation, "Well, you're leaving . . . " And you hardly touched me, she thought.

"Lass, when I'm angry I say so. And I'm not angry, I just can't stand it tonight. I want to take you to bed and I can't. It's best I go home. Away from temptation."

She looked at him. In the moonlight she could see the frustration in his face.

"I've had enough of this," she said. "Come in." She took his arm.

"Well, for a bit . . . but I'll not sit close to you," he said firmly and she knew he meant it.

She shut the door. "Please build a fire. I'll be back in a few minutes."

Bemused, he did as she said. Ten minutes later she drifted back into the room, turning out lights as she went so the room was illuminated only by the fire. He didn't look up until she came to the sofa. His jaw dropped.

She had changed into a nightgown of sheer white lawn. It had long full sleeves, a low, square neckline that all but revealed her breasts, and it buttoned down the front. She'd showered. Damp tendrils of hair that had escaped her shower cap curled around her face and he could smell the perfume of her soap.

He was speechless.

Jean said, "I know, you miss the red rose between the teeth."

Darroch said, "Actually, I was picturing a long black cigarette holder."

"I'll get it," she said and turned, pretending to leave. He seized her and pulled her down onto his lap. What he could see of her aroused him and what he couldn't see was driving him mad. "This gown . . . "

"Is it what you had in mind? You said white and sheer, didn't you? I had it made by my dressmaker in Milwaukee. When I told her it was for a wedding night she said six buttons, no more."

"It's exquisite. You're exquisite." Overwhelmed, he buried his face in her hair and whispered, "I assume this means a change in our relationship."

"Yes . . . if you like. I'm free now, the papers came." She smiled. "Remember I tried to seduce you before, at Hogmanay."

"Aye, and all your relatives kept ringing us on the telephone."

"Aye. So . . . how about it? I turned the phone off. Want to try again?"

"Where?" he whispered hoarsely.

"Right here. By the fire. On the fur rug."

"The rug? Are you sure?"

"That's what you bought it for, isn't it?"

"Aye . . . but . . . how did you know that?"

"You ask too many questions. Anyway, it's all clean down in front of the fire. I swept the hearth today and hung the rug out to air. It will smell of sunshine and peat smoke. Erotic as all get out."

"Did you plan this?"

"No, I'm just naturally tidy."

He was so muddled with love and lust that he didn't know where to touch her first. Luscious, delicious, precious Jean. He nibbled the soft curve of her ear and she sighed. He moved his lips across her chin, then unbuttoned the first button, long fingers drifting inside the neck of the gown.

"Why six buttons?" he murmured, opening the second button.

"Six is my lucky number."

"I have a feeling it's going to be my lucky number too."

The third button went, his fingers feather-light on her skin. She looked down at his hand as it curled around her breast. "I knew you'd be good at this," she whispered.

"I'm just getting started," he said.

On the fourth button her nightgown fell open wide enough to expose her breasts. As he leaned closer the rough fabric of his sweater teased her. "Is this wool?" she said, fingering it. "I don't like wool next to my skin."

He stripped off sweater and undershirt. She smoothed her hands along the strong line of his collarbone, out the broad shoulders, down muscular arms. "You are *miorbhuileach*," she said.

"Me? I'm just an ordinary man. You . . . you are a work of art."

"Oh, really? Who's the artist?" she teased.

"Well, not Rubens . . . you'd have to put on a few pounds. Not Dali . . . you don't have a clock in your belly. Let me look a little more closely . . . " He slipped her off his lap and onto her feet.

He said, "I need to see all of you," and unfastened the last two buttons. Jean lifted her shoulders and the nightgown fell to the floor. She stood naked in front of him.

He leaned back against the sofa and stared at her. Spurred by a mischievous impulse she couldn't control, Jean raised her arms and lifted her hair, letting it fall through her fingers to her shoulders. She posed like a goddess on a pin-up calendar.

His eyes widened. "Wow," he said.

Jean was absurdly pleased. Like all women, she was not satisfied with her body: she thought her breasts were too big, her navel was slightly off-center and she longed for a Scarlett O'Hara waist. But obviously he liked what he saw. "Wow" was the best compliment she'd ever received.

"Turn around," he said and as she revolved slowly in front of him he licked his lips. Then he leaned forward, put his hands on her waist and pulled her to him.

"You are like a sculpture of a Greek goddess. Like Venus. Your breasts are glorious," he said, and kissed each one tenderly.

"From nursing two babies."

Reminded, he said, "We've no form of contraception tonight. Unless you . . . ?"

She said calmly, "I threw all that stuff away when I left Milwaukee."

"Then we might . . . what if . . . "

"Another reason not to wait any longer. I'm forty, I don't have much time left." Suddenly unsure, she whispered, "For a baby, I mean. If you wouldn't mind, that is."

"Mind? Would I mind a baby? Yours and mine? You'd do that for me, Jean?" Unexpectedly his eyes filled with tears. "No, I wouldn't mind."

"Come on, then," she said. "I'm not getting any younger." She stepped away, lowered herself gracefully to the fur rug and lay looking up at him.

"Just one thing about a baby," he said softly. "I want her to have green eyes, the color of the tidal pool off Airgead Head. The color of a Coke bottle."

She laughed. "No, he's going to have eyes like sapphires. Then Eilean Dubh will know for sure who his father is."

He'd thought often and in great detail about this moment, planning a long slow seduction that would leave her dazed and breathless. Now that the moment was upon him, though, he was as hot and eager as a young lad. He was not at all sure he could wait, his need to be inside her was desperate.

He stood and pulled off his trousers but when his hands went to his shorts she whispered, "Let me." She rose to her knees, pulled the shorts down and cupped her hands around him. "You've never let me touch you before," she whispered.

"Because I couldn't stand it." He could barely endure it now. Her caressing fingers promised a world of unimaginable delight. He was terrified she might put her mouth on him and he would lose his mind entirely.

She said, "No more preliminaries. I want you now." She lay back on the rug and stretched her arms out to him.

"There's no hurry," he said, lowering himself to the rug.

"Please," she said.

"You do please me, Jean, so much. You are so lovely and you respond to me with such ardor. Let me take my time with you. We have the night ahead." His hand slipped down, dipped lower, ruffling the curls between her legs, soft as the hair on her head and with the same gold highlights reflecting from the fire.

She said, "I can't wait. I've waited so long to have you inside me. I've dreamed about it, Darroch, and always waked up empty. I don't want to wake up this time; I'm afraid it'll all vanish. This is too *miorbhuileach* to be true."

"Forever it will last, years of loving you." But he too did not want to wait, he burned to have her. There was one preliminary he would not skip, though.

He bent and kissed the exact center of her belly, murmuring softly in the Gaelic against her skin.

Jean's arms went around his neck when he lifted his head. "What did you say?"

"I asked a blessing on our union."

"Whom did you ask?"

"I asked the One Who Listens," he said.

Ah, yes. She thought she knew who that was. "Tell me what you said."

"It can't be said in English. Give me your mouth and I'll give you the words in our language."

Obediently she put her mouth against his and he whispered the words between her lips, heard her sigh and take them in with his warm breath, felt her tremble as the words filled her.

He'd meant to enter her slowly, gently, but she parted for him like the Red Sea parted for Moses and in a heartbeat he was deeply inside and she was tight around him, very tight. He heard her gasp and looked down, fearing he had gone too fast. "Are you all right, Jean?"

He was so large, so hard, he stretched her to the limits of her endurance and it was divine. She took a deep breath and said, "Oh, yes. I am very all right," and gave him a sudden, wide smile.

He smiled back. Why, this is fun, he thought. Not just the pleasure of love fulfilled or lust satisfied, but fun. How serious his last years had been, and how joyful the months since he'd known her. Teasingly he withdrew almost all the way and watched the reaction on her face as he thrust back inside.

"Very all right . . . " Her green eyes were huge and astonished.

He withdrew and thrust again. "Very . . . all right . . . " Her voice trailed off as spasms of pleasure gripped her. She flung her arms back on the rug and arched upwards. He could feel her tightening and rippling around him and he denied his own response for one more deep thrust, penetrating her innermost self.

"Oh . . . " she said in wonder and gave herself to him completely.

His control broke and he dissolved, exploded in rapture, waves of pure delight that enveloped them both, sent them spiraling straight into heaven, their cries mingling in the cool quiet air.

Jean burst into tears.

He came back to himself in sudden alarm, pulling away and staring down at her. "My darling lass, I didn't hurt you?"

"No, of course not. I'm just so happy."

"Ah. *Tha gu dearbh*, it is *miorbhuileach* to belong to each other at last. Now you are mine. Nothing and no one can take you away."

Jean sobbed.

Darroch began to laugh helplessly, gasping for breath as waves of laughter poured through him. What a pair, he thought. One of us hysterical with tears, the other hysterical with laughter. He struggled to a sitting position, his back against the sofa, and reached for her. "Come here," he said, and grasped her by the hips and lifted her over him. He lowered her down with exquisite slowness.

It was like sliding into a volcano. She was molten around him. "Now I'm as deep inside you as I can go," he whispered in her ear. "Do you like it?"

The question was redundant. He could tell she liked it; hot tears scalded his skin, spilled down his shoulders and she shook with sobs even as she began to move upon him.

This time it was as if a lightening bolt had ripped through the cottage. Darroch thought he'd reached a place beyond orgasm, some sort of Tantric plane of bliss beyond imagination. Jean's climax rippled through her, starting deep inside and spreading upward all the way through finger and toe tips. She sobbed.

He laughed, his face against her throat. "Are you always going to weep when I make love to you?"

"I don't know. Are you always going to laugh?" she said.

Darroch had never had a woman yield herself so completely, with such trust. "I love you, Jean," he whispered.

"I love you, Darroch."

He realized she was shivering, the skin of her back cool against his hands, the fire behind her reduced to red coals. "You're cold. Let me take you to bed."

"I'm warm all over and I don't think I can move, I feel so relaxed. No, that's not the right word." She wriggled against him and he gasped with renewed lust.

"Think how much better it will be in your warm cozy bed." He disentangled their bodies and pulled her to her feet. "Get in bed," he whispered. "I'll smoor the fire."

As she went to the bedroom she heard him murmuring to the fire in the Gaelic and she added her own words of gratitude to the One Who Listens.

The bed was every bit as cold as she'd thought it would be and she shrieked aloud as she got into it.

"Mouse?" He came to the bed.

"Cold. Come and warm me."

"Aye." He realized, suddenly, that it had to end. "But then I'm going to leave."

Her eyes flew open in surprise. "Leave? Why?"

"It's Sunday now. In six hours the road will be full of people heading for kirk. And the Bentley's out in front of your cottage. The scandal would be enormous."

"No! I want you here with me. You're my lover now. I want to sleep with you and wake up with you." She set her jaw defiantly. "I don't care about the scandal."

"You would. Remember the last time?"

Her face changed. She remembered. "How long will this go on?"

"Not long, Jean. But for now it's our secret. Sweet and private."

That sounded nice, too. "Before you go, though . . . " she pulled him close. One thing led to another and just before he entered her again he whispered, "You're going to be sore tomorrow."

"Good," she said. "Then I'll have the feel of you inside me all day."

Darroch woke up an hour later and extricated himself from her bed with reluctance. It was very cold in the bedroom. His respect for her increased when he realized she'd been here all winter and had never complained about the cold. He dressed, shivering, in front of the quiet ashes of the fire.

Left alone in bed Jean moved drowsily. She had pleased him. Her forty-year-old, twice-pregnant body had brought her lover great pleasure. He had moaned and shouted his pleasure. And laughed.

And he had pleased her. Her best friend, her adored Darroch, was a wonderful lover. He had come inside her hard and deep, made her his completely, matched her passion with his own. She moved into the warm space in bed he'd left and absorbed into herself the remaining heat from his body.

Jean heard the door close, heard the Bentley purr into life and pull away. She smiled and relaxed into contented sleep.

Fifty-two

A mortal fell in love with a fairy as beautiful as a drop of dew in the sunshine. Let me kiss you, said the mortal, and the fairy offered her mouth. Let me lie with you, said the mortal, and the fairy yielded her body in the deep grass of the hilltop. Marry me, cried the mortal, and the fairy drew away from him. "The People do not wed with mortals," she said . . .

Eilean Dubh fairy tale, translated by Darroch Mac an Rìgh

Darroch sat in kirk the next morning filled with satisfaction. He had headed to his usual place in back, then straightened up and swaggered to the Mac an Rìgh pew.

In the Islanders' minds this meant something significant but no one could figure out what it was. They watched Darroch with avid interest, only turning away when Minister Donald launched into the sermon. Today it was as always Biblically-based, but everyone recognized it as a stinging commentary on the perfidy of the English and their Tory government. It was a text they could all relate to with indignant enjoyment.

Darroch was only half listening. He was remembering the night before. She seduced me, he thought happily. She loves me and she wants me and she seduced me. A foolish grin lifted the corners of his mouth.

In the pulpit Minister Donald glanced up and caught the expression on Darroch's face. He stopped in mid-sentence and stared. When he looked down at his notes again he had lost his place. The congregation stared. No one could remember the last time the Minister had faltered in a sermon.

Between Darroch's behavior and the Minister's, kirk today was an immensely satisfying experience. People lingered in the kirkyard, chatting, for a long time.

Darroch slipped away. He drove home, changed and loped up the hill to Jean's cottage in long easy strides. He rapped gently, then went inside, then peeked into the bedroom. As he had suspected, she was still asleep.

She lay curled in a nest of blankets, her hair tangled around her. As he approached he realized she had gotten up during the night. She was now wearing what appeared to be an enormous flannel nightgown. He raised his eyebrows.

He bent over the bed to kiss her awake. "*Madainn mhath.*"

She opened her eyes, sleepily at first and then wide in surprise. It took her a few moments to orient herself to his presence and he smiled, watching the events of the past night recreated on her face. She turned pink, remembering the best parts.

How beautiful she is just waked from sleep, he thought and reached out a hand to the flannel nightgown. "Something else from your little Milwaukee dressmaker?"

"The Co-Op."

"Isn't it a bit . . . big?"

"Size extra-extra-large. The only flannel nightgown they had. The girls in the Co-Op laughed at me but I didn't care."

He undid the first several buttons. "More than six, I think." Then, as he took in the sheer volume of the garment he said, "There's room for a friend or two in here. Were you expecting company?"

"Laugh if you want but it's wonderfully warm."

"You should have told me how cold it gets in here at night."

"Why? This is Scotland and it's winter. It's supposed to be cold."

He could not argue with that logic so contented himself with unfastening more buttons. Even after doing that he could not find her in the huge gown. "I don't know how you get this off," he grumbled.

"I stand in the middle of the floor, unbutton it and let it slide to the ground."

"I should like to see you do that," he murmured, diverted.

"Consider yourself lucky you've seen this much. I never intended for you . . . or anyone . . . to see me in this."

"I would rather see you without it. Do you think if I started at the bottom and worked my way up I could get it off you?"

"I don't know, no one's ever tried. Sounds like fun, though."

He smiled. "How about a cup of tea first, to fortify me for my explorations?"

When he left for the kitchen she jumped out of bed, ran into the bathroom, washed the sleep away and brushed her hair till it shone. She peeked into the bedroom. He had not returned. She unbuttoned the nightgown, stepped out of it and threw it in the closet.

She got back in bed and pulled the sheet up over her breasts. Then, reconsidering, she pulled it up to her chin and lay demurely waiting.

He brought in the tea tray and poured her a cup. When she reached for it the sheet slipped. Grabbing at the sheet she spilled tea into the saucer.

Vastly amused, but resolved not to smile, he took her cup and wiped the saucer dry. That gave her time to readjust the sheet. She tucked it in above her breasts, leaving her arms free and her shoulders bare.

"What happened to the nightgown?" he inquired.

"I took it off," she said, not meeting his eyes.

"Oh. Good."

While they drank their tea he told her about the Minister's sermon on perfidious Albion, doing his usual wickedly accurate impersonation, making her laugh.

Then he took her cup away. "Jean. Are you hungry?"

"Starving," she said and reached for him. The sheet slipped. When she grabbed at it he gathered her hands in one of his and held them above her head on the pillow. With the other hand he pulled the sheet down. "I haven't seen you naked in the daylight," he said.

She watched his face as his eyes swept slowly over her. "I hope I meet with your approval."

"Oh, yes, *m'aingeal*. Very much so," he murmured and bent to put his mouth against her throat. Sensuality enveloped them, warm and sweet.

He undressed and climbed into bed with her. He had resolved that this time would be delightfully, voluptuously slow but her body against his changed all that. "Ah, Jean," he whispered afterward. "I'm sorry, I just couldn't wait."

"Me neither," she answered. "And I'm not a bit sorry."

After breakfast they wrapped themselves in sweaters and scarves against the cold spring day and walked down to the ocean. They stood, arms around each other, watching the waves crash against the rocks.

"I love this place," Jean said. "I've waited all my life to live next door to the sea."

When they turned to go back she suggested they stop and visit Màiri and Jamie. "Oh, no," he said. "It's Sunday afternoon. I'd not dare disturb them. Ever since the twins left to go to school in Edinburgh they've kept Sunday afternoons as their private time together. In bed. Making love."

"Oh. However do you know that?"

"Jamie told me. One day, when in my zeal and enthusiasm I proposed we have a meeting on Sunday, something about the Playschool, I think. It seemed all right to me, we're none of us the kind of Presbyterians who keep the Sabbath holy, sitting around and reading the Bible. But he was quite explicit on the point."

Darroch remembered the conversation well. A stab of envy, intensely physical, had gone through him when he'd thought of the two of them in bed together, Màiri's bright hair spread across the white pillow. It was a vision as clear as reality and it had nearly broken his heart.

"That's why God made Sunday afternoons," Jamie had said. "Sometimes we start right after breakfast . . . hell, sometimes we don't even have breakfast. That's what keeps me going the whole week. Sunday afternoons."

He knew now why Jamie had told him. You must get over her, Jamie had been saying. You'll not find another woman to love while you're still yearning for Màiri.

Now he had his Jean and now she was all his. He put his arm around her shoulders and whispered in her ear, "What do you think of that as a Sunday afternoon activity, *mo Shine?*"

She grinned. "I think it's *miorbhuileach* and I don't care if I do sound like a gusher."

Hand in hand they headed back uphill. "My bed," Darroch said. "Under the skylight, at last."

Lying with him later, deeply content, she looked up through the skylight into a square of intense blue. A single cloud drifted by. She thought he was asleep, his head pillowed upon her breasts and her fingers wandering lazily through his hair.

But he lifted his head and said, "Let's talk about our wedding."

"Umm . . . what do you want to talk about?"

"Everything. Start by setting the date."

"I don't want to."

Surprised, he said, "Don't want to talk about it? Or don't want to set the date?"

"Don't want to get married."

Shock coursed through every atom of his body. He sat up, stared at her and said blankly, "What?"

Jean moved uneasily but there was a stubborn set to her jaw. "I think we are perfect just as we are." When he looked baffled she added, "Lovers. I like being lovers."

"Lovers?"

The idea had been growing in her head since her divorce and had reached fruition last night. "Yes, lovers. Free and honest. Just between you and me."

When he frowned, puzzled, she added, "Vows in churches and contracts with the state haven't done us much good, have they? Your wife cheated on you and my husband cheated on me. What good are promises like that? What counts between us is what's in our hearts and our heads. We belong to each other and we don't need anyone to tell us it's okay."

"But I want to marry you. I want you to have my name."

She said, "Umm . . . I've been thinking about changing my name."

"Of course. To mine."

"No. I want to change my name to my Island one. My real one, before it was turned into English. I'm not Abbott any more and I'm not Greer. I'm a MacChriathar."

When he hesitated she added, "Women do that here. They keep their own names even if they are married. I've seen it on the tombstones in the cemetery. 'Moira MacQuirter, wife to Ian Ross.' I want my own name."

He ran his hand through his hair in agitation. "But I want you to be Jean Mac an Rìgh. I want you with me in my bed every night."

She said softly, "I love my cottage."

"But, Jean, it's not big enough for both of us. How can we be together . . . "

"We'll together most of the time but we'll each have our own space where we can retreat when we need to be private. I won't move in with you, or you with me."

"No," he said. "I want you with me all the time."

They stared at each other, at an impasse. Lovers, he thought. How in hell am I supposed to handle this?

But the idea was curiously appealing. Coming together in joy, not in duty. Tied to each other by the strength of their love. He lay back down in bed and stared at the sky, trying to work it out in his mind.

"Lovers," Jean said firmly. "Our secret. Sweet and private."

He almost laughed aloud at the impossibility of what she was saying. Was it possible she really believed they could keep such a relationship secret? Already people smiled knowingly at them when they were together, at the way they looked at each other when they sang, the way his arm was always around her shoulders or his hand in the small of her back. There was no way an intimate physical relationship between the two of them would not be quickly recognized for what it was.

The Island expected, wanted, needed them to be married. In many minds Jean was already a Mac an Rìgh, the Lady of Eilean Dubh. Couples promised to each other could be lovers as long as it was clear that marriage would soon follow. Anything else would be incredibly shocking. Visions of a scandal such as the Island had not known for years flooded his mind. Gossiping, clucking, condemning. He shuddered.

He rose on one arm and leaned over her, determined to try reason again.

Jean was not anyone's doormat but after twenty years with a high-strung husband and two independent-minded children she'd learned well the role of conciliator. She changed the subject. "You're getting tense," she said. "Let me rub your back."

"I am not tense," he said, but allowed himself to be cajoled into lying flat on his belly. She climbed on him and began to massage his shoulders.

The bare skin of her thighs on the bare skin of his hips, the soft hairs between her legs tickling his bottom, her strong hands loosening the knots of tension in his back . . . He was caught in an exotic mixture of relaxation and eroticism. After a night and half a day of making love, relaxation won, and he let himself doze off.

Jean looked down at him tenderly. Then she draped herself on top of him, put her cheek against his shoulder and closed her eyes. Just before she drifted into sleep she thought: my lover. And she smiled like a child with a new toy.

Fifty-three

The man who loves a fairy is forever enchanted.
Eilean Dubh proverb

*D*arroch looked at his watch and groaned. Ten o'clock and no end in sight. At this rate the committee would go on wrangling till midnight when the Sabbath began. He didn't think he could stand it. In fact he was sure he couldn't.

At a break in the action when the opponents were trying to think of even more cutting things to say to each other, Darroch stood up, murmuring, "*Gabh mo leisguil*," and made his way to the door. He stopped to whisper in Barabal Mac-a-Phi's ear, "I can't take any more, I'm away. If anyone still wants my opinion, you're authorized to say I'm in favor of the proposal."

Barabal grimaced. "That's supposing they get to a vote tonight. I think they're enjoying themselves too much for that."

Out in the fresh air Darroch stretched and ran a hand through his hair. He hated these meetings; they were always smoky and the room was always close. Several people smoked and another thought fresh air brought colds and the influenza, so the windows stayed shut. He resolved to get off this committee next year. He'd been trying for three years.

He got in the Bentley and switched it on. As it idled he wrinkled his nose, realizing the odor of smoke had followed him. He sniffed fastidiously at himself. The smell was in his clothes, his jacket was permeated with smoke. He kept the windows open as he drove, hoping the odor would go away before he got to Jean's.

He'd known when he'd left the meeting that he was going to her, not home. He hoped she'd still be awake. Although the idea of undressing and sliding into bed next to her was tempting he was shy about doing that. She was from the big city and still nervous about the Island's unlocked-door policy. He did not want to frighten her with an unexpected visitor in her bed in the middle of the night.

Which was why he knocked gently, then eased the door open. If she had gone to bed he would take himself away home. "Jean," he called softly. And then he saw her.

She was sitting on the floor before a blazing fire, dressed in her silk kimono, combing her hair.

The light from the fire turned the whisky-colored hair into a gleaming halo as it flowed back and forth beneath the comb. The bright colors of the silk shimmered and glowed and where the kimono gapped open he could see the long line of her throat and the curve of her breast, and further down, to her belly.

He was enchanted. It was like seeing one of the Island's legendary fairies come to life. "Jean," he called softly as he came in.

Startled, she dropped the comb and pulled the kimono protectively around her. "Darroch?"

"Aye, it's only me. No, stay there," as she moved to get up. "I'll come to you." He hung his jacket on a peg and slipped off his shoes. In his stocking feet he came to the fire and sat down behind her.

"Let me do that." He picked up the comb and settled her between his knees. "I thought you might have gone to bed. That's why I came in so quietly. I didn't want to wake you."

"I stayed up to wash my hair. It takes a while to dry now it's so long."

He ran the comb through her hair and watched the dark wet strands turn golden-red-brown in the firelight, watched the shining cloud drift back to her shoulders. "Nearly dry," he murmured. One hand touched the kimono neckline and long fingers slipped inside to trail over bare skin. He was quite sure she was wearing nothing underneath.

"What is this garment?" he said softly.

"My kimono." She ducked her head. "I didn't expect you tonight or I wouldn't have worn it."

"Why not?" He bent to kiss the back of her neck. Her skin smelled of some delightful flower, rose or lavender. "It's beautiful. It's almost as soft as your skin."

"It's not really decent . . . I've nothing else on."

So modest, and yet every night she had been growing more and more uninhibited when they made love. Last night she had half screamed, half sobbed when he'd entered her and he had every intention of coaxing that delicious sound from her tonight.

"I thought so. What a lot of time that will save," he whispered against her skin. His fingers toyed with the neckline, pushing it off one shoulder. He rubbed his face against the sweet sharpness of her collarbone. "You wouldn't deprive me of the pleasure of seeing you wear this, would you?"

The kimono slipped down and his hand moved with exquisite slowness to her breast. "Or of taking it off of you . . . "

His touch aroused her so much she felt quite wanton. She said, trying to remain rational for at least a little longer, "Did your meeting finish early?"

"The meeting from hell is still going on for all I know. I left when I'd had all I could stand. I wanted you . . . I mean, I wanted to see you. No, I was right the first time. I want you. Now." He pulled her to her feet and put his face against her belly, his hands on her hips. The kimono pooled around his arms.

His fingers moved down her body to slip between her legs and he bent to put his mouth on her. She froze. Her hands seized his hair in sudden panic.

She had never experienced anything so erotic in her life. She threw her head back and moaned. Her knees weakened and it was only his hands on her hips that kept her from falling.

He moved his mouth slowly to the lowest part of her abdomen, just above the pudendum, and looked up at her, relishing the stunned look on her face.

She was suddenly ticklish. He knew it at once and moved upwards, turning his face from side to side so that his evening whiskers rasped against her belly. She squirmed and began to giggle helplessly.

"Oh, lovie," she sighed, pulling his hair. "You know, tickling is a form of torture. It expresses hostility."

He chuckled, his face pressed hard against her belly so she felt his laugh, and licked her navel. "Surely you jest," he said.

She looked down and smiled a little teasing smile.

She let herself go limp and melted into his arms, sliding down against him. He felt one sharp moment of pure sexual madness as her breasts moved past his upturned face. He pulled her down across his lap.

"Why are you wearing so much when I'm wearing so little?" she complained.

He took his hands from her so that he could peel off his sweater. Jean wrinkled her nose. "Ugh, another smoky meeting; it's in your clothes. I don't know how I can tell the smell of cigarette smoke from peat smoke but I can. Take them all off."

She said, "I don't like you sitting in those smoky rooms. It's bad for your lungs."

"Maybe I can use that as an excuse for getting off that committee. It's terrible, with Murdoch the Taxi and Murdoch the Arranger both puffing away like great reekin' lums. My voice is my livelihood. I can't risk it by inhaling smoke."

"I'm glad you left early. I was missing you. And wanting you."

"It's like an addiction, isn't it, Jean. I thought having you at last would ease the need but it's gotten worse."

"Because we know how good it is. Before, we just imagined it."

"Amazing that reality should turn out to be better than fantasy." Her body yielding in his arms was reality.

She wriggled against him. "All these clothes," she grumbled, wrestling with his shirt buttons. He fumbled with his trousers and kicked his feet free of them. "Take off your pretty robe, *mo chridhe*. It's getting wrinkled."

She slipped out of the kimono and lay back naked in his arms. "Lovie," she said shyly, "You gave me so much pleasure, kissing me like that. I've never experienced such a thing before."

Her ex-husband must be an unimaginative lout, thought Darroch. To have had a husband's right to her beautiful body and her sensual nature and to never have made love to her with his mouth. Ah, well, the more he could teach her, so much they could learn together.

He took her slowly and they fused into a perfect crest of desire fulfilled. In his passion tonight he was very vocal in the Gaelic, murmuring against her skin.

"I wish I could talk love talk like you do," she sighed afterward. "It's so limited in English. Teach me what you're saying."

"It's more fun doing than teaching. Ask me tomorrow."

"What? You mean what you're saying could bear the light of day? I'll bet you're reciting your grocery list and it just sounds sexy."

"One dozen eggs," he mumbled against her throat. "A loaf of bread. Washing-up liquid." He squeezed her breast. "And some oranges."

She giggled. "I never imagined it could be this much fun. I love making love with you. I want you nearly all the time."

"Why nearly all the time?"

"The rest of the time I'm asleep. But I think I dream about making love with you because of the way I wake up."

"And that is . . . ?"

"Wait till tomorrow morning. I'll show you."

He sat up. "Jean, I can't stay the night with you."

She was dreadfully disappointed. "Was it something I said?" she joked, to cover her reaction.

"No, it's the bloody car. I parked it in front of your house again. I can't leave it there all night."

"Damn, damn, damn. I want to sleep with you and wake up with you. When is it going to happen?"

"You could come home with me but I've got to get up early for kirk. Best you stay here and I'll come over tomorrow morning."

"It's not the same thing," she grumbled. "Remember the snowstorm? Remember lying in bed together with all our clothes on? That was fun, wasn't it?"

"Considering that it was a dreadful blizzard and I almost froze to death, yes, it was fun. Going to bed with you is much more fun than freezing to death."

"All right, get up, go away. Leave me to cry alone on my pillow and wake up in the morning all hot and bothered. You don't know what you're missing."

The fire was dying slowly. He looked down at her body, warm and willing beside him. "Oh, aye," he said slowly. "Aye, I do." He untangled himself and rooted around on the floor for his clothes. He buttoned his shirt and pulled the sweater on over it. "I don't much fancy leaving, you know that."

She lay back on the pillows, houri-like, and smiled. "Isn't it nice, being lovers."

By unspoken consent they had avoided the subject of marriage during the past week. Now he looked at her. "Lovers have to go home. Husbands get to stay the night."

She turned her head away. "I just need a little time, lovie. Please be patient."

Something else had occurred to him and he played it as a trump card. "What if you get pregnant, Jean?"

"That would be wonderful."

"Pregnant, and not married?"

"It happened to me once before and the world didn't come to an end."

"What would people say . . . "

"They'd get used to it."

He stared at her. "Does the word 'obstinate' mean anything to you? And 'stubborn'? And 'bloody-minded'?"

"I've never heard the last one but I get your general drift."

He gave up. He knew he had to leave before he began thundering ultimatums like one of Minister Donald's Old Testament patriarchs. And it would do no good, she was far too American to be anything but bemused by the Laird voice. He drew himself up to his full height and said with dignity, "*Oidhche mhath, mo Shìne.*"

"Good night, my darling. I love you."

As he reached the door she said, "Umm . . . Darroch . . . Don't forget your trousers."

He looked down at himself. He was stark naked from his shirttails to his socks. He stalked to the sofa and bent to retrieve his pants. Then he looked at her and said mournfully, "Are you laughing at me, Jean?"

Her eyes round and solemn, she said, "Of course not, lovie." Then she smiled. "Is it all right if we laugh together?"

Fifty-four

Fal il e lug 'so bo e lug.
What young girl here is without a husband?
Gaelic pairing song

After kirk next morning the Minister asked Darroch to come and see him. The Minister's requests, however gently phrased, were regarded as commands by the Islanders and Darroch was no exception. He presented himself promptly after the service.

The discussion was to be a momentous one, Darroch realized from the Minister's choice of whisky: a twenty-five-year-old Glenlivet. He savored it, and waited.

At last the Minister said solemnly, "I must ask you your intentions, *a Dharroch*, regarding Mrs. Jean."

The question was totally unexpected. Darroch managed not to choke on his whisky, and put his glass down with elaborate care to give himself a moment to phrase his answer. In tones as formal as the Minister's he said at last, "It is my intention to make her my wife."

"Ah." It was a sigh of relief and satisfaction. The Minister lifted his glass. "A toast, then. Long life and happiness to you and your lady." Darroch nodded his thanks.

After another moment the Minister said, "I did not mean to be intrusive, *a Dharroch*, but Mrs. Jean is a guest on our Island. It is my responsibility to ensure she is treated properly."

Darroch's eyebrow lifted and Minister Donald added quickly, "Not, of course, that I have any suspicion you would behave dishonorably towards her. But it was my duty to ask, as she has no male relative here to look after her."

Darroch noted wryly that despite Jean's demonstrated independence, self-confidence and obvious ability to handle her own life, there was still a man who felt he must ensure she was looked after. She had a vulnerable quality that all the self-confidence in the world could not hide. He wondered if she knew that, and if it would infuriate her if he told her.

The Minister said, "When may we look forward to celebrating this happy event?"

Uh-oh, thought Darroch. "We haven't set a date."

"I hope you will not delay unduly. We must have a care for Mrs. Jean's reputation. The Island will be expecting an announcement."

Darroch thought wildly of stammering some nonsense about waiting periods, divorces becoming final and the like, but to his horror heard himself blurt out his deepest worry. "She doesn't want to get married."

The Minister said blankly, "What?"

"She wants to . . . wait."

"Wait for what?"

"She . . . um . . . wants us to . . . um . . . develop our relationship before we marry."

The Minister said in baffled incomprehension, "She doesn't want to marry you."

"Well, it's not me. It's marriage that she objects to. What might be . . . empty vows . . . even though they're sanctioned by church and state."

The Minister said awfully, "Are you suggesting to me that Mrs. Abbott . . . " She had become Mrs. Abbott, not Mrs. Jean. " . . . might regard a marriage vow made in the house of God as an empty one?"

"No! Certainly not. Not on her part, or mine either. It's just that . . . " He ran his hand through his hair. "Minister, we've both been married in church and we've both had our spouses betray the promises they made. She wants us to make a firm commitment to each other before we stand up in kirk together." There, that sounded better.

The Minister did not think so. He skewered Darroch with his gaze. "There can be no more sacred bond between a man and a woman than that made in the eyes of the Lord and witnessed by His congregation."

Darroch realized he was sweating. "Aye, of course. But we believe the bond we forge between us with our hearts, our minds and our bodies is the basis for what we promise in kirk." I should write that down, he thought, that's good.

The Minister stared at him and Darroch had never seen his eyes so black. "Am I right in assuming you are engaged in a physical relationship with this woman?"

This woman. The situation was deteriorating rapidly. Darroch tried to reassert himself. "Minister, I think that is our private affair . . . " Oops. " . . . um, business and you have no right to . . . "

"*A Dharroch*, as your minister I have every right—the responsibility, in fact—to tell you frankly when you are endangering your immortal soul. And hers, as well."

Darroch thought bitterly that this was all his fault. He should have made a clean break with the kirk and made it clear he did not acknowledge that it had any dominion over his soul. Or his love life.

The Minister was warming to the subject. "Have you thought of what example you are setting? To have such a relationship with a woman to whom you are not married, or even promised?"

"We are promised, it's just not official. She needs time to sort it in her mind. And as for everyone else, they can . . . " They can get stuffed, he thought. Why can't people mind their own damn business?

"The Laird must represent the highest standards. To carry on in this way is wrong." Minister Donald stood up. "I must ask you to consider not only your own spiritual welfare, but the morals of those who owe you respect and who look to you for guidance and example. *Feasgar math, a Dharroch*."

The interview was over. Stunned and shell-shocked, Darroch stood and took the Minister's extended hand. The Minister shook it. "I will pray for you both."

Outside, he sat in the Bentley. Now what the hell am I going to do, he thought, resting his forearms against the wheel. He could not put Jean through another scandal. He could not bear the idea of being denounced in one of the Minister's sermons. And he hated most of all the idea of everybody peering into their private lives.

He wanted so much to claim her as his before the whole world. He had always proudly considered himself a liberated man, valuing independence and assertiveness in the women he'd loved. And now he was behaving like some sort of oriental potentate with a favorite concubine, insisting on complete possession.

Hypocrite, he thought glumly. Next he supposed he'd turn into a caveman, grabbing her by the hair, slinging her over his shoulder, carting her off to bed. His groin tightened agreeably at the thought. Hmm . . . I wonder if she'd like that . . .

He seldom had headaches but pain throbbed suddenly behind his eyes. He needed Jean, he thought, and visualized how she would look after him: a frown of tender concern, cool fingers on his brow and if he was lucky, chocolate chip cookies straight out of the oven, eaten in front of the fireplace.

He sighed in anticipation. And to make sure his headache didn't come back, she'd make him lie, stripped, flat on his belly in the middle of her bed, his face resting on her lavender-scented pillow.

He'd hear the rustle of fabric as she took off her clothes. She'd climb onto him, thighs astride his hips, and massage his back until he lay warm and relaxed, except for the part of him that was very warm and not at all relaxed.

Then he'd turn over under her, put his hand on her hips, lift her and lower her gently down so that she took him deeply inside . . .

With a start Darroch realized that he was doing exactly what the Minister had cautioned him against: he was letting his desire rule his good sense.

He knew quite well he could not carry on a sexual relationship with Jean for long without engendering gossip, rumor and innuendo in epidemic proportions. The Island thrived on gossip and if a story wasn't spicy enough most people weren't above adding a few embellishments. Darroch knew of at least three hot items that were currently circulating. He imagined himself and Jean added to the list and shuddered.

Women never fared well in gossip. Jean would be viewed as either a heartless, immoral tart or a woman wronged, by himself of course. They would not like to believe evil of their Laird, either, but they would, with shocked expressions and hushed voices.

He started the car, but when he came to Jean's cottage he found himself driving on to his own place. He would not, he resolved, share this dilemma with her until he'd worked out a solution. She loved him, he knew she'd marry him but she needed space and time. He would not use the threat of scandal to force her into marriage.

Jean saw the Bentley go by and began supper preparations, expecting him momentarily. When he did not come she phoned him.

He knew who was calling, of course. "Hello, lovie," she said. "Will you be up soon?"

"I . . . I think I'm coming down with something, Jean. Bit of a temperature, achy joints, you know the symptoms. I'll stay away from you so you won't catch it."

"Oh." Her disappointment was obvious and flattering. He felt hot all over and not from a fever. "I'll miss you. Sure you don't want me to bring down something to eat? I could leave it outside your door if you 're worried about being contagious."

"No . . . I'll go to bed and see if I can nip this before it gets worse."

"*Ceart math*. See you tomorrow. Love you, sweetie."

He hung up the phone. Just the sound of her voice, soft and newly seductive, brought back the passion of the last few days and aroused him to an aching hardness.

They were expected to give all this up, he realized angrily. They were to deny themselves the pleasure of each other's body. He was not to make love to her, and he could not tell her why not, and she would be deeply hurt. And because love and sex had both been woven into the intimate tapestry of their relationship they would lose it all.

Back to being friends again, keeping their hands off each other, and both of them frustrated beyond words.

I think I will have a large whisky, he said to himself. Maybe two. Maybe I'll get drunk. His head began to pound again.

The phone rang before he'd had time to do more than taste his drink. Màiri said, in her brusque way, "Jean says you're ill. What's wrong?"

"Nothing physical . . . just a problem I have to solve."

"If you're not sick I need to talk to you about something. I'll be right over." She hung up before he could react.

Maybe Màiri would know what to do. Her instincts about Jean were sound. He remembered a conversation from last week. He'd arrived early to meet Jean in the square and when he'd not seen her he'd arranged his lanky frame on a bench and waited.

"If you're looking for Jean, she's in Beathag's shop," said Màiri, coming up behind him.

"Good, that means croissants for breakfast." He smiled and stood politely. "Will you sit a while?"

"Aye." They sat together in companionable silence until Jean came out of the bakery and started towards the next shop. She was immediately accosted by a young woman in jeans.

Darroch and Màiri watched curiously as the two talked. "Anna Wallace. It'll be something to do with wildflowers," observed Màiri. "It's started, you know."

"What's started?"

"What they do with me. They've started telling her things they want you to know."

He looked at her in astonishment. "They do that to you?"

She could not help a touch of exasperation. Sometimes he was so naive. "Of course. And now they're doing it with Jean."

"Why don't they talk to me?"

"Well, a lot of them do, especially the men. But some of the women think they shouldn't. They say, 'Oh, the Laird's so busy, I hate to bother him. But if you could just put a word in his ear, Màiri, when he's got a free minute, he should know about . . . ' And then they tell me. And I tell you."

"That's why you're always so well-informed. How long has this been going on?"

"Forever."

Jean and Anna were leaning towards each other, their conversation intense. After a bit the younger woman smiled. Then they parted, Anna swinging on her way jauntily and Jean heading for the next shop.

"That'll be a new patch of wildflowers she's discovered and it'll need to be protected," observed Màiri.

"Aye," Darroch murmured. "I hope Jean doesn't mind all this, Màiri."

She looked at him seriously. "It's the duty of the Laird's wife, *mo charaid*. Jean will know that."

As they watched, an elderly woman, tiny, thin and fierce, strode up to Jean.

"*A Dhia beannaich mi*, it's Mairead MacCorkle. What maggot will she have under her bonnet now? She'll talk for an hour. I'd best go rescue Jean." He moved to get up.

Màiri laid her hand on his arm. "Wait. She'll have to learn how to deal with Mairead sooner or later."

They watched as the woman launched into an excited monologue with much arm waving. Jean listened, then spoke. The other woman paused. Jean said something else, then turned slightly, her movement clearly signifying the end of the discussion.

Mairead stood silently for a moment. Then she nodded and produced a crotchety smile on a mouth unused to smiling. Jean smiled back and turned away. Mairead walked down the street, her head held high in satisfaction.

Darroch and Màiri looked at each other. "I don't want to know what that was all about," he said.

"You'll hear, though. Jean will give you the message. She handled that well, Darroch. I don't think you have to worry about her."

No, he wouldn't have to worry about her. She'd accept all that she saw as her responsibilities and she'd do what she perceived as her duty to him and to the *Eilean Dubhannaich*, and she'd do it with love and joy and integrity. I will kiss her in front of the whole damned square, he thought, and set out to catch up with her. When she saw him Jean said, "I'm not finished with my shopping, lovie. Everyone's so talkative today." And she wondered why he grinned at her.

Ah, Jean. If he could take her away for a while, just the two of them, to some place where no one knew them and there were no committees, no gossip, no prying.

What a pity his London apartment was rented for four weeks to an American businessman. But she'd like Paris, or the south of France, or Tahiti . . . Diverted, he thought of a beach and a grass hut and Jean barefooted, bare-breasted, wearing only a sarong knotted loosely about her hips. Sun and sand and pineapples. Pineapples? Perhaps he was thinking of Hawaii.

She was knee-deep in plans for the Playschool roof fund-raiser and it would be like moving the earth to get her to leave.

Brooding, he did not hear Màiri come in. She said, "You do look ill. What's wrong?"

"Come and have a whisky. I could use your advice."

"Not for me, thanks, too early, and for you too. I'll make tea."

When the teapot was cozily ensconced between them she leaned forward and said, "Out with it."

"The Minister." They both sighed. "He wants me to give Jean up." Then, at Màiri's look of shock, he added, "We're causing a scandal and setting a bad example and God knows what else, probably making the cows' milk to sour and the wool to fall off the sheep. Because we haven't set a wedding date and we've . . . um . . . anticipated the wedding night."

He had expected immediate sympathy but she hesitated, looking thoughtful. Alarmed, he said, "You surely don't agree with him."

"To tell the truth," Màiri said slowly, "I've half expected something like this. There's talk . . . "

He looked betrayed and opened his mouth to reply but she went right on.

"You're their favorite topic, you know that, and you've given them plenty to talk about in the last few months. *A Dhia*, we don't need television in this place. Real life provides enough to chatter about and you and Jean have been better than any soap opera. Too bad we couldn't have sold tickets, we'd have enough money to fix the Playschool roof several times over."

"That is outrageous and you know it. I'm entitled to a private life, I'm forty years old . . . "

She shook her head. "Why don't you get married? Surely her divorce is final by now?"

"She doesn't want to get married." He took a grim pleasure in seeing her eyes widen with astonishment.

"What? She doesn't want to marry you?"

"Well, it's not me, she loves me." He was beginning to sound like an echo. "She just doesn't want to be married. Not yet. She likes the idea that we're committed to each other with nothing to do with kirk or state. Free spirits, bound together by love." The explanation was becoming easier with repetition. "She gets quite eloquent about it."

Màiri said softly, "I felt that way about us."

Darroch smiled at her tenderly and took her hand. "Aye. So did I."

"Now, Jamie . . . he couldn't wait to be married. He scarcely gave me time to think."

"So he's told me. He wanted you and he let nothing stand in his way. But Jean's enjoying her freedom so much, Màiri. She's never had a time to be independent; she went from her father's home to her husband's. I don't want to clip her wings. But it's between the two of us, nobody else's business." He set his jaw.

"The Laird's business is everyone's. You must know that by now."

"Aye." He took a deep breath and let his indignation melt away. "Màiri, she wants to have a baby. She won't even try to prevent it."

"A . . . baby?"

"You'd think a woman who'd raised two children to adulthood would have had enough . . . "

Màiri said, "I certainly have."

" . . . but she's determined to give me a child. She's very eloquent on that subject, too." He smiled.

Màiri sat quite still and let joy surge through her. One of her greatest regrets had been that Darroch did not have an heir and she'd felt the guilt keenly. If she had not taken up all his time when they were of marrying age, perhaps he would have found another Island woman who would have been happy to wed him, go to England with him and give him a family and the Island a new generation of Mac an Rìgh lairds.

"I don't want her to be pregnant without the protection of my name. I don't want them gossiping about her." He sighed. "She doesn't care, you know. She says she'll be proud to be carrying my child and marriage has nothing to do with it."

Màiri was thinking hard. Then she said, "Handfasting."

Darroch looked at her.

"A contract between two people, nothing to do with religion or government. Jean will like the idea. It's romantic and old-fashioned, an Island tradition, just her cup of tea. Jamie and I will be your witnesses and Barabal and Catrìona will let the Island know.

"And you can tell the Minister. He will not approve but he will accept it. And if she gets pregnant it will be all right." Privately she thought the Island would put up with any amount of scandalous behavior to have a Mac an Rìgh heir. She knew Darroch wouldn't want to hear that; it would be part of that bloody laird business and it would offend his sense of propriety. But it wouldn't surprise her if there was dancing in the streets and celebratory bonfires if Jean produced the Laird's baby, within or without wedlock.

Darroch said slowly, "Brilliant."

She nodded. "Right, then, best do it straightaway. At our place or yours?"

"Mine. No, Jean's. She loves that cottage and she'll feel in control of the proceedings there. She's more likely to say yes."

"Now that's settled, I'll be on my way and fix Jamie's supper."

"I thought you wanted to talk to me . . . "

She grinned at him. "And I just have, haven't I."

Jean was off to the Playschool early the next day and it was evening before he caught up with her. After dinner they sat cozily entwined on her sofa.

"Jean, I want to change our relationship."

She was instantly wary. "We are perfect just the way we are. We're together. . ."

". . . because we want to be, not because the law says we must be." He could quote it by heart now. "I want more than that. I want us to be handfast. It is an Island tradition." He said firmly, "A beautiful old Island tradition."

He had piqued her interest. She loved Island traditions. "Oh, like Mòrag and Ùisdean. What does it involve?"

"We promise to love each other faithfully for a year and a day. After that, we can marry or we can part. We'll find out whether or not we suit."

"It doesn't involve a church, does it? Or signing anything?" she asked cautiously.

"You and I make our vows in front of two witnesses. Màiri and Jamie, of course. And we won't live together or change your name." But everyone will know you're mine, he thought.

She liked the idea, just as Màiri had predicted. "How sweet. And it's an old custom?"

"Centuries old," he said firmly. "And very practical. There weren't ministers in every village and sometimes people had to wait a long while until the minister got to them on his rounds. It was a way of legitimizing a relationship and children until it was possible to get married."

Her capitulation was sudden and total. "Okay," she said.

Faint with relief he murmured, "Let's seal the bargain in bed."

"Um . . . I'd rather not." When he stared at her in surprise she said, "My . . . um . . . period started this morning. Really."

"Damn."

"It'll be over by Thursday."

"I'm going to Edinburgh Thursday. Won't be back until Monday."

"Damn."

They looked at each other. Finally Jean said, "Well, at least we can make plans. When shall we do this handfasting?"

"Next Tuesday, in front of your fireplace. And then we're going off by ourselves, Jean, for a bit."

"The fundraiser . . . the committee is meeting . . . "

"By ourselves, Jean. To hell with committees. We've earned some time together. Do you fancy Paris?"

"Oh, my. I've never been to Paris. I've never been anywhere, in fact, except here. Could we really? That would be lovely."

"Count on it. I'll make the arrangements." Paris, he thought. A whole week of making love, falling asleep together, waking up together. Or maybe Florence. Yes, Florence, and he'd buy her a ring from a jeweler on the Ponte

Vecchio. He felt like a spider, luring her into his web. One way or another he'd get what he wanted and what he wanted was marriage and he didn't intend to wait a year and a day, either. Handfasting and a ring. That would be a good start.

"Um . . . Darroch . . . we don't have to part after a year and a day, do we?"

He almost laughed aloud, but managed to say solemnly, "No, *m'aingeal*. Only if we don't suit."

"Oh, dear. What if we don't suit?"

"Just think of all the fun we will have had," he said.

Fifty-five

Here, at the heart
Of my universe, glows
Exquisite, absolute,
Love's deep rose.

Alfred Noyes

The four of them met Tuesday night at Jean's cottage for the handfasting. In honor of the occasion Darroch and Jamie were wearing their kilts and Màiri had on a skirt in the MacDonald tartan.

Darroch had asked Jean to wear the green dress that matched her eyes. Now he produced a length of the Mac an Rìgh tartan. "Màiri, please help Jean with her sash."

Màiri took the long slim piece of fabric, pleated one end and turned it back into a rosette. She pinned that to Jean's left shoulder and the other end to her opposite hip, draping the sash across her back, the long end falling down behind against her skirt.

Màiri stood back and looked at her work. "Always pin the sash to the left shoulder, Jean. That's proper for the wife of a chief."

That bloody laird business, thought Jean, but Darroch didn't object tonight. On the contrary, he looked and acted every inch the Laird.

Darroch pulled a handkerchief from his pocket. He untied it to reveal a round silver brooch, the metal twisted into an elaborate Celtic design. In the center a golden-brown stone glinted.

"A brooch for your sash, Jean. It was my mother's. The stone is a cairngorm, a real one. My great-grandfather bought it in the Cairngorm Mountains from the man who found it and had an Island craftsman make the brooch."

It was beautiful, the old silver gleaming with a new polish and the stone with its old-fashioned cut reflecting the firelight. Jean watched as he pinned it in the center of the rosette. "It's lovely, darling."

"Now, *mo chridhe*, come and stand by me. In front of the fire, that's sacred to our love. Jamie, would you fetch my family Bible, please. It's there on the desk."

Jamie brought the large leather-bound volume to Darroch. Unbelievers both, they nevertheless handled the Bible with reverence. Like all Island Bibles it was in the Gaelic, a treasured symbol of their language and culture and the ancient faith of Eilean Dubh.

Màiri held it for them. "Put your hands on the Bible, Jean," he said and when she obeyed he put his hands on top of hers.

He spoke in the Gaelic. She could follow part of it but he repeated it in English for her. "I handfast myself to you, Jean. I will love you and hold you in honor and respect for a year and a day. In all manner of things you are to me as my wife. I swear this to you on the honor of the Mac an Rìghs."

She had thought carefully about what she was going to say, had written it down, laboriously translated it into the Gaelic. All three were looking at her expectantly. But her prepared words went right out of her head and she spoke from her heart. "I love you, Darroch, so much, and I handfast myself to you. I pledge myself to be loyal and loving and a true partner to you . . . for a year and a day." She smiled. "But I hope it's fifty years, darling. Because I'll love you for the rest of my life."

Darroch took her into his arms and kissed her tenderly. "A hundred years, *mo chridhe*. Why stop at fifty?"

Jamie murmured, "Very nice vows. But I rather miss the one that pledges to be 'bonny and buxom in bed.' I never understood quite what that meant but it sounds delightful."

Kisses were exchanged all around. Jamie produced a camera and pictures in various combinations were taken, including one of Màiri and Darroch smiling triumphantly at each other.

Darroch whispered, "It worked, Màiri. I owe you, *mo charaid*."

Màiri whispered back, "Happy to be of service to the Laird." And she grinned at his expression.

The loving that night was especially good. It was as if the beauty and solemnity of the ancient handfasting ceremony had awakened something deep in both of them and they touched and kissed and came together with an unrestrained passion neither had experienced before, becoming one in their love. They fell asleep at last in each other's arms, and for the first time he stayed the night with her.

Jean woke first the next day. Too restless to stay in bed and unwilling to disturb Darroch, deeply asleep, she dressed and went into the kitchen to make tea. There was plenty to do to before the helicopter left: packing and a conference with Barabal to pass on her notes for the next fundraiser meeting.

They were going to Florence, to a cozy *pension* next to the Duomo. She was quite looking forward to it.

The day was gloriously bright and when she took her teacup outside she saw with pleasure that the sky was deep Eilean Dubh blue with huge puffy clouds promising rain later in the day. Trees and plants were beginning to open into spring colors and over in the corner of the cottage, protected from the wind and warmed by the chimney, something glowed a rich dark green. Curious, she went to it.

It was Darroch's mother's climbing rose, the one that had given the cottage its name, *Taigh nan Ròsan*, house of the roses. She'd pruned it ruthlessly, finally turning its wild mass into a controlled but untamed series of ropes that twined to the top of the cottage and beyond. In its sheltered position the stems had turned green and produced leaves a month ago.

Jean looked at it and, surprised, she bent closer.

Darroch came to the door and stood watching her. The sunshine was turning the whisky-colored hair into a bright halo. My Jean, he thought, remembering last night, how she'd trembled and cried out in his arms and how completely she'd yielded herself to him.

He went to her. "*Madainn mhath*. Why did you get out of bed?" he whispered. "I had some delightful things in mind for you."

She could not explain the surge of joyous energy that had waked her, made her want to run and dance, made it impossible for her to lie still. She put her arms around his neck and drew him down for a kiss. When he took her mouth hungrily she responded with equal hunger, then drew back. "There might be someone passing by," she said.

"We're handfast now. Public displays of affection are quite acceptable."

She smiled. "Look, lovie." She twisted in his arms and pointed to the rose.

The climber was covered with buds, most hidden among the leaves, but directly in front of them in a patch of sun a bud had opened into flower, a single white rose surrounded by leaves and thorns.

Darroch touched it gently with his fingers and winced when he encountered a thorn. He said, licking a drop of blood from the wound:

The little white rose of Scotland, the white rose
That smells sweet and sharp,
And breaks the heart.

"None of that Sight business," said Jean. "We're all done with broken hearts." And she put her arms around him and kissed him.

They stood there together in the garden next to his mother's rose while Eilean Dubh woke, confident, self-involved and ready to get on with the business of life.

The story of Jean and Darroch and the Eilean Dubhannaich *continues in* The White Rose of Scotland. *Visit the Eilean Dubh web site,* scottishislandnovels.com *for information on this and other forthcoming novels.*

Acknowledgements

M òran taing . . .

And love to my family, Mike, Michael, Anita, Aaran, John and Carla, for listening to me prattle on endlessly about this writing mixty-maxty. Special thanks to Mike for his moral support, endless patience and delicious cooking, and to John for rescuing this manuscript early on when I did a stupid computer thing. . . twice . . . and for his continuing technical support.

To Donnie MacDonald, from the Isle of Lewis, Scotland, a noted folksinger and half of Men of Worth, who has vetted the Gaelic in this book. *A Dòmhnall,* I deeply appreciate your help.

To Carla for the original cover painting and to John for computerizing it.

To Jane Gordon who drew the map of Eilean Dubh, and knows the geography of the Island better than I do! Jane is a Minneapolis artist who specializes in ceramics.

To Cindy Rogers, my editor, with gratitude for her kind words.

To Lara Friedman-Shedlov, for devising the Scottish country dance "Fàilte gu Eilean Dubh (Welcome to the Dark Island)."

To teachers and friends in the Twin Cities Branch of the RSCDS for all the pleasure and good cheer we've enjoyed in dancing with you.

To Cecile LaBore, the first reader.

I am especially grateful to my dear friend, the talented musician/composer Sherry Wohlers Ladig, for being a perpetual source of encouragement and for liking *Westering Home* so much that she was inspired to write three wonderful pieces of music for it. They were premiered by Sherry's group Dunquin at "An Evening in Eilean Dubh," February 2003, in St. Paul, Minnesota. I hope one day they will appear on a Dunquin recording for all to enjoy.

Thank you, Judith Palmateer, for making me publish this book!

Thanks and love to my little Snowshoe kitty, Twm Siôn, for keeping my lap warm all those long afternoons at the computer!

Notes on the Scottish Literary References in Westering Home

William Dunbar (1460?-1520?) was a poet and court favorite in the reign of James IV.

"The Canadian Boat Song" ("Yet the blood is strong, the heart is Highland, And we in dreams behold the Hebrides") first appeared in Blackwood's Magazine in 1829. It has been attributed to John Galt (1779-1839), a businessman and writer.

Robert Burns (1750-1796) is the national bard of Scotland, revered all over the world.

David Ross was an early nineteenth century Ross-shire crofter and seer. The quote in Chapter Five is from T. C. Smoot's excellent and highly recommended book, *A History of the Scottish People, 1560-1830* (William Collins Sons, London, 1969).

Neil Munro (1864-1930), novelist and journalist, created the very funny Para Handy tales about the captain of the Clyde puffer, the S. S. Vital Spark.

Hugh MacDiarmid (1892-1978), is the pseudonym of Christopher Murray Grieve, one of Scotland's greatest poets. His poem "The Little White Rose" has inspired the adoption of the white rose as the emblem of the Scottish Nationalist Party.

Sir Hugh Roberton (1874-1952), composer and conductor of the Glasgow Orpheus Choir, wrote English words for a traditional tune and called it "Westering Home." The original Gaelic words were about the Isle of Skye, but with Sir Hugh's words ("At hame wi' my ain folk in Isla") it has become the unofficial anthem of Islay.

Sorley Maclean (in Gaelic, Somhairle MacGill-Eain, 1911-1996) is the greatest Scottish Gaelic poet of modern times.

Alfred Noyes (1880-1958) and William Wordsworth (1770-1850) were English poets; Oliver Herford (1863-1935) was American.

I am indebted to Mòrag MacNeill's handy little book, *Everyday Gaelic*, (Gairm, Glasgow, 1986) for hints and spelling when my Gaelic failed me.

The Royal Scottish Country Dance Society, headquartered in Edinburgh, Scotland, has preserved and promoted not only the dances mentioned in this book but hundreds of others since its founding in 1923.

Gaelic–English Glossary

Terms and Phrases

Fàilte do'n Eilean Dubh: Welcome to Eilean Dubh.

Fàilte gu mo thaigh: Welcome to my house.

A Dhia!: Oh, God! *A Dhia beannaich mi!* Goodness gracious me!

A Chatrìona, thoir dhomh-sa an litir. Catriona, give me the letter.

arpag: harpy.

cathair dhan a leadaidh: a chair for the lady.

ceart math: okay.

cèilidh: a social evening of music, dance and storytelling.

a charaid, mo charaid: oh friend, my friend. Plural: *mo chàiradean.*

ciamar a tha: how are you?

Co-Op nan Figheadairean: the Knitters' Co-operative.

craic: talk, chat.

criathar: riddler.

da iawn: okay (Welsh).

dean deagh chadal: sleep well.

deurach: tearful.

diabhol: devil.

eileanach: islander. Plural: *eileanachan.*

eunlaith: birdies.

feasgar math: good evening. *oidhche mhath:* good night.

fiosaiche: a soothsayer, a prophet.

gabh mo leisguil: excuse me.

glé mhath: very good.

grùdair: a man who distills *uisge beatha* (whisky).

madainn mhath: good morning.

mar sin leat: bye for now.

misneachd, mo charaid: courage, my friend.

miorbhuileach: marvelous.

mòran taing: many thanks.

Am Post Rioghal: the Royal Mail. *Fear a' phuist:* postman.
Ard-fhear a' phuist: the Postmaster.
Bhan a' Phuist Rioghail: the Royal Mail van.

mo phiuthar, my sister; *mo brathair,* my brother.

reekin' lums: smoking chimneys.

reiving: sheep or cattle stealing.

seiseanan: music jam sessions.

sgeulaichean: storytellers who recite genealogies.

sgian dubh: small knife worn in kilt hose. Plural: *sgianan dubha.*

s' math sinn: great, terrific, smashing.

tapadh leat, tapadh leibh: thank you. Second phrase is plural, formal or respectful.

thà gu dearbh: yes indeed.

tha mi gu math: I'm fine.

tha mi duilich: I am sorry.

tha mi toilichte a bhith an seo: I am happy to be here.

People

bana-Ameireaganach: American woman.

bhean uasail: respectful term of address for an elderly lady.

Eilean Dubhannach: a native of Eilean Dubh.
Plural: *Eilean Dubhannaich.*

mo leadaidh: my lady.

Sasannach: Englishman. *Bana-Shasannach:* Englishwoman.

Sgiathanach: a man from the Isle of Skye.

Sìne: Jean. Pronounced "sheenuh." When aspirated (an h is added after the s) it becomes *Shìne;* pronounced "heenuh."

Somhairle Mac-a-Phi *as sine:* the elder.

Somhairle Mac-a-Phi *as òige:* the younger.

an Tighearna Dearg: the Red (Socialist) Laird.

Terms of endearment

mo chràdh: my torment.

mo chridhe: my heart.

m'eudail: my darling.

mo fhlùr: my flower.

mo ghille dhubh: my dark-haired lad.

mo leannan: my sweetheart.

mo luaidh: my loved one, my dear.

mo nighean ruadh: my red-haired girl.

tha gràdh agam ort: I love you.

am pòs thu mi: will you marry me?

Weather

Bodach Sneachda: the Snowman, an Island nickname for a blizzard.

'Se là brèagha a th' ann: It's a beautiful day.

Tha e nas blàithe na bha e 'n-dè: It's warmer than it was yesterday.

'Se. Tha i blàth: Yes, it's warm.

Places

a' chreag: a cliff.

àite laighe: helicopter pad (literally, a resting place).

Beanntan MhicChriathar: The MacChriathar hills.

Beinn Mhic-an-Rìgh: MacRìgh's mountain.

Cladh a' Chnuic: Cemetery Hill.

an Eaglais Easbuigeach: the Episcopal Church.

an Eaglais Chaitliceach: the Catholic Church.

an Eaglais Shaor: the Free Kirk.

lòin tràighidh: tidal pools.

Rudha na h Airgid: Airgead Point.

Taigh a Mhorair: the Laird's house.

Taigh nan Ròsan: house of the roses.

Taigh Rois: the Rosses' house.

A note on the Gaelic: in certain circumstances some initial consonants aspirate, that is, are followed by an 'h'. One instance is after the word *a,* the usual form of address which precedes names and titles, and means 'oh'. For example: *A Dharroch* – oh, Darroch.